the Padre Paranoia

A MYSTERY NOVEL

DAVID HARRY

DEDICATION

To Mary, Kat and Hydra; wife, granddaughter and MBF. Without your presence each day life would not be as wonderful as it is. I love each of you and am blessed to have the three of you there for me. May we all go from strength to strength together.

I continue to marvel at the wonderful work performed by our uniformed service people day after day, in almost every country of the world, relentlessly protecting our American way of life. I also marvel at the magnificent job our domestic law enforcement men and women do, most often anonymously, to keep us safe from harms that we cannot even imagine.

For every productive lead they follow there are hundreds that prove fruitless. But if 9-11 taught us anything, it vividly reminded us that one lapse, one trail not followed, one clue, however false it may seem, not run to ground, can prove infinitely painful and destructive. In this regard, paranoia, when used for controlled motivation, is an investigator's best friend. Otherwise, paranoia can become a law enforcement officer's worst enemy.

DISCLAIMER

Everything in this book, except for the establishments listed and a few local folks, is fictitious. The words spoken by any of the locals are, of course, also fictional. Despite its proximity to the drug and smuggling related turbulence now occurring across our border, SPI remains a safe and extremely friendly place to live, work or vacation. Come on down.

Printed in the United States and published by Hotray LLC

Cover: Copyright © Ray Quiroga
Port Isabel-South Padre Press

ISBN-10: 0984678425
ISBN-13 : 978-0-9846784-2 - 6

SOUTH PADRE ISLAND AND PORT ISABEL ESTABLISHMENTS FREQUENTED BY

JIMMY REDSTONE AND ANGELLA MARTINEZ

Black Dragon
Blue Marlin Supermarket
Cafe Kranzler
Clayton's Beach Bar
Clayton's Beach Resort
Gabriella's Italian Grill & Pizzeria

Hilton Garden Inn
Isla Grand Beach Resort
Island Fitness
Island Native Surf House
Laguna Atascosa NationalWildlife Refuge
Louis's Backyard
Origins Recovery Center

Our Lady Star of The Sea
Paragraphs on Padre
Parrot Eyes
Peninsula Island Resort And Spa
Padreritagrill SPI
Pura Vida Cafe

Sea Life Nature Center
Sea Ranch Restaurant
Ted's
UB Captain

Please don't forget to stop by and tell them Jimmy and Angella sent you.

ONE

The action was remarkably clear, especially since it was being observed from an experimental Zephyr ten miles overhead. The scene was a sandy spit of land bordered on one side by the Gulf of Mexico and on the other by what appeared to be a shallow bay. The lens had even captured the wispy clouds seemingly suspended above two men who were walking north, one about twenty to twenty-five yards behind the other. The man in the lead held what appeared to be a large box camera. The other carried an assault rifle with the muzzle pointing down.

Suddenly, the rifle came level with the ground and the gunman's legs flexed into a solid stance with knees slightly bent, elbows tightly tucked. The back of the leader's head exploded, much as would a melon thrown violently against a wall. Then the left side of his body all but disappeared as additional rounds slammed into his torso. The sand turned dark around the fallen body.

The gunman produced a sheet of material from what appeared to be a small backpack and calmly wrapped his weapon. He then laid the wrapped weapon on the sand and went to retrieve the camera box. He studied the box for a few seconds and then wrapped it as well and set it down.

Next, he hoisted the lifeless body onto his shoulder and walked back toward a kayak beached a few hundred yards to the south. He dropped what remained of the body onto the kayak, fished something from the backpack and dropped it on the pile.

The killer then ran up the beach, falling to the sand about sixty yards north of the boat. With hands flashing faster than the eye could follow, he burrowed into the sand, creating a small fortress between himself and the kayak.

Almost as soon as he stopped digging, the boat exploded, spewing debris in all directions.

A few minutes later the killer stood, brushed sand from his face and headed back south. He paused long enough to push sand over the dark patch using the side of his foot. Satisfied, he retrieved the two packages and continued walking south.

"Jimmy, what do you suppose the vic was holding?" My partner Angella Martinez had started the video again from the beginning. She froze the frame, allowing us to discuss what we were seeing. "Can't imagine he'd be taking pictures using a box camera from the dark ages."

"Some kind of recorder, you ask me. Perhaps the Air Force reconnaissance folks could focus on the device; blow it up—pardon the pun—or whatever those wonks do."

Angella advanced the video a few frames and then again paused it. "He's pointing what ever it is ahead of him," Angella said, straining to see if there was anything of interest in the frozen image. Evidently satisfied, she allowed the video to continue forward. "Vic still doesn't sense anyone approaching," she commented. "He seems to be concentrating on something, but I don't see what."

"That's what's puzzling," I added. "Can't figure what he's so intent on seeing. The surveillance camera is ten miles up. If the vic sees anything, so can the camera."

"You suppose they know each other?"

"Don't seem to." That, of course, was a guess. But a guess stemming from my years of surveillance duty in the Texas Rangers; years and years of watching people while hidden in, and under, cars, trucks and vans; sitting in trees and on roofs. Even once locked in an outhouse, my eye pressed to a knothole, squeezing my nostrils against the stink. "Suppose there's footage they're holding out? Killer had to come from somewhere. Had to go somewhere."

"Air Force says we have it all," Angella reminded me, rolling her eyes.

Her skepticism was well founded. We'd been lied to and fed half-truths any number of times in our previous missions working as investigators for Homeland Security. Trusting them was not high on either of our minds. But, as in most things, there are positives as well. The resources of the FBI have proven to be unbelievably good. But, and this is a sore point, we only receive the benefit when it's in their interest to tell us. Otherwise they can be a black hole. Angella, even with several missions behind her, is still a rookie. Some might say I'm over the hill. But truth is, we make a great team.

"There doesn't seem to be any reason for the Air Force to withhold information," Angella said, as if reading my thoughts. "Their briefing went into great detail. Locations, times, speeds, follow-up missions, apparently everything they had. Air Force actually gave us more than they had to. The discussion on multi-spectral imaging and infrared correlation was fascinating. I came away thinking they're playing it straight."

"I came away with a headache," I countered. "Words I can't pronounce tend to do that to me." I returned my attention to the images slowly moving across the screen. The shooter at first held his weapon pointing downward, exactly as I had been taught during Ranger training thirty-some years ago. Not Ranger, as in Texas Ranger my former employer, but rather, Ranger, as in Special Operations Army Ranger. At one time I had been a marksman. Now Angella shoots rings around me.

From far back in my memory the crisp admonishment, "Never point your weapon at anyone unless you fully intend to shoot," flooded my brain. The words belonged to my Special Ops instructor, an otherwise mild-mannered, but highly dedicated, black man. The best instructor I ever had. I'm alive today because of him. But he's not. Killed on a super-secret mission deep in some Columbian jungle. Can't even tell his family he died a hero.

"Pause!" I called to Angella. "Back up several frames. See if we can determine what triggered the killer's reaction."

We ran and reran the segment several times. Neither of us detected anything to spook the gunman.

"Sound is a possibility," Angella ventured. "There's a slight head nod, maybe a twist to the side, by the victim. Doubt that could trigger it."

"With the waves pounding the beach it's doubtful he could have heard much."

"Vic said something. Or possibly that box let out a noise."

"Good point. Let's move on. Keep it slow."

In truth, it didn't make much difference if we watched the next twenty seconds in real time or in slow motion. We had already done both and concluded nothing. The perp's weapon moved in perfect harmony with his body from rest position to shooting position to having been fired. This had not been his first killing, nor, I supposed, his last.

Some techie had superimposed infrared onto the video. The result was that when the weapon was fired, a darkened line extended from the end of the rifle to the victim's head.

In slow motion, the line was reduced to a series of dashes moving frame by frame away from the muzzle of the weapon. The humanity in me screamed for the victim to duck out of the line of fire. It was difficult for me, a seasoned law-enforcement officer, to watch the final frames as the rounds slammed first into the back of his head followed by several more to his body.

"Profiler would describe the shooter as being angry," I said. "One bullet was all he required. But all things considered, I believe he was professionally trained and the extra rounds are designed to throw us off. He had no way of knowing he was on candid camera."

"Looks that way," Angella replied.

The infrared overlay traced a piece of hot metal, probably from an oar handle, or possibly from an instrument in the boat, directly to what appeared to be the back of the perp's neck.

"Pause! Can we determine if that metal hit him?"

Angella stepped the video frame by frame, studying each image carefully. "Here. See here." She pointed to a location at the hairline. "He was hit right here." The gunman's hand had immediately started up toward the impact site, but was back under the sand a few frames later without completing the journey.

Discipline.

A moment later he stood, brushed himself off, touched the back of his head and looked at his fingers. "He's probably checking for blood," I commented. "But it doesn't appear to be slowing him down any."

"Suppose he's on a time schedule?" Angella asked. "He seems to be in a hurry."

"Possibly that's why he fired. Something else could be going down. Any indication of where he's heading?"

"Nor where he came from," she responded. "I assume the same place." The camera on the drone, or as it is officially referred to, the Unmanned Aerial Vehicle, UAV for short, had been shut down at that instant. "They told us the camera had been scheduled to be turned off before flying over the Gulf. Timing issue was the explanation for leaving it on as long as it was."

"My guess is they were looking at oil rigs—or possibly drug smuggling activities. Could be anything really."

"I'm putting my money on this being a CIA mission. Monitoring domestic activities against the rules. But hey, when has that ever stopped those guys? If they can dress that CIA spook, Tiny, as Secret Service, there's no telling what the hell else they're doing." I was referring to the liaison man, Tiny, who Homeland Security had assigned to us on our last mission. We were told he was Secret Service. Turned out he was CIA.

Angella turned off the video player, shifted around to face me, and said, "Let's go over what we have. Frankly, I can't imagine what they want from us."

We were sitting in the living room of the condo I had rented on South Padre Island, Texas. I had found a great place overlooking Laguna Madre bay, since the Gulf of Mexico side of the Island is above my budget. We were on the sixth floor and enjoyed a magnificent view of the setting sun as it painted the sky red over the Texas horizon. In this part of the country, the sun sets fast, but for those brief moments, it's magnificent.

During the day, parasailors, wind surfers, kayakers, and all manner of fishing boats ply the relatively shallow water of the bay. At night nothing disturbs the tranquility of the vista. That is, except on Fridays during the summer when, at precisely nine-fifteen, a barge moored on the bay discharges fifteen minutes of spectacular fireworks.

Angella had spent the night—actually the last month—as my full-time nursemaid while I slowly recovered from an overdose of radiation. The good news, if there can ever be good news when atomic radiation eats you alive, is that I suffered minimal permanent damage. That is, unless you count the inability to spawn further children. I'm certain Angella would disagree, but judging from the mess I've made with my son, my not being able to procreate is nothing to mourn.

I was so nauseous from the radiation that for a while, and despite all manner of medications, I had difficulty holding down water. Bodily fluids have at last begun flowing out of their proper orifices—and doing so at the right time. Solid food is finally processing properly as well. The light fuzz covering my otherwise hairless head acts as a reminder of the morning, afternoon, evening and nighttime sickness that is thankfully behind me.

Through it all, Angella has been rock solid, making me laugh—or at least crack a smile—when I otherwise wanted to roll up and die. We've spent hours walking and talking about ourselves, about our respective pasts, and, most importantly, about the future.

When the subject of her being a cop came up, she simply said, "I grew up around a bunch of rowdy drunks. It was my sister and myself against everyone else. Father had several brothers, all with boys. From as far back as I remember I had to fight for what I wanted. When they started drinking it was lights out. Needed a gun to keep them in check. Cop friend of my dad took me to the range, taught me what I know."

"I should only be half as good as you. Even in my best day you're better."

"Practice, Jimmy. Practice. Anyway, my brothers and cousins never bothered me after that."

A week ago, Angella, sitting on the edge of the bed as she had done every night since taking up her nursing role, leaned over and kissed me goodnight. This had become our nightly ritual before she retired to her own room. But instead of leaving, she turned the light off and slowly circled the bed, pausing at the foot just long enough to allow her slacks to fall away. A few more feet and she again stopped moving, this time unbuttoning her blouse one button at time. The blouse also fell to the floor, followed a few seconds later by her bra. Moonlight reflecting from the calm waters of the bay framed her gorgeous figure perfectly as she slipped into my bed.

The lingering question from my radiation exposure was emphatically answered. All the moving parts worked to perfection.

TWO

"So, what have we learned from the video?" Angella pressed, bringing me back to the working world.

"For starters," I said, my mind still dwelling on the night we consummated our relationship, "We know the video was taken about one-hundred miles north of here, as the pelican flies. We also know the exact time of the shooting, along with the weapon." This was a good start, since all we usually ever have is a dead body. Or, in this case, parts of a dead body.

"That leaves the victim's name unknown," Angella said, adding, "And we don't know who the shooter is. We really don't know where either of them came from."

"We know a couple of other pertinent facts as well," I added. "The shooter appears to be an organized killer. Most likely military trained. We know one of them came by kayak, I'm guessing the vic. We don't know how the perp arrived or departed."

I was musing over the *why* of it when the phone rang. It was Tiny, street name, Kevin Jurald. He had other names, but spooks usually do. "Jimmy Redstone," he roared, "heard you're finished with rehab. Good to have you back!" I could visualize all six-nine of him smiling as he always did. Tiny had also received radiation poisoning as I had, but his was minor.

"I don't put stock in coincidences," I remarked, "so I'm assuming you're calling about the video."

"This is not a secure connection," he quickly pointed out. "Put a smile on your face, Redstone, it's your lucky day. We get to work together again. In fact, all three of us. Me, you and Martinez. I assume she's there with you. Hasn't left your side, so I hear. Tell her hello."

"I'll do that." There was nothing these folks didn't know.

"Powers that be believe we three make a good team. You want to Come here or should I—"

"It's snowing where you are. It's seventy-three down here. High skies. Angella and I were just heading out for a windsurfing lesson. Part of rehab."

"Got your drift. Be there in a few hours. See you for lunch."

"What was that about?" Angella asked when I put the phone in my pocket. "You're agitated."

"Tiny's catching a ride. Be here by lunch."

"I'll eat your cooking if this isn't connected to the video. Someone has their knickers in a knot and it can't be because a drone recorded a murder."

"Look on the bright side," I said, forcing a smile. "It means you've been reinstated." Angella had been implicated—framed is the right word—in a murder, and was on admin leave pending resolution.

"Nice to be the last to know. You up for an assignment? Your hand…"

The back of my right hand had sustained two broken bones. They had been surgically repaired, but my immune system, weakened by the radiation, succumbed to a nasty infection. Miracle drugs had saved my hand from amputation.

I make my living carrying a weapon. Now, I either must learn to fire left-handed or give up my career. I don't welcome either alternative. Angela, while pouring tons of Gatorade down my throat and watching it run out one or another improperly functioning body opening, had lobbied hard for my retirement.

For my part, I was determined to rehab my hand. In case that didn't work, I was learning to draw and shoot as a southpaw. Angella, being excellent with guns, was now my teacher at the range. I was making slow progress.

The issue, at least in my mind, wasn't my shooting accuracy. That would improve with practice. It was my instinct to draw with my right hand. Angella cautioned me several times that I should stop thinking of myself as a wild-west cowboy looking for a gunfight. Instead, she suggested my greatest talent—such as it is—is my ability to assimilate disparate facts into a coherent picture. Theory guy, so to speak.

She didn't exactly express it that way. Those are the words the Texas Ranger PR guru used in a handout to *The Statesman* when I "retired" to join Homeland Security. The Austin newspaper fittingly published the article on the page opposite the obituaries. I suppose I should be grateful they didn't print it on the comic page—or on the obit page itself.

Angella had put it more earthily. "Jimmy, you're not a gunslinger. Your High Noon days are behind you. Get a straw. Suck it up and get on with your life as a Homeland Security Special Investigator. Catch them with your brains—not your weapon."

The *special* in that sentence says it all. Angella and I have worked several assignments that, to say the least, are politically sensitive. Put another way. My phone rings when everybody else is heading for cover.

Rehab has gone exceedingly well. Teran, my trainer at the *Island Fitness Center*, has a never-ending collection of weights, levers, pulleys and ropes. He spends all his energy thinking up body positions and movements designed to torture every muscle a person is supposed to have. His stretching and balancing routines so far have stopped just short of turning me inside out. I must admit, however, that the improvement to my right hand is remarkable—and all his doing.

"You okay?" Angella asked, concern in her eyes. "I'm trying to figure out the video and you...well, you're off somewhere."

"I was thinking about the video," I fibbed, "and why it's here. Went to a lot of effort. Want to go over the video again, or..."

"Or what?" Angella asked, mischief in her eyes.

"...or we take that lesson."

"I vote for the lesson."

"That'll give the video time to settle in, gel a bit, before we meet Tiny."

"I can't bloody wait," she said, again rolling her gorgeous eyes. "Last time we worked with him it was none too pleasant. But, hey, this is a new day." Looking directly into my eyes, she continued, "At least I have you watching my back."

That's not all I was watching of Angella's.

THREE

"How the hell did you get here so fast?" I demanded of Tiny when he walked off the beach and onto the wood-planked porch of *Clayton's Beach Bar* where Angella and I sat munching chips and listening to live music played by classical guitarist Jonathan Dotson. The windsurfing lesson had gone well and I was feeling no pain, having finished my second Skinny Bones. Angella had stopped at one.

"I'm starved," Tiny announced, before even sitting down. "Nice place. What's good?" He was focused on the women's volleyball game in progress in the sand a few feet from where we sat. The bikinis couldn't be smaller. Some might actually have been painted on, a common practice at Spring Break from what I've been told. Angella wouldn't allow me to explore.

"We just ordered burgers," Angella informed Tiny. "Order at the bar. Tell them you're with us."

"What's that concoction you got there?" Tiny asked, nodding in the direction of my empty cup. His nose was crinkled in anticipated disgust.

"Skinny Bones. Captain Morgan spiced. Diet Coke. Lime-juice. Great drink."

"That diet crap ruins good rum! I'll go for a Big Bones."

"Suit yourself, big guy."

Tiny went to order and Angella suggested we move to a table in the far corner that had just become available. I don't know if that table was larger, or if I had spent too much time studying the volleyball game. Either way, we were moving.

"Let's see," I said, "Air miles from DC to SPI about 1500, give or take. Commercial flight through Houston; five hours minimum. Most likely, six. Military, maybe four."

"He spoke to you less than three hours ago," Angella injected. "Made good time."

"Trying to figure how he did it."

"Why are you concerned?" Angella asked.

"Residual mistrust, I suppose. I was wondering if he was already in the Valley. Maybe even up where the execution took place. If the drone was on a CIA mission and if a CIA agent then shows up…well, you do the math."

"My money's on a military transport," Angella said, glancing toward Tiny, who was on his way to join us at the table. "He obviously hasn't eaten. If he was already down here, he would have had plenty of time to eat."

"You talking about me?" Tiny said, approaching the table. "What ever happened to, *Hey, it's nice to see you?* Or, from you, Angella, *Give me a hug?* Southern hospitality being what it is."

Angella politely stood and reached around him. Her head came up only to mid-chest. Angella was not a small woman, but beside this bear she looked like a pre-teen. I extended my left hand, being protective of my right. I preferred not having it crushed in his massive paw.

We sat and Tiny said, "You have no confidence, my friend. I'm aware of the injury to your hand. I was there, remember?"

"Being there and not crushing my hand are not the same."

"I noticed you were using it. That's good, no?"

"That's good, yes," I replied. "Got some residual weakness, but actually it's healing well. Can't yet shoot."

"Hear you're working on it. You have a good instructor."

Was there anything this guy didn't know? Keeping my smile in place, I said, "I see you've recovered from your bout of radiation sickness." I made that call based on his appetite.

"Wasn't as bad as yours. Couldn't keep anything down for over two weeks. But you wouldn't know that to look at me."

In fact, if anything, Tiny looked heavier than I remembered. Angella winked in appreciation of me withholding comment. "Let's clear the air," I said, mindful that with Tiny nothing is ever what is seems. "Either you were already in the Valley or...or you've mastered teleporting. Got here too fast."

"My, you are the suspicious one." His eyes were playful and his face held a *nothing escapes your notice* look.

"Not without reason, I might add."

Before he could answer, little red lights began endlessly chasing themselves round and round the edge of our food pager. Just the way I felt when working with Tiny and the Feds.

Angella motioned for us to remain seated and she played hostess, bringing me a third Skinny Bones and setting a second Big Bones in front of Tiny. I suspected she had instructed the bartender to hold the Captain Morgan for hers.

Tiny launched into his burger and didn't say a word until nothing remained to be eaten. He polished off his drinks and I had the distinct feeling he would have consumed mine, as well as my lunch, if anything had remained on the table.

He wiped his mouth, sat back and said, "Beautiful gig you got going down here. Sand, sun, booze, rolling surf, great music, gorgeous women. What more can a guy want?"

"To be told the truth," I answered, risking the big man's wrath.

Angella's eyes squinted, but she said nothing. It was her equivalent to a kick in the shin.

"Not that I need explain to you," Tiny said, the amused look back on his face, "but in the interest of kicking this assignment off on the right foot, you should know I caught a ride on a T-38C Talon. Andrews to Port Isabel, thirteen-hundred fifty nautical miles. Talon cruises at about seven-hundred knots. Clearance all the way. You do the math."

"How do you…"

"You want to see it? It's parked across the bridge at the Cameron County airport. Air Force has a vested interest in this operation."

"Air Force or CIA?" I responded.

"Plane's still here?" Angella asked, blunting my question, presumably on purpose. "Does that mean you flew it down yourself? Or that you're going right back?"

"Can't get rid of me that fast. I'm certified. Fly copters too, if the mission demands it. But no, this one's AF all the way. They require a babysitter. What we do after takeoff is up to the pilot. I asked nicely and managed to log a few hours. Kapish?"

In Tiny's language, ask is akin to demand.

"Neat little airport," Tiny said, the twinkle returning to his eyes. "In the fifties and sixties, CIA used the airfield for an operation they were involved in not far from there at Laguna Atascosa. Training folks from south of the border. But that's another story. Let's take a walk on the beach. We can talk down by the water."

On the way to the water Tiny retrieved a wayward volleyball and I was surprised at his agility. He moved more like he belonged on a court than behind a desk.

At water's edge, I said, "I suppose even you spooks can't pick up conversation with the surf underfoot."

"Don't be too certain of that, my friend. You'd be surprised what caliber toys we have. Geeks filter out the background noise. Getting better all the time."

"Do we need to check for ears?" On our last mission we were constantly being bugged and I had no intention of repeating that mistake.

"I doubt anyone's on to us yet," he replied. "This thing's been top secret from the beginning."

"Any reason to suspect otherwise?" Angella asked, obviously recalling that microphones had been glued to her gun—and even to her bra.

"None whatsoever," Tiny replied. "No one knows the murder has even been discovered."

"You know." I commented as we walked across the sand. "Once the government's involved there's no telling who knows what."

"If you're referring to me, I got it directly from the top. Have something to show you."

"And what would that be?" I asked, reacting to his tone, as well as to the look in his eye. I had seen that look before and it had meant trouble then. And I had no doubt it meant trouble now.

We walked several minutes in silence, the waves rolling over our feet. Angella was leading the progression and I was trailing behind. Looking out over the endless blue water, it was easy to forget the real world lurked beyond the horizon. Before Tiny had arrived, the real world, with real criminals and real pain, had been a distant abstraction. In Tiny's presence, reality crowded my thoughts.

Single file, we trudged north, just as we had seen the killer and the victim do in the video. The only difference in terrain was that to our west the beach was wide and ended in a sand dune large enough not to be able to see over. I knew Laguna Madre was on the other side of the dune, but I didn't know how far away the bay actually was.

Angella turned to face Tiny. "Okay, big guy, you didn't fly that plane down here to spend leisure time with us. So what gives?"

Tiny responded by producing his iPhone. He shielded the screen from the bright sunlight and held it up so we could see the logo of CNN Headline News. "Recorded last night. Actually, about two-thirty a.m.."

The reporter's demeanor was rigid as she looked directly into the camera. "This just in," she began, taking a deep breath, her lips forming a tight line. "Texas Senior Senator Mathew Donnlevy is dead of an apparent heart attack. His death occurred at eleven-twenty, just three hours ago, and just moments before he was scheduled to vote on the controversial and extremely divisive Senate bill to overhaul the military. Donnlevy's death delivers a fatal blow to those opposed to the legislation."

Tiny turned the phone around, tapped the display several times, and again positioned the screen so we could see. The breaking waves that a moment ago had been so welcome, now made it hard to hear what was being said.

In true equal-opportunity style, a male host appeared and was reminding the audience that Senator Donnlevy was the driving force behind the opposition to the Senate bill. The *Force Redeployment Act of 2012* was the legislation's formal name. Donnlevy had dubbed it *The Great Pacifist Retreat Act*. Unfortunately for the bill's supporters, the public referred to the measure as the *Retreat Act*.

The issue of reducing the military and pulling our troops home was being debated endlessly across the country. With the national deficit out of hand and a Presidential election looming, Congressmen were intent to take money away from any program that did not impact them directly. The President, under intense pressure to reduce spending, was pushing for trillions in savings by bringing our fighting men and women home.

As expected, the conservative talk shows, even though they had been beating the drums for less spending, were leading the battle against the *Retreat Act*. The public was fiercely divided. The rhetoric had become increasingly nasty, with the terms *traitor* and *anti-American* being the mildest characterizations used.

It had taken the administration over a year to reach this stage, and Members of Congress who were up for re-election had their hands full. Many of them believed they would be lucky to be back. Certainly none of them were signing long-term leases in the nation's capitol.

Donnlevy's death was good for the President because it now ensured the bill's passage by the Senate. The House, led by the far right who loathed government spending, together with the left who despised the military, had already approved it.

I digested what we had just seen and then said to Tiny, "What the hell's the death of Donnlevy got to do with a man murdered on the beach north of here? What am I missing?"

"What makes you think they're connected?"

"Air Force sends us the video file. Air Force flies you down here. You show us a broadcast of Donnlevy and the legislation. Follow the dots one-oh-one. Get it on the table already."

"Orders from the top."

"How far on top?" Angella asked.

"The reward for doing a good job for the President is getting to do it again."

"So what's the reward for doing a bad job?"

"Don't plan to find out."

"So, we're going north after all," I said.

"He's coming to you. Figuratively, that is. There's a secure video link scheduled for, let's see..." Tiny studied his watch, squinting in the bright sun to see the dial. "...in exactly three-quarters of an hour."

"And just where—"

"At the Coast Guard Station. Your friend, Lieutenant Cruses is expecting you. He doesn't know what this is about and he won't sit in. He's just the host. We're using secure military communications. Be the three of us on our end."

"You come all this way to drive me a mile to the station." Tiny had his eye-dropper out and we were being drip-fed.

"The Retreat Act would reduce the military to effectively a homeland security force. Guarding our shores, if you will. Coast Guard stuff. The Joint Chiefs are not pleased. Pissed, if you really want to know. With a shrinking global presence, the ranks collapse and promotions stop. That's not good for career-level folks. The President expects hostility."

"You talking about a military take over? A military coup of some sort? Never can happen here."

"And just why not?" Tiny replied, his normal used-car salesman smile dimmed.

I studied Tiny, expecting a signal that he was less than serious. But, in fact, his face continued to harden as he spoke. His eyes told me he believed a coup was possible.

"Military answers to the President," I replied, defending my thesis, all the while fighting the jitters. Here was a man at the top of the CIA. A man who knew what was going on and not prone to idle speculation was advancing a hypothesis of a military take-over.

"Only so long as it wants to answer to the President," Tiny replied. "Ask yourself this. How many tanks—or planes—does the President have? How many Special Forces?"

"All of them," I responded. This conversation made my skin crawl. Treason, or more accurately, conspiracy to commit treason, was a felony.

"Only if the Generals and Admirals follow him. If the Joint Chiefs turn away..."

"You're not suggesting..."

"I'm the messenger. I'm not suggesting anything—yet. But you saw the tape. Someone blew a major hole in that poor guy. For some reason, the video didn't *see* where the shooter came from—or where he went. That seem odd to you?"

"We did question it," Angella responded, stopping short of expressing any further comment.

"So did the FBI. Guy's name is Philip Timberwolf. The dead guy. Lived alone on the coast, just north of Port Mansfield. Maybe divorced, maybe never married. Don't know yet."

Angella interrupted. "So the President thinks the Air Force has more than they turned over to the FBI. Is that what this is about?"

"I don't know what the President thinks or doesn't think. I'm just the facilitator."

"If the military is behind something, then why provide the video to the FBI in the first instance?"

"Maybe the right hand doesn't know what the left is doing? Maybe what's on the tape has nothing to do with a plot. Lot of maybes."

"I buy the right hand, left hand explanation. If a plot is, in fact, being worked up, certainly the troops wouldn't know beforehand. But why send it to us?"

"Good point," Tiny responded, his face relaxing. "I suppose we should wait for the President himself to tell us what's on his mind."

"Knowing you," Angella said to Tiny, forcing a smile, "you wouldn't tell us even if you did know." She looked up into his eyes. "Mind explaining why CIA is involved in a domestic disturbance?"

Tiny was obviously prepared for the question. "There's always the chance this is a foreign-run operation. Government gets nervous when things happen down this way, what with Mexico a stone's throw away, and with...with *things*...coming across the border everyday."

Now it was my turn to get in Tiny's face—so to speak. "I'll call bull crap on that! There's no evidence whatsoever—at least nothing we've seen—even hints in the direction of smuggling. A guy killed taking pictures. A senator dropping dead. Right away everyone's blaming the border—or a military insurrection—or terrorists! Ever hear of paranoia? Got a bad case of it going around."

"What you don't know is that the drone taking that video was on a CIA mission south of the border. Camera was under strict orders to be off out over the Gulf. We don't know if the camera remained on accidentally or on purpose."

"Meaning," Angella said, "someone in the Air Force knew what was going to happen on the ground."

"There's nothing to explain what triggered the shooting. Maybe he was hired to do it exactly when the drone was overhead. Who knows? Listen, all I really know is your friend Cindy McNaughton wants you. You're it, like it or not. And I've been tapped as liaison."

He was referring to retired Marine General Lucinda Westminster McNaughton, who seems to be the go-to person in Washington, at least as far as this President is concerned.

"So, Jimmy. Mommy Long Legs wants you to keep the country safe," Angella hissed, her dislike for the woman taking hold. "I can just hear her now. *Why Cowboy, you're just the man to handle such a sensitive matter. Nobody can do it like you can do it. I just don't know what the country would do without you.*" Angella tossed her head from side to side in mock imitation of the retired General.

There was no denying McNaughton was a gorgeous woman, even at her age. Angella conveniently overlooked the fact that Cindy was the long-time lover of retired four-star General Maxwell Jamison, the man the President calls upon to direct national emergencies—and a man who has no tolerance for nonsense. Angella also conveniently overlooked the fact that Cindy had also requested Angella to work on the team.

"Do I detect a note of jealousy?" Tiny asked, turning to Angella. "She's locked to Jamison, has been for forty-some years. She has her man. She might flirt, that's just harmless shtick. Kapish?"

"Pardon me if your assurances don't give me great comfort," Angella responded. "Your track record is dismal."

"Good to put the past behind us," Tiny replied, regaining his *I'm friends to the whole world* demeanor. "Everything came out just fine. We caught the bad folks, did we not?"

"Don't go there!" Angella wasn't giving an inch. "I don't like the situation. Call it gut reaction. Call it what you want.

Woman bats her hazel eyes, men—you included Tiny—fall over themselves doing her bidding."

"Suck it up," Tiny responded, his smile dimming ever so slightly. "She runs this operation. Your life's in her hands."

"That makes it even worse. Get in her path you'll get run the hell over, is what you're telling me."

"You're off-base Angella," Tiny replied, his face now all business. "Either get with it or resign from Homeland Security—and law enforcement. You try joining a police force, you'll do well getting a job standing guard over tomato cans at the local *IGA*."

Angella was right back in his face. "And you know where you—"

"Enough," I snapped, trying to cut Angella off before she really provoked the big guy. This was a side of Angella I had not seen before. "Let's all be positive, give this a chance. We have a job to do."

"Speaking of McNaughton," Tiny said, "that reminds me. Jimmy, you did a masterful job briefing her sister-in-law, Abigail Johnson. Johnson's series in the Washington Post on the A-bomb threat is up for a Pulitzer. Abby owes you big time."

Angella now focused her attention on me. "And exactly just who is this Abby Johnson? I seem to be out of the loop further than I thought."

In all the debriefing we had been through over the past several months, I had studiously refrained from discussing my off-the-record conversations with Johnson. Those discussions had been sanctioned from above, but only for deep background. I had been warned to keep any mention of them out of the debriefing record. Plausible deniability, or some such rot, is what the brass wanted. It was okay if I was the fall guy, but the damage better stop at my feet. That way, the Attorney General could deny any culpability if he's called by Congress to testify.

"It's a long story," I lamely replied. "She's a Washington Post reporter, Homeland Security Desk. She was tipped off by an informant about the bomb. She told me about that tip along with a couple of other facts. That's what ultimately unraveled their elaborate plot."

"You seem to have a lot of women feeding you information," Angella said. "Should I be worried?"

"All in a days work," I replied. "All in a day's work." I winked in her direction.

Angella did not wink back.

"Time to head to the station," Tiny proclaimed. "Game face time."

Tiny had noted the tension building between Angella and myself and was trying to ease it. The man hadn't risen as far as he had in the CIA being oblivious to the nuances around him. "Not good form to keep POTUS waiting," he called, already heading across the beach in the direction of the dunes.

Angella was again studying the water, as if waiting for the waves to stop rolling over her feet. I gave her time to respond. I wanted to take her hand, pull her close and assure her she had nothing to fear. But I stood my ground. I suppose it's not unusual that two driven people would collide from time to time. But I didn't enjoy the feeling, consoling myself with the thought that Angella was angry with Tiny and not with me.

Angella showed no inclination of leaving the water. I called to her, and when she didn't respond I reluctantly followed Tiny across the beach and out toward the street. This mission wasn't starting well, and if my premonition was any gauge, it promised to get a lot worse long before it got better.

FOUR

The greeting by the Coast Guard Station commander, Lt Mark Cruses, was, as expected, warm and genuine, but brief. He is the son of my former partner and I practically raised him—or so I like to think. We floated mutual promises to get together for dinner soon. I asked about his mother, and his eyes gave away deep concern. He replied, "She's doing fine."

Before I could follow up, Tiny announced, "Time to set up."

Cruses held the door open for us and it was clear he didn't want to talk about his mother. The door closed behind us and Tiny and I were alone in the conference room. For all I knew, Angella was still on the beach. I now had doubts whether she was angry at me, or at the big guy across the room.

Tiny checked his phone for messages. "Five minutes. Boss is on time. That's a new first."

The door opened and Angella was shown in by a young sentry. He tossed a crisp salute in her direction before retreating. Without a word Angella took a seat across from me at the table.

Tiny bent to his phone to respond to an incoming message. Angella took that opportunity to wink in my direction.

My spirits lifted.

The screen came alive and the first face to appear was that of General Maxwell Jamison. "We meet again, Redstone," Jamison said into the camera. "Ms. Martinez, what a special delight to have you with us also." He made it sound as though Angella was a surprise. But nothing is a surprise to Jamison, especially where the President is concerned. Jamison ignored Tiny.

As was seemingly their custom, the conference was being recorded and Jamison apparently didn't want the record to reflect Tiny's presence. I suppose they planned to crop him out of the video. That explained why he had moved around the table and was now sitting off to the side behind me. Nobody knows anything. Plausible denial as an art form. Shit just happens.

The President walked briskly into the room and took a chair opposite Jamison. The camera did not reveal anyone else present. Looking directly into the camera, he said, "Jimmy. Angella. First, let me again personally thank both of you for preventing what I can only call a catastrophe. It is indeed a shame the country can't know what you've both done. We very much appreciate your professionalism and efforts."

He had said almost the same thing when he called me in the hospital. But strangely, seeing and hearing him live held far more meaning. I noticed Angella sit taller as well.

"Thank you, Mr. President. I work with a good team."

"Redstone, Martinez," the President said, tossing his head to signal a new topic. "I have an assignment for you. It's rather sensitive. You have a history of solving mysteries that freeze others."

Not waiting for a response, the President continued, "The sudden and regrettable death early today of Senator Donnlevy puts me in an awkward position. With him alive, the vote on the *Force Redeployment Act of 2010* would have most likely been tied. In such an event, it would have languished until after the election. And, off the record, I actually would have been fine with that outcome. I'm, of course, in favor of the military pulling back to our shores. However, the issue has bitterly divided our country, perhaps even worse than health care did." A self-deprecating smile flicked across his face. "And that's saying a lot." He paused to allow us time to laugh.

Then, his voice regained its serious tone. "If, and I say if because I have nothing to base this on, but *if* his death was other than natural, then we would be in a situation where the killer changed the course of this nation's history against the will of the people. I can't allow a murderer to get away with such tactics. If the Senator's death proves to be military inspired, then the outcome will be even more tragic."

The President paused again. Perhaps he was waiting for a question. Or perhaps he needed time to gather his words. "My plan," he continued when we remained silent, "is to announce a moratorium, if you will, on the vote. I will not sign into law the *Force Redeployment Act,* should it be enacted, until such time as I have positive proof that Donnlevy died of natural causes. Of course I won't put it in those terms, but that will be the effect."

"An autopsy will confirm the cause of death in a matter of hours. A day at most," I replied.

"If this was a normal street death then perhaps you're right. But with the chemicals and other stuff available today to the pros I'm told that medical reports can be, shall we say, deceiving. Under such circumstances nobody will trust a government autopsy." A wry smile appeared on his somber face. "I'm certain, being a

Texan, you're painfully aware that folks are still debating Kennedy's death."

I wasn't sure what being a Texan had to do with the conspiracy theories, but now wasn't the time to bring that up. Instead, I said, "And where do we—Angella and I—fit into this?" Investigating homicides was not a Presidential undertaking. That couldn't possibly be our mission.

"Ah, the sixty-four dollar question. I'll get there in a moment. I believe you received a video of a rather shocking disturbance just north of you. There could be linkage."

"Truax..." Jamison's booming voice filled the room. "...better known as Corpus Christi Naval Air Station, is a main base for our UAV world-wide operations."

"To put it in layman's terms," the President injected, "if that base goes down, the United States is instantly blinded around the world. I'm told even a few seconds could be crucial, particularly if the outage is timed to some event, such as the launching of a hostile missile. Couple that with the passage of the *Force Redeployment Act* and we could be looking at something much larger than the murder of a key senator."

Jamison added, "If we pulled back our forces as the legislation would require, we'd be compelled to rely on our ability to detect hostile actions in enough time to mount a counter-attack. Our detection ability being compromised at a critical instant would put us in grave danger."

"Pardon me, Mr. President," I began, knowing it was not good form to argue with the Commander-In-Chief, but I wasn't buying what he was selling. "Surely, a guy killed on a spit on land miles from anywhere is not enough to—"

"Trust me on this," the President replied, cutting off my comment. "The killer disappeared into thin air. I don't believe I've been made privy to the whole story. General Jamison has said nothing to convince me otherwise. That means it's possible the Air Force—or someone—has doctored the video. I can't tolerate the military…running their own…" He paused to take a deep breath. "If the military have… Let's just say I must get to the bottom of what's going on. And the sooner the better."

I recalled Tiny's concerns of a coup and a shiver again went down my spine. Why weren't there others in the room on his end? The Attorney General, for example. And the Joint Chiefs. General Jamison was retired; that put him outside the normal military command.

My shivers continued. "I assume then," I began, careful of how I phrased my next words, "it is your belief that…that… someone, alone or in concert, is…planning to…to disrupt the government."

"Let's just leave it that I'm being prudent to cover all bases."

"You have the entire Justice Department, why—"

"I trust you two, that's why. This is not something I care to spread around. Press'll be on it in a gnat's breath once Justice gets this. Place leaks worse than an old guy with a faulty bladder. You work alone. For this operation, that's good. I want to know exactly how Donnlevy died. And I want that answer as quickly as possible. If he was helped along his journey, I must know sooner rather than later. Second, I want to know as an absolute certainty if the video killing is related to the legislation in any way. Am I making myself perfectly clear?"

"It's clear, Mr. President. Very clear, indeed."

"In the meantime, should the legislation be passed, I will announce that the signing is to be delayed."

"Mr. President," I said, risking his anger, "with all due respect, proving a negative is extremely difficult."

"Then prove the positive. Prove he died of natural causes. We'll give him a proper funeral and get on with our business."

"How long do we have? Could be weeks, even months, to prove anything either way."

"Time in D.C., in case you haven't noticed Mr. Redstone, is measured in hours. We don't have days, let alone weeks or months. If I wanted weeks—or months—I'd appoint a blue ribbon committee. You have two days. Forty-eight hours."

I didn't understand the urgency. While I was crafting my next question, the President answered the urgency question.

"Next week the nuclear fusion limitation talks begin at Georgetown University. I'm addressing the world's leaders on nuclear proliferation. If we are pulling back, we need to disarm—or seriously curtail—several governments. I'll be demanding tighter controls on fusion materials and other measures I can't go into here. Needless to say, they won't be happy with our demands. If there's even a hint that our ability to detect missile threats and to react timely is compromised, they will ignore me."

"I'm sorry, Mr. President, I'm not following. Forgive me, Sir."

"I'm addressing them at the Capitol Tuesday morning. I did want to announce our arms reduction to encourage others to follow suit. I want this resolved by the weekend. Then, if Donnlevy's death was natural, and if the military is not involved in either of the deaths, we can remain on track."

Crimes aren't solved on a political schedule. And this was all politics. "With all due respect, Sir, I—"

"Listen to me, Redstone. And listen well. FBI made it abundantly clear to me that proving a homicide occurred—or did not occur—can't be accomplished with a certainty within my timetable. I get it. But that's what you're going to do—and more. You're going to prove or disprove a linkage to the video murder. That's why I'm authorizing you and Martinez to use any resources you require. I've instructed the Air Force to provide transportation—as well as full cooperation. Justice and Homeland Security will cooperate as well. They don't know why—they just know to do it. If it turns out Donnlevy was murdered, our peace initiatives around the world will be in serious jeopardy. When word spreads that we've resorted to killing folks who disagree, our moral superiority is gone."

"Mr. President, Sir, real life investigations just don't adhere to a time schedule. I'm sorry, but this could take months."

"Politics happens on its own schedule, Redstone. As I said, I don't have months—and neither do you. Understand?"

"I assume then you're more concerned with what we saw on the video than with the Senator."

"I wouldn't put it that way, exactly. They're different problems indeed. But long term, the Senator will be forgotten. Going blind, should this prove to be linked to the Corpus base, at a critical time is a lingering problem. Get my drift?"

"Understood," I replied, not really understanding anything.

He stroked his chin and ran his hand through his hair, nervous gestures I had seen in the past when he was troubled. When he spoke, his voice was again controlled, mild even. "Let me talk frank. And this is off the record. Not rushing the legislation is political theater, I admit that. But, and I believe this, it's also the right thing to do. At least for a short while. If our defense structure is vulnerable I need to know as soon as possible." The look he shot me reminded me I was not his advisor, but rather his servant.

I wanted to explore that line of thought more thoroughly, but decided against saying anything further. Instead, I asked, "Who's doing the autopsy?"

"FBI forensics team, first thing in the morning. At Walter Reed. He was taken there when he collapsed."

"Mind if we hold off the FBI?"

"I'm not wedded to the FBI. I assume you want the results bulletproofed from charges of government intervention. Have someone in mind?"

"I've worked with Dr. Fedrick Martino from University of Texas Southwestern in Dallas. You can take what he finds to the bank. Man has credentials not even the press can shake. I also suggest doing it a non-military facility. My suggestion would be Hopkins."

"Maxwell," the President snapped, "any objections?"

"No, sir." Jamison shot back, seemingly annoyed, but going along.

"Instruct the AG's office to hold up the autopsy. Find this guy Martino and get him to Hopkins. I want no inconvenience to the Donnlevy family."

"On it, sir," Jamison said, standing and walking off camera. His demeanor confirmed he was pissed. I wondered if his agitation was because I had suggested the public wouldn't trust the military to perform an un-biased autopsy. Or did it go deeper than that?

An unseen door opened and closed. The President then turned back to the camera. "Jamison is, of course, against the legislation. The man is livid with me for supporting military downsizing. But that's to be expected. I can't please everyone all the time. Have to do what I think best for the country. Jamison believes you'll find foul play with the Senator's death."

Angella leaned forward. "Pardon me for asking, Mr. President, but do you want us to go full out on the Senator?"

"I don't fault you for being skeptical, Ms. Martinez. Two of my advisors asked that very same question. Naturally, I want the legislation signed. And just as naturally, and while you may not believe this, I hope to God there was no foul play. If there was, I want the person or persons responsible held fully accountable."

"No matter whom it turns out to be?"

The President's eyes narrowed and his lips moved without sound. He looked directly into the camera. Any softness he may have had evaporated. "And just what are you implying?"

Angella's face turned bright red, and her lips drew into a tight line. But she held her ground. "Only that, Sir, the people who have the most to gain from the Senator's death are your supporters. Perhaps people who work in your office. Someone thinking he or she was doing you a favor."

"I swore to uphold the Constitution of the United States. And I mean to do so. Investigate anyone you want. If Donnlevy was murdered, I want that person tried in a court of law for the entire world to see. Am I clear enough?"

"Yes, sir. Very clear indeed," Angella exclaimed, "No matter where this takes us."

"No matter where it takes you."

FIVE

General Jamison returned a few minutes later and took the President's place. For the first time since I've known the man, his voice did not have a knife-edge to it.

"Angella, Jimmy, I know the President thanked you. But please let me add my heartfelt thanks as well on a job well done. You accomplished what the FBI and Secret Service couldn't. I personally want to commend you both."

"Thank you, General," I replied. "Had a lot of help along the way." In fact, during the operation I had been suffering the gut-wrenching misery of pending failure. "Caught a few lucky breaks."

"Good people make their own luck," he responded. "What counts is that you finished the mission with a positive outcome. The Senator's death is a mess as well. I believe the autopsy will uncover foul play."

"Why are you so convinced?" Angella asked.

"Simple. Donnlevy was too ornery to fall over dead before the biggest vote of his life. And with that Texas shooting..."

"You think they're linked?" Angella pressed.

"What you don't know is that inland from where the shooting occurred is a nuclear-powered generating facility. The victim was taking measurements of some type."

"Nuclear power? In Texas? By the coast?"

"This is not for publication. Hear that Redstone? No deep background shit to your Washington Post friend."

"I understand," I said. "Please continue."

"Not many people know it's there. Could never have been allowed to build it, but for the secrecy. Hid it near a wind generation farm to explain the power lines and transformers and vehicles and shit like that. It's one of the new safe traveling wave reactor types. I'll leave it to your skills to find out why it's safe, but I'm assured it is—to a point."

From Jamison's tone, it was clear he doubted the truth of what he had just said. I accepted Angella's narrowed eyes as my cue to pin the general down. "What do you mean, to a point?"

Ignoring my question, Jamison continued. "Corpus Christi is one of the air fields that houses a portion of our Zephyrs. Worldwide surveillance, as well as drone control, is at Creech Air Base in Nevada. However, Corpus is a major relay point for incoming intelligence from the Atlantic, the Americas, Africa and the Middle-East, as well as a base for part of the Zephyr fleet. They feed Creech as well as Central Command in Tampa."

"This going where I think it's going?" I commented unnecessarily, miffed at being ignored, but knowing the General would only tell us what he wanted us to hear.

"If power were to be interrupted to Corpus, we'd go blind. If the freak...the pending legislation were to pass, then we'd be dependant on electronic surveillance, especially of the Middle-East, for a modicum of advance notice."

"Pardon me, General," Angella broke in, "but the legislation hasn't passed yet. And if it does, it won't be implemented for years. How does a death of one poor guy—"

"President is concerned that if the legislation passes, our allies will gear up with nuclear devices of their own, thinking they can't depend on us for the long haul. He's afraid that when we pull back, someone else will step up. He'll be talking on that subject in a few days, calling for more disarmament. The upcoming joint military mission is timed to demonstrate that even if the U. S. pulls back, we are capable of immediate and effective retaliation. If we screw that up, there's no telling what the outcome will be. It will hamper his chances to obtain buy-off on his plan for world-wide de-escalation."

"The military is against the legislation. It's in the best interests of the military to...let me say...stall—"

"Don't go there, Redstone! The military command is rock solid. Focus on the real problem. I assure you it's not the military."

"You call me in to investigate. Then you tie my hands. I don't—"

"I didn't call you in!" he barked, his eyes as hard as ever. Cindy did. This is her show. I'm just telling you not to waste your time on the military."

"Continue, please," I replied, thankful he was a thousand miles away. Or was he? For all I knew he was in the next room. No. He was with the President and if the President were on the island I'd know it—or so I assumed."

"We're scheduled to test our detection capability against an enemy attack. We can't allow anything or anybody interfering with our ability to detect incoming threats. They will be flying stealth aircraft toward our coast. If even one of the planes man-ages to penetrate our coast, we have a disaster. Need I say more?"

"You draw a tenuous link between a dead guy on a Texas beach and a dead senator in Washington," I said, trying to reduce the tension. "Military doesn't investigate dead civilians—or dead senators for that matter."

"Tenuous is what we live and die by, Redstone. That particu-lar senator was against the pullback. He's dead. A man is blown apart on a beach near a power plant feeding a vital military facil-ity. A person, or an organization, against the pullback could ac-complish a great deal by interrupting power at a critical moment. Linkage or paranoia? You tell me."

"So why us? We have no connection to the Senator. Or to politics, or to—"

"Texas is the freakin' link. Perfect cover to use a Texas Rang-er for both."

Reminding him that Angella and I are now Homeland Securi-ty was senseless. "Are you the point, General? Or should we—"

"Like I said, Cindy's running this. Take your orders...direc-tions...from her."

The panel went blank.

Tiny, coming out from hiding, said, "This fellow Martino, I take it, is good."

"None better. Donnlevy is a Texas senator. You heard the General," I said, nodding toward the dead screen, "it's only fitting to have a Texas pathologist. Better arrange rides for us." I wasn't looking forward to going to the cold north, but it was important for Angella and I to be at the autopsy.

Tiny made a few calls. "Autopsy is scheduled to begin at four AM."

Angella said, "We can copter over the National Seashore where the killing took place and get a look. If need be, we can set down for a closer inspection. Should take two hours max. Then fly to Baltimore from Corpus. Meet you there."

"Too bad I came down in a two-seater, or we could give you a hitch. I'll get your flights arranged." Tiny flipped open his phone and moved across the room to talk.

"What do you make of Jamison?" Angella asked.

"Man's conflicted. He's pissed the President wants to dismantle the military. He's pissed Cindy brought us in. Man bleeds khaki. But he follows orders."

"Man's always pissed at something. Surprised McNaughton puts up with him."

"She's cut from the same tree. A perfect matched set."

Tiny closed his phone. "Coast Guard's taking you up to Corpus and the Air Force will fly you east. You guys need to pack or do you still have stuff in your apartment back in Arlington? I'll have jackets for you on the plane."

Angella shrugged. "Our things are still there. "Unless, of course, they were thrown out. I seem to recall there was a *problem* with the lease."

Angella was in rare form. She was again jabbing Tiny over the fiasco we had faced working with him on our previous assignment.

"Been resolved," Tiny replied, his smile fading only slightly as the barb slid by unchallenged. He was not about to explain away the screw-up. "If you're ready, your ride's waiting." Tiny threw a mock salute and disappeared through the door.

I turned to Angella. Her brown eyes were soft again, all trace of anger gone. I reached for her hand and she pulled it back just out of range.

"Eyes are everywhere. Just because the screen is dark doesn't mean—"

"Been living together for weeks now. You think they don't know?"

"Thinking is not proving." She lowered her voice to barely a whisper. "Later." She turned her back from where the camera was—or at least from where she thought the camera was—and blew me a kiss.

My game face back on, I said, "How about getting an itinerary of everything the Senator did for the week before he died? Everyone he saw, where he ate, the works."

"That's a perfect task for the FBI. Mind if I call Jacobs? Despite all that happened, he seemed a straight shooter."

"Good choice," I replied. I had avoided suggesting Sylvan Jacobs, agent in charge of the San Antonio FBI office, hoping it would come from Angella. Jacobs is a no-nonsense guy and plays it straight. "Tell him to meet us at Hopkins. I'll have Tiny arrange transportation for him from San Antonio."

Logistics out of the way, we boarded the helicopter. It was small, held two passengers behind the pilot and was used, from what I had observed, for spotting drug drops over the Gulf of Mexico. The passenger seat had been removed, as had the door. Observers could sit with their legs dangling in the wind, looking straight down. Anybody sitting that way would make easy targets for a high-powered rifle shot from a drug boat. I didn't volunteer to sit there.

In the air, it was hard to talk over the wind noise. My eyes stung, and when I looked over at Angella there were tears running down her face. At first I thought she was crying, but then I realized my own face was wet as well.

The pilot, a youngster with large ears, said, "Goggles are in the side compartments."

I leaned close to Angella. "We need to talk to all of the Senator's doctors. Have full medical reports delivered to Hopkins, including all medications. Martino will want to review it all anyway."

"I'll go through the Senate Medical staff for that," Angella responded. "Better yet, I'll kick it to Tiny. Put his ass to work."

"Let's keep him out of this for a while, if we can." I replied. This was all moving too fast and I was not yet fully comfortable with the big guy.

"Okay, we'll use Jacobs."

Angella was busy yelling into her phone as we headed north along the sandy coast.

A few minutes later she said, "Don't know how Tiny does it, but Jacobs will join us in Corpus for the ride east. We'll have to wait about twenty minutes, but that still brings us into Baltimore about the time Martino lands."

"Look down there," I said, pointing east. We were flying north over the bay, midway between the sandy barrier island and the mainland. The Texas coast was slowing curving away to the east. "He could have walked or swum from the island. It's not so wide in this area."

"Still, it's a good distance south of where the…the incident took place."

Angella was right to be cautious. The less we said the better. I studied the mainland, trying to spot the telltale signs of a nuclear power plant. I saw nothing but brown soil—or sand. Certainly, not anything that even resembled a power generation facility. Didn't even spot any wires or wire poles until the wind farm, with its massive slowly rotating propellers dotting the landscape.

I leaned forward. "How far to the air field?"

"Up ahead. You'll see it in a few minutes," the pilot responded.

"Do we have time before Jacobs arrives?" I asked Angella.

"A good half-hour."

I again leaned forward, positioning my mouth not far from the pilot's ear. "Take a detour, if you will, Skipper. Fly us over the National Seashore, near the south end."

"You got it."

The helo banked off to the right and made a half-circle. We were now going southeast, and it only took a few minutes to be over the sandy area we had first seen in the video. We were flying about a thousand feet above the dunes and vegetation, but the resolution was no better than the video taken from ten miles up. The wind—perhaps with some human intervention—had cleared away any trace of the mayhem that had occurred below us.

Angella leaned over me and held her camera in the spacious opening. I assumed she was making her own video, but she may have been snapping stills.

"Head inland," I instructed our pilot after we circled twice over the area. The kid flying the 'copter was barely in his twenties and wore a mustache that called to mind Douglas Fairbanks. I doubted if he even knew who Fairbanks was.

"There's a restricted zone on the other side of the bay, inland about ten miles from here," he replied. "Can't over-fly without permission. Shall I call it in?"

"Fly as close to it as you can, then turn north. No need to bother headquarters with this."

We turned west, flew about six minutes and then banked north.

"How wide is the restricted zone?"

"About a mile square."

"Circle around it, if you will."

"Looking for anything in particular?"

"Curious."

"Seeing as though you're HS and all, I wouldn't be talking out of turn if I told you there are rumors of a nuclear plant down there. Just saying."

The way he nodded his head made me think there was more to the story. "You for it or against it?"

"Me, personally, I don't like nuclear power. See what it did in Japan. And right here near the Gulf. Hurricanes and all. Get my drift?"

"Lots of folks agree with you," I replied.

"I like those wind generators better," the kid said, pointing northward in the direction of the wind turbines. He then returned his attention to his gauges as we closed on the restricted zone. I saw nothing unusual. I didn't suppose the military would shoot down one of its own, but I wasn't keen on young Fairbanks getting court-martialed in the process.

SIX

Jacobs was waiting for us when we stepped down from the helicopter. He shook my hand and hugged Angella, congratulating her on her reinstatement.

Our military jet transport to Baltimore was waiting not far away and we were ushered to the base of the steps by an impeccably dressed Marine guard who saluted each of us in turn as we passed in front of him.

Once we were seated, Jacobs said, "Seems you two are the designated hitters. Got the shorthand version from the Director. One thing I'll say about this President, like him or not, when he finds a winner he rides it home. You're the ride. I'm the stable hand."

"Don't know what to make of this. We just flew over the beach where Timberwolf was killed. Nothing much to see."

Jacobs frowned.

"I assumed you'd been briefed," I said, concerned about revealing something I shouldn't have.

"About Senator Donnlevy. You got something else going?"

The cat was out. I told him about the video. He listened carefully. When I finished, he said, "Doesn't tie together. Sounds to me General Jamison is up to more of his..." Jacobs, obviously remembering where he was, lowered his voice. "...more of his clandestine dealings. He's really outside the military, works for the President. Enough said on that subject. I need to see the video."

Angella extracted it from her bag. "I'm not sure I can part with this, but we can watch it together."

"Let's do that later in a more...shall we say...private...setting. What are your thoughts?"

"In all candor," I replied, "we're just doing what we always do. Following the threads. Going where they take us. We're plodders."

"You're not giving yourselves enough credit. But listen, there are stars and wannabes. Sometimes the wannabes have the greater talent. But the public pays to see the stars. Go figure. You get results, *ipso facto*, you're the stars."

"*Ipso facto*. I'm impressed." I chided Jacobs.

"A few *ipso factos*, toss in some *res ipsa locatures*, and an occasional *habeas corpus*, and you got 'em eating out of your hand," Jacobs quipped in a rare moment of relaxation. "It cost my parents well over one-hundred fifty grand for law school, so I can talk that way. Have to give them their money's worth."

I didn't know if this assignment was good for Jacobs' career or not, but he didn't seem worried. The man was a professional all the way. I wouldn't want him on my case. Then I remembered that he had, indeed, investigated me a few years back when I was accused of shooting Badman Tex. From comments he made when we last worked together, I conclude his version of the facts differs from the official findings.

"Where'd you go to school?" Angella asked. "You're not from south Texas. No oil patch in your voice."

"Small school in Columbus. Capital. You probably never heard of it. Capital Law School. Great little place."

"Ohio or Georgia?"

"Ohio."

"You from Ohio?"

"North Carolina."

"What took you to Ohio?"

"Father graduated there. Always talked about a crusty old professor. Name of Sullivan. Had to see for myself."

"Did he live up—or should I say down—to the hype?"

"Best teacher I ever had! Scared the living hell out of me, to tell the truth. But I learned the law. I owe him my career."

"High praise," Angella said, caught off-guard by Jacob's openness—and passion.

"Can't say enough about the man. Died last year. Taught for thirty-five years. Man's a legend. One of a kind."

- - - - -

We napped on the trip east, not knowing when our next sleep period would come. The jet landed at Thurgood Marshall Airport in Baltimore and taxied to the general aviation passenger terminal.

Tiny was waiting for us. "Martino's plane landed an hour ago. He went on to the hospital." Tiny walked us to a government car and climbed in behind the wheel. I sat in front with him. Angella and Jacobs were in back.

"Your folks at Justice did a good job obtaining the releases," Tiny said, directing his comment to Jacobs. "All the medical reports have been entered into the database and are available in a secure e-room. Donnlevy's doctors will consult in person with Martino when he's ready. Donnlevy's Daily Activity Charts, DACs as his camp calls them, are coming on-line as we drive. From the quick peek I took, the guy didn't take a whiz without someone logging the start/stop time."

"Learn anything so far?" Jacobs asked, always the FBI guy.

"Only that the heart attack came on fast. He hadn't complained of pain or any discomfort in the past few days. However, he had been treated in the past for some type of heart problem. No details yet."

Tiny fell silent. We drove to the hospital with no further conversation. Preparing to gather facts surrounding a dead body is never a fun time, and everyone's mood reflected the task ahead.

Dr. Martino was sitting behind a small table in an office the size of a Dallas closet when we arrived at Hopkins. Other than the laptop, a metal table and four wooden chairs, the room was barren. He was waiting for the pathology team to gather. The Senator's body had already arrived and was being prepped in the lab at the end of corridor.

"So we meet again, Ranger Redstone," Martino called from behind the computer. It was close to four in the morning and he was chipper. "And who are these folks?"

I introduced Tiny as being with the Secret Service. No need to go into the CIA connection. Angella was presented as my partner at Homeland Security. "And this is Sylvan Jacobs, FBI."

"So you finally left the Rangers," Martino commented. "How the hell is Texas to survive?" To Angella he said, "I don't often say this, but since I'm on record with the Governor I can't get into trouble. But Jimmy is about the best investigator I've ever had the pleasure of working with. I trust his instincts. You being his partner, I suppose you know that already."

"You give me way too much credit," I said, never comfortable with this line of talk. "Who are we waiting on?"

"I've asked Dr. Lester Stillman and Dr. Glenda Houstein to assist. Glenda trained under me in Dallas. She's one of the best there is anywhere."

I was surprised. Martino usually worked alone, except when he was teaching.

"Don't look so shocked. When the President pulls you out of a Mavericks game, something big is up. Stillman heads the pathology department here at Hopkins, need I say more. You have the A team." He glanced at his cell. "They're ready to go. Joining us?"

"Maybe later. How long you think it'll take?"

"Best guess, three, maybe four hours. In order to rule out human intervention, we must be thorough. Brenda is a nitpicker. Never known her to miss anything. The full tox report will take days."

"I may be able to speed that up," Jacobs said. "Let me know when it's ready to send out."

I said to Martino, "Thanks for coming out. Sorry about the game. You didn't miss a thing. Mavs lost."

When we were alone, Angella said, "I see why you asked for Martino. The man carries himself well. I can't imagine the press taking him down."

"He's as good as they get. Don't know this Houstein woman, but if Martino says she's good, I'll go with that."

Jacobs opened his beat-up black leather case and fished out a small laptop, more in keeping with a net-book than a computer. "I've called up profiles on the Senator's staff. Also got files on his most vocal opponents, who, as you well know, are aligned with the President."

"Already mentioned that to the man," Angella injected. "He gave us the *go for it* pep talk."

"What else would you expect?" Jacobs smiled. "Bet he sounded convincing."

"You think otherwise?"

"The word in the Service," Jacobs responded, "is that he's a straight shooter. But, hey, let's keep our wits about us and rule nothing out. Formula for trouble when you pre-judge."

The computer Tiny had arranged for me booted up without a problem. I turned to Jacobs. "I'll need the link to the Senator's medical records."

"I'll also send info on his staff," Jacobs said, already working his keyboard.

A moment later, both links had arrived. I brought up the staff members. It was longer than I would have expected.

"I'd start with his Chief," Jacobs chimed in. "Man name of Stetson. Hank Stetson. Knew him in another life way back when. Went to the same law school, but he was ahead of me by a year. Interested in politics, not the law. He's made a career latching onto one senator after another. In his mid-fifties. A tough-talking good ole boy. Occupation: Professional mooch."

"Mooch? That a technical term?"

"Personal prerogative."

"Want to observe the autopsy?" I asked Jacobs.

"If I never attend another in my life, that'll be just fine with me," Jacobs replied, a disgusted grimace appearing on his normally bland face. "I'd just as soon read, or better yet, hear, the report. If you want to, by all means go for it."

I turned to Angella, but she pretended to be busy with her computer. To my knowledge she had never witnessed a human body being laid open, all pretext of privacy gone. Now wasn't the time to press the issue.

Tiny, who had been leaning against the wall trying to remain out of the way, came to life when I looked his way. "I'll set up a time to visit with, what's his name? Cowboy Stenson?"

"Stetson. Hank Stetson. Here's his cell number."

Tiny got busy on his keypad and a few minutes later announced, "Stetson's replied. Man's pissed his boss's body was moved without his permission. He's on his way here to set things straight. Should be interesting."

SEVEN

As timing sometimes works out, I was just finishing Hank Stetson's file profile when the man himself came through the door, cowboy hat, boots, oversize belt buckle, the works. All six-feet-five and two-hundred-eighty pounds of him. Before I could say a word, he shoved a hand in my direction. "I'm Hank Stetson. You must be Redstone. I've heard about you. Call me Hank."

After introducing Angella, I turned to introduce Jacobs, forgetting for the moment the two had gone to the same law school. Stetson said, "We know each other. You doin' okay, Jacobs? How's San Antone treating you?"

"As well as can be expected," Jacobs replied. His momentary hesitation made me realize Jacobs disliked the man. Funny how things work out. Jacobs, an east-coast boy, winds up in Texas and Stetson, a Texan, works in Washington. When neither of them extended a hand, I confirmed the bad blood.

Tiny had disappeared, perhaps to the men's room, perhaps to retrieve more files. I assumed he wasn't in hiding, but with Tiny, one never knew.

Stetson faced me. "You the guy brought the Senator up here? You got some tall explaining to do. I haven't informed his wife, wanted to see for myself what's going down. She'd be most upset to learn his dead body was being dragged around the countryside like a side of beef."

"Appreciate your concern, Mr. Stetson," I replied, working to keep this from escalating. "I understand you're the man in charge of the Senator's activities. Just the person we need to speak with actually."

"You understand correct. Whatever you're doing better be good enough to justify kidnapping the Senator. Where I come from we respect the dead. You're a Texas boy; should know better."

"Let me assure you, nothing we do will disrespect the Senator—or his family. He's here because I wanted the autopsy performed quickly and with people who are above public scrutiny."

"You casting aspersions on the military, son? I wouldn't do that if I were you. Not healthy. Get my drift?"

"Just avoiding problems on down the line. Autopsy's being performed by some good ole Texas doctors. Make the Senator right proud."

"Why the hell do we need an autopsy? Gutting him like a fish! Man died of a heart attack, plain and simple. Turned blue right in front of my eyes. Grabbed his chest. Don't need no doctor poking around inside him to know that much."

"A United States Senator holding the critical vote in a hotly contested piece of legislation dies of a sudden heart attack just minutes before the vote. And you don't see a reason to investigate? I'm frankly surprised."

"Just who the hell do you think you are, Redstone? I'm in charge of the Senator and I wasn't consulted!"

"Hank," I said, playing a bit of Texas for his benefit, "your cows are gettin' dangerous close to runnin'. Calm down."

"Don't go getting' fancy with me, son! I'll have your nether parts hanging out to dry sooner you can say your name."

I had enough. "You talk that way, you'll find yourself out in the parking lot."

"Who the hell you think—"

"Let's get something straight," I said, moving inside his private space. "When the Senator died, your stroke died with him. Your choices are simple. Work through this together. Or get the hell out. You keep up the attitude, you won't appreciate the consequences."

"Who the hell gave you authority over a U.S. Senator? Homeland Security has no jurisdiction here."

I wasn't comfortable involving the President, so I lied. "Governor asked me to look into the Senator's death, if you must know. Now what will it be? Work together or get out?"

A puzzled look crossed his broad face. Suddenly he looked tired. "Mind if I sit? To say the least, this has been a most trying day, even considering the types of days we've been having."

I nodded in the general direction of a chair. Angella and Jacobs had remained quiet throughout our exchange. At the mention of the governor, Jacobs had given me a slight nod of approval.

Stetson sat quietly for a moment. I assumed he was considering his options. But he could have been working on some other plan. Then he said, "You looking for foul play. Correct?"

"We're investigating. Not looking for anything in particular. Just want to find cause of death."

"The man was a lightning rod for trouble. Collected a ton of enemies along the way. But this was a heart attack, pure and simple. Know it when I see it."

"You have the log of his activities?"

"I know who he officially spoke with. I don't know who he spoke with privately."

This didn't exactly square with the DAC that Tiny had uploaded. This was Stetson's way of distancing himself from *unofficial* activities. "Could Donnlevy have met with anyone privately that you didn't know about?"

"Certainly. I didn't sleep with the man."

"Did his wife?"

"What the hell kind of question is that? You're overstepping your britches, son. Get my drift?"

"The answer is either, yes, no, or I don't know."

"How the hell would I know?"

"You're his manager. You sure as hell know his sleeping habits."

"I'm not in the bedroom with them."

"Cut the bullshit! We'll do this the long way if you insist. Did he and his wife sleep in the same bedroom?"

"As far as I know."

"Does the Senator have more than one residence?"

"Depends what you mean by residence."

"I said, cut the bullshit! I'll ask the question again. Does the Senator have more than one residence? A simple yes or no will suffice."

"Yes."

"Now we're on a roll. I assume a residence here near Washington and I assume one back in Texas."

"You're right on. His local place is in Georgetown."

"Any others?"

"No."

"See how easy this is?" I chided. "Did they, I mean the Senator and his wife, live in the same house? No, I asked that wrong. When the Senator was east, did his wife live here or did she remain in Texas?"

"In Texas."

"Did he ever mention anything about his sleeping arrangements with his wife? Think before you answer. This could turn into a criminal investigation and false statements will bite you in the butt."

"He never said anything."

"Before I ask this next question, I warn you to tell us the truth and the full truth. Did the good Senator have sex with other women? If you think for one minute we won't find out the truth, you're dreaming."

"Depends upon your definition of sex."

"Shit! You hear me before? Don't you guys ever learn? You define sex for us."

Stetson thought for a moment, his face at first going hard. Then a small embarrassed smile formed at the corners of his mouth. "Let's just say Donnlevy enjoyed younger women."

"How young is young?"

"Is this necessary?"

"Just answer the question."

"Twenties."

"Nineteen?"

"Sometimes."

"Does that mean younger?"

"Sometimes."

"Does his wife know?"

"I suppose."

"Who arranges and how often?"

"Key. Keyston Jenkins."

"Any reason to suspect foul play from any of the women?"

"Wouldn't think that to be so. Key keeps track of all that."

"Anyone in your camp who would wish the Senator ill?"

"Not that I know of. Listen, the old man died of natural causes. Just fell over. I don't understand—"

"I'm only interested in how he died. I have no interest in his sexual activities unless they contributed to his demise. How about reconstructing for us his last week? Work backward from just before he died."

"This necessary?"

"When can we have the first day?"

"Take me about an hour to reconstruct. My computer's in the car. Any chance of getting an office?"

"Tiny will work on it. How do I reach Keyston?"

"I'll have Keys call you. Shouldn't be long; the man never sleeps."

When the door closed behind him, Angella said, "You sure didn't waste time deflating his over-filled balloon. You could almost see the air, or whatever keeps him afloat, leaking."

Jacobs, who had been uncommonly silent during the interrogation of Stetson, chimed in. "That's an act. Seen him do this before. He's lying in the weeds. He'll eat you alive, given half a chance."

"Nice," Angella responded.

"Let's not give him the chance," I said. "Keep him off balance."

"That's not as easy as you might think," Jacobs replied. "Political operatives like him have more lives than the proverbial cat. Like the willow tree, they go with the flow. Bet he has his paws in the next power broker already."

"The Senator's barely cold."

"Doesn't stop these grubs."

"Tell us what you really think," Angella said.

Martino came through the door. He was wearing blue scrubs streaked across the front with a dark substance. "Thought I'd give you an interim report," he said. "Autopsy will take longer than I had initially believed. But, so far, all seems in order. He died of a myocardial infarction. That much we know for certain. Or at least as certain as one can ever know anything. But, of course, that alone only says what you already knew. He had a heart attack."

"Jives with what his chief of staff just said. So what's troubling you?" I asked, reading the look on his face.

"Am I that transparent? I'd very much like to speak to anyone with him when he died."

"What are you looking for exactly?"

"The symptoms he expressed. What people observed."

"Why's that important?"

"We see very little evidence of long-term disabling thickening. Actually, it appears as though his coronary arteries simply collapsed. His medical record suggests he was taking a prophylactic aspirin daily. Doesn't add up. Call it an intuitive feeling if you will."

The door opened. "Just the man we're looking for," I said when Hank Stetson walked back into the room. "Hank, this is Dr. Martino. He's performing the autopsy and has some questions for you. Doctor, this is the Senator's Chief of Staff, Hank Stetson. Mr. Stetson was with the Senator when he died."

The two men shook hands. Stetson volunteered, "Senator Donnlevy died of a heart attack. Anyone can see that. Tell these fools and let's get out of here."

"We have agreement on the heart attack," Martino replied. "Mind telling me where you were in relation to the Senator when you first noticed something was wrong?"

"A few feet away. Why?"

"What did you observe?"

"He was in a heated telephone discussion with Wilkes, that's John Wilkingham. He's the idiot behind this eunuch legislation. We were in a hurry to get to the floor. The vote was in progress. Rare to hold session so late, but this was special. I gave the Senator the cut sign to get off the phone. Time was running out." Stetson closed his eyes as though he was visualizing the events.

"So," Martino probed, "what exactly did you observe?"

"The phone fell from his hand, he started to topple, and before I could get to him, he fell to the floor, hitting his cheek on the side of the desk."

"Did he say anything?"

"Nothing. Maybe a gasp of '*ah*' or something along those lines. One minute he was alive and shouting into the phone, the next he was gone."

"Did he complain of pains, discomfort, breathing problems before that?"

"Nothing."

"Did he place his hand on his chest? You know, like he was trying to massage his chest?"

"I didn't see him do that. I'm certain I would have noticed if he had."

"Anything unusual in his manner? In his movements?"

"Not that I recall."

"In his speech? Tone or patterns different?"

"Nothing"

"Breathing heavy?"

"No."

"Labored in any way?"

"Didn't seem to be."

"Do you know if he had chest pains, particularly at night?"

"If he did, he didn't tell me."

"Would he have?"

"He told me everything else."

"Everything?"

"I believe so."

"What else do you know about his medical health, other than his heart?"

"Nothing. He has regular physicals and he's never said anything other than *I'm healthy as a horse* every time he received the results."

"Anything out of the ordinary happen before he died? Any different food, medications, anything?"

"Nothing that I know of."

I asked, "Anything you don't know of?"

"How the hell would I know what I don't know?"

"Some things you're supposed to know, some things you're not. Did anything happen you're not supposed to know about?"

"The man's dead. Gone! I'm not holding back."

Martino looked Stetson directly in the eye and held his focus for an uncomfortable moment. Then he said, "If anything comes to mind, please let me know immediately. Big or small, just let me know. Behavior, food, anything."

"I'll be sure to do that," Stetson replied. "Am I finished here?"

"As far as I'm concerned, you're free to go."

Without waiting for a reply from Jacobs or I, Stetson left the room.

Angella asked Martino, "Was the Senator sick or something? The way you asked about other conditions makes me wonder."

"He was terminally ill. Cancer had metastasized everywhere. His kidneys were essentially nonfunctional. I find it difficult to believe he managed without anyone noticing. Certainly Donnlevy himself had to know. Almost just as certainly he refused radiation and chemotherapy. I'll find that in his records later."

Stating the obvious, I said, "Stetson says he didn't know. I wonder what else he *doesn't know?*"

"That's what I love about this job," Jacobs said when Martino left. "Nothing's ever easy. Man can't even fall over dead with a heart attack without forensic complications. I'll use some muscle on his personal doctor. We'll get what we need. How about Angella talking to the wife?"

I nodded. "Sounds like we're on our way to the District."

"That's the nexus of this mess," Jacobs replied, "best be there if we want to be in the hunt." He flipped his computer closed. "Off the record, I've asked our San Antonio office to follow up on Philip Timberwolf. Guy lived alone. Not married. Owned the place where he lived. Not much more than a fishing shack. Kept to himself. Not much yet, but we'll build the file. At some point we'll want to go and see for ourselves."

"Let it percolate, we got enough going on here to keep us busy for now," I replied, remembering how we were run in circles up and down the Texas coast chasing the elusive terrorist. The distractions almost worked. I didn't want to repeat that scenario if we could help it. But I also knew from my long years as a Texas Ranger that there was no substitute for direct face time. Boots on the ground, as it were.

"Just saying," Jacobs answered. "They'll be ready when we are."

"I'll talk to Wilkes, or whatever he calls himself," I said. "Get to the bottom of what the legislation is and isn't. The talking jerks on the news give us just enough to make whatever point they're peddling at the moment. Fox portrays the Senator as a hero. To CNN, he's an obstructionist, lost in the Cold War era. Tiny can follow up with Stetson and map the Senator's time line."

The fact was, I trusted Martino's *intuitive feelings*, and sensed we were pulling on all the wrong threads.

EIGHT

John "Wilkes" Wilkingham was a character out of central casting. He carried a good hundred extra pounds on his six-two frame and made no pretext of hiding an overflowing paunch. Ever the politician, he greeted me as a long lost, back-slapping, hard-drinking, buddy. That is, until I told him I was following up on a few facts pertaining to the death of Senator Donnlevy.

"Man dies of a heart attack and right away you government types come sniffing around trying to pin it on someone. Can't bleach the stripes out of you desk jock tigers, now can we?"

"Mind telling me how that chip got on your shoulder? I'm here to ask about the legislation you're pushing and you assume the government's after you. You do something you want to get off your chest?" Confronting a person with their own guilt feelings is exactly the situation that works best for me. Emotions running on overdrive are good for investigators. Most people over-think the situation and dig themselves under.

"I'm sorry," he replied, "lack of sleep. Have you had breakfast? I can use coffee."

Wilkes certainly had not risen to where he was by being stupid. That much was evident by how quickly he gathered himself. His eyes softened, the belligerence replaced by what passed for genuine friendship.

When I didn't immediately respond, he continued, "Been up all night working through the implications of the man's death. President imposed a moratorium on the vote. Suppose you heard that. Our timing is now messed to hell. In politics, timing is everything. Those opposition crazies can now regroup. No telling what damage they'll do. Come, there's a little place around the corner. Not worth a darn for anything else, but they nail breakfast."

Around the corner turned out to be three blocks and an alley. Wilkes explained to me why this legislation was so important. And truth is, while I was initially against the idea of the United States pulling its troops back and disengaging from Iraq and Afghanistan and Kuwait and Pakistan and Korea and countless other places he ticked off, Wilkes made a compelling argument for why bringing them all home was critical to the long-term viability of our country.

"Before the war," he added, "I'm referring, of course, to World War Two, we had it right. Keep to ourselves."

"As I recall, it didn't exactly work out the way we had it planned."

"Temporary set-back," Wilkes responded. "We need to mind our own shores, leave the world to sort out its own mess. How the hell do we know if we wouldn't be better off if Germany had won the war? Right now, the folks running Europe are making a mess of it. Everyone but Germany is broke and we're going down with them."

I couldn't believe this guy. I had never heard anyone with any brains suggest Hitler would have been good for Europe. But I hadn't come to debate with him. "That's not the way the Senator saw it," I said, pausing to give my order to the skinniest waiter I had ever seen. When the skeleton headed off toward the kitchen, I said, "Donnlevy, and the people behind him, believe you're a traitor. How do you answer them?"

My question provoked a deep laugh. "That's perhaps the kindest thing they've said about me. Look, there's no denying I loathe Donnlevy and all he stands for. And I know he felt the same about me. His philosophy that America should impose its views on the world drives me nuts. Look, Redstone, it's absurd to believe democracy is for everyone. A tribal leader in northern Afghanistan is simply not interested in having a rival tribe tell him what he can and can't do. And who are we to say otherwise? We occupy their land. That makes us the enemy. We can't sustain it. And most importantly, we can't afford it."

My resolution to not debate the man was in danger of crumbling. I ventured, "It's worked since forty-five. What's changed?"

"You're conveniently overlooking Korea and Vietnam. Not to mention a dozen other places. Iraq and Afghanistan are fresh on our minds, but there's been many other wars on foreign lands. They're draining us. Our kids are dying on foreign soil. And every time we do it we come away with millions of enemies—and very few friends."

I didn't respond and he went on. "The old policy may have worked at a time when the United States manufactured products they wanted. When we made clothes and tools and cars, the world needed us. They had to listen—or pretend to listen—if they wanted our goods—our glamour. Truth is, our glamour's sagging worse than an aging beauty queen. Now they look to China and India and Japan and Korea to mention only a few for what they need. All we have left to give the world are ideas. Our economy is barely ahead of China and we're slipping fast. Our ideas are becoming second-rate and slipping. The go-go years are visible only in the rear view mirror. Keep this in mind. Ideas, my friend, are useless to a tribal chief fighting for daily survival. We can't sustain it. And the sooner we act, the better we'll be." He sipped his coffee. "Sorry for the rant."

"You've obviously given that speech many times."

"CNN likes to trot me out. Fox'll not touch me, but they agree with me on reducing our costs."

"Donnlevy saw it the other way. His vote would have blocked your legislation. His death works to your advantage."

"As I said earlier, you're here to find out if I orchestrated an accelerated time table. Pardon me for being blunt, but a pig with lipstick is still a pig."

In my mind, the pig in his metaphor was him. I'm certain he saw it the other way.

The pencil-thin waiter slipped a gorgeous frittata in front of me. It had been Wilkes suggestion, and it filled the plate majestically, steam rising to add a pleasurable sensation to the presentation.

But it's difficult to enjoy good food when you're agitated. And Wilkes agitated me. Tribal chief's not requiring ideas is a great sound bite until you realize the chief is most probably using Twitter and Facebook and riding around in a Hummer with missile launchers mounted on the hood. Wouldn't be surprised to find the chief on LinkedIn. He's also most likely feeding his tribe on grain from the Midwest and using medications invented by American companies. A mud slide hits his tent, he yells for American assistance.

I was well into the frittata before the import of what Wilkes had said hit me.

"What makes you believe there was a time table? Or that it was *accelerated?*"

I waited for his response while he dug into his over-stuffed, five-egg omelet. He was finishing the third of three sausages when a text arrived from Angella titled Sarah-Jean. NOT AT ALL WHAT I WOULD HAVE EXPECTED FROM A NEWLY MINTED WIDOW. MORE LATER.

I looked up to see Wilkes wiping something from his jacket sleeve. I assumed the spot was coffee, but it could have been grease. Still busy with the cloth, he said, "Multi-tasking is the thing now. Even you're doing it. Where would we be without all the gadgets?"

"Are you purposefully avoiding my question?" I asked, not allowing him off the hook so easily.

"In politics you learn to answer as few questions as possible and deflect the rest." He used the napkin on his lips. "As they say in court, please repeat the question."

"You mentioned speeding up the time table. What did you mean by that? What time table?"

"I have it on good authority he was terminal. His vote was needed to prevent cloture. The sixty-first vote so to speak. His death came sooner than anyone on his team expected."

"How do you know he was terminal?"

"Revealing sources is never a good idea. I'm sure you know that, Agent Redstone. Just let me say, I trust the source."

"Do you know the nature of what you're calling terminal?"

"I assume some form of cancer. Don't need to know the details."

"How widespread is this *rumor?*"

"I didn't say it was a rumor. A little birdie told me."

"How many others knew?"

"How would I know?"

"Your birdie do a lot of tweeting?"

"Not usually."

"A reporter?"

"We playing twenty questions?"

"Guess how many the birdie told."

"A few."

"Names, please."

"In confidence?"

"No promises, but I'll do my best."

"Clayson and Briley for starters. Who they told is anybody's guess."

Paula Clayson is the Senate Majority leader and Harrison Briley is the House Speaker. "Do you suppose the President knew?"

"Wouldn't be a bit surprised. This President makes it his business to know. Micro-manages everything."

"When did you last see Senator Donnlevy?"

"I was on the phone with him when he went down. We were working on a compromise. Making progress, actually. I thought we had it set, but then the line went dead. Well, not dead exactly, but a thump and then a lot of yelling—commotion really. I heard Stetson's voice yelling, 'He's down. Get a doctor, the Senator's down!' I know it's not funny, but my initial reaction was that he was pulling a stunt."

"And just what was the compromise?"

"It's a bit complicated. But since he was for the military, I proposed keeping the troop and equipment levels where they were for ten years. During that time the country could invest in long-range delivery so that any attack on the U.S. would be met with massive destruction anywhere in the world. Not what I wanted, but something he could buy off on."

"Why?"

"In the end, the President had the votes—and the country—behind him. Our treasure, what remains of it, is being drained. Our babies are dying to save people who won't save themselves. We're good-hearted, but there's a limit."

"Mind telling me what the condition was?" When Wilkes shot a puzzled glance, I clarified. "Medical condition. What was his condition?"

"You mean, what was killing him? As I said, I didn't get into details. I just knew he had a few weeks, maybe a month, no more."

"Heart?"

"Probably not. Heart is not predictable. Liver, kidneys, some form of cancer's my bet."

I looked straight into his eyes. "Did you participate in any manner in hastening his day of reckoning?" Few people can conceal a lie of this magnitude, no matter how hard they work at it. Poker players are the best, but a human death rises to a different magnitude.

Before answering, Wilkes slowly drained his coffee, replaced his cup, wiped his lips and then sat back in his chair. "Truth is, much as I wanted him out of the way, I did nothing. Not the American way. Now is it, Agent Redstone?"

"Wouldn't be my way, if that's what you're implying. But some folks are prone to assist history."

"I may be a lot of things, Redstone, but what I'm not, most assuredly, is a murderer."

"In this situation, you could call it nature's helper."

"Murder, by any other name is still murder. Not my cup of tea."

"No one's said he was murdered. Just investigating."

"Don't take me for a fool. Homeland Security does not investigate heart attacks."

"Let's just say troubled times call for increased diligence."

"Let's just call murder, murder, Agent Redstone. We'll all understand each other better if we do."

NINE

"Mrs. Donnlevy, or Sarah-Jean as she insisted I call her, is a woman in her mid-forties, a good twenty years younger than the Senator." Angella was debriefing us on the patio of the Homeland Security paid-for condo she and I shared in Arlington, Virginia, just across the river from the District. Jacobs and I were sitting on a swinging chaise and Angella sat in a rocking chair, slowly moving forward and back.

Angella paused to consult her notes and then continued. "She confirmed they had not shared a bedroom for years."

"Not surprising," Jacobs said, "given what we know of his propensity for *younger* women."

"Babies, according to Sarah-Jean. Woman's wheelchair-bound. Skiing accident five years ago."

"Your text indicated she was acting strange for a widow. What's up with that?" I asked.

"Not a hint of sadness. In fact, she seemed almost giddy."

"Did she know her husband was terminal?"

"Claims she didn't know, but quickly added she'd be the last to know. When I pressed her, she replied, 'Isn't the wife always the last to know?' I had the impression she knew."

"She obviously knew about his dalliances," Jacobs said.

"That's what the *baby* comment was about. She knew."

"How long were they married?"

"Twelve years, give or take."

"Married after he became a senator then," I commented. "Any children?"

"Not between them. She has a son, by an earlier marriage. I take it he's in his mid to late twenties. She's closed-mouthed about him. Senator had no children."

"You have anything else?" I asked.

Angella addressed Jacobs. "Sylvan, who's Vlad Smol? He called while we were talking. Actually, several calls came in, but she only took that one. His name came up on her cell."

Jacobs entered the name into his computer and while we waited for an answer, Angella continued, "She not only took his call, but spent a good five minutes mostly listening. Said very little, but at one point a large smile flashed across her face. She quickly stifled the smile when she realized I was watching. I asked her who called; she responded, 'A good friend'. She quickly assured me he was a friend of both her and the Senator. Unless I miss my guess, there's a romantic component lurking about."

Jacobs looked up from his laptop. "Vlad Smol's name at one time was Vladimir Smolikoff. Served a stint in the Russian Airborne Corps and then attended Moscow State Technical University. Holds a PhD in astro engineering from there as well as a PhD in systems research from Stanford. Naturalized citizen thirteen years ago. Founded a business selling high-frequency radio antennas to the military. Sold it four years later, netted forty-five million. Funded a new venture, this time software that detects a potential deployment by any military anywhere in the world."

"What the hell does that mean?" I asked, wondering why someone with forty-five million needed to worry about making more money.

"Not sure, but he stands to make tons more if the *Force Redeployment Act* is passed. Foolproof early detection will become mandatory. Vlad's system has passed all the tests. It's on the fast track."

Angella's forehead creased in puzzlement. "Let me understand this. Vlad, or Vad, or whatever his name is, is betting on troop withdrawal and the Senator is—was—opposed to precisely that. So what's he doing hanging around Sarah-Jean?"

"You may have nailed it. Romantic attraction."

"The lady's a paraplegic," Jacobs commented.

"Sex drive, or at least good companionship, doesn't disappear just because her spine's injured." Angella responded, her face flushing. "There's nothing to suggest she's...shall we say, shy toward sex."

I turned to Jacobs. "Any chance of finding out how they met? Vlad and the lady, I mean. Also, let's get more detail on her skiing accident. Was the good Senator with her when it happened? That kind of stuff."

"Shouldn't be hard to find," Jacobs said, his fingers already entering data into his computer.

"You smelling what I'm smelling?" Angella asked, her body alive, like a hound on the hunt.

"Vlad's into early detection. Donnlevy is into military strength. How convenient. Relationships like this are orchestrated. Let's concentrate on where Vlad's money is."

"You thinking Russian mob?"

"Along those lines," I said to Angella as my cell vibrated. Before answering, I said to Jacobs, "Let's get a full workup of his military history. We need to know what this guy ate for breakfast ten years before he left the motherland."

Martino's name was flashing on my cell. I hit the ACCEPT button and Martino began talking without preamble. "Most probably hurried along," the doctor said, his voice low and all business. "Outline available in an hour."

"Thanks. When will the official statement be ready?"

"Several days. But that's just a formality. Nothing will change. We're well within our certainty comfort zone."

"Martino's calling it homicide," I said to the room when the line went dead. "Won't be official for several days, but he's nailed it."

"Any clue as to the perp?" Angella asked.

"He'll have something for us in an hour. Won't address the perp. Just the cause of death—and perhaps the means."

"Tiny's still at Hopkins with Stetson, working him for names and time frames for the past week," Jacobs said. "I'll have him pick up Martino's notes before he leaves. He's been posting the time frames for all the players as he receives them."

"Anything jump out?"

"Senator didn't sleep, judging from the parade for the past thirty-six hours. Steady stream of calls in and out. People coming and going at all hours. Senator was working it, that much is clear."

"All about the legislation?" Angella asked.

"Except for one guy, yes."

"What's that about?" Angella asked, poised to enter the information into her phone notes.

Jacobs consulted his screen before replying. "Man name of Keller. Smith Keller. Stetson listed him as a patron."

"What the hell's a patron?" Angella wanted to know.

"Beats shit outta me," I said.

Jacobs studied the computer before he responded. "Keller's the only person listed as a patron. Patron usually means someone who puts money into the reelection coffers. Bet Stetson's covering something."

"Got an address? When did he visit?"

Silence for a few minutes while Jacobs again studied the computer. "An hour before he died," Jacobs responded, continuing to work the computer. "Listed as being from Pittsburgh. Staying at the Hay Adams. He may still be in town."

"You up for a metro ride?" I asked Angella. "Let's drop by and say hello to this guy Keller. Find out for ourselves what a *patron* is. We can have lunch when we're finished. Or would you rather stay here and catch up on your sleep?"

"I'm going," Angella immediately answered, "I'm not a wimp." Her eyes flashed a warning.

I knew not to press. To Jacobs, I said, "You can work here if you like. Help yourself to whatever you find in the fridge. There's an extra room. Sometimes Tiny stays overnight. Help yourself."

"Already checked out the fridge. Empty as the day it was installed. Never mind, I'll ride with you two into the city and work at our offices. I'll get a visual for you on Keller. It'll only take a moment."

Angella changed into dress jeans and a fresh sweater.

I did likewise.

Walking out of the door, the adrenalin was beginning to take hold. We were on the hunt and I was a new person.

Or perhaps it was just the fresh underwear.

TEN

Showing official badges to a hotel clerk in the District has about the same effect as wearing a chaperone badge at the senior prom. It took arm-twisting and forceful language, but we did finally manage to extract Smith Keller's room number. I instructed the reluctant clerk not to call ahead. When he hesitated, I leaned across the counter, my voice purposefully low, almost guttural. "You touch that phone and I guarantee you won't see the outside of the jailhouse for months."

The man, fear now in his eyes, stammered, "I understand."

"I'll nail your sorry ass to the wall, you get out of line. You understand me?"

This time he nodded, backing away from the counter.

"Give me a key, just in case."

"I can't do—"

"You said you understood. Now start understanding. Give me the key."

He produced a magnetic card, ran it through a reader and handed it across the counter, not saying a word in the process.

We rode the elevator to the third floor and walked down a dimly lit corridor to room three-twenty. It was the last door on the right just before a bend in the hallway where presumably additional rooms were located.

My first knock went unanswered, as did my second. I pressed my ear to the door and heard nothing. I knocked again. This time Angella pressed her ear to the door, held it there a moment and then shrugged her shoulders.

I was about to insert the card in the lock when a man appeared from around the corner. I hadn't heard his footsteps and I guessed the sound had been muffled by the carpeting. He was about my height, six feet, but weighed a good fifty pounds more than I did. I couldn't tell if the bulk was muscle or fat. I guessed muscle from the way he stood, his feet solidly planted, knees slightly flexed. Despite the pleasant smile, he was ready to take me on.

"Pardon me," he said in the friendly manner of a Good Samaritan, "if you're looking for the gentleman in that room, he went down a while ago."

"Do you know him?" Angella inquired. "Are you friends?"

"I'm just in from Houston, don't know a livin' soul. Man came out of that room and asked after a place to eat. I suggested the Lafayette Room downstairs. Told it was excellent."

"Was he alone?

"No one was with him."

"You a guest? What room are you in?" Angella pressed, her demeanor light and flirtatious.

His eyes momentarily flipped toward the bronze numbers on the wall while his smile broadened into that of a guy who believes he just got lucky. "Room three-twenty-five. Just around the corner."

"I'm Angella," she responded, her hand outstretched.

He took her hand, held it a bit too long, then said, "I'm Bill. Bill Snow. Pleasure to know you." His eyes said the rest.

Snow then turned to me. "Bet he's still in the restaurant. I'm going down, show you the way."

Following Snow's lead, we retraced our steps toward the elevator and rode down in silence, Snow standing behind Angella, bending to tie his shoe. I walked a step behind the two of them across the lobby. Just outside the restaurant, Snow said, "Hey, I got an appointment. I trust you'll find him in there." Winking at Angella, he purred, "Be back in an hour."

"You know his name?" Angella asked, her face aglow, her smile widening.

"Never asked," Snow responded. "Catch you later, Angella." He touched her arm before turning away.

"What was that about?" I asked. Being overly friendly was just not Angella's way.

"Guy gives me the creeps," she immediately responded. "Appearing out of nowhere. He knew who we were looking for, but professed not to know his name."

"Carpeting will do that. You might be over——"

"I didn't hear a door open or close either. Creepy's all I can say."

I pulled out Keller's Pennsylvania driver's license picture Jacobs had given us. I turned to get better light and my eye caught Hank Stetson walking across the lobby. At first I thought he was following us. But that idea was dispelled when he continued toward the elevators without glancing in our direction. I turned back to Angella. "Let's go find Keller."

Not many hotel restaurants are busy mid-afternoon, and only a few tables were occupied. Smith Keller was not among the patrons.

"He's obviously not here," I said, "but let's catch a bite. Might return before we leave."

"Expensive place. We can find someplace less—"

"On me. Come." I led Angella to a table off to the side.

It felt good to get off my feet and relax. I was more tired than I wanted to admit. The waiter came for drink orders, and I said, "I'm passing on the alcohol. Coke for me."

Angella just wanted water.

It took an inordinate amount of time for the drinks to arrive. "Sorry, we're light-staffed in the afternoons. Have you decided what you—"

"Hold lunch for a moment," I said, jumping to my feet, I want to check something. I retraced my steps across the lobby to the front desk and caught the eye of the clerk who had earlier given us the key.

"By chance do you folks copy driver's licenses when guests check in?" I asked, annoyed with myself for not asking this earlier.

His face flushed and he pulled back. "I'm sorry, sir, but I must refer you to the manager."

"Make it fast."

He quickly disappeared into a side room.

Angella, who had stayed behind to pay for the Coke, caught up. "What's troubling you?"

Before I could respond, a heavy-set woman wearing a rumpled suit jacket pulled tight across her matronly bust appeared in front of us. The gold tag on her left breast read, KATHLEEN SEXTON HOTEL MANAGER. She reminded me of a horse who had been ridden hard and put away wet. "May I help you," she asked, her voice supporting my horse image. "I'm Ms. Sexton."

"I'm Jimmy Redstone and this is Angella Martinez. We're with the Department of Homeland Security." We flashed our badges. "We're investigating a situation that may involve a hotel guest. Mr. Smith Keller. He's registered in room three-twenty. I was wondering if by chance you have a copy of his driver's license. I'm trying to confirm if your guest is the man we're interested in."

She reached across the counter. "Let me see your picture and I'll see if we have a match."

"Fair enough," I said, unfolding the paper and handling it to her.

She consulted her computer, frowned, made some deep-throated sounds, hit more keys and then said, "Please come with me."

She led us to a small cluttered office, picked a pile of papers from each of two chairs and motioned for us to sit. She went around the desk and adjusted herself in her chair. Leaning forward, she said, "Let's see your identification again."

We again produced our photo IDs and our shields.

"As you can appreciate, this is sensitive. We do copy driver's licenses. You have no idea how many phony credentials we receive in a year. And it's increasing all the time. We also take candids of our guests in the elevator when they check in. Too many people claim they never were here. Seems someone is always stealing their licenses."

"So where is this going?" I was impatient to hear the real story.

"Just explaining why we have all this information. Anyway, here's the story on Mr. Smith Keller. His driver's license picture matches what you have there and so do the candids. The man in room three-twenty is the man in your picture. His daughter is with him." She turned the computer screen so we could see a good-looking woman, age about twenty, possibly younger. A floppy hat covered her hair.

"I put her at seven months," I said to Angella. "You agree?"

"Seven or eight. She's carrying high so she might not be that far along. Wide eyes, high cheeks. Pretty girl."

"Striking," Sexton commented. "Her eyes are so alive."

"His daughter, you said?"

"I know that's what they all say. But this one was telling the truth. No ring."

"Call the room," I said.

Sexton reached for the phone. A moment later, she said, "Sorry, no answer."

Angella leaned forward. "What's the name of the guest in room three-twenty-five?"

"I'm sorry, I can't—"

Before I could get into her face, Angella said, "Let me ask this another way. Do you have a Mr. Bill Snow in room three-twenty-five?"

"That I can answer. Give me a moment." She entered a long string of information into her keyboard, looked at several screens of information, typed in more information, and finally said, "Seems that not only do we not have a man by that name in room three-twenty-five, we don't have a Bill Snow, or a William Snow, or for that matter any Snow, registered in this hotel at all."

Digesting that information, and working through the implications, I said, "I'm afraid we'll have to enter room three-twenty."

She straightened her back and took a deep breath. "You'll have to obtain a Court Order for that. I'm afraid. Hotel policy won't—"

"I pulled the key from my pocket."

"I already have the key. Let's go Angella."

"Not so fast, Mr. Redstone. That key won't work. Mr. Antwain, the man you harassed earlier, gave you a placebo. That's our policy. You could never have entered that room."

"This is bullshit! You're interfering in a criminal investigation! I must be allowed into that room immediately!"

"I'm sorry. Our lawyers tell us to demand a search warrant. I assume if you had one you would have shown it already. So the answer is no."

She was right, of course, but that didn't keep me from being worked up. In an earlier day…well, in an earlier day I don't know what I would have done. But it's true that in an earlier day she would have given us the key.

"What about hot pursuit?" Angella asked. I think she was trying to calm me down more than anything.

"Indeed, I am allowed to open the door to protect life. But we'll need the police. Is there reason to believe a life's at stake?"

Without hesitation, Angella replied, "Certainly." To me she said, "Snow gave me the creeps. He hustled us away from the room."

Kathleen glanced from Angella to me and back again, a puzzled expression on her face. I said to her, "Get the cops up to that room and do it quickly. We'll be waiting outside the door."

"You're a good actress," I said to Angella when Kathleen padded off across the lobby. "You even had me believing something's wrong in there."

"Who's acting?"

ELEVEN

"**N**ow let's go over this again for Tiny," Jacobs was saying. "And this time let's hear it from Angella."

It was after seven in the evening and I was beyond starved, lunch having been forgotten in the events of the day. We were in my office at Homeland Security. Tiny had just walked in, his computer looking like a child's toy tucked under his massive arm. The man could hunt bear with a switch.

"I was following up with Stetson's timeline," Tiny explained when I gave him a puzzled look. "The Senator saw and spoke with a lot of people this week. How the hell the old man did it is beyond me. So what's up? Received your cryptic message and got here as fast as I could."

Jacobs began. "One of the Senator's last visitors was a Mr. Smith Keller."

"That jives with what I got," Tiny said. "Saw the Senator about an hour before he died. I was on my way to talk with Keller when your message arrived. Go on."

"His daughter, Lissalou Keller, was found dead, homicide, in her room at the Hay Adams. Happened around the time Redstone and Angella tried to pay a visit on Keller."

"You have my attention," Tiny said, settling into a chair at the side of my desk. "Now I understand what the flap's about."

"What flap?" I asked.

"You first."

Angella took up the narrative. "Played a hunch. Had the manager call the police. Took them seven minutes to arrive. Met us outside Keller's door."

"What do you mean, hunch?" Tiny asked.

"We had met a man, goes by Bill Snow, in the hall earlier who claimed he saw Keller go down to lunch. Snow claimed to have a room around the corner. In point of fact, he wasn't registered at the hotel. Police found the daughter, Lissalou Keller, nineteen, suffocated. Official term is hypoxia something."

"Fancy word for the same thing," Tiny commented. "Continue."

"Don't yet know exact TOD. Best guess is within fifteen, twenty, minutes of when they found her. Jimmy says he's seen this before. According to him, it was asphyxia caused by something called a carotid sleeper."

I jumped in. "Her larynx wasn't broken and I didn't notice linear finger-nail marks, so my guess is carotid and jugular. Classic blue tongue and petechial hemorrhages on her lips and behind the ears. She most likely lost consciousness within ten, fifteen seconds. Probably was gone in less than two minutes. Whoever did it has strong arms. Typically, it's man versus woman because of the strength it takes."

"This Bill Snow," Tiny said, "what's the take on him?"

"Professional. Man was cool. And fast on his feet. Angella had the presence of mind to ask his name and room. Man never hesitated. But, in hindsight, he glanced around, presumably to see the room number sequence. I noted his glance, but didn't put two and two together fast enough."

"To put it bluntly, we were conned," Angella replied.

"I thought your strength was spotting cons," Jacobs quipped. "Just saying."

"Angella had her antenna up, but I was asleep. I blew it."

Tiny fired up his computer. "I'll go online to get the reports when they're available. Jacobs, you should do the same through the FBI database. It'll make a better court story if we have your records to fall back on. We may never be able to produce mine."

I looked over to Jacobs. His hands were covering his ears.

"Anything else?" Tiny asked.

Angella looked away, her lips worked, but she said nothing. I knew what she was thinking, what she had to say, and how hard it was to form the words. I waited.

"Lou was pregnant. Late term." Tears formed at the corner of Angella's eyes and began to roll slowly down her check. "Pardon me for being..."

"Human," Jacobs added. "It doesn't get easier. We lost two this time. But that's why we do what we do. Catch the perp."

"Thank you, Sylvan," Angella replied, brushing the moisture from her face. "I'm new at this. Tell me it gets easier."

"For some it does. I still have a hard time."

Breaking the awkward silence, I said to Tiny, "Now what's this flap thing you mentioned?"

"Over the autopsy of the Keller girl. I didn't know it was tied to you. I wondered why Martino was involved. Caused a major furor in the DA's office. Homeland Security jurisdiction type of thing. Can you believe it was escalated all the way to the Secretary? Ever the politician, Madam Secretary resolved the dispute by agreeing to have Martino work with the local guy, but—and this is important—Martino is not to slip you, and she mentioned you by name, any information ahead of the locals. In fact, he's not to provide you any information at all, unless the girl's death becomes tied to the Senator."

"How the hell you get all this stuff?"

"Friends in low places."

Jacobs chimed in, "Found it. Report came online twenty minutes ago. White, female, nineteen, name of Lissalou Keller, AKA Lou and Lulu, residence with her parents, Smith and Georgia Keller, Bartlett Street, Pittsburgh, Pennsylvania. Student at Chatham University. Thirty-one weeks pregnant."

Tiny asked, "Is her father accounted for? You said he was not there when you first approached the room."

"He returned to the room just after the police arrived. Man's a mess. Refused to speak with me. Angella had a little better luck. He started to talk, but abruptly stopped. Angella, tell Tiny exactly what he did say."

"I didn't take notes, so this may be a bit inaccurate. He told me his daughter, called her Lu, was a good girl. Never in trouble. He said she was a political science major. Then he said something to the effect of, 'She was doing just fine until she met that snake.' Then he broke off and refused to say anymore."

Tiny added, "It's possible his visit with the Senator was about his daughter. But she wasn't with him on the visit."

"But she was certainly in town." Angella added.

"Yes, but that could have been a social visit to show her around the Capital. After all, politics was her major."

Jacobs said, "Should I have our office follow this, or do you two want to run with it?"

"You guys begin. Angella and I will speak to the father. We'll wait until after the funeral."

"Fair enough. What about Bill Snow? Doubt if that's his name. Any visuals on him?"

I told Tiny about the candids. Jacobs said his office was working on it.

"He's built husky," Angella said. "Make him for six one. Weight about two-fifty, two-sixty. Twenty-eight, give or take. Shoulder-length hair. Dressed in a dark, maybe black, blazer, jeans and boots. Easy smile."

"Texas connection. Said he was from Houston." I injected. "The guy's an easy liar, so who knows about Houston? But that could tie him to the Senator."

"Or to any of a dozen other players," Jacobs said. "Let's see what the cameras have for us." He punched in a series of numbers, brought up one screen after another. Exasperated, he exclaimed, "They're not making the pictures available. Don't know if they even have them."

"Who isn't? The hotel or the police?"

"Can't tell. They're just not here."

I called the hotel and asked for Kathleen. Whether or not she was avoiding me I couldn't determine. After an interminable wait, the clerk finally said, "I passed along a message to call you. That's all I can do."

Jacobs, his brow furled, said, "I can't believe our agents don't have access to the elevator pictures. I'll keep working it."

"I'm starved," I said. "Thinking of having dinner back at the hotel. We may catch Kathleen in the process. If not, we'll track her down."

"I'll grab a sandwich and work the computer," Jacobs said, begging off. "If we don't get this kicked off right, we'll pay later."

"And I'll eat dinner with my family for a change," Tiny replied. "Catch you two later."

I didn't know if they thought Angella and I wanted private time or just that they had other plans. No need to explore motives. Besides, I welcomed quiet time with Angella.

A half-hour later we were seated in the Lafayette Room, reading the menu under candlelight. When Angella ordered wine, I laughed and said, "Thought you didn't drink in uniform?"

"Case you haven't noticed, I don't wear a uniform anymore. Thanks to you—and Chief Duran." She held up her glass. "Here's to the Chief," her eyes moist. "May he rest in peace." She took a long sip, then added, "I hate to say this, but I'm glad his killer died. I couldn't bear to relive it all again at trial."

"I share your sentiment. I know we're supposed to be impartial, protect life, all that stuff. But when a killer shoots someone, especially a cop, in cold blood there's no room on this planet for that behavior. I'm all for an eye for an eye."

"I didn't mean to get you started," Angella said, her tone conveying a desire for a more relaxed dinner. Her eyes held the promise of intimacy.

I put my hand over hers. "Thanks for being there for me," I said. "I need you in my life."

She held up her glass. "To a great team."

"We certainly do make a good team. I've worked with a lot of folks over the years, and you're the best. And I mean that."

"Jimmy," she said, her hand over mine now, "I wasn't just referring to the job. I mean there's a bond between us. I know what you're thinking, I feel it. I want to be where you are, to work with you, to just feel your presence. Living with you this past month has been...well, magical."

"I feel the same way. I promised myself I'd never again get involved romantically with a partner. The last time turned into a disaster. But this is different."

"Do you really mean that? Or are you telling me what I want to hear?" She used her free hand to dry her cheeks. But more tears replaced the moisture she wiped away.

"Have you known me to say what I didn't mean? I'm in love with you, Angella." I hadn't intending on saying that, but it was out now and nothing I could do to retrieve it. I didn't want to rush her so soon after her divorce became final. Tears were now streaming uncontrollably down her face. She pulled her hand away, ostensibly to retrieve a tissue.

For the longest time she remained silent. Every minute of that time seemed an eternity. Then she said, "I willed myself not to leap from one relationship to another. I wanted time to find myself, to settle into a new life. So what did I do? Like a fool, I fell in love with you. Oh, Jimmy, I'm more in love with you than you can possibly know."

"So why the tears?"

"I could glibly say they're tears of joy. But truth is, it's a mixture of happiness and...and fear. I'm afraid something will happen to you. You were lucky to live when Trich's father cut your throat. Then the radiation exposure nearly killed you. It's dangerous what we do. Being married is a liability—for both of us."

Married! I hadn't even thought of marriage. I was in love with Angella, yes, but that's as far as I had taken the concept. My first marriage had been a disaster. The thought of a second was... well, not teed up.

"Oh, Jimmy. I'm sorry. I can read it in your face. I took a big leap forward. But even if we're not married, even if we're just lovers, isn't that the same?"

Her hand was back in mine now, but the vibrancy was gone. "I suppose it is," I lamely responded. "Emotionally, anyway. But marriage implies so much more."

"Forgive me for getting ahead of myself. I just want you to know I'm in love with you, and wherever it leads I'm prepared to go. I want you close to me."

The remainder of the dinner was a blur. I'm prepared to testify that it was the best dinner I ever had. But if pressed, I couldn't say what I ate or what it tasted like or even what was said. We finished off a full bottle of wine and had started into after-dinner drinks when Angella picked up my hand, kissed it and said, "You want to continue consummating our relationship, then I suggest you ply me with no more alcohol."

"You suggesting we take a room here?"

"The sooner the better." Angella winked. "I couldn't be more ready."

TWELVE

"**O**h, Mr. Redstone," hotel manager Kathleen Sexton called as I approached the front desk to check in for the night, "just the person I wanted to see. If you and Ms. Martinez care to come back to my office, I think you'll find this interesting."

The pleasant buzz of dinner was instantly gone. I could feel it in my own reaction and could see it in Angella as well. Her lips and eyes had lost their allure and were now set hard. This is the look I have come to appreciate as her game face.

Sexton closed the door to her office and took her place behind the still messy desk. She leaned forward and rotated her computer to face us. "Is this the man, I believe you called him Snow, you were talking with earlier today?"

There was no question the cameras had captured Bill Snow. The movements, the height, the clothing, the gestures, all matched. Everything was there except his face. He had known where the camera was located and in every shot his face was turned away.

"He must have used the steps, because there is nothing in any of the elevator candids," Kathleen informed us. "Knew what he was doing, most certainly."

"But he rode down with us," Angella commented.

Sexton hit a few more keys and there we were, Angella and I looking somewhat bewildered. Snow was behind Angella, face downward tying his shoe.

"Have you given these to the police?" I asked.

"About an hour ago. Said they were useless for their purposes."

"Appreciate your effort, Ms. Sexton. If you uncover anything else, please call." I handed her a card and followed Angella back to the lobby.

I retraced my steps to the front desk to get a room. Angella caught my eye. There was no mistaking her look. The mood had passed. I walked over to her and before I could say anything, she leaned close. "Let's go back to our own place. Our own bed will do just fine."

I nodded, but before we got though the front door, Jacobs called to say that Keyston Jenkins, the Senator's procurement person, maintained a list of young women, presumably for hourly rental. Tiny was in the process of escorting Jenkins to our offices and Jacobs was planning to meet him there.

- - - - -

We were seated in my office when Jacobs arrived, followed within five minutes by Tiny and a weasel-looking man of about thirty-five who was introduced as Keyston Jenkins, Senator Donnlevy's procurement specialist.

When we were all seated, I said, "Now Keyston, would you tell us exactly what function you performed for the Senator?"

He looked first at Angella and then at me. "You sure you want that considering—"

"Considering there's a lady present. Forget about the lady. Tell us everything you know. You hold back anything, anything at all, and I promise you'll spend twenty years in prison thinking about it."

"I didn't do anything wrong. You can't hold me."

"You got a law degree? Funny, that wasn't what it said in your file. It said you dropped out of high school before your senior year."

"I know my rights."

"Then you know you can't lie in a federal investigation. You lie to me and you're going to jail. Got that?"

"I don't have to say nothing!"

"That's not a good idea. I find you propositioned even one girl under eighteen and then see how long you're gone. Maybe for life. Maybe even longer."

Panic shot across his face. The Senator liked them young, and if this weasel did his job right, many of the girls would be under age. We had the makings of a star witness.

Angella nodded when she realized I had hit on the right tactic. Fortunately for Jenkins, underage sex was not what I was commissioned to investigate. Except he didn't know that.

What came out of him over the next two hours made even my callused blood run hot. The fact that a sixty-seven-year-old respected U.S. Senator would have sex with women in their twenties was bad enough. But to hear how he continued to demand younger and younger women, some barely in their teens, made my skin crawl.

"He's not the only one!" Jenkins finally blurted out. "There are several others."

Jacobs flipped his recorder on. The FBI would follow up in that regard. But for now we were focused exclusively on the death of Donnlevy, and anything beyond that was noise as far as Angella and I were concerned. As Jenkins spoke, the list of women grew longer. Within fifteen minutes, there were enough names to make one wonder how the recently departed Senator managed to get any work done at all.

"Let's focus on Lou Keller," I said, catching Keyston by surprise. "Don't give us that canned confused look, son. I'm not buying it. You were in charge, so you know about Lou." Her death had not yet been reported, so he didn't know she was dead—unless, of course, he was the cause.

"Name's not familiar," he said, showing no indication that he knew she had died.

Angella brought a picture of Lou up on her screen. He exclaimed, "Oh, her! I knew her only as Lulu. Not Lou, but Lulu."

"No last name?"

"Just Lulu. From Pittsburgh."

"Tell me all you know about her. Hold back nothing, you know what's good for you."

"Political science fanatic. Wanted to be near politicians. She found me and asked for an introduction to Donnlevy."

"By name?"

"Yes, she asked for an introduction. I don't know if she wanted a sex relationship or just to meet him. I told her I could arrange for it."

"What are you not telling us?" I asked, playing off his eyes.

"It would cost her."

"You talking money or something else?"

"Money."

"How much?"

"Two thousand for a private meeting."

"She pay it?"

"She was going to, but somehow the Senator heard about it and shit hit the fan! Never seen the old man so angry. Almost got my ass fired. About a year ago it was."

"What else you know about Lisa...Lulu?"

"Nothing."

"You arrange for the meeting?"

"Yes."

"When?"

"I said, about a year."

"Can you get closer than that? Month, anything."

"Nope."

"Where?"

"Customary place."

"Where's that?"

"Usual Georgetown place."

"His wife not there?"

"Not where he lives, the pad he keeps. That's where I bring them."

"Where's she stay?"

"Who?"

"Senator's wife!"

"In Texas. Midlothian. Near Dallas. They have a spread there. Really nice place. Been there once."

"You meet her?"

"Yes."

"What's her name?"

"Sarah-Jean."

"What's your take?"

"Got a lover. Some rich guy, starts companies, that sort of thing. Dude's weird."

"In what way?"

"Talks funny. Keeps to himself, that sort of thing. Heard him talk some foreign gibberish to a guy."

"Ever see him with Sarah-Jean?"

"Yes."

"Anyone else?"

"Some weird guys."

"In what way are *they* weird?"

"As I said, foreign language stuff. Don't look friendly. Always in pairs, looking around, that sort of stuff."

"You ever speak to them?"

"No."

"To him?"

"Once. Creeps me out. Reminds me of a bantam rooster."

"You know Sarah-Jean before she married the Senator?"

He looked away, thought about it, then said, "I arranged for them to meet."

"How long ago was that?"

"Married about ten or so years, so that was about eleven years ago. Look, I can't help it if the old man likes girls. That's his business. Wife likes men. That's her business. I'm a broker, bring them together. What they do after that is their business. Nothing wrong in that is there?"

"There is if the girls are under age. Go to prison for that."

"Only do it for the Senator."

"And his friends?"

"Just the Senator."

"You get paid well?"

"Well enough."

"By whom?"

"Stetson."

"Out of what fund?"

"I don't know, man. The checks are good. Don't ask no questions."

"You ever visit Stetson in the Senator's office?"

"Hell no, man! That'd be like suicide."

"Where do you meet him?"

"Phone, text, that sort of thing."

"So where do the checks come from?"

"Deposited directly. Don't know."

"You have no idea where they come from or who writes them?"

"I didn't say that. Putting words in my mouth I didn't say."

"So you know where the checks come from?"

"Course I do."

"Where?"

He looked around the room as if calculating his chances of making a break for it. Apparently satisfying himself it was foolish to try, he replied, "Well, not exactly where, but generally. In the train building."

We all looked at him puzzled. "You know, the big station in town. Got an office there. Not far from here actually." He paused to see if we understood, then added, "Yea, Union Square. No Union Station. It's in Union Station."

"What's in Union Station?" Jacobs inquired.

"Stetson's office. Where the checks came from."

We all fell quiet, watching him look from one to the other, hoping to find a friendly face. After a while, I asked, "What's your job title?"

"Facilitator."

"Facilitator. So you facilitated a meeting between Lulu and the Senator about a year ago."

"Yes."

"Did they have sex?"

"I don't know what they did. That's none of my business."

"The truth is, you do know what they did. You made it your business to know what they did."

"How you figure that?"

"You know his wife Sarah-Jean has a lover. You know that and you're not even in Texas. I figure you make it your business to know everything that happens. I bet you have pictures—the works. Knowledge is power sort of thing."

I was playing to his vanity and he was enjoying himself. But he still shook his head. "With Lulu I didn't know."

"How many times did you arrange for meetings between Lulu and the Senator?"

"He wanted me to bring her to him on Friday nights when classes were out. She stayed the weekend. Did that a lot."

"What's a lot?"

"Four, five months."

"Why did he stop seeing her?"

"Don't know."

"Was it because he got tired of her?"

"Said I don't know."

"Was it because she got tired of him?"

"Dude, I told you all I know."

"He told you to stop bringing her, isn't that right?"

"How do you...hey...what's this all about? I don't like this. Man, I want out of here! I want a lawyer."

"Just answer my question. Why did you stop bringing Lulu?"

Keyston Jenkins looked around the room for help. No one moved. No one said anything. Finally he said, "I guess it was because she was pregnant."

"You guess? Was she pregnant?"

"Yes."

"Was it her idea to stop seeing him?"

"Don't know."

"Did he tell you to stop bringing her?"

"I said, I don't know."

"Did he replace her with someone else?"

"No."

"How did she take that?"

"What?"

"Being cut off from him."

"She called me all the time. Had to change my number."

"Why didn't she just go herself?"

"She tried. Got turned away at the door."

"Who turned her away?"

"Stetson."

"When was that?"

"Last week. Maybe ten days. Stetson was furious with me. I had nothing to do with it. We had some words."

"What was the result of the words?"

"I was friggin' fired! Alright! I was fired! After all the good work I did for the Senator, I was fired!"

"You know a guy named Bill Snow?"

"No."

"Here's a picture. Ever see him before?"

He glanced at the picture. "Can't say as I have. Can't see his face. Can't say as I've seen anybody like that."

"You have anything more you care to tell us?"

"Told you more than I should have, but I'm pissed at the Senator."

"He's dead."

"I'm still pissed. Got my ass fired for doing a good job. That's bullshit! If I get my hands on Stetson, I'll—"

"You'll what?"

"Never mind!"

"Procuring underage woman is not something a man should be proud about," Jacobs injected.

"That's bullshit!" Jenkins snapped. "Senator gets what he needs. That's the American way."

"Don't plan on leaving the country anytime soon," Jacobs cautioned him. "You understand me?"

"I ain't going nowhere, so you have no worries."

"See that you don't. Now get your sorry ass out of here."

THIRTEEN

Dr. Glenda Houstein called the next morning. She had been the one to spot the abnormality of the Senator's death. I interrupted her detailed medical briefing and asked for the short layman's version. She sounded upset not to have an audience for her meticulous and inspired work. "In short, he suffered a sudden collapsed heart. This typically occurs at night followed by days of distress. Another way this could happen is as a result of an intake, by injection or pill, of scopolamine. He was on an aspirin regiment and I would not have expected this result."

"You lost me. Sorry."

"Seems he was not on the aspirin for several days, so the scopolamine worked. In the end I'm prepared to call this premeditated murder by someone having access to stop the aspirin as well as to administer the scopolamine."

"When would the scopolamine have been administered?"

"Just before he collapsed."

"Why so elaborate?"

"Not traceable. If he hadn't fallen and hit his face I'd not have known."

"Why's that important?"

"People on aspirin or other anticoagulants tend to hemorrhage under the skin as a result of a trauma, even in the face of a heart attack. Petechiae is common in aspirin users, especially as a result of a head trauma. He had essentially no hemorrhaging. That was my first clue. No need to get into the rest now."

"Is it premature to inform the President?" I asked, wondering where this was leading.

"No. We can file the report later today or hold it until you give us the green light. We can always blame the hold on the tox report."

"Hold it for as long as possible. No rush until we have a perp in mind. Thanks for the heads up."

"You can thank Dr. Martino. I'm just following his orders. Oh, by the way, the other case, the female. She was carrying a male child. Between thirty and thirty-two weeks, just as her father reported."

Houstein had no way to know that Tiny had already given us that unnerving fact. I took the opportunity to confirm what had been nagging at me all night. "Is it your opinion the baby could have lived on its own had we gotten to the mother in time?"

"Most certainly. Perfectly formed, healthy fetus. You didn't hear it from me."

"Thanks again. I owe you one."

- - - - -

Jacobs had spent the night at the condo and had gone for coffee and pastry. I filled him in on the conversation with Houstein when he returned. Then I called Tiny. We were just finishing breakfast when Angella joined us.

"How can you two eat that vile stuff? A couple eggs, some toast, maybe, but not that Danish from the convenience store. Stuff'll kill you."

"One or more of us needs to stock the fridge if we're to eat healthy," I said. "Besides, this is better for you than eggs."

"How do you figure?" Angela asked, her head cocked to the side.

"Following doctor's orders. Lay off the eggs, high in cholesterol."

"These things are worse. And you know it full well."

"Doctor never mentioned Danish," I replied. "Besides, eggs are...bland."

"Then you just haven't had my omelets," Angella responded, winking at me when Jacobs' back was turned.

"Promises, promises," I responded, blowing a kiss. "By the way, Houstein just confirmed Lissalou being between thirty and thirty-two weeks."

"Boy or girl?"

"Boy."

Angella's lips tightened into a grimace and her eyes squeezed shut. It took a moment before she gathered herself. "Where do we go from here? That's not our investigation."

"We were just discussing next steps. We're planning to talk with Sarah-Jean's boyfriend, Vlad. Want breakfast first?"

"An OJ and I'm good to go."

"Sylvan's ahead of you. In the fridge. Forgot to ask, why was she in town? That slime Jenkins told us Sarah-Jean never visited Georgetown."

"My bad. I didn't ask. It didn't seem important at the time. My impression was she was here to support her husband in the critical vote."

"Why this time?"

"Can't answer."

"Maybe Vlad can shed some light. We're set to meet him in an hour. Senator's body's been released, so the center of attention will focus on Arlington where the Senator, patriot that he was, will be buried."

Angella cocked her head, "Do I take it you're no longer a Donnlevy fan?"

"Who said I ever was?"

"He supported everything you stand for."

"The under-aged sex, frankly, turns my stomach. Too many girls are victims. I investigated a sex slavery ring a few years back. Talk about vile stuff. Girls ten, eleven, having babies. And that's the best of what happens to them! Nasty people in that trade."

Angella drank her juice and retreated to the kitchen to rinse her glass. I followed her with the thought of snatching a quick kiss and a hug. But Tiny interrupted, calling to say he would skip Vlad and catch us later.

I relayed the message to Jacobs, who studied his computer one last time before closing it. He jotted down a few notes and then slipped the computer into his bag. "Let's go," he called, "I'm driving."

Fifteen minutes later we were circling the city to the east and on our way up to Aspen Hill where Vlad had a condo. It was a forty-five minute drive in light traffic. The community was convenient to both the District and the airport.

On the way, Jacobs said, "Got some info from Texas. Your dead guy, Philip Timberwolf, indeed lived alone. His only known hobby was storm chasing. Into it big time. Known to drive hundreds of miles just to be in the eye of some twister. Lately, he had shifted his focus to tropical storms—and hurricanes."

"What did he do for a living?" Angella asked.

"Drove a truck. Now retired."

"Retired? How old was he?"

"Forty-two."

"Sure he didn't own the trucking company?"

"Driver. No other record."

"That's odd," Angella commented.

"I agree. Nothing to show how he earned his money," Jacobs replied.

"No. I mean about chasing hurricanes. This is not hurricane season. There are no storms anywhere in the vicinity and haven't been for several months."

"But it could explain what he was holding," I said. "Some type of meter to detect storms, or pressures."

"Can't be doing much detection if there's no storm," Angella answered.

I pulled out my cell, looked up Cindy McLaughlin's name and touched the screen. Angella leaned over my seat from the back to see who I was calling. She let out a grimace when she realized who it was.

Cindy answered on the first ring. "Cowboy!" she announced, her voice a bit louder and friendlier than I had expected. The thought crossed my mind that she was playing to someone in her presence. I'm not sure if she was warning me—or possibly warning them. "How the hell are you? Heard you were in the city. Expected your call. What took so long?"

"So you know about our visit to the hotel?" I asked, trying not to sound defensive.

"Of course. I take it you require my services."

"I wouldn't put it that way, exactly. But it would be helpful if you could round up a few things for us. First, on the day Timberwolf was killed, and for the few days on either side, I want to know the weather situation, particularly on the Texas Gulf coast. And I'm not just referring to time and temperature. I want to know about storms, high level, low level, water conditions, everything meteorologically going on."

"Have Tiny obtain what you need from the national metrological office."

"I want more than he can get. I want to know what the Air Force has. What the Coast Guard has. Anything any service has, I want. I also want their actual observations for before, during and after, say three days either side."

"That it?"

"For now."

"Any report on the main event?"

Now I was certain she had company. I had learned not to hold back information, but I was not yet ready to impart leaked information. "Nothing yet. I believe they're waiting for the tox screen on the Senator."

"I trust this is the latest?"

"Most certainly is. I'll keep you in the loop."

"You do that, Cowboy, and all will work just fine. Tell Angella hello for me. Goodbye."

The fact that she had said *goodbye* was a tipoff she had been playing to the house. I doubted if her visitor had been Jamison. That man never said *goodbye*, or *hello,* or anything else that could pass for a friendly greeting. I'd settle for a grunt from him.

Angella didn't comment on Cindy and I decided to say nothing more. We drove in silence until we turned onto Vlad's street.

Angella said, "For a guy with big bucks this is a pedestrian neighborhood. Not that I wouldn't love to live here, but this is not what I had expected for someone with fifty million, more or less, in his pocket."

"Each to his own," I absently commented, still thinking about my conversation with Cindy, wondering why if she couldn't talk she even picked up the call.

Vlad answered the door dressed in jeans and a black turtle-neck pull-over. He was mostly bald and what little hair still remained was shaved clean, leaving a grey shadow rimming his head. He would have reminded me of Mr. Clean, except he was no more than five-two on a good day.

His condo was smaller than I had anticipated, but the furniture appeared expensive. A built-in sound system was playing background music featuring a piano.

"Nice haircut," he said to me. "We share the same barber." To Angella, he said, "Sarah-Jean spoke about your visit, but omitted to mention how attractive you are. A pleasant surprise. Come to sun-room we talk."

He led the way through the house to a surprisingly large glassed-in porch facing a compact well-planted backyard area, most of it in hibernation. The furniture was metal with white cushions and looked comfortable.

"Anybody for Vodka? The good Russia kind if you prefer." Having no takers, he sat back. "Your show."

By our prior agreement, Angella took the lead. "Sarah-Jean said you sold a business. How about the elevator version?"

"Invented small antenna having high gain and exceptional efficiency across wide frequency spectrum. The spectrum fits in the range critical for military communications. Allows for small field units with long battery life. Lockheed was important customer.

Bought company. You know Lockheed?" We all nodded that we did, and Vlad continued, "From womb to bank, total four years."

"Internet says you walked away with over fifty million," Angella said.

"Made money before company sold, so it was more."

Jacobs, who usually remains silent while Angella and I ask questions, leaned forward. "You say the spectrum just happened to be in the military range. Was that coincidence or—"

"You are FBI, right?"

Jacobs nodded.

"Look in files. Been investigated, I think you say, all the way to Saturday night. Made lucky guess."

Jacobs didn't follow up, so Angella asked, "How long have you known Mrs. Donnlevy?"

"Sarah-Jean. Little longer than eight years."

"So you knew her before her accident?"

"Yes."

"Where you lovers before the accident?"

"She's a married woman. I think your question is not placed right."

"This is not a social call, Mr. Smol," Angella replied. "Just answer the questions and we'll be out of your hair. Sorry, poor choice of words. But anyway, we'll be gone sooner if you cooperate."

"Sarah-Jean and I...say we are close friends."

"Were you with her when she fell?"

"At lodge. Not on hill. From Russia, but don't ski. Attending to business. Wasn't told about accident until later."

"Was the Senator with her skiing?"

"Was with some child! Disgusting."

"You know the girl's name?"

"Keyston has names."

Angella pretended to consult her notes, not giving away what we already knew. "His full name."

"Keyston Jenkins."

"What role did Stetson play in all this?"

"Overseer. Stetson ran operation from top to bottom. Knows everything."

"Does that go for your relationship with Sarah-Jean? Did he know what was going on?"

"Of course. Was no secret. Managed press like back home. Papers treated Senator well. Stetson gave reporters what they needed. They returned favor."

"What's your new business venture?"

Vlad looked away, studied a bird perched on a feeder. When he answered, it was in a more serious tone. "Global detection of troop or missile movements. Foolproof."

"If the *Force Redeployment Act* passes, you stand to make a ton of money?"

"I already made what you say, a ton of money?"

"Is it fair to say then you were a supporter of troop withdrawal?"

"America must come home, get out of Europe. Get out of Middle-East. Designed my system long before they talked of withdrawing. Senator and I did not see nose-to-nose on this. In private, he called it *Traitor's Treachery*. We had long arguments."

"Did you know Wilkes came to him with a proposal at the last moment?"

Vlad again studied the bird feeder before responding. "Who is Wilkes?"

"You don't know him?"

"Should I? Troop withdrawal will happen. A matter of when."

"You plan to marry Sarah-Jean now that the Senator's gone?"

"No comment."

"Why was she here this week? We understand she hardly ever visited."

"Ask Sarah-Jean."

"Any guess?"

"None."

"Anything to do with you?"

"She'll be the one to say that."

"Did you spend time with her when she was here on this visit?"

"I had business to take care of."

"Is that a no?"

"Yes."

"Yes, what?"

"It is *no*."

Angella glanced over at me as if to say, *anything you want to ask?* I had noticed a slight hesitation before Vlad had denied being with Donnlevy's wife this week. Not enough to tell me he lied, but enough to put me on notice. I leaned toward him and said, "What if I told you Mrs. Donnlevy visited this condo the afternoon before the Senator died? Would that refresh your memory?"

"Didn't happen."

"Was she planning on leaving the Senator?"

"Her plans are her plans."

"And to just make sure we have this right. The two of you never discussed marriage."

"Never is a long time. Discussed living together, what it would be like."

"Long-term plans for marriage?"

"Not considered it."

"This new business of yours. Detecting troops. How does it work?"

"Troops are only part. Weapon launching, planes taking off, ships sailing. Anything military moving."

"How does it work?"

"Secret."

"I assume you have some type of early warning detection system."

"Mr. Redstone. You work for United States government. You know meaning of secret. My knowledge of antennas and spectrum came in handy."

"Anything more you want to tell us on any other subject?"

"Back home, we don't talk easy to government."

"You're not home. You're a United States citizen."

"I fail to know the difference."

"I'll ignore that remark. Do you have partners? Business partners, in your new company?"

"Work on it alone."

"No partners."

"Correct."

"How about financing?"

"Myself."

"No foreign governments. Nothing?"

"Cannot do business with your military with foreign money."

"Is your answer no? You do not have foreign money in your company?"

"Correct. If we are finished, I have—"

"If I told you Senator Donnlevy was terminally ill, would that come as a surprise?"

His eyes said it all. Vlad Smol had no idea.

FOURTEEN

At exactly noon, the President sent a formal request to Congress to hold up any further voting on *The Force Redeployment Act of 2010*. He asked for a seven-day moratorium, citing respect for a fallen patriot. He wisely made no mention of the murder investigation.

Tiny was driving Angella and me to the airport. Jacobs was in the FBI offices cross-checking leads and arranging for me to visit with a storm tracker expert from Texas A&M. I had expected to be headed to College Station, but Jacobs informed me the professor was based in Galveston. "Be sure she's cleared to receive the Air Force video," I had reminded Jacobs before we left his office.

Angella, after listening to the President's short radio message, observed, "As far as I can tell, the death of Lou Keller has not yet been tied to the Senator."

"That's good," Tiny responded. When that happens, our life will get complicated."

"How so?" I asked. In these matters the big guy seemed to be clairvoyant.

"Reporters won't leave it alone. More importantly, right now the perp, or perps, don't feel any heat. Once the news is out, they'll regroup and tighten up. May even leave the country."

We pulled up to the American Airlines drop-off gate. Angella patted my shoulder as she climbed out of the car. She was booked on an American flight to Dallas to search news archives for stories, and more importantly, gossip, about the Senator and Sarah-Jean. "Wish me luck," she said, "I'll miss you." I had the distinct feeling she wanted to kiss me goodbye, but had thought better of it in front of Tiny. Why she hesitated I don't know. Tiny, and most likely the entire Secret Service, knew we were sleeping together. I refused to believe they would stoop so low as to have videos.

When she disappeared inside the terminal, Tiny said, "Tell me again why Angella is going to Dallas? Anything she can find there I can get here."

"With all due respect to your super powers with the computer, and whatever other methods you spooks have for gathering information, not everything is online. I want her going through everything they have at the *Dallas Morning News* and other local papers like the *Observer*, the *Voice*—even the *Dallas Business Journal*. She'll catch the *Sun-Telegraph* over in Fort Worth as well. I want to know everything there is to know about the Senator and his lovely wife. If there's anything Vlad or Sarah-Jean are not telling us, we'll find it."

"Wasting your time," Tiny commented when he dropped me at the Continental terminal.

"Perhaps, but I've spent a lifetime going down rabbit holes; one more won't hurt." I closed his car door, took a step and then thought of something. I motioned for him to roll down the window. "How about you digging through old archives yourself? I'm talking about government stuff. Never know what gossip we might find. Go through the Senator's legislation. Get into the man's head."

"Anything in particular?"

"I want everything. But...what's bothering me...Vlad seems to be making a living on the U.S. military. Guessing which frequencies they'll use, guessing about troop pullbacks, that type of stuff. See if the dearly departed Senator was on any committees, or sponsored any legislation, along those lines. Could he have passed the frequency information to Vlad? The relationship with the Senator's wife might be a cover. Check the Senator's bank accounts. Trace Vlad's money."

Tiny frowned. "This latest legislation is perfect for Vlad. The troops come home, early warning becomes critical. But Donnlevy is opposed."

"Could have been for show. These guys are masters of deception. Like boxers. Nod left and knock you down from the right."

"Maybe it wasn't the Senator who was off the reservation. Maybe one of his staff."

"Good point. Follow them all."

- - - - -

I met with Dr. Hydra Buttercroft at Texas A&M. From her Curriculum Vitae I knew she was fifty-two years old, held a PhD in experimental and theoretical physics from Ohio State and was a tenured professor who maintained an aggressive teaching schedule in both physics and astronomy. Her list of publications went on for several pages on topics I had no hope of understanding. I couldn't even decipher the titles.

In person, Buttercroft appeared more like my grandmother than a college professor; except that her skin had more intersecting lines than a Google map. It was evident the woman spent a good part of her life outdoors. The sun hadn't been kind to her. She was a slight woman with the hand strength of a mountain climber, as I painfully learned when she shook my hand.

"I've reviewed the video and I suppose you know there's not much to work with," she began after the normal introductory remarks. "But I can tell you this much, the man with the box—"

"Name's Timberwolf. Philip Timberwolf."

"Strange how putting a name on him makes this so very personal. I abhor violence, Mr. Redstone. Just so you understand where I'm coming from I will tell you straight out that if you were not working with the President, I'd not speak with you about this. With that as a disclaimer, Mr. Timberwolf is holding a spectral analyzer. My guess is he's monitoring a radio noise storm. We call such storms NS for short. If I say anything you don't follow just stop me. Or put your hand up. I'm a teacher at heart and waving hands get my attention. I can't teach if you don't understand. Fair enough?"

"Fair enough, Professor. Fair enough." I had come here apprehensive, concerned that my limited grasp of science would hinder my understanding. But her natural teacher personality put me at ease.

"I must say, there is controversy over NS spectral signals. Recent observations seem to vary from accepted understandings. This calls into question a hypothesis regarding nanoflares."

My hand went up.

"Putting it simply, NS give off energy signals. These signals are in the form of energy waves. Similar to the waves in an ocean, but they are mostly invisible to the human eye."

My hand was up again. "Does that mean humans can actually see energy signals...waves?"

"Yes and no. We see energy waves in the nanometer range, three-eighty to seven-forty, to be exact. Waves in this range are observed as color, from violet to red. I must add, however, the human eye only sees the waves indirectly. Waves in this range hit objects, such as paper, or plastic, or a tree branch, and the object absorbs many of the waves. That's why objects become hot in the sun. They retain the absorbed wave energy. The waves that are not absorbed by the object are the ones that impact the retinas and cones in our eyes. Following so far?"

I nodded, not sure that I was, in fact, following. But her enthusiasm had captivated me.

"Our brain then translates those reflected waves, the waves not absorbed by the object, into color. So when we see a green leaf in reality all wavelengths, except the green wavelength, have been absorbed into the leaf. The leaf has reflected waves in the green range. But this is getting off subject. The important fact is that NS events yield waves across the spectrum, primarily much higher than human vision. But not always."

It was clear from her animation that Professor Buttercroft was passionate about her subject.

"So what is the controversy?"

"Recently it was reported that the NS wave lengths are longer than we thought. This is in conflict with the accepted theory that NS events are primarily short, or nanoflares."

"If Timberwolf couldn't see anything, then what was he looking for out there?"

"He was recording, so I suppose, the wavelengths of NS events. I have checked the Crimean Astrophysical Observatory and indeed during the time in question there were several NS events."

My hand was up. "Crimean? Like in Russia?" I immediately thought of Vlad and his connection, if any, to Russia.

"Ukraine. The observatory is one of the oldest and most respected in the world. They follow NS events, among many other things. The *Bulletin of the Crimean Astrophysical Observatory* is one of the most respected in the world."

"Is this new?"

"Opened in forty-seven. Published in English since seventy-seven."

"And that place is where?" I had my phone ready to copy this all down.

"Lovely place called Nauchny, Crimea, Ukraine. Don't bother taking notes. I'll text you the information."

"That would be a big help, Professor. Thanks."

"Call me Hy if you will. Professor is so formal. My students call me Hy—at least to my face. God only knows what they call me at other times." For the first time since meeting the woman, she allowed a small smile.

"Hy, what exactly would Timberwolf do with the recordings? I mean, since he couldn't see anything, how would he know what he got? Or even if there was anything out there?" I had visions of the guy spending time on the beach and then coming home to find he had recorded dead air.

"First of all, he must have known from the observatory when the NS events were anticipated. Their predictions are not usually off by much. So it is unlikely he would get a total null condition. I would have expected him to wear earphones to hear the detection."

"What do you make of the lack of earphones?"

"Perhaps his recorder was giving off the sound."

"What do you suppose he'd do with the recordings?"

"One recording, or even a few, would be meaningless. But over a period of time he could compare his findings to determine if a consistent pattern emerged."

"For what purpose?"

"Don't know what he had in mind. But if he had his own data over a period of time, then he'd use it possibly to predict weather patterns. Many of us believe NS events foreshadow weather events. Certainly, if the energy spectrum was to be concentrated in a particular frequency range, a correlation could be explored."

"Would you have time to accompany me to Timberwolf's cabin?" I asked, knowing I was in this far over my head. "I'd like you to decipher any equipment he may have."

"And where would that be?"

"South of here. Area around Port Mansfield."

"Fishing village. Our oceanography students often work out of there. It would be my pleasure, Mr. Redstone. I'd love to know what he's recorded." She smiled one of her rare smiles. "Could A&M possibly obtain his data?"

"Can't promise. But I don't see why not. So far, no one else has come forward to claim it."

"In that case I can arrange for the school helicopter to take us down there, if you wish. Take about an hour to arrange, and about a half-hour flight. Then, if you wish, we can go over to the island where he was...working. Don't suppose there's anything to see, but you might want to investigate for yourself."

I treated the professor to lunch while we waited for the helicopter pilot. I learned enough about spectral analysis and weather patterns to have earned a Ph.D. myself. I wondered how

Dr. Redstone would sound. The ring of it was wrong. Dr. Jimmy was more my style.

The truth is, I conveniently ignored the fact that despite how many times she explained it to me, I still couldn't follow why apple skins reflect red but are not intrinsically red. No wonder I had a hard time with science. Who ever heard of blue apples?

The FBI had sealed the door of Timberwolf's cabin and it didn't appear disturbed. They also had installed a lock. Jacobs had given me the combination.

The lock opened easily and I stepped into the small room. Hy was directly behind me, anxious to get at the equipment we had seen in the FBI photos. Our first task was to inventory what was now in the cabin with what the FBI had found when they had first entered.

It only took the professor a few minutes before she pronounced, "It's all here. Any problem with me firing up the computer?"

"Go for it." I said. "This is my scene now."

She dutifully began booting the machine. "See here? This is an auxiliary memory bank." She pointed to three large boxes on the floor beside the desk. "These puppies can hold a ton of data. I don't know where this guy came from or what he was doing, but he certainly has a large memory capacity." She nodded in the direction of some misshapen metal boxes on the table across from the computer. "This is sophisticated equipment. Timberwolf knew what he was doing. You say he was a truck driver?"

"That's what I was told."

"He may have driven trucks, but he didn't learn how to use this stuff at driving school. This is post-doc equipment. I'd love to have some of this in my lab. Any chance of making that happen?"

"Unless someone comes forward to claim it, I can't imagine why not." I didn't have authority to give Timberwolf's equipment away. We could sort that out later.

Hy began tapping keys and then looked up. "Something's not right here."

"How do you mean?"

"Won't boot."

"Is it password protected?"

"Not even to that level. It won't boot at all."

"What could cause that?"

"Only thing I know is that someone wiped the drive clean."

"Can you boot it back in your lab?"

"We can try, but my guess is it will be futile. I'll have the pilot load it. We'll have room for the computer and the memory drives, but not the rest of this. Have to send a van for that."

"I suppose this all makes sense to you?"

"It's mostly recording equipment for different frequencies. Different antennas, that sort of thing." Hy then moved across the room to where equipment was lined up on a long table. A moment later she said, "It's a no go. The memories have been physically removed. See here."

I looked to where her finger pointed and saw an empty slot. "Looks like a camera memory slot before the memory is loaded in."

"Close. There is permanent memory inside, but it's accessed through this slot. You need the code on the external memory to activate the permanent memory. We can duplicate this back home, but only if the internal permanent memory has not been wiped clean. That would render the access codes of little importance."

"There's not much of a cell signal out here, so we'll have to wait until we're back in civilization until I can get the FBI to pack this up."

"This *is* civilization, Mr. Redstone. Just not your definition.

"Let's go over to the island. See what we can see."

"Judging from this dead end, I can't imagine it will be much."

- - - - -

It was late when we landed back at Galveston. Professor Buttercroft carefully supervised the unloading, making sure all the equipment we had managed to stuff into the helicopter arrived safely in her lab. I waited for her to begin her evaluation, but she begged off, explaining how she would require assistance from a computer expert if this was to be done properly.

When I balked, she said, "Don't worry, Mr. Redstone, it's only numbers we'll find. He'll not know where they came from, or even what they are. If we don't do it right, you'll get nothing. He's an expert on this equipment."

It was no use arguing with her, so I reluctantly went to the motel and called Angella.

A sleepy voice answered.

"Sorry, Ange, I...I just wanted to tell you how much I missed you."

"Where have you been? Been trying to reach you. Is something wrong?"

"What ever happened to, *glad to hear your voice,* or *I miss you, or...*"

"I love you, Jimmy Redstone. How about that? Will that do?"

"Now you have it right. I needed to hear it."

"Something's wrong. I can tell."

"Not wrong in that way," I replied. "I mean not with me."

"With what then?"

"This whole matter. Been at Timberwolf's cabin and out to the island. Nothing either place. I mean, except for a bunch of specialized equipment, cabin's got nothing. Some bare minimum clothes, some frozen meals in the freezer, bottles of water and Gatorade, some power bars, a few publications from a Crimean observatory. Nothing else. No pictures, nothing personal."

"What about the island? Find anything?"

"Nothing out there either. Reminds me of South Padre Island. I mean the beach north of town. Nothing but sand, some scrub brush, and more sand. Who the hell is this guy?"

"That's why I was trying to call you. *Morning News* files gave me what Tiny already had. However, a local paper, *The Observer,* had a picture of Timberwolf."

My antennae shot up, as did the hairs at the back of my head. "You've got my attention. Keep it coming."

"Thought you'd be interested. But that's not the best part. The picture was taken at a reelection reception for the Senator."

"So there *is* a connection."

"Hear me out, Jimmy. It gets better. I love this work. The reception was hosted by Vlad." Angella paused, waiting for me to process this tidbit.

I could hear the drum roll building. She was holding the best for last. "And?"

"Only his name isn't Timberwolf. It's Zolyar. Sergy Zolyar."

"Sergy Zolyar. Russian?"

"Actually, Ukrainian. And get this. He was an astrophysicist." The drum roll was in full volume now. "And?"

"And...and...he was a co-founder of Vlad's first company."

The music stopped. A curve ball caught me looking. "So why did Jacobs tell us he was a truck driver?"

"Why do the Feds ever tell us anything? I checked this out with Jacobs. He claims the full FBI report on Vlad had just come to him and he hadn't had a chance to digest it. He called back about fifteen minutes later. Confirmed Timberwolf and Zolyar being one in the same. Met Vlad in the Army."

I took in that bit of information and blended it with what I already knew about Vlad and his background. "I assume by Army you mean the Russian Airborne?"

"Not exactly. Can you say sniper school? Seems Vlad and Sergy were in the same squad."

My mind was out of gear and spinning wildly, doing no useful work.

"Oh," Angella said, interrupting nothing useful. "Did Tiny get to you?"

"No," I replied. "What's up?"

"Funeral's set for tomorrow at Arlington. I'm catching the first flight east. Gets me there by ten. Funeral's at eleven. I miss you. Hope you can make it."

"Not sure I can get there in time." I had been planning to drop in on Professor Hy. Picking her brain seemed like a good use of my time.

"Let Tiny work his magic. Air Force is always going somewhere."

"Tiny didn't answer a few minutes ago. I'll try again. Don't hold out much hope."

"I miss you. Kisses. Love you."

FIFTEEN

As it turned out, my Air Force flight, such as it was, arrived ahead of Angella's. She was scheduled to land at National. I touched down at Andrews. In fact, Angella's plane was delayed just long enough so that I stood with Jacobs on an immaculately manicured hillside in Arlington Cemetery among the grave markers of our fallen heroes. The Marine honor guard was off in the distance slowly making its way along a gravel path escorting the caisson carrying the Senator. I was time-sharing my attention among the slowly moving procession, watching for Angella and listening to Jacobs.

I finally caught a glimpse of Angella's trim figure striding up the winding road from the parking area, hair bouncing with each step. For the moment, I allowed myself to relax.

She kissed me on the check. I turned to give her a proper welcome home kiss, but she leaned back and whispered, "Later." She nodded in the direction of the procession. The flag-draped casket had been unloaded and was now moving toward the grave.

We stood at attention, our hands locked together, while twenty-one rifle volleys sounded across the otherwise silent burial ground.

Then the speeches began. I motioned Jacobs to follow Angella and I back away from the crowd. Tributes from the speaker's podium floated over our heads while Jacobs explained what he knew about Timberwolf. I refrained from using obscenities out of respect for the hallowed ground upon which we stood. But that didn't keep the anger from my voice.

"Calm yourself," Jacobs finally admonished, "nothing's intentional."

"Let's see. You call it unintentional that the FBI withheld the fact that a man shot through the head by a sniper was himself a sniper? Or that the dead man was in the witness protection program? Or that he was a former partner of the dead Senator's wife's lover?"

"The Bureau sometimes moves slower than we'd all like," Jacobs commented.

"Knock off the bull...the...the double talk. You want me to believe that you, Sylvan Jacobs, Special Agent in charge of the San Antonio FBI office, wasn't told a murder victim was being protected by the United States government?"

"Believe what you want," Jacobs snapped, "I didn't know. Period."

"Now that you know, tell me the why."

"You know he was Vlad's former partner. Apparently, Vlad, or someone working for Vlad, was slipping money to Donnlevy."

"Somebody other than Zolyar?"

"Zolyar, from all the FBI knew, was not involved. FBI went to Zolyar and threatened to revoke his citizenship on some technicality if he didn't cooperate. They wanted the Senator and were willing to give immunity. Zolyar began to cooperate, but apparently a couple of body-beautiful types pay him a late night visit. Next morning he tries to purchase a gun. Fingerprint check tips off the FBI and they move him into WP after extracting a promise from him to testify."

"I don't recall a trial."

"That's because there wasn't one. Timber...Zolyar didn't quite remember enough hard facts to warrant an indictment. Everything fell apart. Note in the file indicates someone got to him."

"So they just turned him loose?"

"Something like that. Gave him a new identity and kicked him out the door."

"And no one thought this important enough to tell us?"

"Got caught in the cracks, all I can say."

"You son..."

Angella yanked my arm and I moved away from Jacobs enough to catch my balance. A couple of heads had turned.

I turned back to issue one last barb when the proverbial shit hit the fan in the person of Abigail Johnson. I had seen her earlier, but thought, wrongly as it turns out, that she had not seen me.

"Hello, again Mr. Redstone," she announced. "Can I buy you lunch? My way of giving you an in-person thanks." I must have glanced toward Angella, because Johnson immediately stuck out her right hand in greeting. With the left she thrust a business card toward Angella. The card said *Washington Post* in the center and below it the words *Homeland Security Desk* were printed in bold letters. "You must be Angella Martinez. I trust you were okay with my stories."

In point of fact, Johnson had treated Angella softer than she had me.

Angella, wearing the smile she reserved for *have to* situations, shook Johnson's hand. "It is nice to meet you in person. Jimmy told me about your role in helping us resolve the situation." She paused, glanced at me, then added, "But truth is, I'm not comfortable around reporters."

"Some people are not comfortable around cops," Johnson replied. "I suppose you could say it's a learned taste." Turning to me, Johnson said, "Will you join me for lunch? You're invited as well, Ms. Martinez. Say thanks to both of you."

"I'm afraid not," I replied, "but it's the thought that counts."

Not one to give up, Johnson asked, "In that case, can we find a quiet place to talk?" A conspiratorial smile spread across her otherwise plain face. "This is important."

My immediate thought was to find Tiny and have him deal with her. But typical of Tiny, he was nowhere to be found when we needed him. He had driven me from Andrews and his car was parked only a few feet away. Unfortunately, it was locked.

My hesitation gave Johnson the opportunity to add, "I know your instinct—and training—is not to speak to the press. I respect that. But two things you should know. First, I'm paid to produce. I will produce, with or without your cooperation. Second, I'm willing, at least for now, to talk to you off the record. As you well know, I keep my promises."

"We're here for a funeral. Pay our respects. Nothing more."

"Nonsense! For starters, you both have impressive offices at Homeland Security on the investigations floor." She bent down her first finger and started on the second. "Couple that with the fact that you're at the funeral of a Senator who mysteriously dropped dead just as he was about to answer the roll call to lock the veto on the Force Redeployment Act. Or, as the Senator dubbed it, *The Great Pacifist Retreat Act*." Another finger was bent over. "And third, you are attempting to get into the car of Tiny Jurald. He's CIA, working in the guise of Secret Service. Tiny's good at what he does, but he's not good at being incognito. Man his size gets noticed."

As if to prove the point, Tiny's head appeared over the heads of the folks gathered around the widow. Even though he was fifty yards away, there was no mistaking his profile. He was moving in the direction of Vlad Smol, the widow's lover.

Smol had separated himself and appeared from this distance to be reading grave markers, unconcerned with the funeral of Senator Donnlevy. Tiny reached the little man and handed him a piece of paper. Tiny waited while Smol absorbed the contents. I wasn't certain, but it seemed that Vlad's head shook sideways as he reached up to hand the paper back to Tiny.

Johnson's eyes had followed mine. "As I was saying, you two are here working the crowd. You're drinking your own Kool-Aid if you think I don't know what's going on."

"Since you already know what's going on, you don't need to speak with me."

Angella dug her nails into my arm.

Johnson ignored my remark, and replied, "As I said, we can talk off-the-record, or I can go with half a story."

"What half?" I asked, wanting to know what she had. I didn't want to give anything away that was not on the street. "What are you talking about?"

"Senator didn't die of natural causes. You've interviewed Wilkes and God only knows who else. Tiny's over there badgering the wife's lover, for God sakes. A million stories are in the air. If I covered the society desk, I'd latch onto the fact that the dirt hasn't even covered the husband and the lover is waiting for her in the cemetery. For the political desk I'd be asking why the father of a pregnant teen was one of the last visitors to see the Senator alive. But I cover Homeland Security, and you're working with the President. Tiny's the President's Secret Service liaison to the CIA. He only works on critical issues. I simply want to know what gives."

"Angella and I are from Texas. Governor asked us to pay our respects. We're here as private citizens."

"I call bull shit. You're a lot of things, Redstone. But you're not the Governor's representative. Politicians never send cops to represent them. Optics are wrong."

"Just here on behalf of the Governor," I repeated, fooling no one.

"And Tiny's selling raffles to a church car wash! It's a mistake to play me for a fool." A heavy scowl now replaced her broad smile. "There's a story here and I want it."

"Excuse me, Ms. Johnson," I replied, "we have nothing further to talk about." I started in the direction of Tiny.

We took two steps before she called out, "I allowed that bullshit fake airplane crash to slide by because I agreed with you I'd panic the country otherwise. You play ball with me, I'll return the favor. The President's holding a conference on nuclear material control. That A-bomb episode shook him. Is this connected to the bomb? Was Donnlevy killed because he found out the truth and was blackmailing the President?"

That froze me in mid-stride. Another curve ball. I hadn't even considered that angle. Working with the Feds, nothing was ever what it seemed. The fact was, Abby Johnson had helped us solve the A-bomb investigation. I had repaid her, but obviously more compensation was due.

"You want to talk," she pressed, "or continue bull shitting me?"

"I'm here to pay respects," I replied. "If you think Tiny's working the crowd, ask him."

"Ask me what?" Tiny's voice boomed. He was now standing a few feet behind Johnson. "You taking my name in vain? Oh, Abigail, didn't see you over there. How are you this fine day? Covering funerals now? How the mighty fall. Long way down."

She wheeled toward him. "Please explain to your friends I can be trusted off the record."

Tiny responded. "Johnson is a reporter first and foremost. Truth, as she believes it, is paramount. But, off the record, she's as good as it gets."

Johnson turned to me, her eyes asking for my cooperation.

"Nothing to talk about," I said.

"Senator banging underage woman change your mind?"

When the shock wore off, I said, "I'll be in my office in an hour. Maybe I'll think of something to talk about by then."

SIXTEEN

An hour later Abby Johnson swept into my office. Angella, seeing her arrive, came across the hall. Tiny had dropped us at the front door, characteristically begging off the interview.

"Can we talk privately?" she asked, glancing toward Angella, who had taken a seat off to the side and slightly behind Johnson. "I find that off-the-record discussions are best one on one."

Angella, anticipating my response, stood to leave.

"We work as a team," I replied, "so we'll talk as a team. Treat Angella and I interchangeably if you will."

Johnson looked from me to Angella and back to me, giving herself time to weigh the pros and cons. "Okay. Let's start by cutting the cat-and-mouse shit. You asked me here hoping I'd lead you to my sources. I've spent twenty years in this town, Redstone. Five Pulitzers, countless other awards. I know everyone who even thinks this stuff. You think I'd be careless enough to fry one of them? Truth is, I pick up a word here, a word there and soon I have a picture. No single person is a source by him or herself. I don't believe Donnlevy died of natural causes. Frankly, neither do you. I know he was terminal. Kidney something. But he was helped along. The autopsy report, by pathologists you suggested might I add, have not been released. That's enough in my mind to confirm foul play."

"How do you know I suggested the pathologist?"

"Two to be exact. You think for a moment the bells don't go off when Johns Hopkins needs help on an autopsy? Didn't happen by accident. And why Homeland Security? The only way HS would have authority to investigate is by order of the President. So, why not the FBI? I ask a few questions. So what do we find? A nineteen year old, most likely carrying the Senator's child, dies at the Hay Adams. You were there when she was found. A coincidence? I hardly think so. And who do you suppose performs the autopsy? None other than Martino and his assistant, Glenda Houstein. Checked them out. Reputation as the best forensic pathologist team in the Southwest. So now we have two Dallas-based doctors doing post-mortems on District murders. And you expect me to believe nothing is going down?"

"You have it all. Can't add anything further."

"Confirm I have the facts right."

"Off the record?"

"That's what we agreed."

"Right on. And might I add, impressive."

"I'll accept that as a compliment coming from you. I assume you're aware the Senator has been having underage sex with several partners?"

"It does seem highly likely."

"Thanks for being honest. My sources say several members of Congress are also involved in similar activities?"

"Same answer."

"Are you willing to tell me who arranged for the Senator's activities in that regard?'

"Slime by the name of Keyston Jenkins." I had to give to get. Tossing Jenkins' to the wolves was no major loss. The sooner he was rolled up the better we'd all be.

Johnson made a note of the name. At least I was ahead of her on one fact—or so she made it appear.

"What can you confirm about the Senator's relationship to Roberto Alterez Santiago, a Mexican National known to be a drug lord based in Matamoras?"

To say I was stunned is an understatement. Santiago was the man who had cut my throat when Angella and I had intercepted a smuggled A-bomb. Johnson knew about the operation because I had briefed her. I had no suspicion that Santiago was linked to the Senator. If that were so, then the implications were beyond huge.

"I'm sorry," I managed to say, "but everything about that aspect is classified."

"What aspect?" Now Johnson was momentarily confused. But she recovered before I did. "That's the reason the President asked you and not the FBI, isn't it? There's a connection to the drug trade. And here I was thinking he was covering up the A-bomb scare."

"You have it wrong," I said, hoping to get this back on track. "I gave you the full story on the smuggling. That's over. This is not a smuggling issue."

"But Santiago is under house arrest in Mexico. That would take high-level approval. I have good reason to believe there is a connection between the Senator and Santiago."

"Beats me," I replied. "Above my pay grade as they say."

"I'll accept that—for now. What can you tell me about Joy Malcolm?"

Angella broke in. Am I off-the-record as well?"

"You are," Johnson confirmed, turning in her seat to face Angella. "You have something?"

"What I know came from police reports and is not classified, so far as I know." Angella glanced in my direction. I nodded. "Malcolm checked into rehab. She needed to detox, that's for certain. But that's not why she's there. She took a picture and caught a murderer walking with the victim shortly before the vic died. She went into hiding. As far as I know, she's still there."

"Go on," Johnson said, when Angella seemingly was finished.

"She's under ATF and ICE investigation for drug smuggling and dealing. It's an ongoing investigation. We are not involved."

This is off the record," I lamely reminded Johnson. "Please don't violate that agreement." The more we spoke with Johnson, the more agitated I became. I had never worked this way, and it felt wrong. Old dogs and new tricks came to mind. I was the old dog.

"Don't worry, you've given me nothing I didn't already have. Except for Malcolm being in rehab. Wondered where she had gone. There's no real story yet, just speculation. Not a national security issue as far as I can determine. Look, as the man said, I'll make you a deal you can't refuse. As before, I'll hold what I have if you promise to give me an exclusive when it's resolved, whatever it is."

"I'm new to this world, so I don't know the rules. Don't know if I can honor the exclusive. What happens if the President slaps a confidential order on it all?"

"That's my problem, not yours," Johnson answered. The look on her face implied that she'd find a way to publish regardless. "You give me the story exclusive and the paper will deal with what we can publish. Your name will be withheld."

I reluctantly nodded.

"Let's go on the record. What can you tell me concerning the dead woman, one Lissalou Keller? Goes by Lou."

"Nothing about her directly. But I'll provide a video of, shall we say, a person of interest. No quote, mind you. And no TV usage. The video is background only. You okay with that?"

"Anonymous source will do. You saying the person on the video is the killer?"

"I can't say that for certain, but I'd be surprised to learn he's not. Again, no quote."

"I always protect my sources. That's how I get what I get. My lips are sealed."

"It's not your lips I'm concerned about. It's your pen."

SEVENTEEN

"**S**old out to the devil," were Angella's first words when Johnson departed. "Hope this doesn't bite us in the butt."

"President asks us to do a favor, then proceeds to give only half the facts."

"You're the detective," Angella said, using her calming voice. "After last time, he thinks you can ferret out anything. I choose to believe it's not him."

"Who then?"

"Take your pick. Jacobs? Tiny? Jamison? And that's for starters. Oh, and add your good buddy Mommy Long Legs."

Angella's smile flattened when she mentioned McNaughton. Changing the subject was a good idea. I said, "Have Jacobs research the Donnlevy connection to Santiago. Could be something. Or could be Johnson's baiting us."

"Whatever she's doing, she caught your imagination."

"She makes sense. It never did add up that the President would call us simply to determine if a senator died of natural causes. That's the FBI's job."

An hour later we had our answer. "It always amazes me," Jacobs was saying, "as to what's right under our noses and you never see it until it's pointed out."

"Like a dead guy being in witness protection and you not telling us," I replied, continuing to scratch the scab.

"Bag it already, Redstone! I told you I hadn't been informed. Want me off the case, just say the word and I'll get my ass back to San Antone. Otherwise move on."

"What did you find on the Donnlevy Santiago connection?" I asked, not taking the bait.

"Donnlevy spent over forty days in Mexico in the last two years alone. He crosses over at Brownsville with a non-specific destination of Matamoras. No hotel, resort or residence was listed in either the U.S. Customs or Mexican databases."

"Proving yet again senators do, in fact, have privileges the rest of us don't enjoy."

"FBI has no authority to investigate a senator in Mexico without specific authorization. Nothing more I can get at this time."

"What about hot pursuit?" Angella asked, obviously toying with Jacobs.

"Nothing hot about this. Cold as the dead Senator. Tiny might be able to help though."

A thought came to me. I said to Angella, "Call Trich and see how she's doing. Casually ask whether Donnlevy had ever been a visitor to her home."

Trich is the fiancée of SPI Coast Guard Station Chief Mark Cruses and works at the Brownsville hospital. From what Angella and I could determine, she was not involved with her father's drug dealings.

Angella retreated to her office to make the call.

Jacobs said, "Let's assume for a moment Donnlevy and Santiago are buds. Where does that lead?"

"You're trying to find the end of the string without unraveling the knots," I commented. "Shit, I thought we were finished with that bomb-traitor business. Doesn't make sense that Donnlevy, a staunch supporter of our military, is involved in a scheme to bring down the government."

"How does anything fit into anything?" Jacobs replied. "Now look who's jumping ahead. Santiago and his gang were convenient to use for the smuggling. They were not part of the terrorist plot. Most likely didn't even know what was going down."

"Maybe Donnlevy just wanted to embarrass the President and never meant the bomb to go off."

"Could be," Jacobs said, not sounding particularly enthused about that hypothesis. "Donnlevy is tight with General Jamison. Jamison ran the special ops. Both of them support increased military spending. Maybe they intended for the bomb to scare the shit out of the public. That could have been enough to defeat the legislation."

"Doesn't track," I answered. "If they wanted the bomb found, Jamison would have darn well allowed it to be found. Didn't need me in the middle."

"Maybe and maybe not. The operation might have run amok. Clearly, Jamison lost track of the bomb. By the time he tracked it down, the operation was out of his control."

"I'm thinking something else is going down," I replied when Jacobs fell silent.

"The sixty-four dollar question remains: Why was Donnlevy killed? Correction: Why were Donnlevy, Timberwolf/Zolyar *and* Lou Keller killed?"

"You have a theory?" I asked Jacobs.

"Nothing concrete. Need to find Bill Snow, or whatever his real name is. Need to know why Lou died?"

"Maybe they're not connected," I postulated, my heart not in that theory.

"And politicians always tell the truth."

"Just had a delightful conversation with Trich," Angella called to us from the doorway. "She and Mark Cruses are back together. He's being transferred to New Jersey. A place called Sandy Hook. She's looking forward to her new life with him. Says Mark wants her to move as soon as he's settled."

"What about Donnlevy?" I asked, preferring to deal with the matter at hand and not with the romantic entanglements of Coast Guard Lt. Mark Cruses.

"Your hunch was right. Donnlevy is a long-time friend of Trich's father. Goes back before she was born. Donnlevy and Santiago go deep-sea fishing all the time. Trich was sad to hear of the Senator's death."

"Not surprising they go fishing," Jacobs said. "Out of earshot. Surely Donnlevy was briefed by INS on Santiago. Most likely also by the FBI. I'll need high-level approval to access the files. Curious the Senator continued their friendship."

"She's upset," Angella continued. "Her brother died this week. She doesn't know it's from radiation poisoning and I didn't tell her."

"I know it's crass," I said, "but can't say I'm sorry. Anything else from her?"

"Just girl stuff about the wedding plans, that sort of thing."

"Just thought of something," I said. "Sorry I didn't think of this earlier. Text the image of Bill Snow to her. See what she knows."

"Already did. She knows him only as Snow. Works for her father from time to time taking vegetables to the States."

Jacobs looked up. "As they say, the plot thickens."

"I must have missed something," Angella said, "What plot?"

Ignoring Angella's question for the moment, I said to Jacobs, "I assume you have access to the Senator's financial records. Both personal and contributions. Follow the smoke."

"Maybe we'll find the fire," he called over his shoulder as he brushed past a somewhat bewildered Angella heading for the FBI building a few blocks south.

Tiny called to say the remainder of the equipment from Timberwolf's cabin was on the truck.

"I thought the FBI was overseeing the transfer," I commented to Tiny, puzzled as to why he was involved.

"They are. I'm the expeditor. Handle travel arrangements for people and freight." He laughed. "Jacobs asked me to follow up. My question: How do we know memory's been wiped clean?"

"Professor Butterball inspected it."

"What makes her a computer expert?"

"Good point. Can you arrange for an FBI computer forensics expert to inspect it before we release it to the university?"

"Anticipated it. The equipment was diverted to the FBI lab. We also rounded up the stuff you took up there last night. Need a chain of evidence. You know better than to leave it unattended."

"Thanks for having my back," I replied, not happy with myself for allowing the equipment out of my control. Lapses such as that allow perps to run free.

"That's what I'm paid to do," the big guy said. "Anything else?"

"Ange and I should go to Pittsburgh to interview Smith Keller, Lou's father."

"Hold a minute."

In fact it was closer to ten minutes, but when he came back on the line, he announced, "Trip's arranged. Going commercial. Flight leaves in two hours."

"Fill me in?" Angella said when I hung up. "We're going where?"

"Pittsburgh. Talk with Smith Keller."

"His daughter's funeral was this morning," Angella said, her eyes turning moist. "Shouldn't we wait?"

"Hours count in these types of cases. Don't have the luxury. Waited too long already. Goes with the job."

"Sounds as though you're more interested in finding her murderer than the Senator's."

As I was learning, Angella was a step ahead of me in understanding my motivation. "Maybe one in the same," I replied. I was covering myself while knowing Angella was right. The Keller killing bothered me more than either of the others.

"I was thinking about her this morning while we were at Arlington. Lou was buried about the same time as the Senator. A young life, with everything to live for, lost. Actually, two lives lost. Do you ever get used to it?"

"I care. That's what channels me." What I was not willing to admit was that perhaps I cared too much.

EIGHTEEN

Pittsburgh, a city tucked into the foothills of the Allegheny mountain range between three rivers, is one of those cities that tricks the mind into thinking it's a sleepy backwater. The drive from the airport into the city took us past shopping malls and businesses carved into the hills. Ahead I could see a massive-looking hill or the base of a small mountain. I couldn't tell which. The highway appeared to be heading straight into grey shale when we suddenly dipped downward. But instead of curving around the mountain, the roadway ran straight into a well-lit tunnel bored through its heart.

A moment later the mountain spit us out onto a bridge suspended over one of the rivers.

Angella, following our progress from the airport on her cell phone map, announced, "Monongahela below us. Downtown straight ahead. Allegheny River is over there." She pointed slightly to my left. "And that's the headwaters of the Ohio." Her outstretched arm moved further to my left.

Indeed, the entire breathtaking downtown fanned out directly in front. Three Rivers Stadium and Heinz Field lined the far banks of the Allegheny River.

"If I recall, this area is called the Golden Triangle. Imagine getting on a raft and floating down to the Mississippi. That's what…"

"RIGHT TURN AHEAD," the GPS announced, directing us onto a road that snaked alongside the Monongahela, heading toward a part of the city known as Squirrel Hill.

Angella was acting as tour guide and pointed out the reclaimed land that had once held the steel-making Bessemer furnaces. Coal coming down the river in barges fueled the massive furnaces that once had been instrumental in building this great country.

"Is Pitt around here anywhere?" I asked Angella. "They have a great basketball program. Love the cheering section. Call themselves the *Oakland Zoo*."

She studied the map. "You're in luck. Oakland exit is just ahead." She pointed to a quickly approaching exit ramp. "What they call the Cathedral of Learning will be only a few blocks away."

It was now after nine and the traffic was almost non-existent. I moved into the right lane and then immediately onto the off-ramp. We lumbered up a long, steep, cobble-stoned street, row houses tight on either side. At the top we could see, directly ahead, the top of the towering cathedral.

Pitt didn't seem to have much of a campus aside from the commercial buildings of a bustling city. We quickly passed the Cathedral, and a few miles further on we passed Carnegie Mellon University.

A few more miles and we were in Squirrel Hill where Smith Keller lived. As an accommodation to him we had agreed to meet at his friend's law office on Murray Avenue. This was to be a private meeting between just the three of us. I had preferred meeting at his home, but he had insisted that his wife was not yet ready to talk about what had happened.

"Murray Avenue is a block ahead. Next light, turn right." Angella said. She beat the GPS by a few seconds. "The office is about five blocks down on the right."

My cell sounded.

Tiny came on the line. "Lab says the computer has been wiped clean. Professional job. No residual, nothing to recover."

"So why are you so upbeat?" I asked, sensing Tiny was holding back the good news part of the report.

"That's the computer. But on the actual recording equipment they only took the memory keys. The keys allow access to the actual recorder memory. They mistook the keys for the main memory."

"Can the memories be read without the keys?"

"Experts can reconstruct the keys—or so I'm told."

"What about Galveston?"

"Your friend, Buttercroft, says she can't, but claims one of the students is a master at hacking. Not something she should be overly proud about—but it is what it is. Jacobs put his foot down, said that the FBI would coordinate any attempt at reading the files. Buttercroft seemed entirely too interested in getting her hands on the devices. She obtains much of her grant money from the Air Force. Need I say more?"

"Suggestions?" I asked, knowing Tiny never presents a problem without a solution.

"Kicked it around with Jacobs. With your permission, we'll deliver the devices overnight to Dr. Singh. That's pronounced Sing with an h. S-i-n-g-h. He's at Pitt, just a few miles from where you're meeting Keller. They just lured him away from Carnegie Mellon. World's expert in data recovery."

"Just drove past the campus. I assume you already made arrangements."

"Not until you give the green light.'

"Go for it. Tell Singh with an h that Angella and I will come by to see him mid-morning. Say ten-thirty."

"Got it. Good luck with Keller."

Murray Avenue, like many streets in Pittsburgh, is steeply sloped. At this time on a midweek night there were only a few cars moving about and the sidewalk was deserted. We parked across from a synagogue and walked up the hill past an all-night news and tobacco shop, making our way toward the law firm of Katz and Associates located on the second floor above a Jewish bookstore. The tobacco shop was the only business open.

I rang the bell and immediately heard the answering buzz of the electronic lock. Someone had been waiting for us. A metallic voice instructed us to open the door and come up.

At the top of the stairs we were greeted by a middle-aged man wearing a wrinkled white shirt, open at the collar, and trousers held up with suspenders. His face was in dark shadow, in need of a shave. A small round blue-and-white knitted piece of material was perched on the back of his head. He held out his hand. "I'm Chester Katz, a friend of Smith Keller."

We shook hands. "I'm Jimmy Redstone and this is Angella Martinez."

He reached for Angella's outstretched hand, then said, "Smith asked me to meet you folks. What a terrible loss. Such a nice girl. Bright and always cheerful. Called me Uncle Louie. We're not related. The Dyson's aren't even Jewish, but we've known each other since we were boys. Went to Alderdice, played chess, that sort of thing."

"Is Mr. Keller here?" Angella asked, "I don't see him."

"He'll be here in a moment or two. I have a conference room down the hall where you can be comfortable. May I get you anything? Water? Maybe some pop from the fridge? Afraid the coffee's empty."

"Nothing, thanks. So you knew Lissalou. Do you know who the father was?"

A puzzled look crossed his face.

"She means," I added, "the father of the baby."

"My, you are direct, Ms. Martinez. One doesn't go around asking young women such questions."

"Sometimes," Angella responded, her smile still pleasant, "young women tell their uncles things they might not tell anyone else. Did you have that type of relationship with Lissalou?"

Katz's face colored and at the same time softened. "At times I did, yes."

"Was this one of those times?"

"Not exactly. She spoke to me about the Senator. She worshiped the man. She was planning to intern for him next semester. She worked the phones for him."

"Do you believe he's the father of the baby?"

"The Senator? That's hard to...Is that what this is about?"

"Just asking questions. Please don't jump to conclusions."

"I can't imagine Donnlevy having relations with Lissalou. My good God, she's a baby! Not even twenty yet. He's...he's over sixty-five!" He wiped a tear from his eye. "Pardon me. I feel as if I lost one of my own. I have three daughters, and if one of mine—" He wiped away more tears, fighting a losing battle.

"Pardon me. This has been a long day. A very emotional day, to say the least."

"We're sorry to intrude," I said, "but it is important that we speak to Mr. Keller."

"I advised him against it. He doesn't have to speak to you now—or ever."

"I wouldn't go so far as to say never. If we are to have hope of finding the perpetrator, then the sooner the better. Already too much time has elapsed."

"He gave a statement to the Washington police. What more do you need from the poor man?"

In all honesty I didn't know. "One never knows what was overlooked. Are you representing him?"

"Not in this. I'm a real estate lawyer. House closings, mortgages, rentals, that sort of thing. Make a nice living. No house calls."

"Those pictures are magnificent," Angella said, admiring the many photos of flower gardens decorating the walls. The radiant colors brought life to what otherwise would have been a drab office.

"Thanks," Katz said, a flicker of light coming into his eyes. "That's my real passion, photography. Get out every chance I get. It's ironic, the one hanging on the far wall in the conference room was taken in the very cemetery where Lou was laid to rest." Katz's eyes misted over again.

The picture he was referring to appeared to have been taken from outside the cemetery and captured roses and day lilies and several other flowering plants in full bloom.

"That's Homewood Cemetery and all those plantings were put there by a neighbor. Believe his name's Laurence. Guy has a green touch and a great eye for color balance. That area was mostly weeds before he began cultivating the ground. Now it's an attraction. I understand he moved away, but he certainly left behind a legacy.

The front bell rang and Uncle Louie reached under his desk and pressed a button. The door opened, then closed. Heavy footsteps hung in the air, one after the other, as Smith Keller slowly made his way to the second floor.

Katz intercepted him at the top of the steps, saying, "You certain you want to do this? If not, I'll just ask these folks to leave. They have no right bothering you. Especially not tonight of all nights."

Keller stood silent, his shoulders hunched forward, looking slowly from Angella to me and back again, his thin face lined in misery. His lips moved, but nothing audible emerged.

Gathering himself as best he could, drained of emotion, he rasped, "Thank you Ches. You've done enough for our family. I will talk to these people. If it helps in finding my baby's murderer, then how can I refuse?"

"I'll wait in the other room. Just call if you need anything."

"Go home to your family, Chester. Go home to your girls and kiss them for me." He pulled out a soiled hanky and wiped his face. He blew his nose and shoved the cloth back in his pocket. "I'll close up behind. Go home and enjoy your family."

Katz stood for a moment, indecisive. Then he said. "Call me if you need anything. I'll come right back." In a moment his retreating footsteps were heard going down the steps. The door once again opened and closed. Silence filled the room. An uncomfortable silence no one wanted to break, least of all me.

Keller looked up from the floor. His sad eyes were red and puffy, moisture lingering in the corners. "I trust you've read the report I gave the police," he began, "so why did you come all this way? What's so important you had to take me away from my family tonight of all times?"

"I know this sounds trite, but from painful experience, the longer we wait, the less likely we are to catch the person who did this to your family. We'll make this as fast as we can so you can get back home."

Tears streamed down his face and he made no effort to wipe them away.

"Angella and I are sorry for your loss. We can't replace your daughter, and we can't reduce the pain, but we can help find who is responsible," I was trying to sound sympathetic, but making a poor showing of it.

"You're not the police, so who are you? FBI?"

"Homeland Security. We are looking into the death of the Senator."

"Homeland Security? Does that mean Donnlevy's death has to do with terrorism?"

"We don't yet know."

"What does my baby have to do with terrorists? She was no terrorist. She's a sweet child."

"Please, let's start at the beginning. Before Lissalou came to know the Senator, did you know him?"

"Yes. I contributed to his campaign."

"But he was from Texas."

"I thought he was on the right track, conservative and all that. I liked what he stood for."

"When did you first contribute?"

"When he ran for re-election, about five years ago."

I then proceeded to march him through his relationship with the Senator. Keller was in the wholesale food business, specializing in produce. His biggest customer was Giant Eagle, based here in Pittsburgh. His company did well, "Nothing spectacular, but a nice living," is how he put it.

Angella leaned forward, a sudden urgency in her face. She brought the Snow picture up on her cell phone and turned it to face Keller.

The result was as though we had touched a cattle prod to his genitals. Blood drained from his face. He jumped up and paced around the small room. After several rounds he slumped back into his seat.

We waited for him to explain himself.

The soiled hanky came out. He dabbed his checks several times and crumpled the silk material into his fist. Again his lips moved silently. When he finally spoke, it was with a great deal of effort. "Where did you get that picture?" he asked, his voice barely above a whisper.

"A more important question is, who is he?" I responded, deflecting his question.

Keller went silent again. More hanky. More wiping. He was up and pacing again. We waited while he decided what he was willing to tell us.

Finally, he said, "His name is William Dermitt. Goes by Snow."

"Please tell us about him."

Keller again slumped into the chair. "I met Snow down in Mexico several years back. He works for a grower, name of Santiago, in Matamoras. Snow handled deliveries of vegetables from Santiago. He was Santiago's expeditor, making sure the orders arrived when promised. His job, and he was always good at it, was to get the produce here on time and unblemished." Keller wiped the corners of his eyes and then said, "He treated me well. My produce was always first-rate, very little waste. I built my reputation on his ability to expedite my orders. I was able to capitalize on this and that's why I've done well."

"Go on," I encouraged. Clearly, Snow was important in his life. And not just because of vegetable deliveries.

"He met my daughter and they…"

"And they, what?" I pressed.

"I have nothing further to say on that subject! My God, I just buried her. Can't you respect that?"

"Wish we could. But her murderer is running loose. We need all the information you can provide."

"I have nothing more to say on that subject." He slumped into a chair.

I leaned forward. Our faces were not more than a few inches apart. I smelled alcohol on his breath. But I also smelled fear. "Please continue, Mr. Keller," I coaxed. "You might want to consider revising your story as to why you supported Senator Donnlevy. You can start by telling us exactly when and where you first met him."

Again the hanky, this time to the forehead. "I knew the Senator through my Mexican vegetable grower. Goes by Santiago. I think his full name is Roberto Alterez Santiago."

"Why did you lie about that when I asked you before?"

"I didn't lie," he mumbled. "I just didn't say."

"Why?"

"Didn't think it was important."

"What relationship did you have with the Senator?"

"I refuse to answer any more questions."

"That's certainly your prerogative. But it won't end with this conversation."

"I did nothing wrong. I need say nothing more."

Keller was on the verge of bolting. I wanted to glean from him as much as I could before we lost him. My plan was to have

Sylvan Jacobs and the FBI follow up. They would make Keller's life a living hell if he didn't cooperate. But for now, the Mr. Nice Guy approach was called for.

I leaned back, giving him space. "Smith," I began again, this time using my best buddy voice, "We're here to find the killer. Snow was seen outside her room. We want to speak with him, see what he knows. Do you know where we can find him?"

Smith Keller looked up, his bloodshot eyes meeting mine. "Snow finds you. You don't find Snow," he said, convincingly.

"Do you know who fathered Lou's child?"

"Donnlevy."

"You're positive?"

"Yes."

"What makes you so certain?"

"I know. Leave it at that."

"Why did you visit the Senator the night he died?"

"He refused to see Lou. I wanted to see what I could do. I knew he'd see me."

"What did you want him to do?"

"Acknowledge the baby."

"Does that mean he had never acknowledged the child?"

"He stopped seeing Lou."

"Why was she in D.C. with you?"

"She wanted to see him. He agreed to see me, but only without her. But she insisted on coming to Washington anyway."

"Were you blackmailing the Senator?"

"I refuse to answer any more questions!" he exclaimed, new life pumped into him. He stood. "This discussion is over."

I got up, and Angella followed my lead.

Keller was halfway down the stairwell, his heavy footsteps reverberating off the walls. Angella called after him, "Your daughter's gone. Honor her memory by helping us catch her killer."

The footsteps stopped. Without turning to face us, he shouted, "He owed me! The son of a bitch owed me! And this is the thanks I get! Now leave me alone!"

NINETEEN

"One room or two?" I quipped as we entered the lobby of the Hampton Inn, not far from Pitt. The Keller interview had emotionally drained both Angella and I.

"Two," Angella said without hesitation. "I'm whipped. No need to advertise."

"You think for one moment our relationship hasn't been duly noted by Tiny and his crowd?"

"I'm not concerned about Tiny. No need to help anyone else along. Make them work for what they get."

I wasn't sure if *them* meant the bad guys or the Feds. Both sides qualified equally. "See you in the lobby at nine. We can catch breakfast and then head out to visit Singh."

"Works for me."

I leaned over and kissed her cheek.

I didn't hear it and certainly there was no flash to signal that a picture had just been taken, but I felt a tight twist in my stomach. I quickly looked around and saw two groups of people talking among themselves. All men and all were dressed for business, their ties now hanging loose around their necks. Off to the side, a college kid was talking on his cell. One man, much too heavy for his height, stood in the news shop thumbing through a magazine. All appeared normal. But then, good operatives always appear normal.

"What's that look about?" Angella asked.

"Bad feeling is all. Keep your door locked. Don't answer without calling me on my cell. See you in the morning."

- - - - -

Professor Singh was in his mid-fifties. I had served in the Army with a kid named Singh. Lekh Singh. Went by Lee. Short guy, dark skinned. All Lee ever talked about was how he missed India. Turned out he and his family fled India when he was two. So it surprised me when Dr. Singh turned out to be tall and light-skinned. And unlike the Singh I had known, this man had a calm demeanor bolstered by a genuinely pleasant smile. A good-look-ing guy with perfect English.

"I knew a Singh once," I commented, "way back in another life. From Southern India, I believe."

Professor Singh's smile broadened even further. "My family's from Sri Lanka. I came to this country when I was five." He must have read the puzzlement on my face because he added, "Sri Lanka's an island just off the southern coast of India."

"I remember doing a report, you know the type when you go to the board and draw a map. Freshman year in high school. The name changed from...from..."

"Ceylon," Singh coached.

"…Ceylon," I repeated. "I drew the outline of the island. The teacher asked me to put it into context of a land mass. I was stumped."

"Please, Mr. Redstone, Miss Martinez, tell me why you are here. It all sounded so mysterious."

Dr. Singh listened patiently until I finished. Then he said, "The equipment arrived about an hour ago. It's in the lab. The recoding equipment is missing the memory security keys. I suppose that is why it is here."

"Precisely," I said, recalling what Professor Buttercroft had said about accessing the memory through the slots.

"Perhaps I can help," Singh replied. "But I won't know until I examine the devices more closely. Didn't want to do anything until we spoke."

"How long will that take?" Angella inquired, leaning in close to hear the soft-spoken professor.

"With any luck, I'll have an answer for you by mid-afternoon. I have a lecture in an hour and then a meeting. Let's say three. We can discuss my findings at that time."

- - - - -

"You're in luck, Mr. Redstone, Ms. Martinez." Singh began when we walked back into his office at exactly three. "In this equipment, the portable memories are only used to identify the user. The real data is stored internally."

"Were you able to read it out?" I asked, anxious to know where we stood.

"Most certainly. I've made copies for you on these drives." He proceeded to hold up two thumb-sized flash drives. "These each hold twenty gigs." He handed the drives to me and then said, "I don't know how much good the data will do you though."

"What's that mean, Professor?" Angella asked.

"Just that it's all frequency data. He apparently was monitoring a NS. Actually more than one, judging from the volume of readings."

"NS means noise storms," I said for Angella's benefit, proud of myself for remembering. "Timberwolf was recoding space noise."

"What is interesting, Singh added, "is the surprising amount of low frequency interference overlaying the latest recordings."

"What's the significance of that?" I asked.

"That will require further analysis, I'm afraid."

"So why is it interesting if you don't know what it is?" Angella asked.

"Just that he was out on an island. The reason one goes to all that trouble is to be free from interference. Puzzling is all."

"How long will it take to analyze the data?"

"Depends upon how long it takes to get basic data for the times in question from the Crimean Observatory. I plan to compare their readings with the readings on these disks. That will provide a starting point. Then I can filter out much of the chaff, so to speak."

"Can't they just send the data?" I asked.

"The red tape is insurmountable. Could take weeks, even months."

"Please send me a text listing exactly what you require. I'll see if we can work some magic. Send it to the number on the card I gave you."

"Good luck. Nothing cuts through the paperwork. Tried everything in the past."

"Got a friend," I replied. "Should work."

"Pardon me for being a skeptic, but I'll believe it when I see it. Don't expect anything from me until, say, six."

"That'll work. I'll try and have what you require by morning."

I had no idea if such a time frame was possible, but that problem was Tiny's to solve.

"As I said, I'll believe it when I see it."

"Professor, one other thing. Please perform the work yourself and keep the results private."

"Those were my instructions."

"Also, please keep the disks in a safe. Is that possible?"

"Certainly." He led us to a corner of the lab and pointed to an ancient fortress the size of a small desk. I doubt if it was bolted to the floor, but I'd like to see the size of the machine that could lift it out of here. Have to take down the wall. "This secure enough? Do this all the time for the government. No worries."

Walking out to our car, the sun had set and the chill in the air reminded me I was in Pittsburgh and not on South Padre Island. I had grown fond of that sand spit and my new life down there. Right now SPI seemed far away.

A shiver snaked its way down my spine. Maybe it was simply the damp air. Maybe it was something more.

TWENTY

We enjoyed a late dinner and sat at the bar nursing beers at the airport Hyatt Regency. My hand rested softly in Angella's as she sipped the last of her drink. She leaned forward and kissed me. Then she said, "You mind terribly, if we sleep in our own rooms tonight?"

"It would be nice to have you next to me," I answered, trying not to show my disappointment. "Last night the bed seemed so... so empty."

"Hey, don't give me that *woe is me look*. Tomorrow night we'll be back at the beach and..."

"And..."

"Use your ample imagination, big guy."

I started to respond, but Angella put her finger across my lips. Her eyes told me to back off. Knowing when to retreat has never been my strong suit.

Angella stood and I did the same. Out of habit I reached for my phone and found a text message from Dr. Martino

time-stamped several hours earlier. INSULIN VIAL WAS TAM-
PEREDED WITH. INSULIN REPLACED. SELF-ADMINIS-
TERED AT ELEVEN EVERY NIGHT.

I held the phone so that Angella could see the message. "Now
we know how," she commented.

"And when," I replied.

"All's left is who."

"And why?" I said. "Never forget the why."

"I suppose we'll know *why* when we know *who*," she replied.

"Or the other way around."

"I'm too tired for this," Angella said, blowing a kiss. "See you
in the morning. Lobby at five."

- - - - -

Angella looked as though she had spent the night in her
clothes. She had made a halfhearted attempt to run a comb
through her hair, but apparently had given up.

"Say one word and I swear I'll kick you where it hurts."

"Do that and you'll be sorry."

"Frankly, right now I don't give a gnat's skinny butt. I didn't
sleep five minutes."

"What's bothering you?"

"Smith Keller, that's what. I couldn't sleep thinking about our
interview the other night. Took it a day to gel, but something's
wrong with that man. I can't tell if he was blackmailing the Senator
or what. And his reaction to Snow, was…well, over the top."

"It's fear. He's convinced Snow killed his daughter. He must
believe he's next."

"That's where I came out. But why?"

I checked my watch. "We have time. Let's talk over coffee."

"Go through security first. The hotel is slow. Besides, when I'm in the lobby, I get the creeps. Like eyes are on me."

We walked to the airport, passed easily through security, and not until we were in the Starbuck's line did we speak again.

I leaned close to Angella, making it difficult—but not impossible—to pick up our conversation. "I also spent time working through the Snow angle last night. Can't figure why he'd be in the hotel, other than to be in the vicinity of LissaLou."

"So that puts him in the ace spot for homicide. He lied about knowing anyone."

"You think it was before or after?"

"Not following."

"He kill her before he intercepted us—or after? Cool customer either way."

"Psychopaths often are. All in a day's work type of thing."

Angella fell silent, sipping her coffee and apparently thinking through the possibilities. "Lou knew the Senator. Snow had a relationship to the Senator and to her."

"You going somewhere with this?"

"Thought so for a moment. But lost the thread. If we can tie Snow to the data, then we can tie Timberwolf's murder to the Senator."

"Too much of a leap—so far. I've asked Jacobs to have the FBI labs try to match Snow with the image from the island video. FBI's also looking for him, but no luck so far."

"You get the feeling the FBI only finds who they want to find?"

"Seems that way at times. But this is a big country and professional troublemakers tend to have several picture IDs. Wig, a little creative makeup, and TSA doesn't have a chance. Remember how Te Burner ran free all over south Texas, even when we knew where he had to be?"

"Don't get me started on that." Angella's eyes went intense. "I don't harbor fond memories."

She was referring to the nasty time Burner had given us. And how suspicion had fallen on her.

We leaned against a railing. I took her free hand in mine. "Tell me this. And I want it straight. The time we spent together in South Padre Island that wasn't…that wasn't…just you being nice to me? Angella playing nurse?"

"God no!" Angella exclaimed. "You really think so? I want you more than anything. I'm just…afraid I guess. What we do is dangerous."

"We'll be fine," I replied, trying to sound more upbeat than I felt. "Keep your wits about you, we'll be fine."

"Wish I could share your optimism. I'm just…well frightened."

I leaned over and kissed her. "That's your plane they just called. You better get going."

She kissed me on the cheek, took a last gulp of coffee and threw the rest in the trash can. What do you mean, my plane? We're both—"

"Got to thinking about the widow Donnlevy. Going to Dallas. Want to talk to her in person, lean on her a bit."

"I can do everything I need to do from Texas. I'm going with you."

"Wish you could. Tiny has a long list of folks we need to interview. You need face time with them. I'll catch up later today. Should be there by nine at the latest. Catch a late dinner."

Her face twisted into what looked to be a pout. She said nothing.

I had two hours to kill before my flight to Dallas. I treated myself to a full breakfast, read *USA Today,* and then decided to read the *Washington Post* to see what, if anything, my new best friend Abigail Johnson was up to.

Her by-line appeared under the heading of Homeland Security, and she was in rare form. The good news is that she honored our agreement. The bad news is that she broke the story about under-age sex and the Senator's ties to known Mexican drug dealers. And while she didn't come right out and say it, she hinted strongly that the dealer, whom she called a Regional Czar, was recently involved with smuggling contraband into the country. She stopped short of discussing the aborted bomb episode, but she let it hang that terrorists might be hiding in the country.

I located an airport network TV and found a seat directly facing the screen. Within fifteen minutes, a breathless reporter, a microphone in her hand, stood in front of the Capital building. "This morning's *Washington Post* broke the news that the FBI is investigating allegations that the late Senator Donnlevy had sex with underage women. CNN has just learned that Donnlevy was not alone. According to usually reliable sources, several other members of Congress are involved with underage girls. The White House has refused comment and inquiries are being directed to the Department of Justice. The FBI will neither confirm nor deny that it is currently conducting an investigation. Senate Majority leader Paula Clayson has refused to comment, saying only that the Senate does not confirm or deny rumors. Senator Mathew Donnlevy has been linked to a death of a nineteen-year-old pregnant woman at the prestigious Hay Adams hotel. The young woman, LissaLou Keller of Pittsburgh, apparently visited the Senator often on weekends. Sources have speculated that Senator Donnlevy was the father of the unborn child. District police have not released the results of DNA testing. That's all we have at this time."

"Thank you, Tracy," the news anchor sweetly said. "We'll be back to you shortly." Turning toward the camera, the reporter continued, "This story first appeared in the *Washington Post* and the reporter, Abigail Johnson, when interviewed earlier today, refused to disclose her sources. She did, however, adamantly defend the story. Please stay here for all the breaking news."

I found it fascinating, but not entirely surprising, that the news coverage focused on the sex and entirely ignored the terrorism aspect with terrorists possibly still in the country.

I called the Widow Donnlevy as a courtesy to arrange a time convenient for her.

"There is no convenient time!" she barked. "I already spoke to your associate, a Miss...Miss..."

"Martinez. Angella Martinez. I'd like to speak with you personally."

"Must I? I mean, under the law must I? I just arrived home and need time for myself."

"This is a national security matter, Mrs. Donnlevy. It's important I speak with you." I fudged a bit. "I prefer that we talk in the privacy of your house." Innuendo sometimes works better than a threat.

"Vlad told me about your talk with him. There's not much I can add."

"That'll be my problem then. Wasted trip and all. My flight lands about one. How about two? I promise I'll be out of your hair by three."

"If I must I must. Come and waste the taxpayers' money. Goodness knows everyone else is doing it, so why not you as well?"

TWENTY-ONE

The plane actually landed twenty minutes early. I used the extra time to check in with Jacobs and Tiny. Still no news on Snow. But Tiny had a report back from Singh.

"Obviously the Crimean Observatory sent the data overnight. Singh said it would take months."

"Let's just say I have friends," Tiny replied.

"In the Ukraine? At the Crimean Astro...whatever it is?"

"I've been in this business a long time. Lots of favors are due."

"So you bypassed government channels is what you're saying."

"Let's just say this was a personal request to a friend."

"So what's the report from Singh?"

"Thought you'd never ask. The dead guy Timberwolf was recoding noise storms. Timberwolf's data is a perfect match to what the Crimean Observatory recorded."

"Is that the full story?" My question was prompted by the knowledge Tiny only gave up what he had to.

"As far as space storm data goes. But, and here's where Singh didn't have the answer, the recordings also held readings in a range unique to commercial electrical power-generating stations."

"Commercial generating stations? What's that about?"

"Singh didn't know, except to say that some of the most prominent readings bore the signature of controls used with nuclear energy power generation."

"That jives with what we heard. There's a restricted zone down that way. But certainly not on the island."

"That's not what the data says. Singh matched Timberwolf's recorded NS signal data to a precise land-based location. He did it by mapping Timberwolf's data with the observatory data and adjusting timing for physical location differences. The nuclear control signals came from the spit of land where he was killed."

"There's not a nuke power plant out there. So what gives?"

"You're the detective. Kapish?"

"You telling me I'm wrong?"

"I'm telling you this is not a secure connection."

That could only mean there is a nuclear plant somewhere out there. Underground? The vision of the Japanese reactor meltdown came to mind.

Tiny continued, "I've sent the findings to Jacobs. He'll have the FBI go over it. CIA also has the data. I'll keep you posted."

My question was, what came first? Was Timberwolf recording NS events and just happened to record nuclear energy generation sounds as incidental findings? Or was he recording nuclear energy signatures and covering his work with NS events?

And how did Timberwolf know about hidden nuclear energy generation facilities in the first place? Who else knew about Timberwolf's work? He was in hiding, but who was he hiding from? Questions were plentiful. Answers were scarce.

I parked the rental car in Sara-Jean Donnlevy's spacious circular driveway. The house and grounds were impressive, even for Texas. I didn't think I could have seen another house if I used binoculars—or even a telescope. Some states cover less territory.

A wheelchair ramp snaked from the front door to the driveway. Before I climbed out of the car, Sarah-Jean emerged wearing what appeared to be a tie-dyed polo hanging loose over a pair of cut-off jeans. The pattern on the polo contained vivid blues, reds and yellows and seemed to be in the form of an ever-decreasing swirl that sucked my eyes into her well-endowed chest. For a woman in a wheel-chair, she looked to be exceptionally well-fit.

Her handshake proved the point and I was lucky she hadn't injured my still-tender hand. "Come, we can talk in the back. The birds are feeding and we won't be disturbed by the gardener back there." Without waiting for my reply, she performed a tight wheelie and charged off on a path leading around the side of the house. I had trouble keeping up with her.

Sarah-Jean waited for me in the gazebo, where a bowl of corn chips and a pitcher of margaritas were already on the table. "Thought we might as well enjoy ourselves. I long ago learned to make the most of what life hands me."

She was indeed a different breed of cat from what I usually investigated. She was flamboyant, yet at the same time her eye-piercing concentration told me she was deadly serious. "Your home and grounds are magnificent," I said, keeping the conversation on neutral ground, at least for now. "You've gone to a lot of trouble and I certainly appreciate your hospitality."

She filled my glass and topped up her own. Then holding her drink high, said. "Here's to the most honorable Senator. May he be forever blessed with a thousand naked virgins." She took a long swallow and added, "All under the age of sixteen."

"I take it you didn't approve of his life style," I replied, trying to assess whether it was the alcohol talking, or if she was always this way.

"That's a complex subject, at best. Let's understand, I'm not exactly the model of propriety. I chased him—and married him—for his money. Hey, I'm not saying anything you don't already know. I'm told you're very good at what you do. So I assume you've read the newspaper accounts. Shit, the *Dallas Morning News* ran a series on me for God sakes. Oh, don't get me wrong. I gave him everything his little heart desired. That is, until his heart desired what I couldn't give him." She swept her arm around at the yard. "He was good to me in return. All this and more. I was ready to settle down, forget other men, concentrate on him. That worked for a few years until his appetite drifted to younger women."

"Was that before or after your accident?"

"Before. I'm twenty-one years younger than him. But he wanted women in their twenties. I suppose I can understand that. But when he slipped below eighteen he and I parted ways, so to speak."

"Was Vlad your lover before your accident?"

"Vlad warned me you would ask that. Why is sex so important to you? Can't you leave it that Vlad and I were just friends?"

"Frankly, I don't know what's important and what's not. I need a complete picture." In fact, over the years I had come to understand that the two biggest drivers to criminal activity were money and sex.

"You'll never get a complete picture," she countered. You should know, nobody tells the truth, the full truth and nothing but the truth. Even under oath they don't."

I hadn't come all this way for philosophical discussions, so I pressed my line of thought. "Was Vlad with you when you fell?"

"He was at the resort. But not with me on the mountain. Actually, I remember so little of it. Hit an icy patch, lost control, went off into the tree line. Lucky to be alive. Vlad has seldom left my side since. He's not here now, but that is rare."

"Will you two be married?"

"We have not discussed it, but I can't imagine not."

"Do you have children?"

"Not with Mathew. He never wanted children."

"By your answer I assume by another man."

"A boy. The result of too much booze and not enough sense when I was twenty. I've paid dearly for that roll in the hay. Woke up with the creep draped over me in some fleabag motel room. I managed to slip out of bed and lock myself in the bathroom. I called to him through the door. Told him to get out before I called the police. Said I had better sense than to sleep with him."

Sarah-Jean's eyes had gone into the middle distance, lost in a distressing private thought. The fleeting moment passed and her eyes again came alive. "At first he said nothing. I repeated my threat to call the cops. That's when he said, 'Woman, you invited me here. Get real. Deed's done. Come out and enjoy the second act.' I vomited what little remained inside."

She drained her glass. "Nine months later, to the day, his kid popped out. Ended my college career and sucked away my dreams of making it on my own."

"I take it you didn't marry him."

"I don't even remember his name. Don't recall ever hearing it."

"And your son's name?"

"I prefer to keep him out of this."

"I'm afraid that won't be possible. If he's not involved, then nothing will come of it."

"You won't be getting his name from me. That much I can assure you."

"Shouldn't be hard to find."

"Go find it then!"

"When was the last time you saw your son?"

"I have no intention, Mr. Redstone, of discussing my son in any context. Now move along with your questions or finish your drink and leave."

I sipped my drink, taking time to observe Sarah-Jean Donn-levy, a still beautiful woman who held herself proud despite the wheel chair. She was certainly in command of herself and knew exactly what she was doing. I leaned back in my chair. "The name Sergy Zolyar mean anything to you?"

"Co-founded Vlad's first company."

"Seen him recently? Say within the last year?"

"Lying rat! Hell no I haven't seen him! Comes around here, I'll...I'll...never mind. I don't wish to discuss that scum."

"Seems I hit a nerve. Care to explain?"

"It's all in the government's files. Go look it up."

"How about your version?"

"Simple. He was cooperating with the Feds pertaining to some bullshit story that Vlad was bribing my husband to get advance frequency allocation information. I don't pretend to understand all that technical mumbo jumbo, but I do know Vlad did not bribe my husband."

I had to agree with Sarah-Jean on that point. The Senator was a rich guy. Jeopardizing everything made no sense. "After Zolyar began cooperating what happened?"

"He disappeared. No trace."

"Did Zolyar have assets? I mean that he could have taken with him?"

"Really don't know. I presume so."

"So you haven't heard from him since he disappeared?"

"Not a peep."

"I understand you hardly ever visited your husband's home in Georgetown. Yet you were there the night he had his heart attack. Mind telling me why at that time?"

"I wanted to show my support. He was working non-stop and I thought I could help."

"Why this time?"

"Vlad asked me to help."

"Vlad? I thought he was in favor of the legislation."

"Oh, no indeed. Vlad was opposed. Didn't think it was good for the country to pull all the troops home. If the bill passed, yes, his business would grow faster. But he's a rich man, can afford to wait. Even without the troop pull-back Vlad was positioned to do well. Vlad's a genius at what he does. He would never bet on one piece of legislation."

"If the troops remained deployed as your husband wanted, why would the government need Vlad's detection system?"

"As I said, I don't follow all the technical stuff. But Vlad is convinced the increased deployment of drones will require us to have world-wide monitoring. His is the only real solution."

"But the United States already tracks its drones. Why add Vlad's system?"

"I'm talking about terrorist-controlled drones. They are the next major threat to this country. Did you know that some of those drones are as small as...", she looked around, "...as hummingbirds. Maybe even as small as a dragon fly."

"And his system can track something that small?"

"We never discussed the exact specifics. But he claims he can detect drones."

Changing the subject, I said, "Vlad made a lot of money on his last company. What did he do with that money?"

"How the hell would I know? He doesn't discuss his finances with me."

"Is he well-off?"

"Of course."

"You never talk about finances?"

"We have better things to do with our time than sit around and match stock portfolios." Her flirtatious wink was intended to tell me she was still sexually active. I interpreted it as her trying to distract me from the subject.

"When you and Vlad take trips, travel, who pays?"

"I do, why?"

"Do you pay for him as well as yourself?"

"Usually, I buy the tickets. He pays for meals and things."

I dropped this line of questioning because we could get financial information on Vlad a number of different ways. But I was setting the stage for the real question I wanted answered. "Since you bought the tickets, I must assume you have your own access to money. Is it your own account or a joint account?"

"I really don't know. I just do what I want and the bills get paid. The Senator is…was…not a poor man."

"Any idea of how much he's worth?"

"I told you, I don't sit around discussing finances."

"With Vlad. I'm speaking of your own finances. You have any idea of what you are personally worth?"

She looked off into the distance, apparently studying a pair of mockingbirds pecking at a feeder hanging from a tree limb. This was one of the days Dallas is famous for; high deep blue skies with a hint of cloud painted on as isolated specks.

After what seemed several minutes, Sarah-Jean quietly said, "I have no separate accounts. The Senator, I'd say, is worth fifteen, maybe twenty, million."

"What plans did he make, like with a will, or anything?"

"Are you asking what I will receive? The answer is, all of it."

"How do you know? Did your husband tell you? Do you have a copy of his will?"

"His lawyers handle all that. We've had discussions." She studied the mockingbirds until they flew off, checked her watch, then announced, "I believe your hour is up, Mr. Redstone. My, how time flies when you're having fun. I think you know the way out. I'll just remain here and perhaps a hummingbird or two will make its way over to keep me company."

TWENTY-TWO

I drove in the direction of DFW airport, not yet decided about my next course of action. Follow the Donnlevy murder or concentrate on Timberwolf? I didn't yet know for certain if I was working on puzzle pieces from the same puzzle or from different puzzles. One thing for certain, however, was that if there were two puzzles, then they shared the same color palette.

Angella called. Her first words were, "Enjoy your visit with the jolly widow?" I could hear the chuckle in her voice. "Bet you obtained nothing of value from her. She's a piece of work."

"Charming. Filibustered for an hour, then threw me out. Didn't much care for her husband. Knew about the under-aged girls. Had a son when she was twenty. Claims it was a one-nighter. Knows Timberwolf/Zolyar. Says she hasn't seen him since he disappeared. According to her, both Zolyar and Vlad had a lot of money. Speaking of money, she inherits it all, or so she claims. Run a full financial report on Vlad. Something Sarah-Jean said caused me to think the man is not as financially well-off as we believe. Oh, and Vlad, according to Sarah-Jean, was not in favor of the troop pull-back."

"That doesn't line up."

"She says Vlad had money and could afford to wait. They would deploy his system sooner or later."

"Shouldn't be hard to find that out."

I proceeded to fill Angella in on the information Tiny had passed along concerning the noise signatures on Timberwolf's recording equipment.

"So what does a nuclear power plant have to do with Snow, drugs or the Senator?"

"We're in the answer business," I mumbled, "but all we have are questions." I redirected the conversation back to my interview with the widow. "Sarah-Jean married the Senator for his money. Said so. She could have murdered Lou for the same reason. She has the arm strength, but I doubt if she could manage the leverage. But possible."

"Motive?"

"If the baby was a child of the Senator, then the baby could have cut her out entirely, or at least by half. Some states provide for children."

"You leaning that way?"

"Can't foreclose anything."

"When I showed her the picture of Snow, I expected her to say something to the effect that she had seen him around once or twice. She immediately said she had never seen him in her life."

"You're not buying it."

"Something in her manner. I can't place it, but it's real. She's hiding something. She's also hiding the reason why she was in Georgetown. She hated the Senator, made no excuses for it. But yet wants us to believe she was supporting him in his campaign to defeat the legislation even though her boyfriend didn't much care one way or the other. That is, if you believe what she said. Doesn't compute."

"Where you going with this?"

"She wasn't there in support of him. Don't think her vocabulary owns the word *help*. She wanted something, and whatever it was it couldn't wait until the vote was over."

Angella and I spoke a while longer. Then she said, "Hate to cut you short, Jimmy, but I gotta run."

"What's up?"

"Spoke to Trich an hour ago. She's acting funny. Professed to not know what I was asking when I brought up Snow. Had no idea what exactly he did for her father. I had the distinct impression she wanted to say more but she wanted me off the phone. At one point I asked her what was wrong. She whispered, 'can't talk'. When I pressed, she responded, 'Need to see you in person as soon as possible. Hurry!' Then the line went dead. I'm at National about to board Continental through Houston to Brownsville. Get in at nine-forty."

"Meet you there. Catch up with you in Houston. Your flight is three hours, mine's an hour."

"I was hoping you'd say that. Got to go. They're boarding."

"Love you," I said, the words slipping out easily.

"Love you also. Bye."

I called Continental to book the flights. Both legs, Dallas to Houston and Houston to Brownsville, were sold out. I called Tiny to see what he could do.

Ten minutes later he called to say I was confirmed on Continental to Houston, but was wait-listed on the second leg. He assured me I'd get a seat. You can always fly in the cockpit, same as a Federal Marshal, he assured me.

I was looking forward to being back in South Texas with Angella. South Padre Island, with its mix of people, from brain surgeons to bartenders, had grown on me. Angella and I hadn't discussed it, but after her divorce she had put her house in Port Isabel up for sale. My plan is to have her move in with me on the island. I don't know what her plan is.

I thought about the logistics of seeing Trich. Angella and I would arrive in Brownsville around eleven-fifteen. We could either go across the bridge to meet with Trich late tonight or go first thing in the morning. Given the turmoil between the Mexican government and the drug cartel, which Trich's father controlled, the sooner the better. Angella would control the timing.

I called Jacobs and repeated what I learned from Sarah-Jean. He promised to immediately check the finances of all concerned. He assured me he'd put some folks on locating Sarah-Jean's son.

At one point in our conversation, he said, "I don't say this lightly, Jimmy, so hear me out. Mexico is not a safe place right now and getting worse. Our law enforcement people have become targets. Can we arrange to speak with Trich another way? Perhaps at the hospital in Brownsville where she works?"

"I'll ask Angella, but I doubt it. Something's gone wrong over there. According to Angella, she's scared, can't talk."

"I'll alert BEST. Get you some cover."

Jacobs was referring to the Border Enforcement Security Task Force. In theory, the task force was designed to bridge the information flow gap between the various federal and state agencies. But in practice, the gap was just too wide.

I found myself rubbing my barely functional right knuckles. Not that a shootout is the answer, but the thought of being naked without proper use of my weapon was discomforting.

Tiny called with disturbing news. "I have it on good sources," he said, "the President has ended the investigation. Donnlevy was going to die anyway, and he no longer cares if his demise was rushed. His backers are furious he stalled the legislation this long. Since you haven't turned up evidence of a terrorism connection, he's turning the investigation over to Justice and the District police."

"That's bullshit!" I shouted into the phone.

"That's Washington," Tiny calmly replied. He waited a few beats before dropping the other shoe. "I'm expecting Madame Secretary to be in touch with you at any moment. You and Angella will be reassigned. Senator will be off limits."

"When did you get that info?"

"Few minutes ago. Why?"

"My bet is the widow Donnlevy got to the President. She was not thrilled about my probing her life."

"She's off limits to you now. You overstayed your welcome."

"Not until I have official word," I replied, more pissed than I had at first realized. "That woman is up to it further than...than the wheels of her chair!"

"Be careful. Her husband may be dead, but she still has considerable stroke. I'm surprised McNaughton hasn't been on the horn to you. Cindy and Sara-Jean go way back."

"Think she got to Cindy?"

"You're Cindy's idea. Doubt if she'd drop you."

"My line's been busy."

"That wouldn't stop Cindy if she wanted you."

I changed the subject. "As you know, we're going to see Trich tonight, or in the morning."

"President doesn't give a flip anymore. The Mexico connection is off the table as far as he's concerned. Your mandate is Timberwolf."

"Mexico *is* dealing with Timberwolf," I said, grasping at threads. "They're connected through Snow."

"You saying Snow's connected to Timberwolf? In what way?"

"Not prepared to say exactly just yet."

"Just so you know," Tiny said, not challenging me further on the Snow/Timberwolf connection, "the news about under aged sex didn't do much to put you in favor with the Washington crowd. You did something no one else has been able to accomplish. Brought both parties together. They all want your scalp. FBI's caught with their shorts down. You're into the feed corn now. Johnson refuses to reveal her sources. But word on the street has it that it came from you."

"Some value came from it after all," I responded, trying to hold my temper. "First time they've agreed on anything."

"Good luck with Trich. And watch out for Santiago. He's one slippery bastard. Mexican government's stepped up their crackdown on the drug folks and they aren't going quietly. It's hell down there now. And you, my friend, are in the cross-hairs."

TWENTY-THREE

The plane's wheels bounced onto the runway at Houston's Intercontinental airport and my head snapped forward. I had fallen asleep the moment the plane lifted from the ground in Dallas. My phone was still off and so far as I knew I was still officially investigating the Senator's death. That was my story and I was hanging by it.

Angella's flight from National had been scheduled to land at almost the same time as mine, but the overhead board now showed a twenty-minute delay. I had left her only this morning, but it seemed a lot longer than that. Thinking about Angella gave me a pleasant tingle, and, truth be known, I was silently whistling a corrupted version of *Piano Man* remembered from my high school years.

Instead of waiting in terminal C where her plane was scheduled to land, I decided to walk over to the B terminal where the Continental regional jets to Brownsville were based. My goal was to register with Continental to be sure my name was high on the standby list. I wanted to avoid playing my Homeland Security trump card if possible.

The young man working the gate check-in assured me I'd get on the flight, but it was too early for him to release seats.

Thirty minutes passed. Then forty-five. Then an hour.

Still no Angella.

At ten-fifty my name was called. The gate agent handed me a ticket. "You're in luck, Mr. Redstone. We have a couple of no-shows. You can board now if you wish."

"Has the flight from National, flight three-five-nine, landed? I'm waiting for someone from that flight."

He dutifully punched in the information and studied the screen. "It's in," he announced. "Landed a bit late, but was at the gate twenty-five minutes ago. Gate forty-two, the C terminal."

"Can you check if a passenger was on that flight?"

"I can't do that, sir. I'm very sorry." His resolve to follow the rules was tempered by a forced smile.

The smile turned genuine when I flashed my Homeland Security shield. "Sorry, didn't know," he said, apology in his voice. "What's that name again?"

"Martinez. Angella Martinez. That's Angella with two lls."

"Just a minute." More information was punched in. A puzzled expression crossed his face. After what seemed an eternity, he looked up from the screen. "She was definitely on flight three-five-nine from National, but she hasn't checked-in here. She's one of the no-shows. Sorry."

I barely heard the word *sorry,* as I ran from the gate area, sprinting as fast as I could in the direction of the C terminal, all the while trying to study the faces of people coming the other way. I wanted desperately to see Angella coming toward me.

But we did not pass.

I could have taken the Terminal Link train, but jogging seemed faster. Possibly Angella was on the train, but I had no way to check the terminal and the train at the same time. Knowing her, she would never trust the rather slow train when she was running late.

Running through airports may have been okay for OJ Simpson, but it was difficult now. People seemed to take delight in moving slower when they saw me coming, often stopping to stare. "Take it easy, buddy," one man called, "you'll knock someone down." Rarely did anyone step out of the way, as though it was my fault I was late for my plane.

I arrived at counter forty-two just as the agent, a woman in her fifties or early sixties, thin as a noodle with a face pinched flat as though it had been caught in an elevator door, was about to begin calling passengers for a flight to Las Vegas.

"Pardon me," I said, flashing my shield, "are all the passengers off the flight from National?"

"Oh my, yes. We're now boarding for Las Vegas."

"Is that a continuation?" I was hoping against hope that Angella had fallen asleep. Or possibly she took sick. Anything. "Could there be people remaining on board from the National flight?"

"No, sir, there's not. Mind if I see that badge again?"

"Homeland Security." I again flashed my shield, at the same time, saying, "I'm looking for a passenger. Her name's Angella Martinez."

"Did Ms. Martinez, that *is* what you said her name was, did she do something wrong?"

"I *must* find her. I need your cooperation."

"I'll call my supervisor. Please wait over there." She pointed to the area where the passengers were lining up to board.

"I need to speak with the crew of the airplane now. It's an emergency."

The thin face snapped, "Sir, I said please wait over there. I must speak with my supervisor."

"I don't have time for that bull shit! I want on that plane and I want on it now! It's important."

"Sir, please come this way." She had suddenly become all sweetness and charm, even though her face was pinched even tighter. Her eyes showed fear. She led me to the far side of the counter away from the boarding passengers. "If you'll wait just a moment, I'll have the Captain come out to speak with you."

"The Captain won't know anything. I want to speak with the flight attendants. Anyone who might have seen her." I hastily scrolled through my phone camera files desperate to find Angella's picture.

"Okay, sir, just a moment."

Instead of a uniformed airline captain, two uniformed TSA workers approached, accompanied by three Houston police officers, one with his hand on his weapon.

"Would you please come with us, sir," the police officer wearing a white shirt asked. "We can discuss this in private."

I again reached for my shield. My movement triggered two of the police officers to pull their weapons. Several passengers pulled back in shock. Others ran to the side. One guy dropped onto the floor. "I'm an officer with Homeland Security," I announced, my voice louder than I had anticipated. "My associate was on the flight from National. She was going on to Brownsville. She never made it to the—"

"We'll discuss this in private," the head officer repeated. "Keep your voice down."

"Something's happened! I need to find Angella! She's——" I broke free and started to run back toward terminal D.

I managed two steps before a TSA guy and a police officer had my arms pulled back. Two weapons were leveled at my head.

I went limp. They relieved me of my Berretta. If I thought I was naked before, now I really was.

I was talking faster than normal, but was helpless to slow down. Angella was in trouble and these jackasses were busy examining my shield and my ID picture and asking pointless questions pertaining to my age, my address, who exactly I worked for. Several minutes were wasted until the head guy even asked about Angella.

"Age?"

"Forty."

"What was she wearing?

"Don't remember."

"Hair color?"

"Brown."

"Eyes?"

"Brown."

"Height?"

"Five-six." I tried to get to my phone to show them a picture, but they had a solid grip on my arms and refused to ease up. "Enough!" I shouted. "Pull it up in your database! We're registered with Homeland Security. What's wrong with you folks? She got off that plane and disappeared!"

"Perhaps she missed her flight, is all," the head-guy volunteered. "People go missing all the time. Only they're not really missing. Just someplace else."

"She didn't miss the flight on purpose! For God sakes, she's a Federal Officer, not a dingbat!"

"Let's go to the TSA office," one of the TSA guys said. "This is better handled in private. Will you cooperate or must we cuff you?"

"Have you at least confirmed my credentials?" I demanded, not at all understanding their behavior.

"Being done now as we speak. Have it by the time we get to the office."

Once in the office, the TSA guy dismissed everyone except the white-shirted Houston police officer. The TSA guy introduced himself as Justin Rover.

"Let's go over this again," Rover said. "You arrived from Dallas on Continental at gate thirty-six in terminal C. Why didn't you meet her there? Her flight was scheduled for gate forty-two."

"I told you, her flight was delayed. Have you confirmed I am who I say I am?"

"That's why you're not under arrest. Now let's go over this so we get it all right."

"Right would have been to listen to me immediately and locked down the airport! God only—"

"We've been over this several times, Agent Redstone. Just do it our way." He paused, and when I didn't say anything, he continued. "So then you went over to terminal B. Did you walk or take the train?"

"Walked."

"And you waited at gate B seventy-three for Continental flight two-six-five-four to Brownsville. Is that the ten-fifty flight?"

"Yes."

"And Angella never arrived at terminal B seventy-three, is that correct?"

"Yes! For the tenth time, yes! She got off the National flight and disappeared."

"Settle yourself, Agent Redstone." It was the Houston cop joining in. He was a big black man and sported a stylish mustache on a wide smooth face. His badge read Carver. The shoulder patches proclaimed him sergeant. "People miss flights all the time. And for many reasons. Very few of those reasons are sinister. Maybe she became sick and went to the hospital. Maybe she's sick in the restroom. It happens. People do strange things. You, of all people, should know that."

"Was she taken to a hospital?"

"Matter of fact, no. No ambulances have been dispatched in the past two hours."

"She would have called me." Then it struck me like a hot branding iron. I had been dodging headquarters and hadn't turned my phone back on until I retrieved her photo. My face grew hot as I checked incoming messages. This was one time I wanted to be embarrassed, wanted to hear her voice say, I don't feel well, went to the hospital. Or better yet, to a hotel. It's amazing how long it takes to scroll through the various screens when you're desperate and your fingers behave like left thumbs.

No texts, but two voice mails. One was from Jacobs, which I ignored for the moment. The other was from Angella.

My heart raced as I hit the call-back number. Her voice came on the line, "Jimmy, I'm in Houston. Flight was late. Just saw Snow walking out of the gate area. I'm following. If you're in Houston come quickly. Heading toward terminal B. More to follow."

My heart stopped.

Then it raced harder than ever. I was breathing heavy and couldn't focus clearly. Rover continued to ask questions that I couldn't understand.

Carver guided me into a chair and returned a moment later with a cup of water. Slowly the room came back into focus.

I brought up Snow's picture on my cell. "She saw this man and is following him. He's dangerous. That was over an hour ago." I checked my phone to be sure there were no more messages from her.

There were none.

I had a thought. "I assume you have cameras around the airport. Can we see tapes?"

"That will take time," Rover replied, a trace of concern taking shape. "She's an agent also. Is that what you said earlier?"

"That's what I've been trying to tell you!" I wanted to add *bonehead* to the end of the sentence, but managed to hold my tongue. Losing one of their own is never a good note to have in your personnel file.

"I'll do what I can to expedite the process." It was beginning to dawn on Rover that he had screwed this up. "System's designed for immediate review, maybe go back a half hour or so. Over an hour is more difficult, but can be done."

"Time is what we don't have," I needlessly said. "Please do what you can as fast as you can."

"What's that time period again?" Rover asked, now deadly serious.

"She landed at ten-seventeen, terminal C forty-two. Called me at ten-twenty-two."

"There are several camera feeds, but since we know the terminal and the time, we can focus in. Matter of calling up the right database." He bent over his computer and worked the keyboard.

A short chunky no-nonsense woman entered the room and Rover stood taller. Her name was Lisa Cooperton, and she was the Houston TSA regional head. A moment later a uniformed

Houston cop, who introduced himself as Lt. Galton Ortiz, followed Cooperton into the small room.

I briefed them both, trying to provide as few background facts as possible, especially about Snow. But at some point, probably sooner rather than later, this was going to escalate to Washington. Maybe already had.

It took about ten minutes before Rover was able to bring up the right images. During that period, Cooperton positioned herself away from us and proceeded to text for several minutes.

Rejoining us, she looked at me quizzically, removed her glasses, and said, "I take it you're the same Jimmy Redstone who set off that firestorm last fall up in Dallas." Not waiting for an answer, she turned to Ortiz and said, "This man closed down Love because some guy who he claimed to be gunning for the President was on an incoming plane. Man turned out to be benign. Some damned General even scrambled jet fighters. All came to nothing."

Focusing back on me, she said, "We're talking about the same person, are we not? I don't suppose there are two Jimmy Redstones running loose in Texas."

"One and the same," I answered, not liking where this was heading.

Saved by the bell. Rover found the images and called us over.

There was no mistaking the silhouette of Bill Snow. He was sitting in a terminal as though waiting to board a plane. He remained stationary until ten-nineteen, when passengers began entering the terminal from the jetway. He stood, studied the deplaning passengers for a few moments, and then at ten-twenty-one he turned and walked slowly toward the main concourse. Angella appeared from the jetway, looked around, took several steps and then suddenly moved to her right. She retrieved her phone from her carry bag and began dialing. She said a few words into the phone and then put it back in her bag. The time on the video matched the time on my phone.

A chill ran down my spine.

Snow stopped under the large flight information board. When Angella again began walking toward him he ambled off, as if he was just another passenger catching a flight. In fact, he was a fisherman preparing to reel in an all too eager hooked fish.

In a few seconds the screen went blank.

"They're heading toward terminal B," I said. "Is there another camera that—"

"It's also the way to baggage claim and the exit," Rover said. We don't usually worry about movement in that direction. "We'll see what we have."

We had been joined in Rover's office by a technician who, using the keyboard and mouse, selected another file. The mouse curser moved to a clock image displayed at the bottom of the screen. In a moment Snow came into view. Angella was closing from behind.

Snow seemed unaware of her presence, but he managed to keep just far enough in front to prevent her from catching up. She seemed to be looking around for help. Whether she was looking for me or a cop, I couldn't determine.

Snow began moving faster and Angella broke into a jog to keep up. She turned a corner in pursuit and we lost her.

The techie dialed up another file.

Nothing.

Another file.

Still nothing.

"That's all we have interior. I'll try exterior."

"Repeat that last segment," I commanded, when the first exterior segment came up. I was afraid it would confirm what I thought I had seen. If so, that would not be good news.

When it came back up, I said, "In slow motion."

The camera was focused on the pedestrian walkway in front of the airport. A corner of the frame caught the cab line where a number of people were standing. One by one they climbed into cabs and disappeared.

Then, out of the shadows moved the distinctive shape of Snow. Only now two bodies were huddled together, his jacket wrapped around both.

"Zoom in on the cab stand. Those people there!"

The techie said, "One person. I only see—oh, you're right. That coat's around a man and a woman. These things don't have all that good resolution. Let's see if we can get this closer."

As the image grew, it also blurred and soon became unintelligible. But there was no doubt of what we saw. Snow had maneuvered Angella into the cab just before it drove away from the stand.

"Get the cab number," I shouted.

Sergeant Carver was already barking orders into his police radio. "We'll have the cab driver on line in a few minutes," he said. "But I promise it'll be a dead end."

I knew what he said was accurate. Snow was clearly a professional and knew how to disappear better than Houdini.

I kicked the wall, knowing Angella was not going to be found anytime soon. And if Snow turned out to be LissaLou's killer, it was unlikely I would ever see my partner—and lover—alive again.

I slumped in the chair willing myself to think it through piece by piece. I had to work on it as I would any other missing person case, focusing on the pieces and not on the ultimate result. But that proved impossible. All I could see was her wonderful smile. All I could feel was the comfort of her hand on mine, the warmth and pleasure of her body comforting me.

I went out front and called Jacobs. It was after two on the east coast, but he sounded as though he had not been sleeping. Reporting the kidnapping of my lover was unlike anything I had ever done before. It was as though I was discussing a nightmare, not really sure I had it all correct, the facts slipping away in confusion and inconsistency.

When I fell silent, Jacobs, his voice devoid of emotion, said, "I'll put the Houston FBI office on it immediately. They'll coordinate with the locals, but also run their own operation. Need for you to calm down, Jimmy. I'd get you off this now except I need you to get your sorry ass down to Mexico and interview Trich. No one else knows her like you do. She trusts you. Find out who all knew Angella was coming. We need to know if Snow is working alone or with others."

"He didn't kidnap her to ask her to the fucking prom!" I snapped. "Hell with Mexico! Something's going down up here and she—or I—must be mucking it up." Angella is in Houston and I didn't want to leave without her.

"Get your butt to Mexico! Don't waste time in Houston. We have people who know that city inside and out. If she's there, we'll find her. All stops off. I promise you that much. Trich may be the best link to Angella."

"Feels wrong. I'm sorry."

"Angella's family. It's difficult to process properly when a family member is in harm's way. Do it my way. And besides… besides, and you didn't hear it from me, you're officially off the Senator's case. You have no cover. Be careful."

"I can't think straight and you're telling me to be careful."

"Do you want me or Tiny to join you? Can be there in the morning—or sooner if you want."

"Maybe as this progresses," I replied, "but not right now. I need you to concentrate on Angella. I'll be okay with Trich." In truth, I just needed to be alone, to do what I had to do—and do it my way. This was not the time to follow orders from Washington. Angella, my Angella, was in trouble and I wasn't leaving Houston.

"Listen to me, Jimmy," Jacobs said, his voice not leaving a trace of doubt as to his seriousness, "and listen carefully. Either you follow me on this or...or I'll have you detained. Get the hell out of Houston. Don't muck this up. Either do what we need you to do, or—"

I snapped the phone off. Put my hand up for a cab and climbed in.

"Where to?" the driver asked, his foreign accent barely registering.

Truth is, I had no destination in mind. No place to tell him I wanted to go. Jacobs was right. I was as useless as a snow blower in the desert.

I handed the puzzled driver five dollars and told him I changed my mind.

Heading back to the terminal, all I could focus on was Angella. Her birthday was coming up and I had been struggling to come up with an appropriate gift. Now, gifts seemed trivial. All I wanted was to see her alive.

TWENTY-FOUR

I found the police lieutenant and inquired, "Any luck with the cab?"

"The one from the airport is easy. He reported taking them to the Galleria area. Here," he shoved his report toward me, "read for yourself."

Liberty driver 7815 reports taking a tall man and a woman companion from IAH to the Galleria. As they approached the destination, the man ordered the cab stopped, passengers disembarked, cab fare placed on back seat. Time of discharge: 22:55.

At 23:05 *Fiesta* driver 0293 reports picking up a couple matching the description from the Galleria and dropping them at Toyota Field at approx 23:13. Mavericks, Rockets basketball game had just ended. Driver reports woman tried to say something but he could not understand.

When I looked up, Lt. Ortiz said, "Those are my personal notes. I took the report over the phone. I'm thinking either a gun or a knife was used to restrain your partner. Could be drugged."

I suggested going to the ballpark, but Ortiz insisted a thorough search of the area had turned up nothing. "Eighteen thousand people excited about an overtime win, and you expect someone to notice someone acting strange? With the amount of beer consumed at those games, it's a wonder anyone gets home alive."

"Someone picked them up from the game."

"Trying to get cab information will be a long shot at best. Probably jumped into a gypsy cab. Those guys won't even acknowledge they were there."

The trail was cold and, unless something broke, I could do nothing. This was the advice I had given many times to crime victims. Coming in my direction it was totally unsatisfactory. I knew Jacobs was right, but that didn't make it any easier.

I slumped in a chair waiting for the next flight to Brownsville leaving at six in the morning. I had had about five hours sleep in the last forty hours, yet my eyes were pinned open. My head swiveled with every approaching footstep. I saw four, four-thirty, four forty-five, then five. Morning passengers and shop workers were coming into the terminal and I studied every shadow.

Five-fifteen passed, five-thirty. The trickle of people had now grown, but still no Angella. No message from her either.

Suddenly, a hand was on my shoulder, the fingers digging lightly into my comatose flesh. My eyes opened, confused as to where I was. A woman's hand was shaking me. I heard my name.

I sat up. Angella was standing over me, talking to me, encouraging me to follow her.

Relief flooded through my tired and disoriented body. I jumped to my feet, while at the same time reaching out to touch her, to pull her tight against me. To kiss her.

But Angella had stepped back several feet and now wore a blue uniform blouse. I blinked my eyes to clear my vision. I concentrated on the nametag. It read Elizabeth.

"Mr. Redstone," the soft voice of the woman floated in, "sorry to wake you. You'll miss your flight unless you hurry. We're all boarded and ready to go."

"What time is it?" I sounded foolish, still partially disoriented.

"Six o'clock, sir. Flight's ready to go. We saved you a seat in the first row."

I looked around one more time vainly hoping to catch a glimpse of Angella racing to the gate, her long legs effortlessly propelling her across the terminal.

My cell startled me. It was Jacobs, sounding as if he had been awake all night, which he said he had been. A team of FBI investigators were culling records, watching videos, talking to hack drivers known to be anywhere near Toyota Field. He continued, "Trich will meet you at the bridge. Sounded anxious, maybe even frightened, but with Snow gone she feels better."

"Talk to me about Snow."

"He was upset with her for talking to Angella. Then suddenly around six last night he left. We now know he flew to Houston from Brownsville under the name of William Dermitt. The good news is that he didn't have weapons with him. We're suspecting drugs. More when you land."

"Come along, Mr. Redstone," Elizabeth urged. "Pilot wants to take off. This airport gets busy about now and he's concerned about giving up his slot."

I looked over my shoulder one more time as if Angella was about to appear. Keeping a hostage alive and in hiding is a difficult task and not worth the risk unless the kidnappers have a very good reason for doing so. I could think of no good reason. Logic then argued that she was dead. But I wasn't going by logic.

Forty minutes later we landed in Brownsville and I took a fifteen minute cab ride to the B & M International bridge linking Brownsville and Matamoras across the Rio Grande River. These two cities, perhaps more than any other two cross-border cities in North America, have inter-linked economies that depend on each other for survival.

Even this early in the morning there was a line of cars at least a mile long going south into Mexico. Nothing seemed to be moving. The pedestrian line was not as long, but even it was at a standstill. This traffic backlog was the direct result of the war being waged between the drug cartels and the Mexican police. The cartels appeared to be winning. As Jacobs had warned me, Mexico was not a safe place to be at this time.

Jacobs called. "One piece of news," he announced. "About an hour ago a night guard leaving one of the office buildings across from Toyota Field reported his car, a Civic, missing from the parking garage. We have a video of Snow and Angella walking down the ramp into that garage. Angella was moving her feet, but appeared to be sleep-walking. We'll probably find the car abandoned at some strip mall."

My stomach tightened even further. "I need to help find her," I pleaded. "I should be in Houston, not down here frying my brains at the border."

"Good chance they're not in Houston," came his calm reply. "We're on it big time. He's going to a lot of trouble keeping her with him. Could have killed her any time. Stay positive."

"This line's going nowhere," I said. "At least work some magic getting me across the border."

"Where are you exactly?"

"At the back of the pedestrian line."

"Wearing?"

"A tan shirt. Tan hat. I picked up the hat at the airport. Says SPI on it. In memory of where Angella and I met."

"A bit soon for memorials. Keep the faith. Which bridge?"

"International. Faith is all I'm going on."

"Stay in line. I'll see if I can shake the trees, have Border Patrol assist you."

One thing I can say for Jacobs, the man's well connected. Within five minutes a scooter pulled alongside. The uniformed guard motioned for me to climb on behind him. There wasn't a handhold, so when he accelerated I grabbed his ample belly to keep from flying off.

Thankfully, the ride lasted only about thirty seconds. I dismounted in front of the guardhouse and the driver signaled for me to follow him inside. Another guard checked my shield and ID, ran my name through a computer, and said, "Be careful over there. The Army can't tell the good guys from the bad. I frankly don't believe they care. One notch to them is as good as another. And Americans are fair game for either side. We can't come get you like we could in the past, so watch your back."

With that, the door opened and I was on the pedestrian bridge crossing the Rio Grande River. In point of fact, I was the only pedestrian on the bridge. Talk about targets. I could almost feel the bright red target on my chest. Now I know how the bull feels going into the ring. But at least he has horns.

A cluster of people waited at the end of the bridge. At first all I could make out was a sea of sombreros bobbing about. As they came into focus I saw a few ball caps. Finally, faces became defined.

But not Trich's face. She was slightly taller than the average Mexican, so I tried to find her that way, but without success. Coming off the bridge, I continued walking straight ahead into Matamoras, hoping she was waiting, perhaps just inside one of the many stores. After fifteen minutes it was obvious she was not where she was expected to be.

I knew the way to her father's compound. In point of fact, it was less than three miles from where I stood. But given the circumstances, with the Mexican and American governments cracking down on drug dealers, going to Trich's home was not a good plan.

"I spoke to her a little over an hour ago," Jacobs said when I got him on the line. "Hold and I'll see what I can find." The line went silent as if he had hung up.

I continued to scan the faces, one by one. With a start I realized the image I was trying to match was Angella's and not Trich's. Angella was about five-six and well proportioned. Trich had a dark complexion and carried a more rounded appearance, at least before she stopped eating out of worry over her fiancée. I adjusted my mental image and resumed searching the crowd. But Angella's face kept forcing itself into my mind's eye. I clenched my fists until my nails cut into my palms, but that didn't clear my mind.

"Can't reach her," Jacobs said a few minutes later. "Not even voice mail. I tried text, but it won't go through. I'll check one more source."

Again he was gone.

When he returned, he said, "Mexican Government cut off cell phone service in preparation for a raid on Santiago's place.

Don't know if the raid took place, but the phones are down. Whatever you do, don't, and I mean don't, go out there. They've issued orders to shoot first."

I thought shooting first was a tradition down here, but I withheld comment. "I can't just walk the streets of Matamoras. Need a plan."

"Find a place to have breakfast. Sit tight. Pretend you're on stakeout duty and observe. That's all you can do for now. I'll work it from this end. Be back at you."

An hour passed. I was the only patron remaining in the little place where I had woofed down the best refried beans I had ever eaten. I was now nursing my third bowl, this time without the melted white cheese topping. The place was beginning to fill for lunch. The proprietor looked in my direction for the third time, this last time with eyes that clearly indicated I had overstayed my welcome.

I found a T-shirt and junk jewelry shop and killed another hour browsing. Across the street was a furniture store where I sat in a dozen chairs, fooled with several lamps and generally made a nuisance of myself. Nothing materialized.

Finally, my phone buzzed. It was Jacobs. "Still no word from Trich?" he asked.

"Heard nothing. Saw nothing."

"Remain in town. I'll keep working it. On the Angella side, some news." His voice was passive, giving away nothing.

I couldn't bring myself to speak, so I waited.

"Motel in Galveston. Maid was changing the sheets, found blood."

I waited, steeling myself for the bad news. I didn't trust my emotions so I turned away so the clerk could not see my face.

"Maid says someone smeared blood on a sheet. Manager called the Galveston police, said the blood looked to be numbers.

Sergeant knew about our alert notice and contacted the local office."

I managed to say, "Blood? What do you mean blood?   How much?"

"Hold on, Jimmy. We'll have answers in due course. Speculation is bad for the nervous system."

"All I have is speculation!" I wanted to kick something, but I forced myself to remain under control.

"You're not exactly impartial, Jimmy. Stay calm. Need you rational."

My antenna shot up. "You trying to tell me something?"

"Nothing that you don't already know. You and Angella are… close. It's only natural. Your task at this point is to concentrate on Trich. She may hold the key to Angella."

"You know something you're not saying?"

"You know what I know."

"Trich's not here, I tell you. I've looked everywhere."

"Do it again. Go back to the crossing and start over. Something's wrong, but she'll get to you if possible."

I walked back to the river, turned and slowly retraced my steps. I walked past the furniture store, this time limiting myself to window shopping. Then on to the bakery, where I eyed the lime *très leches* cakes.

A shadow passed over my shoulder. The shadow sported a large brimmed hat that concealed its face. My focus moved from the pastries to the man behind me who was now slowly walking down the street away from where I stood. Clearly, he had paused long enough for me to notice him, and when I moved my head he continued on.

No harm in following, but perhaps it was wishful thinking, me grasping at any slight hope. I lost him when he turned a corner. I crossed the street and worked my way back toward the pastry store. He was gone, and what little hope I had quickly faded.

I waited a few minutes and when the man did not reappear, I went inside and bought one of the *très leches* cakes. More to occupy my mind than because I was hungry.

Stepping back outside, the hat reappeared. This time I followed more closely, carefully keeping him in my view. I dropped the cake in a waste bin without taking even one bite. I needed both hands available for contingencies.

Midway down the block the hat turned into an alley. That must have been where I lost him the last time. The alley was narrow and filthy from garbage falling from containers spaced every few feet. The unmistakable smell of urine insulted my senses, along with God only knows what else.

He was at the far end, and, but for the hat, I would not have recognized him. He paused until he was sure I was following. He then climbed a flight of steps, more in the nature of a fire exit than an entry. Above me, I could see the hat pass through a second-floor door.

I hesitated. Jacobs' warning to be careful rang loud and clear. Years of working these situations had taught me the value of backup. Gold letter rule: Never, under any circumstances, allow yourself to be lured into an unknown building. I studied the surroundings and saw nothing suspicious. I was certain no one had followed me. But, as I had learned the hard way years before, if they know where you're going, there is no need to follow you.

"Jimmy," my former partner, Mark Cruses Sr., had scolded me, "a trap can't work if there's anything amiss. The professionals know how to set traps that even the best of us won't sense. Just never, ever follow anyone inside an unsurveillanced building. You're a dead man if you do."

Heart versus years of training. Classic conflict. I knew what was right, but playing it safe was not in my DNA when the life of someone I loved was in the balance. Jacobs had convinced me that finding Trich could be the window to rescuing Angella. So I followed the hat–wearing shadow up the steps.

I paused before going through the doorway, giving my eyes and ears time to adjust. I heard noting, not even the footsteps of the man I was following. Go through the door slowly or quickly? Standing or rolling? The worst thing I could do was to over-think it. That was precisely what I was doing.

I yanked the door open and moved quickly through the opening. Out of instinct I crouched low and moved against the left wall.

Everything went black. Nothing moved. Hot damp air enveloped me and I felt as though I had been wrapped in a hot, wet blanket.

I hadn't expected it to be so dark in the hallway. The transition from bright sunlight was disorienting and my muscles tensed for an assault. Involuntarily, I reached for my gun with my right hand, but it was positioned with the handle facing forward, ready for a left hand draw. Not good at all.

I heard footsteps. Then a child crying. Then more footsteps. I pressed hard against the wall, keeping as low as I could without lying on what I assumed would be a filthy floor. The damp air masked the direction of the sound. I strained to hear something that would orient me.

Nothing.

Suddenly, from not far in front of me, someone spoke. It was a native Spanish speaker. "*Señor, por favor sígame.*" Shadows began to form in the direction of the voice as my eyes slowly adjusted to the darkness.

"*Por favor, de esta manera*," the voice came again. I could now make out the outline of the man in the hat. He was not ten steps in front and frantically waving for me to follow him.

Garbage and feces littered the passageway, making **walking treacherous. "¡***Vamanos!* ¡*Rapido!*" **he hissed over his** shoulder when I didn't move fast enough.

Then he switched to heavily accented English. "Please hurry, Señor. *Importante.*"

My foot kicked something soft and yielding. I thought I heard a slight moan, but newspaper covered whatever it was. I stumbled, but caught my balance against the splintered wood of the wall. I listened for the moaning but heard nothing.

Then the squeak of a door opening—or closing. I didn't see it, but there was no mistaking the sound of ancient hinges. A faint shadow outlined the door, which opened inward.

Without warning I was pushed into the opening and the door swung closed behind me. Whoever pushed me remained outside.

What little light my eyes had been using in the hallway was gone. I didn't immediately sense the presence of other people, but the stench of human excrement masked other smells. The shadows could be furniture or—"

A faint light pattern on what I assumed to be a wall betrayed something—or someone—moving toward me. I softened my knees bracing for attack. The Berretta was in my left hand as I swung around to get a clear shot.

Then the movement was gone as suddenly as it had appeared. My eyes were acclimating, but there wasn't enough light to make out anything but shadows. The floor didn't seem to be as filthy as the outside passage had been, but still I was uncertain of my footing.

I had been brought to this place for a purpose, either good or bad for me, but right now I was in middle land, not knowing if I was among friend or foe. A perfect formula for disaster.

Had Angella been brought here? Not likely by car. However, speedboat was a definite possibility. Drug smugglers are experts in logistics, but even as good as they are, moving her this quickly would have been problematic.

What about the bloody sheets back in Galveston? A distraction? Evidence of foul play?

Focus, I forced myself. Focus.

Tentatively, I moved forward. I put my gun back in the holster for fear someone would grab it in the dark. My leg bumped a chair and it toppled over. I quickly moved away from the sound, found a wall and pressed myself tightly against it.

Faint. Ever so faint, came the sound of breathing. I faced the direction I thought the sound was coming from and listened intently.

Muffled, but real. Ahead, and seemingly in a different room.

I found a doorway and paused. The breathing noises, mostly wheezing, grew slightly louder.

"Come into the bedroom." The voice was low, a bare whisper above the breathing sounds. "I'm here." The voice was female, but husky. Low in the throat husky. Definitely not Angella.

Trich?

I moved toward the voice, using a sliver of light from a boarded window. Whoever it was seemed alone in the room.

Breaking my silence, I said, "Identify yourself."

Labored breathing.

"Who's in here?" I called again.

"Thank God you came, Mr. Redstone. We are alone." She coughed, then said, "My prayers are answered."

"Trich? Is that you?"

"I am here."

It was definitely Trich's voice. But hoarse, painful sounding. She sucked in air and her lungs wheezed with fluid. It was clearly difficult for her to talk. I moved to the side of the bed. From what little light there was, I could make out dark rings under her eyes. She had been beat around the head and God only knew how badly she had been injured.

I put my hand on her neck and felt her much too rapid pulse. She pulled away.

"Trich, what happened?"

"Whisper, or they'll find me. Please, I beg you."

I lowered my voice. "Did someone beat you?"

"Don't look at me. My face is damaged. I am so ashamed. Will Mark still love me if I am disfigured?"

"Of course he will love you. Please tell me what happened."

"They are coming for my father. I denied it to myself all these years. But it is true. They say he deals in drugs—and other things. They gave him time to get my mother and the servants out."

"What other things?"

"Bad things."

"What bad things."

"Smuggling. Terrorists."

"Koreans? Al-Qaeda? Taliban? What?"

"Koreans. Also some from Iran. Bad people."

"Who did this to you? Was it one of them?"

"Snow. He heard me talking to Angella. I tried to whisper, but he must have heard me. He is a bad man."

"Do you know where Snow is now?"

"I overheard him say Houston. Something about Angella."

"Are they bringing Angella down here? Is your father involved?"

"Just to help bring people into your country," she wheezed. "He's a farmer."

It was clear Trich still did not see her father for what he really was.

"You need medical help," I said. "Need to get you out of here."

"Miguel, the man who brought you here, he owns *la farmacia* below us. I got his son a job at the hospital in Brownsville. He will keep me safe—if anyone can."

"I'll help you. Tell me what you want."

"It is not safe for me in Mexico. My papers have been cancelled. I can't cross into your country. I need new papers. I want to be with Mark. I miss him." She turned away and her battered body heaved with her silent crying. Her breathing came in gasps.

I touched her arm, and her body went into spasms.

"Please be gentle. I hurt everywhere."

I wouldn't be surprised if Trich had internal injuries. I leaned close and realized her face was swollen, her eyes barely open. Her breathing was shallow, labored. "You need a doctor. Is one coming?"

"Please, no."

"I'll bring one to you."

"Don't! They'll kill me."

"Who will?"

"Snow. Other people. You must go now."

Trich's eyes pleaded with me to leave. Her broken body called for my help.

"If you remain, they will find me and then they will kill me. Migel will take care of me until I can get to Brownsville."

"How can I get in touch with you with new papers?" I was thinking more in the line of medical help. Without it she didn't have much chance of surviving.

"They took my cell. I think it best if you reach Miguel, the son, at *la farmacia* in the hospital in Brownsville, the hospital where I work. He works midnight to seven every day. Just ask for Miguel, tell him to tell his father. Do not tell him where I am. He will come to see me and that is not good."

"They may already know where you are. Let me help you out of here."

"They do not know. Miguel would not have brought you here if you were being followed. He is wise to them. Please go now. I cannot much longer talk."

"Do you know what they want with Angella."

"Snow...I know nothing more."

I bent to kiss her, but her lips were so cracked and swollen I thought better of it and blew her a kiss.

"Thank you for coming, Mr. Redstone," she wheezed. "Mark told me often I could trust you. You are a good person. Tell him I love him."

TWENTY-FIVE

"She'll not survive if we don't get her out of Mexico!" I repeated my plea to Jacobs for the third time in as many hours. He was working to obtain a commitment from INS to reclassify Trich to allow her to enter the United States. The best he received from them was that the matter was being reviewed upstairs, whatever upstairs meant. I viewed that answer as a polite way of saying, "Kiss my butt!"

I continued petitioning Jacobs, listing the reasons we should move on this, from urgent medical attention to obtaining leads on terrorists, to helping find Angella.

Every hour that passed without finding Angella was one more hole in my heart. I was finding it difficult to maintain focus and not yield to despair. I had counseled loved ones numerous times in kidnap situations to not give up hope, to remain positive. Now, those very same words made me angry. I was fighting hard to keep myself in check, knowing I was losing the battle.

"We're working it," Jacobs patiently explained. "I've asked Tiny to work his magic, and he assures me everything's being done that can be done. It's not just the U.S. that's involved here. The Mexican government must be brought on board. As you well know, our relations are strained by the drug crackdown."

"Strained or not, we have a life to save."

"We have many lives to save," Jacobs retorted, his patience clearly wearing thin. "I'm sorry. That was uncalled for."

"You're speaking of Angella. Okay, give it to me straight. How bad is it?"

"The blood's been analyzed and she's one clever woman. The writing was her attempt at your cell number."

"How much blood?"

"Hang in there a moment. It's actually good news—in a way. The blood is mixed with traces of cotton and rayon. Lab is positive the numbers were written with a tampon using menstrual blood. They expect to have a brand name within the hour."

In a perverse way, that made me feel better. At least in my male mind that explained her reluctance to spend the night with me. I suppose a shrink would counsel that it's not about me at all. But that opens a long conversation that I'd rather not have. When I didn't respond, Jacobs asked me where I was now located.

"At the airport in Brownsville, waiting on a plane to Houston. Where should I be?"

"I suggest going over to SPI. Stay down there close to Trich. We'll eventually get the paperwork done. Relax as best you can. Angella's certainly no longer in Galveston. Most likely been moved down your way."

"How the hell am I supposed to relax when that barbarian is doing who knows what to my partner? Relax my ass!"

"If you don't settle yourself I guarantee you'll be pulled from the case. I'll do it myself if need be. You're going to get someone hurt and it won't be pretty."

"Since when do I work for the FBI?" I was using Sylvan Jacobs, Special Agent in charge of the San Antonio FBI office, as a colleague. Now he was my boss.

"President pulled you off the Senator's investigation. But you're still on the Timberwolf killing. There is presently no clear indication that Timberwolf's murder involves national security. But cross-over is possible. So I——"

"Just give me the bottom line before my damn battery gives out!"

"What ever happened to patience?" Jacobs rhetorically asked. "I worked a deal with the Director. It's now a fully joint operation. FBI and Homeland Security."

"Nice of someone to tell me. Always the last to know."

Ignoring my outburst, Jacobs continued, "Something else. This may mean nothing, but I personally don't like the fact that Mark Cruses was transferred from the SPI post up to New Jersey. Moving him out of the way is just too...shall we say, convenient."

"What are you thinking?"

"Nothing in particular. But it doesn't sit well with me. First they put him on house arrest. Then they give him his command back. Then——"

"They didn't give the command back voluntarily. I asked McNaughton to look into his house arrest. She's the one pulled the strings on that."

"I guessed as much," Jacobs replied. "But then a few months later they sent him packing up to Sandy Hook."

"His commander, that guy Boyle, was pissed when Mark got the command back. Maybe it's just revenge for me going over his head. Don't like that guy. Military or not."

"Maybe Boyle had a hand in it. Maybe not. I'm just saying, it makes me stop and think."

"I'm thinking about calling McNaughton to see if she can arrange leave for him. Mark needs to be with Trich."

"I'm okay with that. But be careful what you tell Mark."

"Any problem if I get Tiny down here?"

"Thought you'd never ask. He's on his way. Be there in two hours."

"You guys got it all figured, don't you?"

"That's what they pay us for."

Jacobs made his point. There was a reason he was the head FBI guy for south Texas—and Tiny was trusted by the President to get it right.

- - - - -

Forty-five minutes later I was cruising through Port Isabel, having treated myself to a rental Corvette at the airport. The roof was down and the wind cooled the air blowing across my head. On a whim, I swung off the main road and headed toward Angella's house located on one of the many canals that snaked though the fishing village.

At first I couldn't remember which street; they all looked alike. I had mentioned to Angella when she had shown me her house how surprised I was that every house, except for a few expensive brick homes, looked to be in need of a paint job. She cautioned me not to judge until I tried to maintain a house in salt air. "What the salt doesn't eat, the wind blows away," she had said.

"Marine hardware simply means it will cost more and last a little longer. Rust is the enemy. Rust is undefeatable."

Then I remembered the Spanish-style mini-mansion that was located at the end of her block. I drove around until I located it. Turning onto her street served only to increase the hollowness in my heart. I slowed to allow several boys, none above the age of twelve, all carrying fishing poles, to pass. They were on their way to the canal to try their luck.

I spotted the house and stopped across the street. A for-sale sign was planted in the scrub grass that passed for a front yard. I sat for several minutes alone with my thoughts, wondering if I would ever again see Angella alive. I pounded the steering wheel in frustration, knowing that finding her was out of my control. The FBI, with over fourteen thousand sworn officers, was the world's greatest investigative body. If they couldn't do it, it couldn't be done. I wanted to believe all fourteen thousand of them were actively pursuing every lead. As I saw it, nothing was more important than finding Angella alive. I refused to dwell on what they thought.

"Think positive," Jacobs had counseled. But it's hard to remain positive sitting in front of the empty house of your kidnapped lover. I reached for the shift lever, intending to drive across the causeway to the island and drown my sorrow in a few Skinny Bones. I had in mind the back deck of *The Sea Ranch* where the waters of Laguna Madre could, along with the alcohol, have a calming influence.

I pulled away from the curb and at the far end of the block, just before I turned the corner, I gave one last glance in my rear-view mirror. A car was moving slowly down the street and pulled over almost exactly where I had been parked.

I turned the corner and found a place to park. By the time I trotted back to Angella's street the car was empty and the driver not in sight. I increased my pace, not knowing what to expect.

Then I had the shock of my life.

A really pleasant shock. My heart raced and I broke into a full-out run, my eyes misting from excitement.

Angella stood on the small porch of her house, facing the door, her back to me. I wanted to call to her, but I couldn't form the words. I took the steps up to the porch two at a time, anxious to wrap my arms around her, to pull her tight and never let her go.

Hearing me coming, Angella turned.

Something was wrong.

Then it came to me; Angella never used the front door. She always used the side entrance into the kitchen. I remembered her saying, "Don't even know why I have a front door. Don't even carry a key."

I froze, sensing a trap, but seeing nothing. It was Angella, appearing heavier through my blurred vision, but Angella none-theless. She took a step toward me and I calmed down. It was Angella's walk, Angella's arm movement. Same slight tilt of the head, down and to the left. Same hair coloring. Same everything.

I opened my arms to receive her. But she pulled back.

Her face came alive. "You're Jimmy!" Angella exclaimed. "I'd know you anywhere!"

It never ceases to amaze me how difficult it is to refocus when a hypothesis is built on a premise that turns out to be false. The mind struggles to make it all come out right, even going so far as to suspend belief. Magic is built around that phenomenon—as is bunko.

My initial belief was that Angella had been swollen from a beating. Now I was working on her also having been brainwashed into not recognizing me.

"You *are* Jimmy, are you not? Tell me you're Jimmy."

I froze.

"Hey, who are you? Studying me that intently, not saying anything, frightens me. Tell me you're Jimmy." She backed away from me and stood with her back pressed against the door, her cell phone in hand.

When I didn't respond, she said, "I've just called nine-one-one. You better leave."

"Who...who are you? I thought...I thought you—"

"Oh, now I understand. I'm..." Someone must have answered the call, because Angella said into the phone, "Sorry. Everything is okay." She listened for a moment and then, presumably, in answer to questions she was being asked, responded with the address and a description of me. Then she said, "Name's Jayme Partridge. No, I'm okay. False alarm. Sorry."

She flipped her phone closed and took a step toward me. "You look just like your picture. Angella told me all about you. She's so—"

"And you are?" I stammered, fighting a dizzy spell.

"Her sister. Can't you tell?"

"I thought you were—"

"Everyone gets us confused. Jayme. Jayme Partridge. Come, give me a hug."

Definitely thicker, I noted when I hugged her. But same intense brown eyes. "You twins? She never men—"

"Two years apart. I shouldn't admit it, but she's my baby sister."

"You fooled me. I mean I thought you were Angella." I still hadn't recovered from the surprise.

"I take it Angella's not home. I came a day early. Her birthday's tomorrow and I wanted to surprise her. Know where she is?"

I didn't want to outright lie. But I certainly couldn't tell her Angella had been kidnapped. "Out of town for a few days," I said. "Job-related stuff."

"Know when she'll be back? I have a key, but I don't want her to walk in and find someone unexpected in her house. She might shoot me by mistake."

"Not likely," I said, still trying to work through how much to tell her sister. "She's been staying on the island."

"That rat! She didn't tell me. You two, you're…engaged?"

"No."

"Planning to?"

"I wouldn't be surprised." My answer came with a mental asterisk: *if she lives*. The last twenty hours has driven home a truth I had been suppressing. I need Angella in my life more than I care to admit. "I'll tell her you're here when I talk with her. In the meantime, make yourself at home."

"Changed my mind about staying here. Without Ange, the place is dead. I thought it would be fun spending a few days with her. You know, girl talk. Frankly, about you mostly. I knew from her tone I wasn't getting the full scoop. She's so closed-mouthed about everything. I told her to take her time, play the field. Didn't listen. So she's living with you already. I can see why."

"Nursemaid, mostly."

She studied me from head to foot, then said, "You look healthy enough. Ange must be some good nurse."

"Can't complain."

"I'm happy for her. First marriage didn't work out—for either of us. She didn't waste any time. Been three years for me. Nothing in sight." She again looked me over before saying, "Hey, enough of this. I'm heading to the island where the action is. Any suggestions?"

"*Clayton's Beach Resort.* Had lunch on their beach patio not long ago." With all that has happened, I had lost track of the days. "Swinging place. Music, volleyball, the works."

"Great. I'm ready to party."

"Call me if you need anything. I'll be in and out." I handed her a card.

"Sure everything's okay? Ange doesn't answer my calls or my texts. Shame on her for going silent on me."

"Mine either," I stupidly said. "Might be a while."

"Is she on assignment?"

"Let's just say, she's tied up."

"And what, miss her birthday?"

"May have to celebrate without her this year."

"Sounds important. I mean, what she's doing. She won't say much, but I gather you two have had a few...shall we say... adventures."

"That we have," I answered. "That we have."

TWENTY-SIX

I drove across the bridge on my way to the *Sea Ranch* thinking of Angella and her sister. They both had the same fire, but Angella managed to channel hers into her work. Jayme seemed to be firing in all directions. It would take a strong man to corral her, assuming she really wanted to be tamed. *Clayton's Beach Bar* is jumping. Good place for her.

Once on the island, I abandoned my plan of getting sloshed and instead stopped at the *Island Native Surf House*, a neat place located next to *Gabriella's,* and bought a bathing suit, some cut-offs, a few tees and a giant bottle of suntan lotion. I eyed the surf boards and other water playthings, but remained with my basic plan of spreading a blanket on the beach and napping while waiting for Tiny to arrive.

I never made it past the changing stage. Not because my cell went off, but because when I stripped off my pants it all caught up to me. I literally fell into bed.

Pounding on the door woke me. Sounded as though the wall was coming down.

"You look like hell!" Tiny exclaimed when I finally managed to answer the door. "I'm hungry. You up to eating or what?"

I checked my watch, disoriented as to the time. It was exactly six. I had slept three hours. "Give me a minute, I'll join you."

At six-thirty we were seated at *Gabriella's*, a great home-cooking Italian restaurant at the south end of the island. Tiny's Margarita was quickly sucked dry. His hand was in the air waving to the waiter, an industrious young man who seemed to be everywhere at once.

"Whoa," I said, "you planning to eat or get pissed?"

"Didn't know we were playing *Mother may I*. You got a thorn under your saddle, get it on the table."

"Sorry. Didn't intend it to come out that way. This sitting around while they have Angella is for crap! According to your account, nothing much is happening with Trich either. We're friggin' impotent!"

Tiny lifted his empty glass. "Here's to Viagra. A double dose."

"What's that supposed to mean?" I was not following the big guy and was in no mood to be toyed with.

"Look, Jimmy, we're on it. Got more resources than you can imagine working all the angles. We'll find Angella. It's just a matter…"

Tiny fell silent as the bartender approached with his refill. I ordered Pasta a la Tonno and Tiny went with Italian meatloaf. When the waiter walked off, Tiny switched to a different topic. "Focus for a moment on the Timberwolf killing. What do we have?"

"Timberwolf was out there recording something. Appears to be sun bursts, but he captured frequencies that could have come from that secret nuclear power generation plant. What we don't know is whether he was an innocent guy caught in the wrong place or an agent of someone recording power plant noises under cover of pretending to record space noises."

"You troubled by anything?"

"A million things. Start with the fact he's an astrophysicist. Guy knows what he's about. Add in he's a former partner of Vlad. And—"

"Don't forget he's a Russian. That's where I get my jollies. Teethed on the Russians."

"So tell me, why did the nuclear power plant talk get mixed into the soup? It's on the mainland, not on that barren spit of land."

"Tell me what you know about the nuke facility," Tiny said.

I caught a hint that he had something more to say on that subject, but didn't want to go first. I waited for him to continue, but he sat sipping his drink. One thing about Tiny, he's disciplined.

A large bowl of salad was set between us, along with bread and a plate of olives and cheese. I spooned salad onto my plate, still waiting for Tiny to continue.

The silence was broken by a large, good-natured man who introduced himself as Duane, the husband of Vickie, the owner and chef. "Everything good here?" Duane inquired. "I see you ordered the meatloaf. You'll enjoy it. Once you've had Vickie's, you'll never eat meatloaf anywhere else."

"That's going to make my grandmother crazy," Tiny replied. "Won't be able to explain it to her."

"Bring her down to the island and let her taste for herself. She won't go home."

"May just do that," Tiny replied, making the last of the olives disappear.

"Enjoy," Duane said, moving on to another table.

When he was out of range, Tiny said, "We know there's a whole friggin' nuclear power plant less than twenty miles inland from where Timberwolf was killed."

"Not according to the video," I said.

"Conclusion?"

"Doctored video," I dutifully responded.

"Or it has a cover impervious to flyover video."

At first I dismissed Tiny's comment as science fiction. But as I thought about it further I was reminded that during the last big war, the Boeing field in California was covered with netting and made to appear from the air like a housing sub-development, complete with cars and people. "I'll buy the cover—for now," I said. "There's a no-fly zone right about that location. So where does that leave us?"

"Facility's sole mission is to supply power to the base."

"Why does the military require their own generation?"

"Military never trusts anything civilian without foolproof backup. That base is one of the key facilities of our global un-manned surveillance. If the power goes down, we go blind around the world."

"You flew down here to tell me that?"

"Partly. And partly to help find Angella."

"And partly what else?"

"Fact gathering. That's what I do. I don't pretend to have your deduction abilities, Jimmy. I'm a facilitator, a sounding board, that's all."

"And perhaps babysitting me."

"Perhaps that also," He winked. "You've been known, shall we say, to take things in your own hands. You do that this time,

McNaughton will have your hide. And I mean that literally. Don't cross her."

Food being served saved me from making a fool of myself by saying something I would regret. And it gave me time to think. Military going blind means they couldn't defend an attack. Who benefits by that? Certainly our enemies do. But that begs the question. Who are our enemies?

I outlined my thoughts to Tiny, who said, "Can't focus on external, foreign. That's CIA territory and, as a practical matter, not really possible from what we have. Focus domestic."

"The legislation is a starting point. If we pull back our forces then we're vulnerable at home. Need *eyes* to see. The early warning concerns of the sixties resurfacing. Take away those eyes then…"

"Keep going. Getting interesting."

"Vlad. His technology is used for early warning?"

"You're on a roll."

"Senator Donnlevy was against pull-back. Could the Senator have been planning to show Congress what would happen if we go blind?"

"Possibly, I suppose. But not his style."

"But then, if it was the Senator, shouldn't he have done whatever it is he was going to do before the vote? And what does all this have to do with Timberwolf and his recordings?"

"Bingo," Tiny said.

"That's why you're here. You and your pals back at the mother ship can't figure that part out? You had all the rest."

- - - - -

When I woke it was night. Tiny was sleeping in the guest bedroom and the apartment was quiet. I felt empty and forlorn without Angella. Not knowing where she was or what was happening to her was eating me from the inside out. My stomach felt as though the horse was still kicking.

I again thought of the many times I had consoled a kidnap victim's spouse, my words of comfort falling, for the most part, on deaf ears? Child kidnappings were the worst. You could see the parents' eyes go dim, then after a day or two without hearing from their child, the eyes would be stone cold dead.

We—or at least I—hadn't received a single lead. From what Tiny had said over dinner, the trail was cold. Iced, was how he had put it. Iced. As in, Angella's on ice.

I walked to the window and looked down on the lighted pool. Ripples were running from one end to the other. The bottom was painted inviting blue and seemed so relaxing, seductive. Just a few days ago Angella was sitting down there waiting for me. The remembered image again brought tears to my eyes.

There were footsteps in the hall just outside the door. Woman's footsteps. I rushed to the living room, hoping the door would swing open and Angella would materialize. But no open door. And no Angella.

I pulled on a shirt and trousers and headed out for a walk. I crossed Padre Boulevard with not a car in sight. Once on the beach, I removed my shoes and dropped them in the dunes. I turned north at the surf line, allowing the water to ripple over my toes. Fingers of light from the rising moon danced on the water. I lost myself in thought.

I must have traveled several miles before I realized I could no longer see the glow of light from civilization. It seemed an eternity since Angella and I had spent a night in a tent out here in the early stages of a murder investigation. It had been our first case together and we hardly knew each other. It now seems we have always known each other.

I stood facing the water, studying the horizon, again reviewing the twisted path, beginning with our viewing of the Timberwolf murder, to Angella's kidnapping, to my visit with Trich. I was no closer to understanding what the Timberwolf murder had in common with a lethal drug administered to Senator Donnlevy than I had been when the President commissioned us. Dots touched all the players, but even with a force fit, the pattern remained incomplete.

The best I could achieve was to lay the Senator's death squarely at the lifeless feet of his widow, Sarah-Jean. I have Snow down for the death of the Keller girl. And possibly Vlad for Timberwolf. Three murders, three perps. Didn't feel right.

Start again. If Keller's unborn child was, in fact, Donnlevy's, then the child would be in line for inheritance from the Senator. Sarah-Jean would be out a lot of money. By her own admission, that's why she married him. As clear as if she were standing next to me, I heard Angella remind me, "But not if the child was never born."

"Then," I responded, as if Angella was working this with me, "that argues for Sarah-Jean being Lou's killer, and not Snow."

Angella's voice continued, "Isn't it you who always says to follow the money? Sarah-Jean benefits from the girl's death. That logic says Sarah-Jean killed Lou and the Senator."

"Widow had two choices," I answered. "Kill the Senator before he changed his will. Or kill the girl, eliminate the baby."

"Or do both to be doubly certain," Angella added, her voice growing fainter. "Think about it."

"What is that supposed to mean?" I asked.

No response.

I no longer felt Angella's presence working with me through the possibilities. She had been so close I could feel her presence. Now I was empty again. Alone.

"Angella, I love you," I shouted into the wind. "Yes, Angella, I'll marry you. I'll marry you and retire if that's what you want. Please, oh, God, just come back!"

TWENTY-SEVEN

"**W**here the hell you been?" Sylvan Jacobs, as was his custom, began without preamble when a signal finally appeared on my phone. "Been trying to reach you for hours. You okay? Tiny said you weren't in your room when he got up."

"Out walking the beach. Thinking."

"Thought we lost you like we lost…anyway, got some news. Tox report on the Keller girl is negative. No trace of drugs of any kind. Prelim financials on Vlad show him broke, or near broke."

That caught me by surprise. "Thought Vlad made——"

"Over eighty million, actually. Blew a wad on new ventures and spent big-time on drugs. Detoxed and seems clean now. Oh, and a big chunk went to Timberwolf."

"So he needed the legislation to save his company. Sarah-Jean led me to believe otherwise. Senator was blocking the bill. Kill the Senator——"

"Whoa! You're out in front of your headlights."

"I've wanted to believe the wife did it, but with Vlad having money I had doubts. With Vlad broke we have a new equation."

"Now factor this in," Jacobs said. From his tone I knew what I was about to hear would impact my thinking.

"Reliable source indicates a prenuptial between Donnlevy and Sarah-Jean. Senator could cut her out anytime, by making a will. Prenup expires end of this month."

I digested what Jacobs had just said, then added, "Widow's in trouble if Donnlevy cuts her off. You say the prenup allows that?"

"That's how I understand it. I also understand Donnlevy was fixing to make the will. Cut her out entirely. In Texas that's allowed provided he earned the money before they were married, which he did."

"Bingo! Senator lives, the bill dies, she gets cut out, Vlad falls on his face, she's out in the cold, wheelchair and all. You getting a warrant?"

"She's not going anywhere. We have twenty-four-seven surveillance on her. We have Snow for the girl. The man was careless. Got his prints from the hotel room. What we don't have is why?"

"Don't overlook the fact that if Lou's child was the Senator's, the child would inherit." I was giving him further reason to arrest Sarah-Jean, but where that left Snow I hadn't calculated.

"One major problem," Jacobs interjected, holding the beat long enough for me to pay attention. "Baby wasn't the Senator's. DNA didn't match."

"Snow and Sarah-Jean didn't know that," I answered, reluctant to part with my thesis.

"Still make the widow for it, but not so strong."

"The numbers are scrambled," I said, trying in vain to work through the mental gymnastics.

"What numbers? What the hell you talking about?"

"When you do *Sudoku,* you think you're almost to the end and then every number you try causes some other number to be wrong. That's what we have here."

"What are you saying exactly? It's too early in the day for gymnastics."

"The pieces fit if Snow and Sarah-Jean are linked. Then I can see why Snow would have killed the girl. Wife kills the Senator for his money and Snow eliminates a possible heir."

"You thinking the widow paid him?"

"That's what stumps me. We'd be able to trace the money. She has nothing of her own—or at least that's what she told me. But the father had a bad reaction when he saw Snow's picture. I still have Snow for the girl."

"That's what our profilers said," Jacobs confirmed. A neat way to let me know I wasn't the only one capable of working the puzzle. In fact, based on his comments, the FBI was ahead of me.

I remained silent, hoping for news of Angella. But nothing was forthcoming. So I broke down and asked Jacobs about Angella.

"Nothing much to report other than the car was found in a place called Surfside Beach, south of Galveston."

"Anybody see anything?"

"Do they ever?"

"Let some old guy take a whiz in a dark alley at midnight and see how many people call it in."

"That's safe," Jacobs said, his demeanor as serious as always. "People don't call the police when there's chance for blow-back. Human nature, I suppose."

"Darwin at work. The folks who make that call are gone. With them we lost the *snitch on a bad guy* gene."

"Now you're a scientist," Jacobs replied. "And a bad one at that. Go get some rest."

"Rest isn't what I need. What I really need is to find Angella."

"We're working it. You're not. And keep it that way. Call you when I have something."

Walking south, I continued thinking about possible links between Snow and Sarah-Jean Donnlevy. A mile later, just as the first rays of sun broke through the overcast, it hit me. "Lined up again!" I shouted into the wind.

An old couple, him with baggy pants, a plaid shirt and an ancient wide-brimmed canvas hat resting on his ears, and her in a heavy cotton pink workout outfit, looked at me like I had just been let out of the nut house—or whatever the politically correct name is these days.

Jacobs answered on the first ring.

"Thought you went back to bed. What's up?"

"Follow me for a moment. I first met Snow in the hotel when he interrupted us from going into Keller's room. He shook my hand and I damn near leaped out of my skin. I put it down to my hand being sensitive from the bullet wound. When I met Sarah-Jean the same thing happened. My hand hurt for a good hour. I concluded it was because of her using a wheel chair. Of course she'd have a strong grip. I mean I was thinking about gene pools earlier and it popped into my mind. Like mother, like son. I like Snow as Sarah-Jean's son."

Jacobs didn't respond initially. When he did, it was a compliment of a sort. "Didn't see that one coming, Jimmy. But it's certainly a possibility. So far, we haven't found any connection between Sarah-Jean and any child anywhere. We'll work it backward from Snow. See what we get."

- - - - -

Ten minutes later I left the beach, walked a block over to Padre Boulevard, turned south and headed for the police station. As luck would have it, Acting Police Chief Lt. Jose Garcia was just climbing out of his car when I arrived.

"Hey, Redstone," he called, "Good to see you. Come, join me for coffee."

"Sounds good, actually. We having it here or going somewhere?"

"The stuff the Sergeant makes will take years off your life, assuming you can drink it in the first place. Let's head up to *Ted's* and get us a real breakfast. Pecan Pancakes with the pecans cooked inside. Finest anywhere."

"Good thought. Love that little place. They're the best."

It was still relatively early and *Ted's* wasn't yet full, so we were seated without wait. "Pecan pancakes, I said to Karen. Three. Coffee." Garcia ordered the same but added a couple slices of bacon.

"Some FBI type called last night," Garcia began when Karen walked away, "to fill me in on what's going down. Any news on Angella?"

I shook my head.

He continued, "You know, we hated to lose her to Homeland Security. But when the Governor calls, you don't say no."

"I have a hunch, though," I said, knowing I'd need his help if I were ever to find Angella. "Hear me out. My gut tells me she was brought here last night. The car was found in Surfside. They brought her down here overnight by water. I don't know if they stopped here or in Mexico." I couldn't tell Garcia how close I had felt to Angella while I was on the beach. He'd dismiss me as a lovesick kid. But I had felt her presence and I now knew she was still alive.

"If she's south of the border I'm afraid for her. Nothing good's coming out of Mexico right now. Santiago might have helped us, but the Mexican government is closing in. His rein is over."

I hadn't realized how plugged in this little town was. "You sure keep up with what's going on."

"Got to. What happens there, happens here. They get run out, they come here. By boat, car, across the river, whatever. A few of their low-lifes have been seen here on the island. Bet more will show. But nothing seems to be going down."

"I can't believe they'll take her to Mexico. My hope is she'll be brought here." I was skeptical that anyone in authority down here would know she had been smuggled in. After all, an A-bomb managed to be brought ashore even with full military surveillance. I was convinced the bad guys could move an army in and out undetected.

"FBI asked us to be vigilant. The Coast Guard's on alert. Every law enforcement body in the valley has been notified. I can say with full confidence Angella did not land on our beaches last night."

"I was out there and didn't see anybody patrolling. How can you be so certain?"

"You never got far enough north. The activity, if there was going to be any, would have been a good two miles beyond where you were."

Now he had my full attention. "How the hell you know where I was?"

"I told you, the Coast Guard was alerted. You came up on a surveillance run. Believe me, on any given night they know what's out there. Bringing a person ashore is not as easy as it seems. Drugs are a different story. There are a number of sophisticated techniques for getting them in. But there's a limit to how long a human can live in a sealed bag."

"That means they could have dumped her overboard."

"Lots of could haves. Not likely, though. Could have left her in a trashcan someplace up north. They want her alive for a reason."

"Let's hope so," I said, relieved to hear someone else agreeing with my thoughts.

His plate now empty, Garcia pushed back his chair. "Can I drop you anywhere? Got to get to the office, see what the day brings. If you need anything, you know how to find me. Good luck finding your partner."

TWENTY-EIGHT

Garcia and I walked out of Ted's together. I called Tiny to tell him I'd be back to the condo in a half-hour. First I wanted to stop at the Island Fitness gym across the street and say hello to Teran. Well, it wasn't just hello I wanted. Teran usually knew what was going on in town. I wanted to pick his brain, hear the latest rumors of who was doing what. He, together with his friend Billy, had opened a new coffee and smoothie bar, **called the** *Pura Vida Café* and if there were any rumors going around, they'd surface there.

After speaking with both Teran and Billy a few minutes it was clear nothing out of the ordinary had happened—or he wasn't saying.

"Redstone," a blonde in too-tight sweats called from the bar area. She had something red, frothy and cold-looking in front of her. "I was looking for you."

Her face was vaguely familiar, but lack of makeup is sometimes a perfect disguise. It took me several seconds before I placed her as one of the women Joy usually hung around with at *Louie's Backyard*. "Hi," I said, approaching her seat. "You're a friend of Joy Malcolm."

"I'm Savanna Latworth. Go by Anna. I've been looking for you. Hey, get yourself a mixed-berry drink and join me. Billy adds a touch of peanut butter and some other good stuff. It's all good."

"Just ate. Some other time."

"Come sit with me," she said, patting the wooden-slated seat next to her. "Been hoping to find you."

My antenna went up. "Not many people know I'm here."

"Joy said you'd be at the gym if you were on the island. Not that I can't use a workout." She patted her ample hips as if to emphasis the fact. "Joy wants you to come see her."

I knew Joy was in rehab at *Origins Recovery Center* but didn't know much more than that. How's she doing?"

"As well as can be expected. She's working hard at getting clean. None of us knew she was a druggie. We all thought... she just drank too much. Her husband walked out on her. Poor woman."

"She have visiting hours or what?"

"Hour in the morning, starting at nine. Then an hour beginning at eight at night. They keep the rest of the day open for lectures, that sort of thing."

From what I knew of detox centers, the lectures were more like therapy sessions. "I'll try and get over to see her," I said, not holding out much promise.

"It's important. She's asked several times to find you. She has something to tell you."

"Thanks for the message," I replied, not sure if I cared what Joy Malcolm had for me. I also wasn't certain her only problem was substance addition. Her need for attention troubled me, as did her obsession with murder victims.

"Please visit Joy," Anna pressed. "I'll tell her I spoke to you."

"Can't promise, but I'll try to stop by."

"Sooner would be better," Anna replied, not letting me off the hook. She checked her watch. "It's nine now. I'll go with you if you like."

"That won't be necessary," I said, dismissing Savanna Latworth. At least she hadn't batted her eyes and wiggled her ample body as Joy had tried several times.

I walked down the outdoor steps to the street intending to go back to the condo, take a shower and get ready for the day. On impulse I pulled out my phone and called the condo instead. Tiny answered and I said, "I'll be delayed. Going to see Joy Malcolm. Fill you in later. Do me a favor. Set up a time with our Coast Guard friend, Captain Boyle. I want to speak with him."

"You mean Mark Cruses' boss? The guy who put Mark on house arrest?"

"He's also the guy who transferred him—or had him transferred—to Jersey. Boyle's in Corpus. Set something up at eleven if you can. Need about fifteen minutes of his time. Phone conference will do."

"Your wish is my command," Tiny answered, obviously peeved. At what I didn't know. And truthfully, I didn't much care to find out.

Origins turned out to be located in a former bed-and-breakfast across from the movie theater and directly on Padre Boulevard. I gave Joy's name to Mrs. Marilyn Balognes, the receptionist according to the nameplate on her desk.

"You're in the wrong facility," she promptly announced, obviously happy to see me gone. Men only here. Women's center is over by the bay. Opened not long ago. Here's a street map."

"Not that far. Please call and set it up for me."

"And who shall I say is wanting to see Ms. Malcom?" Balognes asked, her pencil ready to write my name on a prescription pad.

I gave her my name and she consulted her computer. Twenty or so key strokes later she said, "I see here your name is on Ms. Malcolm's friends list. Go ahead over. I'll tell them you're coming."

The facility was magnificent. Looked to be a former motel or bed-and-breakfast, but completely redone. Everything was polished and new looking. In this salt air it wouldn't remain pristine for long.

"If you'll take a seat in the den right through that doorway, I'll inform Ms. Malcom you are here," the receptionist said before I was even through the door. "Please understand, she is not permitted to leave the building and don't provide her anything to eat or drink."

"I would think you'd be more worried about drugs than food," I commented, puzzled at the no food and drink rules.

"That's Angel's job," she responded pointing to a small Pit Bull napping by the den entrance. "Angel never misses. You come in here with drugs, you're not leaving. Period."

"I hope Angel doesn't get confused," I muttered mostly to myself.

"Just take a seat, Mr. Redstone. Joy will be along in a few minutes."

- - - - -

"Hi, there, handsome," Joy called from the doorway. "I'm so glad you came."

Her demeanor was in sharp contrast to the last time I had seen her, when she went from full on to full stop and back again in a matter of moments. When she was in the on mode it was as if she were high on a substance with not a care in the world, even to the point of sexually suggestive. Now, she was tense. Perhaps apprehensive is the better description. Her eyes darted around the room, as if expecting something to happen. The mischief her eyes had previously held had been replaced with wariness. But she wore a genuinely pleasant smile and seemed under control— for her.

I hugged her and she pulled me tight against her chest. It was uncomfortably long before her grip eased. She stepped back about a foot, batted her eyes, and said. "Thanks, Jimmy, I needed that." Tears appeared in the corner of her eyes and rolled down her checks. She casually wiped them away, as if crying was a common occurrence. "This place is wonderful. I'm almost done here. Get out in a few weeks."

"You doing okay?" I asked, not knowing why she wanted me to visit and trying to give her no reason for concern. "You look great."

"Can't really complain. I put myself in here, and I can walk away. But I'm not leaving until...until they say I can. I want the drugs gone forever."

"You're doing the right thing. You look good." A little white lie is not always the worst thing. "Keep up the good work."

Her eyes stopped moving and focused directly on me. Her head tilted slightly to the side. "I'm here because of you, you know. You're the reason."

"Me?"

"You saw through the act. You made me face it head on. I thought I had everyone fooled. They all thought I drank too much. Alcohol's great cover for cocaine. At least it was for me. Had my act down pat. But didn't fool you. Thanks."

I didn't have a ready reply, but I didn't need to say anything because she reached out and threw her arms around me again and again pulled me against her body. Not in a suggestive way, but more like a mother hugs a grown son.

She pulled back and, her voice barely audible, whispered, "They were after me."

"Who was after you?" I replied, relived to have a natural topic to follow up on. "For what?"

"The killer. The serial killer. He knows I...I gave you the pictures." Her eyes began to dart again, this time directed to the front window. "You're on the island again. Who will it be this time?"

"There is no serial killer, Joy. I now live here." That seemed to calm her. At least her eyes refocused on me. "I like it down here."

"Tell me you caught him. Tell me he's not coming back."

"There is no..."

"I knew you'd deny it. But I know better.

"Who's after you? Who knew about the pictures?"

"The guy who killed the Coast Guard medic. He knows I have his picture."

"He's not going to bother you. I promise."

"How can you be sure?" Her eyes were darting back and forth again. This time she stepped back, as if she were contemplating running from me.

"He's dead, Joy. Dead. Can't bother you—or anyone—anymore. The guy whose picture you took is dead."

"You certain? You're not just saying that to make me feel better?"

"Certain. Have to take my word. But he's gone."

"I'm not happy to hear about dead people, but he frightened me. Pardon me," she said, tears again running down her checks. This time she didn't bother to wipe them away. "Jimmy, I don't know whether to love you or hate you. You exposed me, made me feel...well, to be honest, awful about myself. But you did a good thing for me."

"I'm sorry you're struggling, but we both know it's for the best."

"That's what my counselor says. Some days it works. Other days are hell!" She wiped her cheeks and then continued, "You know, it's not only the drugs, but coming to grips with my life that's so hard. They make me face myself, and that's not easy."

"You're doing well and soon you'll be out and feeling good about yourself." I was out of my league and struggling to select the right words. "You'll see," I said, as upbeat as I could muster. "It'll all be worth it in the end."

"I hope so, Jimmy. I hope so." her eyes sparked with a hint of mischief, the same look I remembered from before. Involuntarily, my weight shifted away from her. "But I liked my life the way it was, you know. I had fun. Lots of laughs. Everything was going so well. And then...then it crumbled when John left."

I debated reminding her of how miserable she had been before he left her. She had told me so herself. She had been ready to throw her husband out. But that was her counselor's job to make her see reality. Instead, I said, "You asked me to come. Let's talk about that."

She again lowered her voice. "A friend of John's came by last week. He said John was never coming back. He's sick in a hospital in Mexico, near death."

Now the tears were really flowing. I put my hand on her shoulder but maintained my distance. "He loved me, you know. I mean really loved me. He's never coming back."

"I'm sorry to hear that," I said. "I know you loved him as well."

"I did. Except he left me alone so much. Off somewhere all the time. His friend told me something I didn't know. He had a daughter by a previous marriage. Name of Patricia May. Pretty name. Patricia May. They're in Mexico and can't get out. The friend said you could help get his daughter out."

"The friend knew me?"

"Yes. Said you'd been to the daughter's house. Said you could get her out of Mexico if anyone could."

"Who is this friend? What's his name?"

"I saw him when he came to visit John. But I was never introduced."

"Pardon me, Joy, but we're telling the truth here. You must tell me the truth. Was this man your supplier?"

She glanced at the floor, then over my shoulder to the window. Then back to the floor.

"If you want me to help, then I must have the truth—all of it."

Joy looked up, drew her lips tight. Then she relaxed, as if a weight had been lifted. I had seen that look many times before. It's what every interrogator works to achieve. "I suppose it does no harm to say it," she began. "When he visited John he always had some for me."

"But he wasn't your regular supplier?"

"I had no regular supplier. Different people all the time. I'm not certain, but I think John arranged it."

Her eyes told me she was telling the truth. "Thanks for being honest. Go on."

"Nothing much else. Except he came by to see me yesterday again. He said to tell you about explosive conditions."

"He named me directly?"

"Jimmy Redstone, the cop. That's you, isn't it?"

"What's an explosive condition?"

"Patricia May. He said Patricia May is an explosive condition. He said to tell you to hurry."

"Is that all he said?"

"That's it. I had to pass it along."

Now it was her turn to step back. As she did so, I noticed she seemed to have gained weight. But as she moved it was clear she was actually looking more fit than I recalled. Coming off drugs often does that.

"I have a class now, must go. Please come back. I don't have many visitors. In fact, only Anna comes. The others…well, they're too busy to bother. Please come see me. In a funny way, I consider you…well a friend."

She turned abruptly and disappeared though the door.

I walked out to the receptionist, a woman in her mid-sixties who looked as though she might have used the services of a re-hab center once or twice in her life. "You keep a visitor log for guests?"

"Of course we do."

"I'd like to see the log for Joy Malcolm."

Without even looking up, she began, "It is our policy…"

I was holding my Homeland Security shield in front of me when her eyes eventually came away from her computer screen.

"Oh, my. I didn't know. I …I must…ask you to wait while I call my supervisor. My gracious, what did our Ms. Malcolm get herself into?"

"I'm interested in her visitors, not her. Is it possible for a visitor to not be in your computer?"

"Oh my, no. That just can't be. Please wait just a moment. I will be back in a jiffy."

The receptionist never did return. Instead, a short paunchy guy came through the door. He introduced himself as Doctor Andres Sanchez. Apparently he was the head person at *Origins*—or at least at the women's dorm.

"Medical doctor or otherwise?" I asked.

"Otherwise, Agent Redstone. I'm a PhD. I understand you want to know who has visited Joy Malcolm."

"That and who's on her approved list."

"I'm afraid we can't reveal that information."

"And just why not?"

"It's confidential. That's why not. Now if you'll just leave us, I have work to do."

"Not so fast, pal," I said. This is a national security investigation and I'm requesting your cooperation."

"The people in this facility are under treatment. The last thing in the world they need is someone snooping around. So please leave us. You have no authority here."

"Not only am I not leaving, but neither are you until I receive a list of Joy's visitors and everyone on her visitor list. You understand me?"

He reached for the telephone.

"Mind telling me who you're calling? I might save you some time."

"Police."

"Ask for Lt. Garcia. He's acting chief."

Sanchez slammed the phone down. "Get out of here. You're trespassing!"

"Got to do better than that, Doctor." I reached for my phone and called Jacobs. "Need a search warrant for *Origins Recovery Center* on South Padre Island," I said into the phone loud enough for Sanchez to hear. "The only items I'm interested in are the approved visitor list of Joy Malcolm and a list of all visitors she's had since she entered this facility. I'm at the location—women's facility—now. Have with me a Dr. Andres Sanchez who claims to be the head person. I don't want him tempted to erase any information, so have the locals send a uniform to babysit until the warrant arrives."

Jacobs and I exchanged additional information, primarily me telling him why the information I was looking for plays into our investigation. I conveyed that information in a whisper, my back turned to Sanchez.

"How long will this take?" Sanchez asked when I hung up. "Sessions are underway and my presence is required."

"Don't know. Might be an hour. Might be a day. Might even be a week. Judges and the FBI move at their own speed."

"I don't have that kind of time. Have programs to run, other stuff. This is bull shit! Get the hell out of here!"

"Bet you teach your patients to mind their tempers. I suggest you heed your own advice, Doctor."

"Show me your shield again," Sanchez demanded. "How the hell do I know you're for real?"

"I'm for real alright," I said, producing my badge and ID. "I'm for friggin' real."

He examined the shield thoroughly, then turned his attention to the photo ID and official seal of The Department of Homeland Security. "Okay, you win." He walked over toward the computer.

"Not so fast," I called after him. "If you're thinking of printing out the information, it's too late for that now." In fact, I would have taken what he had to offer, but Jacobs had warned me not to. He was worried about having the evidence thrown out as having been obtained under duress. It seems that once the ponderous wheels of justice begin to grind there's no short cut to the end.

"But I must get on with my patients," he pleaded.

"Afraid not today," I said, happy to see a police car pull into a parking space in front. A woman wearing the brown uniform of the SPI police department stepped out. She proceeded to walk into the lobby.

My mind flashed back to the first time I had met Angella. She was dressed exactly this way, weapon, handcuffs, two-way radio, spare ammunition and all. Only Angella was taller and slimmer.

"Which one of you is Redstone?" she barked. The name Lopez was pinned to her shirt.

I nodded.

"This the man I'm to baby sit?" she asked, pointing to Sanchez.

"That's him. Don't allow him to touch the computer or call anyone. Search warrant is on the way."

"Understood," came the terse response. Officer Lopez was not happy to have pulled this assignment. But that's what cops do. This was better than standing in the sun all afternoon, so why she was so pissy about it I didn't understand.

TWENTY-NINE

"What the hell's Boyle doing on the island?" I said to Tiny as we were being escorted into the Coast Guard meeting room where the Captain was to join us. My understanding had been that our meeting had been set up as a video connection, with Boyle up in Corpus and us at the station here on the island. Our escort, a kid seemingly not old enough to shave, had informed us about Boyle being here in person.

"With Mark dispatched to New Jersey," Tiny responded, "the Captain must be back down here running the operation."

"Makes you stop and think," I said.

"Maybe," Tiny answered, ever the peacekeeper, "just maybe, Boyle's here for no other reason than this is where the Coast Guard needs him to be. Things don't always have to be complicated."

"I hope you're right," I replied, "I just hope you're right. But keep in mind. Even paranoids have enemies."

"About a third as many as they think."

"Gentlemen," Boyle said, "we meet again. Redstone, great haircut." The corner of one lip turned up in what for him passed as a laugh. "Kidding aside, that was good work on tracking and defusing the bomb. Not the military's finest day. But in the end a satisfactory result, thanks to you."

"Thank you, Captain," I said, "got help from all concerned. Real team effort." Better to say what he wanted to hear and not what I wanted to tell him. Angella had suggested that the only way the two of us would ever clear the air was to go a few rounds. I was ready. My right hand wasn't.

"You called the meeting," Boyle said when we were all seated. "So what's up?"

"First, Mark. His fiancée is in serious condition in Mexico. We're working to have her brought over to Brownsville for medical treatment."

"I'm well aware of the effort. Causing problems with our southern neighbors. Go on."

"Can you arrange leave for Mark to visit her when she comes over?"

"Above my pay grade. Ask your friend McNaughton. She seems to have the ear of the right people." His condescending tone made it clear he was baiting me.

"Last time I went to her you pitched a fit. Thought I'd try you first. Give you a chance to support your men."

He jumped to his feet so quickly his chair fell over backward. I followed his lead.

Only Tiny remained seated, the beginnings of a smile forming under his eyes. He was settling in for a good time, preparing to enjoy the show.

"That's not the first time you've accused me of not supporting my folks," Boyle said, his face beet red. "That's uncalled for and inappropriate. If I wasn't on duty, I'd..."

Tiny stood. At close to seven feet, he towered over both of us. "I suggest you both sit down. This is not the time, nor the place, for foolishness. Kapish?"

I sat.

Boyle bent to pick up his chair. I had the sense he was debating throwing it at me. Tiny glared down at him.

Reluctantly, he set the chair upright and sat. "Okay, Redstone, the floor's yours. Get off your chest what you came for. Then get your sorry ass out of here."

My legs tensed. Tiny, still standing, looked directly at me. I settled back. "Will you support Mark getting leave to visit Trich?"

"I like Mark as a person. In fact, he's one of the best officers we have. But, and here's the rub, his girlfriend is the daughter of Santiago, a known drug lord. Not a night goes by we don't chase and intercept a vessel run by Santiago. We can't have Mark in charge of the operation. If nothing else, optics are wrong."

"With all due respect, Captain," Tiny injected, "that's not the question on the table."

"I know damn well what's on the table! Don't need you telling me how to run my business. Either of you." Boyle took a deep breath. Then another. Then he sat back. "I was clearing the air, so to speak. Let me say this. I won't veto the leave, but I'll not initiate it."

"You won't block it if I can get it arranged?" I wanted to be certain I understood him properly.

"You understand correctly."

"Next, I understand you told Lt. Garcia that Angella was not smuggled onto the island last night."

"Correct again. You're two for two, Redstone."

Ignoring his taunts, I asked, "What makes you so certain?"

"Surveillance. That's what we do, my lad. We watch vessel traffic along the shore. Nothing moves we don't observe."

Boyle's posturing didn't exactly square with all the drug and people smuggling going on. "Could you have missed something?" I pressed. "There's a lot of water out there. You seem so certain."

"Trust us to do our jobs, Redstone. You're not the only person working this. I'll wager my record is better than yours, given I've never been the subject of—"

Tiny shifted his weight. His face set hard.

I held my seat.

"Never mind," Boyle said, his eyes relaxing. "Just trust us to do our jobs.

"I need to know why you're certain she wasn't brought ashore."

"What you don't seem to grasp is that CBP is out there with us twenty-four seven. They board—"

"Customs and Border Patrol? We're not discussing checkpoints! What's that got—"

Boyle pushed back his chair again, but this time rose to his feet slowly. He walked to a sideboard, retrieved a remote control unit, and returned to the table. Several wall-mounted monitors came alive. At first, it appeared that Boyle was showing us the video of the Timberwolf killing. Except, this time we were seeing a high-level aerial view of the Texas coastline from north of Galveston to Mexico. I assumed the white lines just offshore were waves breaking on the beach, but I wasn't certain. Overlaid to the right of the white lines, and scattered everywhere like an inkblot test, were greenish smears of various sizes. Small orange dots were interspersed among the green ones.

"The green images are vessel tracks of everything moving last night along the coast. This screen shot is a twelve-hour composite from eighteen hundred hours to oh-six hundred. Here, I'll put identification information on each vessel."

The screen then filled with names, many of which were shrimpers. There was one processing ship and several had foreign-looking names that appeared to be Japanese or Chinese. The orange dots remained name-free.

"The orange are CBP vessels. There's a large Marine Unit based in Port Isabel. They work with us to intercept suspicious vessels, check for papers, do safety inspections, that sort of thing. Those folks are good."

When I remained silent, Boyle, using a laser pointer, highlighted a series of green smears near the top of the display. "See this track? They're ships leaving Corpus and going straight out into the Gulf." The laser dot moved north. Here are two vessels sailing from Galveston, most likely on their way to service oil rigs. Notice the orange dots in the vicinity. These down here," he said, moving the red pointer dot southeast, "are commercial fishing vessels. These out here are overnight fishing charters."

The pointer moved further south. "Here's SPI, and note one charter going out and two fishing vessels coming in. That's exactly in keeping with our log of shoreline activity."

The green images then rearranged themselves. "Let's focus on one sector and follow two vessels moving down the coast. The time is twenty-three hundred." The screen then stepped through a series of images. In each image the green spots were positioned further south. "Two things of note. First, a CBP patrol intercepted each of these but saw no reason to intercede. Second, note that at zero-five hundred the first vessel came into Laguna Madre, passing just south of the island and into the bay through

Brazos Pass. And at zero-five-fifty the second vessel did the same. Nothing was lost overboard. Nothing stopped along the way."

"What are those dark lines where the two boats are?"

"Rock jetties bounding either side of the Brazos Pass."

"And those white dots scattered on what I assume is the beach south of the jetties. What are they?"

"Shacks and people on Boca Chico Beach," Boyle answered. "Brazos Island runs right down to the Rio Grande. Mostly undeveloped. A few primitive huts. No water, electric, nothing. Fishermen mainly. One of the shacks fell over this past winter." A smile crossed Boyles' face. "If you were a Civil War buff you'd know the last land engagement of the war was fought down there in eighteen sixty-five. Actually fought thirty-four days after General Lee surrendered. Union lost that last fight."

"Could Angella have been landed down there?"

"Not according to our surveillance. And not according to CBP."

"Could anything have been dumped overboard and floated in?" I asked. I knew from past experience weapons had come into the country in just that manner.

"That's a possibility as you well know." Boyle pushed another button and white dots appeared on the screen. "This overlay, the white dots, are heat signatures. Anything with human cargo—assuming the cargo is alive—would show on the image. Believe me, this is ultra sensitive, and might I add, ultra secret. It will pick up a person swimming underwater."

"How does it know humans from sharks and things underwater?"

"Humans are warm blooded. Fish are not."

"Dolphins are warm blooded," I responded, sensing Boyle had been dodging the question.

"Yes, and matter of fact their skin temperature is roughly that of humans. Maybe a degree less, but not much. But dolphins don't remain at the surface. They come up for air and then dive. So the system is designed to eliminate dolphins and other warm-blooded sea creatures from the image. Not perfect, but pretty good."

"So in theory, at least, she could have been smuggled ashore if her heat pattern was made to simulate a dolphin."

"In theory, I suppose anything's possible." Boyle pushed more buttons and another overlay came alive. This time it was a high-level video showing white ripples abutting a dark area. A few white dots were scattered along the dark area. "Last night happened to be bright. But it really makes no difference. Have some problems in heavy rain though," Boyle said. He cracked a smile, the second I had seen from him. "This dot is you in the surf north of SPI."

The video slowly focused in on the white dot and the figure of a human emerged. Zooming continued until the form of a man came clear. The man was standing in the surf facing what clearly was water.

"Tell me when you recognize yourself," Boyle said.

"That is most definitely you, Redstone," Tiny said. "Can't mistake the way you hold your head since you went and got your neck cut."

"I didn't know I was tilted to the right," I responded, "But that's me."

"That's you alright," Boyle confirmed. "We knew it was you from a heat signature of you we have on file. The infrared system identified you from the heat images without human involvement. Now do you understand why I'm sticking with my original state-ment? Angella Martinez was not smuggled ashore last night, or at any other time. I'll bet my command on that."

I really would have loved to win that bet—for many reasons. I glanced at Tiny, but read nothing from him. "Okay," I said, "I concede. Angella was not smuggled onto SPI by boat." I was not yet ready to concede she hadn't come in some other way. After all, a few boats did enter the bay.

Changing the subject, I asked, "Does this mean you can use heat-sensitive images of a crowd and identify individuals?"

"Wish it were so," Boyle replied. "But can't yet do that. Person must be isolated and, truth be known, this only works when there's a significant temperature differential between the object and the surface. Near water is perfect."

Tiny said, "Jimmy, we got what we came for. I've seen enough. You got anything else you want?"

"Nothing more," I said.

Boyle got up to leave.

"Oh, yes. I do have a question," I said, trying to sound casual. "It's not exactly Coast Guard business, but you spend a lot of time on the water so you probably know the answer."

"Shoot," Boyle said. That might not have been the best choice of a phrase, but I let it pass.

"While I was walking down the beach I saw a shooting star. Only it was going west to east. Lasted only a few minutes."

"ISS." Before I could ask what the hell ISS meant, Boyle continued, "International Space Station. At zero-four-fifty last night. Low in the southern sky."

"That's it."

"Sky's full of man-made satellites," Boyle volunteered, obviously relieved to be discussing something other than Coast Guard business. "They're always passing overhead. Just have to know where and when to look."

THIRTY

"We've studied the airport tapes," Jacobs said, his voice coming from my cell phone loudspeaker. Tiny was driving us back to the condo and I had called Jacobs to fill him in. "Snow was alone on the initial capture. He clearly was waiting for her. Arrived from Brownsville about two hours before she landed. He apparently knew she was coming into Houston and knew the flight. You know about the transfer at the ballpark. After he left downtown with Angella we think someone else joined them. If Snow visited Joy Malcolm, then Angella was alone with somebody for some period of time. Maybe still is. We also believe Angella has been drugged."

"Who's this other person? You not saying for a reason or you don't know?"

"Don't know who, but reasonably certain it happened."

Not a good report and my spirits fell even further. I sat quietly as we headed north, passing City Hall and police headquarters. I had Tiny swing one block west to the bay and continued north toward my condo. The woman's section of *Origins* was only a block from where I lived and I noted the police cruiser still parked outside. Jacobs had just informed us the warrant would be signed within the hour. He had already dispatched a computer expert from ATF who would be on-scene within thirty minutes.

"Go back over to the main road," I instructed Tiny. "Want to stop at *Paragraphs on Padre.*"

"What the—"

"A book store. Angella says it's a delightful little place. Run by Joni and Griff. I need a book."

"It's 'bout time you settled down. You looking for that Civil War stuff? Trying to catch Boyle wrong? Can't imagine you reading mysteries. For that matter, nix the history as well. What the hell do your read?"

"Just drive. I'll let you know when I require a summer reading list—or a shrink."

Tiny pulled to a stop in front of the store, constructed in the form of a home. Several flags were waving in the breeze. "Remain in the car or come with me?"

"I'll wait. Got some calls to make."

Griff was behind the counter, a computer screen positioned in front of him. Joni was off to the right of the store talking with a customer. Two small dogs were napping in one of the reading chairs.

I approached Joni, waited for her to look in my direction, and when she did, I asked, "Have anything on satellites? The kind in orbit."

Joni looked at me puzzled.

"I'm interested in finding orbit times, capabilities, that sort of thing."

"I don't believe we have what you are looking for," Joni said. "But Griff might be of help."

"Heard you talking to Joni. I just *Googled* satellite books," Griff said when I approached the counter. "Here's ten." He turned the screen around and showed me the list.

"This one," I said, pointing to the third one from the top, "looks promising." It was titled *Introduction to Satellite Communication*. "Don't know if this is what I want, but I'll give it a try."

"I can have that one for you," Griff replied, "if you're willing to pay special handling, tomorrow afternoon. If not, three days."

"Tomorrow will work. Is there anything showing the times when satellites are visible?"

"I suppose there is. But you can get that information on your phone if you have one of those smart phones."

"Seems you can get anything electronically these days," Joni commented. "Here. I found a children's book of the planets and the night sky. It has pictures of various man-made satellites. Don't know if this is what you are looking for."

"I'll take that as well," I said. "It's a start."

While I was paying, Joni said, "How's Angella? Tell her I have the book she ordered."

"What book?" I asked, curious that Angella hadn't said anything.

"That's between her and I."

"I'll tell her to come by for it," I answered, taking a deep breath to hide my concern. I couldn't imagine what she could have ordered. I had not seen her reading in all the time we were together.

Back in the car, Tiny said, "You bought a children's book on the nighttime sky! "Now I'm convinced you've gone over the edge."

"I'm happy to hear you had doubts," I responded. "Just a little something in case I have to read you to sleep."

"Just might take you up on the offer. Where to now?"

I checked the time. "Still forty-five minutes until the search warrant is signed, let's—"

"Wrong. It was granted five minutes ago. Jacobs just—"

"Okay. Head back to *Origins*. Let's get Joy's visitor list."

- - - - -

Talk about disappointments. An hour later, after going through *Origins* electronic files and then their paper chart files, the list of people who visited Joy numbered exactly two. Savanna Latworth. Every day, exactly at nine. Stayed the full hour. And one visit by William Dermitt, alias Snow. I had convinced myself that someone else, perhaps someone I could lean on, might have visited her.

I turned to officer Lopez. "Please assure me that Dr. Sanchez has not left your sight."

"Only to go to the men's room."

Oh, shit, I thought, here we go. "Did you accompany him?" I asked.

"Not inside, not on your life."

"But you walked him to the door and stood outside. Correct?"

"Door's right over there," Lopez replied, pointing toward the back corner of the lobby. Her tone told me she had reached her limit. "He went in, did his business, he came out. End of story. Get off my back."

I walked across the lobby and poked my head in the bathroom. No extra doors, nothing fancy.

"Satisfied?" Lopez asked when I turned back to face the group.

"With the fact that this is a bathroom, yes. Not with the fact that only two names are on the list, no." I turned to the forensic expert, a woman in her mid-thirties who could have passed for a teenager. "Agent Wainwright," I said, "any possibility you over-looked a file?"

"Been doing this for eight years. Never missed anything yet. No reason to start now. I assure you, the only names that match the search warrant are the ones on that paper."

I wanted to ask her how she would know if she had missed anything, but the clenched jaw and tight lips told me to back off. I glanced at Tiny, who had positioned himself next to the front door. His expression told me I was making a fool of myself. And indeed I was. That's the price to be paid when things don't pan out the way you think they will.

"Okay," I said to no one in particular, "show's over. Dr. San-chez, you can go back to your duties. Sorry to have interrupted your day. Agent Wainwright, thanks for your time. Officer Lo-pez, you did a good job. Nice working with you." I took my exit and Tiny followed, but not before he tossed a look over his shoulder to the others as if to indicate he was not responsible for my actions. If he didn't tower over me by a foot, I would have decked him.

- - - - -

Back at the condo, I called Jacobs to check on Trich.

"We're still working it," he said, sounding somber. "Have rea-son to believe she'll be moved to Brownsville late today. Just need one more sign off. This one in Mexico."

I thought about the logistics for a moment. "And just how will she be transported? The woman is seriously injured and under quarantine."

"Mexican Government will coordinate. Coast Guard SEAL evacuation team is standing by. They'll be in the air in a matter of minutes once we receive the go-ahead."

"SEALs? Why—"

"McNaughton insisted on it. That's why. Need I say more? Trich is deteriorating fast. There's been more...violence. Time's not on our side. I'm told they'll be on scene within ten minutes of the paper being signed. That is, of course, if the Mexican government allows it."

"Can they be trusted?"

"The SEALs?"

"Of course the SEALs can be trusted! I mean the Mexicans."

"That's what State is working out now. A Mexican team will work with our folks. Meet them on scene type of thing. I'll let you know when it's worked out. We'll need the exact location from you. I'll send you a blow-up, building by building. Use your computer and pinpoint the exact location. We'll do the rest."

"Okay," I said, wishing I was moving into action. "Now let's concentrate on finding Angella."

"Easier said than done. I was hoping to interrogate Santiago. But the Mexican government is adamant they want him tried in Mexico. Allowing him to leave is politically unwise. However, we did have a major breakthrough. The Mexicans won't raid Santiago's place while Angella is being held. Had to cash in a bunch of chips on that one."

"How long we have?"

"What makes you think there's a deadline?"

"There's always a deadline."

"Twenty-four hours."

THIRTY-ONE

A quick shower and back I went to the police station. Tiny remained behind at the condo, his nose in his computer.

"I met with Boyle this morning," I told Lt. Garcia when I finally got in to see him. I was cranky after cooling my heels in the hall for over an hour and my tone was sharper than it should have been. "He played us videos to back up his contention that Angella did not come ashore last night. But if you don't mind my asking, what made *you* so positive? I assume you hadn't seen the videos."

"Let me put this to you more graphically," he snapped, apparently not happy with my questioning of his sources. Or perhaps he was thinking I was questioning his competence. "She may have come ashore, but not alive."

Garcia now had my full attention. I slumped back in his battered visitor's chair. "You have reason to believe that might have happened?"

"Ordinarily, I'd tell you it was fifty/fifty. But, frankly, there's little chance anything came ashore. Paco Santino, I believe you

know him from when you worked the smuggling case with Angella, is still recovering from radiation burns and not working the
beaches. Drug infiltration has gone way down. We stop ninety
percent of the stuff now."

"He's that good?"

"Man's a genius when it comes to inventing new ways to
move the stuff. He's an idiot in the rest of his life, but running
drugs, there's never been anyone like him."

"So why isn't he in custody?"

"Can't get anything on him. He's that good."

"Just shoot him."

"I'll pretend I didn't hear that. So why are you here? Told
you all I knew earlier."

"Had a hunch. Remember that house we raided? The so-
called staging house, the one over on Gulf Boulevard?"

"I know the house. Go on."

"Any chance of getting a peek inside?"

"It's for sale. Call the realtor. Nothing wrong with looking
around if they let you in."

"For sale?"

"Once we busted the operation, Feds had no reason to keep
the house. All painted, fixed up. Maybe you can buy it and retire.
We'd love to have you as a resident." I studied the man to see if he
was serious or busting my chops. I leaned toward chop busting,
but couldn't get a good read.

"Maybe I will. Then I can vote."

"That a threat?"

"Wouldn't dream of it."

He stood. "Let me know if I can help you any further."

"I'll do that," I said, easing myself from the ancient chair.

"Good luck," he called as the door closed behind me. I had most definitely worn out my welcome.

- - - - -

I parked in front of the Gulf Street house while I waited for the sales agent to appear. She had sounded as though she had been sleeping when I called, even though it was after noon. It took self-control to refrain from pushing the door in and searching the place without her. Another few minutes and I planned to do just that.

Five minutes later I was halfway to the front door when a car pulled up. "Hey, I know you!" the woman stepping from the car yelled, "you're the guy from *Louie's Backyard*! Seen you there a couple of times with that lady cop. Didn't recognize your name when you called."

"I'm Jimmy Redstone," I said, extending my hand when she came bounding up the walkway. "You Saundra McKenzie?"

"I am. Pleased to meet you. You thinking of moving to the Island? That'll make Joy happy. Joy Malcolm. She likes you. Husband walked out on her."

"You a friend of hers?"

"We have laughs together at *Louie's*. She's...well, she's away for a while. Had a few problems. She'll be back. You planning to live here permanently?"

I paused for a moment, wanting to make my answer sound right. "Thinking about it."

"Don't think too long. Places like this go fast. A few steps from the water. Good rental value. Priced aggressive."

"I assume you have the key," I responded, trying to break off the sales pitch before she really got rolling.

Taking the hint, she proceeded to the front door and inserted the key.

Nothing.

She pulled and pushed and twisted to no avail.

"Sorry, Mr. Redstone. I was just here yesterday and it worked fine. Don't know what's wrong."

"Here, let me try."

Nothing I did worked. "Got the right key?"

"Can't imagine what's wrong."

The lawn was mostly sand and gravel. I searched for a rock large enough to break a window. Nothing out front. Around the side I found what I was looking for. A brick was lying lose under the portico. Someone may have used it before I did.

"Hey, don't do that," Saundra frantically yelled when she realized what I was about to do. "I think I had the keys mixed up. Here's the right one." She inserted the new key. Still nothing moved.

The rock went through the window and Saundra screamed. She stopped screaming long enough to shout, "You're fully responsible for this, I hope you realize! When the police arrive I'll—"

"Stay out," I snapped at her. "Go sit in your car. Lock your car door."

"I'm not—"

I flashed my shield. "Now get in your car and stay put!"

She marched to the street and slammed the door behind her.

I cleared the glass, reached my arm though the opening and opened the door. Berretta in my left hand, I began searching the house, room by room, taking my time. My ears were alert to any telltale noise, whether from the first floor or the second. I heard nothing, not even a police siren in the distance.

The living and dining rooms were easy, no furniture and no closets. A small half-bath was positioned next to the kitchen. Empty. Under the stairs there was a door that I supposed was a broom closet. I pressed myself back against the wall trying to keep out of the line of fire of anyone hiding under the stairs.

I yanked the door open.

Nothing moved.

The opening was lined with metal shelves, all empty, except for a few paint cans.

Next came the kitchen. I checked under the sink, in the cabinets and in the refrigerator.

Now for the second floor, where all hell had broken loose the last time I was in this house.

I took the stairs slowly, pausing to listen intently, all the time knowing that a true professional like Snow would never allow me to know where he was. He would fire through the wall at the slightest sound.

I heard something move.

It moved again. This time the sound had come from just above my head on the landing.

A soft rustling sound. Then it repeated again.

And again.

It sounded like plastic, perhaps painter's plastic, on the hall floor. But I couldn't be sure.

I butt-walked up the stairs, keeping a low profile, all the while listening to the movement of the plastic—or whatever was moving.

I carefully moved onto the hall landing and again paused listening for human sounds. I peeked around the corner and caught a quick glimpse of a narrow hallway with room doors on either side. There was no place to hide in the hallway. Once I turned the corner, I would be a sitting target for anyone up here. My only chance of avoiding being hit and of getting a shot off first was to remain low.

The noise indeed had come from plastic on the floor. Nothing else seemed to be moving. I elbow-crawled down the hall toward the first door, trying not to cause any additional movement of the plastic.

The first bedroom was empty. I was halfway down the hall to the second of the three bedrooms when a door burst open and the plastic along the hall began to ripple. I rolled against the wall and took aim at the door.

No one came out of the room, but I was exposed with nothing between me and the open door.

"Redstone!" Saundra's voice startled me. "Where are you? I found the key. It fell out in my car. Sorry. Where are you?"

I couldn't answer for fear of becoming a target.

"Where are you?" Saundra again called. "Are you upstairs? What do you think of the house? It's lovely isn't it?"

I couldn't allow her to come up the steps, so I yelled, "Get out of the house! Get out now!"

"I need you to sign in. I'm coming up. You can't be here without—"

"Stay down there! Get outside."

"What are you doing up there?" Saundra replied. "Come down or I'm coming up."

The commotion did not produce anybody from any of the rooms. I leaped to my feet and rushed forward toward the open door, intent on shielding Saundra from any gunfire. That, above all, was my sworn duty.

The room was empty.

I quickly checked the third bedroom and then turned back to join Saundra, who had just turned the corner behind me.

"Well, what do you think?" she asked, not allowing my rock throwing episode, nor my admonishments, nor my gun, to interrupt her sales pitch. To her, I was a live one on the line.

"This is not it," I mumbled, "I didn't find what I'm looking for."

"You're not going to shoot me," she laughed, "for not having a key."

I put my weapon away.

"This is indeed a nice property. I know you will enjoy living on the island. Are you certain this is not for you?"

"Certain."

"What do you have in mind? I'll find it for you. I'm sorry this doesn't work for you."

"Not as sorry as I am," I replied, walking past her and out to the street. "Not nearly as sorry as I am."

THIRTY-TWO

"**G**ood news," Jacobs exclaimed, uncharacteristically up-beat. "Paperwork's been signed. Assuming the location information you provided is accurate, Trich will be on U.S. soil within the hour. Hospital is standing by."

"What the hell took so long?"

"You're welcome," Jacobs replied, sarcasm hanging heavy.

"Okay. Thanks."

"Had to brief the Senate terrorism oversight committee. Talk about micro-management. She'll be in Brownsville... hold a minute, my other line is ringing." Jacobs was back in a moment. That was McNaughton. SEALs are in the air."

"You certain Trich's safe passage has been assured? I don't want—"

"As certain as anyone can be with all the crap happening down there. Border Patrol's been notified. Mexican army's in place. This is a major operation. McNaughton insisted the President give them authority to go in hot. They'll fire if necessary.

Trich is the daughter of the drug lord. Can't imagine the cartel folks harming her. Snow's the one we have to worry about, and he's not down there."

"How do you know where the hell he is?"

"Caught a break a few hours ago. Can't say much on this line, but we've got a trace on his cell."

"So where—"

"Can't say more."

It's taken me a while, but I've learned that when Jacobs says no it only goes downhill to press. "So what are they doing about Santiago? Is he continuing on house arrest? Do we still have twenty-four hours?"

"That's what broke the logjam. He's agreed to surrender as soon as Trich lands safely at the hospital. Trading his life for his daughter's so to speak."

"First decent thing that man's done." I again visualized his knife blade cutting into my neck. An involuntary shudder went down my spine. "That means I can't shoot him on sight."

"You don't have the full story," Jacobs said, "Hold judgment."

Jacobs hint that Santiago may not have been as bad for the U.S. as I had thought was intriguing. There was time for the full story later. Now I was focused on Trich.

"My line is ringing," Jacobs said, "I'll let you know when she's in Brownsville."

I called the Brownsville hospital and asked for Miguel, Jr. I was told he wasn't in. I had forgotten he worked the midnight shift. I left word for him to call me.

A text arrived from Jacobs. **Snow in 956 area.**

956 is a large area, covering Port Isabel and SPI, as well as many other towns in the Valley. But, Snow's a professional, and professionals don't allow their phones to be traced. And what

had he meant by telling Joy that Trich was an explosive situation? More questions, fewer answers.

I fell asleep thinking of where Angella might be. I was out for maybe an hour, maybe two, maybe more. The truth was, I didn't know how long I had slept when the phone jarred me awake.

Jacob's upbeat voice said, "Preliminary report from Brownsville is she's in critical condition. Throat badly bruised, trouble breathing, eyes swollen closed. Possible broken leg. Some internal bleeding."

I was groggy and assumed Tiny was talking about Angella. "Did she say any more? Anything on who kidnapped her?"

"Kidnapped? Wake up, Redstone. It's Trich. She's unconscious. Was when the team arrived."

"Prognosis?"

"Guarded."

"She has information on terrorists smuggled into the country. We need what she has. We also need to know why Snow went after her."

Jacobs took a moment before he responded. "If they've already smuggled in a second bomb, then it's only a matter of time 'til they blow it."

"We're missing something," I said. "If they have a bomb, then why mess around with Angella and Trich, and where does Snow fit in?"

"We spend our lives missing things," Jacobs replied, sounding exhausted. "World Trade Center came down because we didn't connect the dots. It's just not as easy as it appears. After the fact, it seems trivial. Talk to you later."

Tiny begged off and I drove myself to Brownsville. On the drive I again went over all the facts I could muster. I added in surmised facts and still it made no sense. My mood was sour when I climbed out of the car in the hospital parking lot. Two orderlies were taking a smoke break on the front steps. I walked past them into the hospital and made my way directly to the emergency room.

The receptionist checked her list and responded that no one by the name of Trich Santiago—or Patricia Santiago—had been admitted in the past few hours.

I produced my Homeland Security shield and said, "I want to see names of all the people admitted within the last three hours.

"Sorry, I can't allow—"

"Get the hospital president or whoever runs this place on the phone. And do it now!" I demanded.

She shot me a look that conveyed a very clear message to the effect that if she possessed a gun, she'd shoot me. She didn't, but I did.

A few minutes later she printed a sheet of paper and slid it across the desk to me.

It was easy to spot Trich. There were twelve admissions, nine of whom were men, and of the three women, one was pregnant and about to deliver and the other sixty-eight. That narrowed it to a twenty-nine year old female name of Jane Doe. How very original.

I pointed to Jane Doe. "Where is this woman now?"

She entered the name in her computer. A moment later she said, "I'll have someone come see you."

"Tell them to make it quick. Which way to the men's room?"

She pointed behind me. "Go out of the waiting room, turn left. At the end of the hall on the right."

"I'll be right back. Tell them to hurry."

"I'll do my best."

I was standing at the urinal when the orderlies I had seen out front came in. One of them bumped against me on his way to the toilets. I finished, walked toward the sink and my knees collapsed. My feet were locked against the floor as if lead weights had been placed on top. I fell forward and was unable to raise my hands to protect myself from the rising floor.

- - - - -

I looked up at a sterile white ceiling. Tubes snaked across my body. An IV was dripping into my arm. I was within a curtained area with movement not far away.

"Hey," I called, my voice weak, "where am I?"

No one responded.

"Hey," I repeated starting to sit up. When I did, my head spun out of control. Nausea quickly forced me back down. I dry-heaved several times. My throat was raw and my head hurt.

A woman wearing a white jacket appeared at my side. "Glad you're awake, Mr. Redstone. Don't try to sit up. It'll take at least another hour for the drugs to work out of your system."

"What's going on?" I demanded. "Why am I here? Where's Trich?"

"Whoa. You were found on the men's room floor. Thought you had a heart attack, but the tox screen showed a combination of scopolamine and curare. Wonder you're not dead."

I vaguely remember falling. I couldn't move, couldn't talk. Then nothing. "What happened?"

"At one point in time, curare was used on arrows for paralyzing prey. Seems to be going around."

"Going around?"

"Another patient earlier today, had the same screen."

"Shit! Was that by any chance Trich?"

A puzzled look crossed her face.

"Jane Doe. Brought here from Mexico."

"Yes, that's her. How do you—"

"How is she? Where is she? I must see her!" I tried to sit up and the nausea again overwhelmed me. "Give me the whole picture."

"Can't, privac-"

"I'm Homeland Security, check my—"

"Saw it on the chart. Okay. Fractured tibia. Why are you interested in her? She do something?"

"Internal injuries?"

"When she was first examined, the initial assessment was internal trauma. The intake x-rays revealed an internal mass. Machine must have malfunctioned. On follow up, the mass was gone."

"Was she awake when she came in?"

"Unconscious. May have been sedated by the transport team. She squeezed my hand. She's aware, but in no pain."

"Has she said anything?

"Nothing's on her chart, if she did."

I pulled myself up and immediately felt dizzy. The room spun and I fell back onto the table. A moment later I tried it again. Same result, but this time instead of lying down I bent my head forward.

It took a moment, but the spinning slowed slightly.

"I wouldn't get off the table if I was you, Mr. Redstone. You'll fall and—"

I was already moving, albeit wobbly, across the space to the curtain. I grabbed the IV pole for support and hung on while a wave of dizziness peaked.

"Disconnect me. I have business to attend to."

"Can't do that without doctor's orders."

"Either you do it or I will."

"Not allowed. Please get back in bed. You'll get hurt."

I ripped the tape from the IV needle and slid it out of my arm. Unfortunately, in the past year I've watched them do that to me numerous times. I was a pro by now at getting disconnected from all the machinery.

"Please don't do that!" the nurse demanded, "you'll injure yourself."

It took a few minutes, while I peeled the sensors from my chest. Blood dripped from my arm where the needle had been. I looked around for a bandage.

"Here," the nurse said, holding out a cotton ball and some tape. "Hold the cotton over the opening and use the tape to secure it. This is most unusual—and dangerous. Please—"

I was outside the curtain, wobbly, but moving forward.

"Please come back and lie down." The nurse's voice floated in the air behind me. I felt as if I was in a cave filling with water and the harder I fought the worse it became. It was hard to move my limbs against the pressure.

I leaned against a wall, again waiting for a wave of dizziness to pass. When it did, I called to the nurse, my voice disconnected from my body. "Which room is she in?"

"One floor up. Recovery. Please sit down before you hurt yourself."

I found the stairwell, wrestled the door open and sat on the bottom step waiting for the fog to clear and the dizziness to subside. When it was tolerable, I slowly made my way up the steps, taking them one at a time, hanging tightly to the handrail. It took all of my concentration to avoid falling backward. The steps seemed to stretch out ahead of me, rising forever on their way to heaven. I paused several times, holding tight to the banister to keep from toppling over.

Finally, my feet hit a flat area and I forced myself to let go of the railing and move toward the door. Another wave of disorienting dizziness swept across me and I fell forward, slamming my forehead into the door. I slid to the floor.

The dizziness persisted and I didn't dare try to stand. I sat there for several minutes before my visual focus returned. Slowly, I pulled myself up and leaned heavily on the door. I worked my way out into the brightly lit hallway, still disoriented and dizzy.

"Recovery room," I managed to mumble to an orderly pushing a cart. He pointed in the general direction of where I was heading. After several more cautious steps I was opposite a room that held four beds, all with monitors and tubes dwarfing the patients.

"Where are you going?" a stern voice from the cloud demanded.

I fumbled for my shield, flashed it, and mumbled, "Doe, official business. Which bed?"

"Third on the right," came the disemboweled reply. I was having trouble focusing, let alone standing unaided. I leaned against the wall to catch my balance. My vision was dancing and the room was rocking. I fought the urge to vomit.

"The Doe woman," I heard from the direction of the desk, "came through better than we had initially expected."

I focused as best I could in the direction of the voice. A white-jacketed middle-aged bald guy was speaking to the nurse while running his finger down a chart. "Fever's down, heart rate lowering, BP in range." He jotted something on the chart and handed it across the desk to a nurse. "Her throat appears to have been abraded from the inside. Vocal cords swollen. Keep her quiet. The initial X-rays showed a mass. Redo showed negative. Unless something changes, I expect a full recovery. Only it will take time." He then went to her bed, checked her bandages, made a few more notes on the chart and left.

When he was gone, I made my way to Trich's bed. It was clear she was sleeping, her breathing labored. Oxygen tubes snaked from her nose and intravenous liquid dripped steadily into her veins. But even if she had been awake, it was clear from what I had just heard she couldn't talk.

One thing was clear, she had more injuries than when I had last seen her in Mexico.

I bent and kissed her forehead. In doing so, I realized her eyes were swollen closed. Her nose was puffy and streaked with red and black splotches. I couldn't be certain, but it appeared it had been broken. When I get my hands on Snow I'd return the favor—in spades.

The nausea was clearing, and if I walked slowly I could do so without the aid of the wall. The hall clock showed twelve-fifteen. Hospitals run twenty-four seven, so it's hard to know day from night, but thinking back to the various events, I knew it couldn't be noon. Unless I had skipped an entire day.

I made my way to a window, and the lights in the parking lot were on. I must have been out a good six hours or more. Hard to believe.

I found the pharmacy and asked for Miguel. After a while, a woman who I had seen before, but could not place, came out. "Mr. Redstone, Miguel is not here tonight; I'm Eileen, Trich's friend. I used to be a pharmacist before I was certified as a sonographer. I'm filling in for Miguel."

That's how I knew her. She had performed a sonographic exam on Mark Cruses at my request.

"I'm sorry, I didn't immediately recognize you. I thought he worked every night."

"Usually he does. But he had a death in the family."

"Please don't tell me it's his father."

"Afraid so. Earlier today. I understand it occurred about two hours before they got to Trich. Thugs broke into his pharmacy and killed him."

"Was it a robbery or what?"

"Authorities believe they were looking for Trich. She's here, you know. They have her listed as Jane Doe. Something to do with Mexico and drugs. That's all I know."

"Please have Miguel call me when he gets back. I must speak with him."

"I'll do that. Nice seeing you again."

Before I could respond, the phone rang. It was a little past one in the morning, two o'clock in the District, but Jacobs sounded as if he just had his morning coffee. "You feeling better?"

"Doing okay."

"Understand you got jumped. Losing your touch. I trust the drugs wore off."

"Feel like shit, you really want to know."

"I've seen the surveillance footage. Definitely Snow. And two other men we don't know."

I added, "Wearing jeans and tees. One had on a green three-quarter arm length tee and the other, I think it was grey, had some writing on it."

"So you saw them."

"They were smoking on the front steps, didn't think much about them; both were scrawny looking. You're right, I'm losing it."

"Doesn't take much strength to stick you with a needle. Snow was with them on the way out."

"If I ever get my hands——"

"No time for that now. Need you back home. I'm arranging a plane as we speak."

"What's up?"

"Got a lead on where the second Korean is holed up. Get over to the airport. You can sleep on the plane."

"What's that got to do with Timberwolf—or Angella?"

"You're not on the Martinez file. Not much of a tie to Timberwolf. But you're the designated hitter for the bomb threat. So they want you back in Washington."

"They want me away from the action around Angella, that's what they want."

"Think what you will. But get over to the airport, I'll have a ride waiting."

"So what's the hurry?"

"Something's going down in the next twenty-four, forty-eight hours. Don't know for certain what it is, but recall the President is delivering a major speech on Nuclear Fusion Reduction to heads of State thirty-two hours from now. International coverage. Prime targets. CIA's picked up deep vibes. Fits with what we've been getting."

"I can't leave Angella." I protested.

"We're working that. There's nothing you can do at this point. Court orders for an addict's useless visitor information and breaking windows won't find her."

"How the hell——"

The line went dead. How in the world Jacobs in D.C. knew of my activities on SPI baffled me. The realtor certainly didn't call the police, not after I handed her a hundred dollars to replace what couldn't cost more than fifty.

Fifteen minutes later, an even more animated Jacobs was back on the phone. "We may have just caught a break. Actually two. I'm talking about Angella. Tiny's folks picked up a call placed to Mexico from her cell. Short story, the signal originated from Port Isabel."

"Was it her voice?"

"Tiny doesn't think so, but they're not sure. The spooks never give us all the info, so we're running a bit blind on this."

"One transmission means nothing. They can't find her from just one."

"Maybe not, but we can be ready for the next one. If they have something planned soon, then there'll be more activity."

"Other piece. You said two breaks."

"Angella sightings. Some friend of Joy's was overheard at a place called *Louies Back Something*."

"Backyard. *Louies Backyard*. A local watering hole where Joy hung out. We ate there a few times."

One of the SPI cops overheard this friend talking about seeing Angella having a burger at the *Parrot Eyes*? Know it?"

"Across from *Teds*. Neat place. Do water sports. Jet skies, parasailing, that kind of thing."

The line was silent.

"What are you not telling me?"

"When Lt. Garcia investigated, she was gone. A woman answering her description was seen leaving with a local by the name of Bill Stallings. Part-time bartender, full-time playboy. Answers to Buffalo Bill."

"Not like Angella. Unless she was following him like she followed Snow."

"I wouldn't think so. She didn't check in with us so we doubt she was released. Maybe running something for Snow."

"She'd not do that, unless…unless she thought they had me and she's doing it to protect me."

"You might be onto something. Snow wanted her for something. We've been looking for Stallings. Not in any of his usual haunts. None of his regular friends have seen him since yesterday. I'll let you know when we get anything."

"I'm heading to SPI. The hell with coming east. Whatever you need, I'll do it by remote."

"McNaughton won't be happy."

"Hell with that! I'm tired of being babysat. Angella's my partner, and my…friend. I'm in this whether they like it or not."

"Don't get cross-wise with her or the Bureau. Not a good idea."

"You done lecturing? I have business to take care of."

"One last item. Been a busy night. The intelligence we picked up gives us a high degree of confidence that the bomb threat, or whatever it is, is being run by some well-placed Iranians. Secretary of State delivered a strongly worded message to Ahmadinejad. Two Iranians attached to the Pakistani embassy hurriedly left the country a few hours ago."

"Pakistan? What's that—"

"We don't have diplomatic relations with Iran. They maintain something called an Interests Section at the Pakistani embassy."

"So the threat is off."

"Can't say anything for sure. They may have finished their business and it's in someone else's hands now. Who really knows? Must assume nothing has changed."

"That it?"

"Isn't that enough?"

"Nothing's enough until Angella is safe."

Jacobs not responding was harsher than if he had spoken. He was communicating how wrong I was. No one's life is more important than the safety of the country. I had debated this very topic going all the way back to my Ranger training days. Nice concept—except when it's your lover's life you are discussing.

THIRTY-THREE

Highway forty-eight leading east to Port Isabel was desolate at this time of night. On my right, separated from the road by several large metal structures, was the Brownsville shipping channel. Near the channel sat three off-shore drilling rigs, welding arcs flashing in random patterns within their massive towers. The silhouetted bulk of a large freighter loomed out of the darkness. I suppose it was waiting its turn in the shipyard—or to be scrapped.

Further east, what I took to be sand flats lined both sides of the highway. Signs warned against blowing sand.

A shadow, perhaps a fox or maybe a coyote, darted across the road. I twisted my head too quickly and was rewarded with dizziness. The center divider snaked in front of me and I hit the brakes, trying not to slam into the undulating concrete barrier. My vision cleared about the same time as the car stopped. The divider was straight again and stretched off into the darkness.

Shaken, I drove slower, thinking of Angella on SPI. Based on what the Coast Guard had showed me, I knew they were right. But I also knew she was close. The reported sighting confirmed my sense of her being close by.

The road sign warned of reduced speed as I entered Port Isabel. I again thought of her house and meeting her sister. Angella had been unhappy there with her former husband.

A thought came and went.

Then came again. The call that Snow had made using her phone had originated from this area. Could Angella be at her own house?

Bingo!

I almost wrecked the car reaching for my cell. "Jacobs!" I shouted into the phone when he answered. "Numbers all fit! It's perfect. Angella's being held at her own house. The woman you're trailing on SPI is her sister. She's staying at a place called *Claytons*. Sister's name's Jayme Partridge."

"Don't know anything about a sister. I'll relay that information. But you could be right about her house. It fits with another piece of info that came in about two hours ago. Can't say much about the technology on an open line, but we know Angella's phone is in Port Isabel."

"Perfect! Snow's holding her at her own house!"

"Hold a moment. I'm looking up Angella's address and then...then...never mind. Tell you when I see you. Call you when I have something."

It didn't take ten minutes and Jacobs was back on the phone. "Hit a break. Confirmed the phone is now in her house with eighty-percent certainty."

"Hell, I've shot people with less certainty than that!"

"Don't remind me. Park in the Wal-Mart lot. Stay put and wait for the locals to come get you. Because it's a residential area, need to clear a ton of hurdles before we can go in. It'll take a while, but McNaughton's on board, so it'll happen."

My head cleared. Funny what adrenalin will do. I pulled into the Wal-Mart lot expecting to see a bevy of police cars scattered about. Instead, it appeared to be business as usual, albeit it was three in the morning. Fishermen were already stirring, although I can't imagine what fun there is in getting up so early and climbing into a wet boat hours before sunrise. I suppose a snapper on the grill at noon after an early morning chase has a far different taste than does the one I buy from the market. I'd rather sleep.

I settled in, much as I would do on a stakeout. I was trying to feel upbeat and positive, but underneath the bravado lay the simple fact that based on what Snow had done to Trich there was little real hope of finding Angella uninjured—or even alive.

I put a ninety percent certainty factor on Snow knowing the phone he was using had been traced. Snow didn't stay alive in his line of work being a fool. But there was a chance he didn't know that phones can be traced even when they're not in use.

With the engine off, the car became a bit stuffy, so I opened the door hoping to catch a breeze. It helped, but not enough. I knew I needed sleep, but the thought of Angella being close kept me pumped. I climbed out of the car and walked carefully across the parking lot, testing my balance and clearing my head.

A young couple pulled into the lot, drove up close to the front door. A moment later they both bounded out. The car had Kansas plates and a Jay Hawk on the rear window.

Probably drove straight through, some eighteen to twenty hours, getting ready to start a vacation. Most likely across the causeway on the island.

Twenty minutes later, the young couple emerged from the store pushing a shopping cart filled with bags of groceries, two cartons of water and enough beer to float their car. He was carrying a large green bag over his shoulder and I recognized its shape as that of a tent bag. It reminded me of the tent Angella and I had used on our first assignment. That now seemed ages ago.

I have never been kicked in the gut by a bull, but I imagined the feeling I was experiencing was similar. A knot welled up inside me and it felt as though the bull was still kicking. I ran back to my car, stumbling twice as my body wanted to move faster than my spongy legs could propel it. I started the engine and reached for my cell. It rang in my hand.

It was Jacobs. "You in the lot?"

"I'm here, listen—"

"Good. Stay put. Police didn't want to congregate in the lot and tip them off. When something breaks I'll let you know."

"Angella's house is on a canal that opens to the bay. That's why the Coast Guard didn't detect anyone coming ashore. They didn't have to land on the beach. Pulled right up to her house."

"You done?"

"What do you have?

"We have a team of Rangers, FBI and Coast Guard SEALs standing by. We're moving them in position low key. Got a solid land perimeter. Nobody's going anywhere. But water's not yet covered. This may take another hour to set up. Try to get some shuteye. I'll call when things are in place."

"It's four in the morning. It's already been a long night. We don't have an hour."

"They're not getting away. Trust me. Get some sleep. We'll not go without you. And we can't go until we're ready."

"If they realize they're trapped, they'll kill Angella! We don't have an hour."

"We won't go a second earlier than we're ready. She's not the only life we need to preserve. Now hang tight."

No matter how many times you participate in a raid, especially when a hostage is involved, it is impossible to control the adrenalin. This was no exception. I was angry for not thinking of it sooner. How much pain and suffering they had inflicted on Angella in the meantime I had no way of knowing. I was vividly aware of Trich's battered and broken body, her swollen eyes and throat, and I envisioned Angella the same way. The image tore at me relentlessly.

I kicked the floorboards and pounded the wheel to relive the tension, all to no avail. Sitting in a mostly deserted parking lot, doing nothing to help my partner, the woman I loved, was more than I could tolerate.

I mentally replayed the video Captain Boyle had shown us; the one with the white heat dots and green smudges. I recalled our conversation about Boca Chico Beach and how isolated it was. Then a horrible thought occurred to me. That deserted beach had shelter, primitive huts Boyle had called them, and would be perfect for holding a hostage. Snow could well know about the telephone company tracking and could have just planted the phone in the house.

I started the motor. Sitting here doing nothing was no longer tolerable. I knew better than to intercede at this point, but sitting in an empty parking lot was not the answer. I drove east toward the causeway bridge. I glanced to my left in the direction of Angella's house. I saw nothing out of the usual. Two blocks later I turned to the right, drove several blocks, swung to the left and hoped I had the right street.

I was looking for *Our Lady Star of the Sea* church. If ever I needed the comfort of a church, this was it. I also needed a more direct route for my prayers. Over the years I've wavered on the necessity for organized religion. For that matter, I've sometimes been skeptical of the unseen, unproven, unexplained concept of God. But yet, here I was, desperate to offer prayers, to ask for divine help, not for myself, but for Angella.

I was on the wrong block, but when I circled back I saw the church tucked in among homes. Angella had driven me past the church, showing me where she had been married.

I parked a half-block away and walked briskly toward the front door. It was locked. A small sign instructed anyone with an emergency to ring the bell on the side entrance. Presumably, the bell was wired directly to the Deity.

I dutifully walked around to the side and reached for the bell. My finger hesitated while I thought out what I planned to say to whomever answered the bell. Nothing good came to mind. Instead of ringing the bell, I knelt beside a lawn sculpture of Mary cradling her baby. I prayed for Angella to be delivered safely back to us. And while I was at it, I tossed in a few additional prayers for Trich. Then a few for Mark. A couple for his mother. And finally, a few extra for good measure for Angella. At least out here there wasn't a roof to slow the prayers. Speed of delivery is what was required. The response was out of my control.

Back in the car I called Jacobs.

"Hold on a few minutes longer," he admonished. "Everything is almost in place. Just working out the final timing."

"Had another thought," I said. "Boca Chica Beach is perfect for—"

"You're about six hours behind Tiny on that one," Jacobs replied. "First, the road into the beach has a checkpoint. Second, we swept the beach five hours ago to be on the safe side. Other than some drunk fishermen, and two illegal Mexicans holed up in a hut, it proved to be a dead end."

"Glad you guys are sharing. Anything else you forgot to tell me?"

"Just a few minutes more. We're about to go in."

Jacobs few minutes turned into a half-hour. Then an hour. Convinced they'd go in without me, I slipped the car into gear and drove slowly back toward the parking lot. But instead of turning left, I crossed over the main drag and followed the path I had traveled not long ago. I circled around Angella's block looking for signs of activity.

I knew I wouldn't see flashing red and blue lights atop a myriad of police cars as is typical in movies. That's not what happens prior to a raid of this nature. But I did expect to see a few dark vans, possible a utility truck, hanging about. Instead, I saw nothing giving rise to any suspicion of the pending operation.

Was Jacobs leveling with me? Or had they been playing me, keeping me isolated in the Wal-Mart lot for some other purpose? In my Texas Ranger days I would have called my boss, Lt. Contentus, for clarification. He may have been a lot of things—gruff around the edges, blunt, hard-nosed, some would say a genuine A-hole—but he always, and I mean always, had my back. Unfortunately, the way I feel, it seems that if I give the guys I now work with my back there is a better than even chance they'll blow a hole through it.

I turned onto Angella's street. Here again, I saw no sign of activity. Her house was dark when I drove past, but I did notice something odd. The For Sale sign was gone. Vandals may have ripped it down, but from what Angella had told me about Port Isabel, that was a low possibility. If Snow was using it for a hideaway, then he would surely have taken the sign down.

I parked several houses away. My intention was to sit in the car a while to see if an operation was being mounted. If it wasn't, I was going in myself. I would not allow Angella's fate to hang in the balance while the ponderous wheels of government red-tape churned. I couldn't live with myself if anything—

My cell went off, startling me. The display read Jacobs. I tapped the green accept button and before I could say anything, he barked, "What the hell you doing? Get the hell away from there!"

"I'm going in," I replied. "I'm not sitting by while—"

"Not alone you're not! You take one step outside of your vehicle and a sniper will disable you. Trust me on this. You're in their sights. Put the car in gear and drive away. Now!"

I again studied the area around me and saw nothing unusual. But there was no doubt Jacobs meant business. Obviously something was going down or he wouldn't know what I was doing. "Promise you won't cut me out. She's my partner."

"I'm not promising you shit! Get your ass away from there immediately! You know the odds of someone being injured in a SWAT raid. We don't get the timing right there's no telling what might happen. Circle the block. Go back toward the boat parked on a trailer at the end of the street."

"Saw it on the way in," I replied. "Didn't make it for—"

"Get moving! That's the control point. Park in the lot by the main road and walk back to the boat. You know the drill, be casual." He was some fifteen hundred miles away, yet he knew my every move. I had made a fool of myself in front of an entire audience. Breaking protocol as I had would be unthinkable, even for me, if my sense of balance as to right and wrong had not been suspended by my concern for my lover.

The only smart thing I could do now was leave without throwing a finger.

THIRTY-FOUR

I drove past the boat. It was a typical fishing boat of the kind seen all over town. Relatively flat bottom, outboard motor. This one sported a large cabin. A small Mexican-looking guy was busy removing a flat tire from the trailer. I hadn't noticed him when I drove past before.

Jacobs had reminded me of the unfavorable odds of injury or death accruing during a hostage release. The number ninety-two had been drilled into my head. Ninety-two percent of the time when a SWAT team goes in for a hostage rescue, someone is injured.

I parked in the lot as instructed by Jacobs and started back, glancing around to see if I could spot the snipers. A slight movement caught my eye. Two blocks away and directly in front of Angella's house, a bulge was barely noticeable among the wires high up in a utility pole. The movement I had seen was on another pole; the bulge was slowly moving upward.

I approached the boat trailer and the man working on the tire hissed, "Get into the cabin from the far side. There's a ladder over there."

Four men were inside, electronic gear spread on every surface. A small TV screen showed the front of Angella's house and I supposed the camera was mounted on one of the utility poles. A second screen showed the back of the house and the dock. I had no idea where that camera was located.

"Nothing's moved, in or out, for at least two hours," one of the men, who I assumed to be in command, said. "Snipers in position. Land perimeter is secure. The waterside is not yet fully secure. Figure another five minutes, ten at most. We're using the military satellite for communication, they can't possibly hear us. FBI in D.C. is coordinating. Everything's on video. Some lady general's on line as well."

"You guys have some fancy electronics—can't say as I've seen all this stuff before—or even know what it all does."

"Probably haven't. Homeland Security, Border Patrol, ATF. Ever since that A-bomb scare, the stuff's been pouring in. Can't keep up with the training."

"You local?"

He stuck out his big hand. "Guillimo. Johnny Guillimo, with the Texas Rangers. Took your place."

"Glad to meet you. Surprised the locals are letting you run this."

"As I said, being run from back east. Guy name of Jacobs. San Antonio FBI head. I'm just coordinating. Hey, see that green light?" I looked at his display. "The red light is the target. The green light shows the approaching friendly vessels. In this case, fishing boats. The solid green one will be the first on the dock. The other ones, the ones that are flashing, will follow. They'll put six people on that dock in a matter of seconds. There's a boat tied up out back. We think that's how the target plans to escape. Target's boat will disappear when the operation begins."

"How long now?"

"The countdown has started. SEALs are out of the plane and in the air as we speak. That's why this has taken so long to set up. Had to get them in position. Then we needed to wait for the wind to be right. Worst possible thing is to begin the operation before they land. They'd be target practice for Snow."

The display showed one hundred twenty and counting downward in one-second intervals. "Does that mean two minutes to go?"

"That's it."

I started for the door.

"Hold it. You're to leave at thirty seconds. And walk, don't run."

"I won't get there on time." I protested.

"You're not going in first. These guys are highly trained to protect the hostage. You come in behind them." He studied the screens for another several seconds and then said, "Thirty-five, thirty-three, thirty-one, go!" Guillimo pointed to the door. "Walk. You'll mess up the timing if you don't."

I fought the urge to run toward the house. I had forgotten how long thirty seconds can be when the adrenalin is pumping and you know all hell is about to break loose.

Twenty. I was keeping count in my head. I was still a block away and just turning toward the water. I strained to hear the sounds of a boat engine, but nothing registered.

Fifteen. I was closing too fast, so I slowed.

Ten. A car, a black station wagon, moved slowly past me, heading in the direction of Angella's house. I was now a half-block away, separated by five small houses.

Five. A second car turned onto the block from the other direction. The street was now sealed, both cars moving slowly. I heard the faint sound of a fishing boat's engine. Then in the distance a second engine started up, both muted against the slight breeze.

Nothing was visible in the sky.

Three. The first station wagon turned into Angella's driveway.

One. The doors opened in the first car. Five black-clad figures poured out, crouching low as they ran across the small lawn, their elbows held tight against their sides, their assault weapons in firing position. They were joined by five figures from the second car. At the house, they spaced themselves around the perimeter. Three figures stacked themselves on opposite sides of the door, one behind the other. The person nearest the handle, which was to the left, was going in first. That much I knew. But after that there were several tactics that could be employed to secure the room immediately inside the door. The one thing I knew they wouldn't do, was stop in the door frame. Timing now between them was critical. Anyone on the inside knew that to breach the house, they had to come through that framework.

Zero. An ear shattering pop and brilliant light flooded my senses. The stack beside the door had disappeared and several more black forms raced onto the porch and froze in their place. Nothing moved.

I looked skyward in time to see several parachutes descending from the south, their color blending perfectly with the dark early morning sky. The first SEAL landed on the roof, his parachute immediately disappearing. Four others landed within seconds.

Then black-clad forms descended from the roof, each disappearing inside through a different window. All this was happening from above while shadows swarmed through the front door.

I ran across the lawn and entered just behind the last of them. No sounds came from the second floor. No gun shots. No running feet. No barked orders. Nothing.

A man across from me signaled that the first floor was clear. Almost simultaneously the signal was relayed that the second floor was also clear. The house was empty.

I was now frantic. "What about Angella?" I shouted at a commando coming down the steps, his assault rifle pointed down.

"A hostage has been identified and secured. She's on the second floor. Back room. No one else in the house."

I pushed past everyone and took the steps two at a time. I was breathing heavy when I reached the second floor, and the nausea returned with a vengeance.

I slumped against the wall, struggling to regain balance. I sat to keep from heaving.

Several men in black stepped over my legs on their way to the first floor. One man, wearing a microphone headset, bent toward me and asked if I required medical attention. I waived him away.

He spoke softly into the mike. "House is clear. No casualties. Only the hostage and Observer One remain. Hostage drugged, breathing labored. Oxygen begun. Trauma to face, fractures. Observer One down. Refused assistance." Transmission finished, he followed the others down the steps.

I forced myself to stand. The dizziness had subsided, but I still had to use the wall for balance. I made my way down the hall and into the room where the activity was centered. Angella was lying on her back on an unmade bed, a sheet covering her body. There was blood on her forehead, but it appeared to be dried. Her face was a mass of bruises, her eyes puffy.

I said a silent prayer as the vision of Trich, lying unconscious in the hospital, flashed before me. Angella's hair was knotted and filthy. Her right arm appeared to be under her side. A pool of blood had formed and her palm, which was bent at an unnatural angle, rested in the congealing liquid.

"It's broken," a voice from over my shoulder said. "Probably compound from the looks of that blood. Don't touch her. Movement could do major damage. We'll use ultrasound to determine the extent of her injuries before we move her. Vital signs are stable."

I looked behind me and was startled to see two SEALs standing over me. I assumed they were two of the men I saw parachute onto the roof.

One of the men placed a stethoscope on Angella's neck, nodded, and proceeded to move the instrument to her chest. He listened for a while and then nodded again. "No change. That's good."

The other man said, "It's good to see you up and around, Agent Redstone." My puzzled look prompted him to say, "Thanks for the note you sent my command. You didn't have to do that, but we appreciate it."

"I'm sorry, I don't—"

"Over on the sand flats. Your neck was severely lacerated."

"Oh, my." This was the man—actually barely out of his teens—who had saved my life a few miles from here. He had literally held my carotid artery together while I was airlifted to the hospital. I reached out to shake his hand.

He pulled away. "Sterile."

I patted him on the back. "I can't thank you enough. You saved my life. All I can say is thank God for you."

"Thanks, sir. Just doing our jobs. Right now we need to attend to her."

"Sorry, I said, stepping back and to the side.

Silently, with nothing but hand motions and an occasional nod, they worked on Angella, recording blood pressure and heart rate and extracting several vials of blood. They moved quickly, and thoroughly.

"We need to do the sonogram now. Please step out," the SEAL said.

I wanted to remain, to hold her hand, to kiss her. But her life was at stake and I trusted these guys.

After what seemed like an hour, but was closer to five minutes, I heard one of them say, "Clear."

They must have then turned her over because the same voice a few minutes later said, "Some bruising on her back and legs. She might have fallen or been beaten because her butt seems to have experienced trauma." He then continued, "Sugar level's low. No recreational drugs, coke, crack, cannabis. Alcohol level is okay. Blood is saturated with drugs we can't identify. High level of codeine."

"Agent Redstone, you may come back in now," the voice called.

I rejoined them in the room, and Angella was again on her back. The man closest to me said, "She isn't feeling pain and won't for a long while. High level of codeine and some other drugs our meter doesn't recognize."

"Scopolamine and curare," I said. "I've seen this movie."

"What the hell?"

"Knocks you out instantly."

"I'll bet."

He then fished out a small package, tore it open, pulled out what looked to be a fat spaghetti noodle. When the noodle hit the air it self-inflated to form a splint. He then cleaned the lacerations and gently slipped her arm inside the inflated bag, pulling it tight.

"Arm's immobilized. No need to treat the wound any more than we have. It's sealed and the doctors won't have to spend time removing bandages and cleaning off anything we apply."

When he moved her hand, I could see that it was tightly clenched. Clearly when she lost consciousness it had been important to her to hold onto whatever she had. "Would you bag her hand," I asked.

Both men looked surprised at the request.

"Evidence," I added. "She seems to be grasping something. Looks like flesh. Wouldn't want to have the evidence contaminated."

"No problem."

I watched for another few minutes while they worked on her. Their movements were efficient and well coordinated. These men knew exactly what they were doing. Unable to contain myself any longer, I blurted, "What's the verdict? Will she make it?"

"Heart weak, but steady. Breathing labored. No other surface trauma other than her face, right arm and buttocks. Don't know about internals for certain, but all seems well. She's remained stable since we arrived."

"May have broken her arm when she resisted the needle."

"What needle?"

"She was drugged. Seen it earlier in Mexico."

"You guys bring Trich out to Brownsville?"

"Been a busy day. This related?"

"Possibly." I couldn't tell him anymore because there was no clear connection, just my strong hunch.

"You want her moved to Brownsville also? Our orders are to deliver her to Hopkins."

"Is she stable enough for the flight?"

"The drugs should start wearing off in three, maybe four hours. Her arm requires medical attention, but it's stabilized and can wait. Nothing's urgent at this moment."

"Hopkins seems a long way to go."

"There's a plane to D.C. waiting at Brownsville. A helicopter's standing by in the old Wal-Mart lot. About thirty minutes and she'll be loaded and ready to fly."

"Thirty minutes to get her to Wal-Mart? Walk there in ten max."

"No, sir. We'll have her, and you if you wish, on the jet and cleared for takeoff from Brownsville in thirty minutes. That is, if you shut the hell up and let us do our job."

"Aye, aye!" I shot back. "Let's make tracks."

THIRTY-FIVE

Angella had not yet been brought aboard the big jet. I was getting edgier by the moment. The helicopter was not more than twenty yards away, and orderlies had been moving back and forth between the two aircraft.

I continued to dismiss the thought that something had gone terribly wrong. I had stood beside her when she had been transferred from the ambulance to the helicopter, and her breathing had been steady. The small heart monitor strapped to her chest had displayed what appeared to be a steady EKG. But something could have changed that. Goodness knows, she had drugs of every variety in her body, many of which could be deadly in their own right.

I was pacing the cabin when the cockpit door opened. The pilot walked purposefully toward me. "Been a change of plans," he announced, his clipped words telegraphed that we were not about to have a discussion. "Washington ordered your partner transported to the hospital here in Brownsville."

From the corner of my eye I saw the helicopter's blades begin to move. Slowly at first, then gaining speed with each revolution. Its steps folded upward, sealing the cabin. I ran to the door foolishly thinking they'd wait for me. I was on the top step when the helicopter's wheels broke contact with the ground and rose several yards. The big machine then tilted to the right as it gained altitude.

The pilot, standing behind me just inside the cabin, said, "I was instructed to bring you to Washington. Please take a seat."

I didn't immediately follow his order. Not so much because I intended to disobey him, but I was struggling to understand why the plans had changed. Was Angella in a medical emergency? Or was this Washington just being Washington?

The helicopter quickly became a fading dark area blending with the background as it moved out over the tree line. From my perspective, they were dangerously close to the Rio Grande River, and I was uncomfortable with Angella being that close to Mexican air space. I wanted her as far from here—and Snow—as possible.

"Please take your seat, sir. We need to close the door for takeoff." The pilot's voice broke though my thoughts. "As I said, I'm to fly you on up to Washington."

I turned to face him. He was a pleasant man, medium build with eyes that seemed to twinkle, as if he had just told himself a private joke. In a lowered voice he said, "Off the record, sir, I am not authorized to restrain you. And in fact, I wouldn't if they had asked. You can come inside and ride on up with us. Or, if you prefer, go over to the hospital with her."

I asked what had happened to cause the shift in plans. But he cut me off with a slight wave of his hand. "Sorry, sir, can't answer questions. Go now, or take your seat." He turned and headed back toward the cockpit.

I raced down the steps and across the tarmac.

In the cab on the way to the hospital, I called Jacobs.

"I just heard you changed the plans," Jacobs announced when he came on the line. "The meeting here in D.C. was to discuss the video and Singh's findings. Wanted you here for the discussion."

"Singh?" I repeated, momentarily confused. The adrenalin rush from the raid, followed by my bolting down the steps of the aircraft, hadn't mixed well with the drugs already in my system. I only hoped the disorientation would be temporary.

"Pitt. The data from Timberwolf's recordings," Jacobs said, sounding impatient.

Timberwolf? It wasn't ringing any bells.

"Redstone," Jacobs said, "you with me on this?"

"Sorry, Sylvan," I responded, "been a tough night. Lack of sleep, drugs, causing me to block." As I spoke, the video of the killing came back, but it seemed so long ago. An old movie mostly forgotten. "I'm with you. What about the findings?"

"If you recall, the analysis seemed to indicate frequencies matching those found in nuclear reactors." Jacobs, heeding my reduced concentration ability, spoke slowly. I appreciated the gesture. "Not only do they match, but they are the precise control frequencies used to cool the reactors in the event of a potential meltdown. You following?"

"Keep going."

"You remember how the Japanese reactors required vast amounts of water when the plants were taken out by the Tsunami? Same here. If the reactor goes into crisis and those control frequencies are blocked, then there could be a lack of cooling and...and...problems."

Problems! Cooling! Control frequencies! It was going over my head. "Why are you telling me this now?"

"Redstone, you on something? That's your assignment. Air Force wants to know what the H is going on out there. You up for this or should you go on block leave?"

"Right now I'm focused on Angella. That Timberwolf stuff is—"

"Angella is not your assignment! You best focus on getting those drugs out of your system. Want a bed at the hospital?"

That was the last thing I wanted. "Hell no! This will pass. Need a few hours."

"Focus on Timberwolf! Trich is covered. Angella's covered. Trust me on this. They're in good hands."

"Trust you, I'll—"

"Don't say it, Redstone. Just don't say it. Listen, we found Angella and got her out. She's in good hands. You concentrate on Timberwolf. Understand what I'm saying? On Timberwolf."

"I hear you," I replied, refraining from reminding him it was I who pinpointed Angella's house.

"Hearing is one thing. Understanding is another."

"I understand."

"Now get on task, and remain on task. You get caught off-reservation, God help you."

- - - - -

Angella was in the operating room having her arm set when I arrived at the hospital. I went to find Trich, but she was still unconscious. Mark was sitting in a chair next to her bed and jumped to his feet when I entered the room. We hugged like father and son. "How's she doing?"

"Doctors are positive," Mark replied, belying what his demeanor told me. "They don't yet know if she'll have eye damage. They think not. Her throat trauma was superficial, but will take awhile for the swelling to go down. You saved her life. Thanks. I owe you big time."

I wondered how he knew I had been involved, but decided not to press. "It was your Coast Guard SEALs who saved her life."

"I only got a three-day leave and I hope she's awake before I have to go. But Mother will be here later today. She'll take Trich back to Austin with her. We're not leaving her out of our sight."

"Times are different," I said. "They used to allow you a week for attending a loved one."

"It's not my new commander. She's great. But all leave is curtailed. The military, and this includes the Coast Guard, is about to go on full alert. We're participating in a massive multinational exercise."

"Coast Guard as well?"

"This time, yes. I can't say much about it, but there is a simulated attack on the east and Gulf coasts."

"Starts when?"

"Tomorrow. Good news is I can report to the SPI Station. They're short-handed down here and back east I'm too new to be of any real help. If I can wrangle time off after the exercise, then I can get over here and see Trich. Even if only for a few hours."

This wasn't the time to break the news to him that Trich might be arrested for aiding her father's drug business. The involvement of Senator Donnlevy and possible other Congressmen had rekindled their interest. If nothing else, she was a valuable witness.

I said to Mark, "Tell your mother hello for me and I'll see her later today."

"She's looking forward to seeing you. I told her you had been injured and she baked you a pie. She's bringing it with her."

"Can't wait to dig in," I said. The thought of a Nora Cruse pie made my mouth water. It also reminded me of how hungry I was. "I'm going down for some breakfast. Want to join me?"

"Love to but...but I don't want to be away from Trich even one minute. Please understand."

I understood only too well.

- - - - -

"How's Angella doing?" I was on my second plate of scrambled eggs when Jacobs called. "Wake yet?" he asked.

"Won't be for many hours. Her arm is being set now. Other than that, it looks good." I was grateful she was alive. "I'm told her face wounds are not bad. Looked horrible when I saw her, swollen and black. Eye's puffy. I'm told it's not as bad as it appeared." Or perhaps that's what they want me to believe. "Saw Mark Cruses. Looks beaten."

"From what I gather, he's resilient. Anything further?"

"Nothing, other than I'm going to get some sleep. Oh, one other thing. I want Angella watched twenty-four-seven. Locals are okay with me, but use your folks if need be."

"Paranoid, are we?"

"You'd be also if you'd been drugged by these thugs. This isn't over. Something's going down. I just can't figure what."

"A room's been booked for you. Motel you stayed at once before. Don't say the name. Just get over there and they'll be ready for you."

"Now who's paranoid?"

I'll let Tiny know where you are. He'll come by for you."

"Why do you suppose they allowed her to live?"

"That's the sixty-four dollar question."

Or had they left her to die? Snow didn't seem to have any problem in that regard.

THIRTY-SIX

I awoke to a banging sound. Pounding actually.

"Get your lazy butt out of bed and open this door!"

I was fuzzy and disoriented. By instinct, I remained quiet. My Berretta pointed at the door.

"Get a move on, or I'll push this shack over. Kapish?"

My mind cleared. Tiny's familiar voice broke through the fog. I holstered my weapon. "Hold on," I called back, testing my legs and being pleasantly surprised to find the dizziness had passed.

"What's so urgent?" I asked Tiny when I finally managed to open the door.

"Potty. Nature's calling," he said, disappearing into the head.

When he emerged, I said, "I just remembered, I bagged Angella's hand at the house. Hospital probably got it all screwed up. Angella was grasping something. We need forensics on whatever it is before it becomes contaminated—or lost. Flesh, unless I miss my guess."

"SEALs got you covered. They forwarded the bag to the FBI. In the lab as we speak. Jacobs is working it."

"You didn't come all this way to take a whiz. What gives?"

"We have a reliable report that a major disturbance—can you say terrorist attack—is set for tomorrow when the President makes his speech."

"How reliable?"

"Checked out positive. We have names, even an address where the terrorists were staying."

"Past tense?"

"You got it. What made this even more convincing is that the operation is built around a Korean. Sound familiar?"

"The one we know, Tae-Hyun, is dead."

"Precisely. His mission was to detonate a rogue suitcase A-bomb. Remember, our initial intelligence was that at least two bombs made it into the country. You tracked down one of them."

I unconsciously ran my fingers over the scar on my throat as Tiny was talking. Angella had pointed out to me that when my agitation level rose, my hand went to my neck. She called it my vulnerability point.

"We never found the other one," Tiny continued, "because either there was no other one or because it wasn't leaking radiation."

"Dead end," I said. "My thought is no radiation, no second bomb. Period. End of story."

"What if, just what if, the radiation leak had not been accidental?"

"This your theory, or is Wash—"

"Told you, I gather facts. Leave the brains to others. It's their theory, not mine."

"Are they saying the one we captured was a Trojan horse? To make us think we could track them by radiation?"

"The idea was to make us believe there was only one. That way we wouldn't be on guard for others. Kind of like *out of sight out of mind*. Governments tend to be that way."

"Do they expect a WMD at the President's speech?"

"All I know is that HS is advancing the theory of the second bomb."

"Okay, so what about the Korean connection? They obviously have a name and a location for him. Well, maybe not a name, but you said they knew he was here."

"Raided the place early this morning. Gone. Radiation was negative."

"So what's the plan?"

"Every CIA snoop in the world is working his or her ass off trying to uncover leads. Nothing so far."

"Bomb can be anywhere," I said, not really getting my heart into this. We had captured the top people. Our intelligence had confirmed that fact. "The Iranian handlers left the country. What's changed?"

"HS is going on the assumption that once the bomb was put in place, there was no further need for the handlers." Tiny's enthusiasm for the party line was as weak as mine.

"Find the igniter," I said, "you don't have to find the bomb."

"Trust me, they've turned the country upside down. Theory is the igniter never came into the country. They've been looking for possible material at every entry point. X-raying everything we can get our hands on. Bags, people, animals, you name it. Nothing."

"There's an all-hands meeting later today to deal with the issue."

"That why Jacobs wanted me east?"

"Got it."

"And they think I'll walk into the meeting and put a plan into place to find the igniter. Just like that."

"Not alone you won't. But a team working together might. I'll say this, they believe that if you—or somebody—doesn't find a solution, and if they're right about the bomb, then Angella's recovery will be a non-issue to everyone but you."

- - - - -

Angella was in a private room when we arrived back at the hospital. Her face from just below her eyes to her chin was covered with a white breathing mask. Her puffy eyes were closed. Her vital signs were improving. The nurse suggested she'd not be awake for at least a day. Like Mark had done with Trich, I chose to sit next to her. She didn't appear to be in pain.

Tiny excused himself to get some lunch, and I passed on his offer to bring me back a sandwich. I must have dozed off, because I had a dream that Mark Cruses' mother was in the room with me holding a wonderful-looking pie.

My eyes came open. Beside me stood Nora Cruses, tears running down her cheeks. "I didn't want to wake you, Jimmy. You looked like you could use the sleep. I thought I saw you walk down the hall, but it took some time to find the right room."

I stood and embraced her. "I suppose you've been to see Trich," I said. "She's had a rough time."

"Poor girl. That's so awful what bad people can do. Mark told me she fell down a flight of steps. But I know better. He forgets I was married to a Texas Ranger. I've seen far too many battered women."

"I'm sorry this happened to Trich," I said.

"Mark is beside himself. He doesn't want to leave her. He's thinking of resigning from the Coast Guard. Please, Jimmy, please don't let him do it. He's good at what he does. The country needs him. He's a good boy, always has been. A good boy."

"I'll talk to Mark, see what I can do," I promised, thinking all the while that he wouldn't be the first to put love above duty.

"I know Mark loves her. She's a nice girl, but…but you know, Jimmy, I think she comes from a not so good family. I love my son and I'll do everything for him. I only hope he knows what he's doing?"

"He's a good boy, Nora. He'll figure it out."

"If only his father was alive. He'd take care of it. My Mark would know what to do. Mark Jr. always listened to his father." Nora continued to talk, but tears and sniffling blocked most of what she was saying.

A few minutes later she stepped back and said, "I shouldn't be burdening you with my problems, Jimmy. Here," she said, reaching into her tote bag and producing one of her famous, at least in my circle of friends, apple pies. "This will cheer you up. Here, I'll just run and get some plates."

"Funny," I said. "I was dreaming of seeing you standing here with that pie. That's what woke me. Thank you. It's my favorite."

She bent and kissed my cheek.

"Now I have something to blackmail you with," Tiny, his deep voice in full throttle, said from the doorway. "A good-looking woman kissing you right in front of Angella."

"Guilty," I replied. I introduced Nora Cruses to the big guy, saying only that he was a friend.

"I'll cut you a piece of apple pie, Mr. Tiny," Nora said, "but you must promise not to eat it all. It's for Jimmy. Baked it special for him early this morning."

"I promise, Mrs. Cruses. Scouts honor."

"Be certain to eat only one piece and then keep away from the pie. Hear me?"

"Promise," Tiny said, a twinkle in his eye. "I promise."

Nora refused to join us in the pie and never once took her eyes from Tiny. I don't know if it was his size, or if she really didn't trust him.

- - - - -

"Brought you your book. Actually, I brought all the books you ordered," Tiny told me after Nora returned to Trich's room. "Should I read you a bedtime story while we're sitting vigil?"

I had forgotten about the books. I took the children's book from Tiny and flipped it open. Mostly pictures were inside, but enough words to teach me that a great number of objects circle the sun, but only one natural object, the moon, circles the earth. But the moon has company to the tune of over twenty-five hundred man-made satellites circling overhead. The satellites have many different shapes and range from large, such as the International Space Station, the one I had seen over the Gulf of Mexico, to some smaller than my car.

"If you enjoy children's books so much, I'll bring you a load of my kids' old books," Tiny chided, when I hadn't looked up in over twenty minutes.

"What if, and follow me on this," I began, "Timberwolf wasn't recording sun spots or whatever comes from outer space? And what if he wasn't recording nuclear control signals? What if he was recording satellite signals?"

"Where does that take us?"Tiny asked. "I'm not hearing anything that winds my motor?"

"That, my big friend, is what I don't know." I reached for the books Griff had sent over and settled back to try to absorb words I had never before heard. Words such as *geosynchronous*, *geostationary*, *earth's sidereal day*, *satellite's sidereal day*, and on and on. In high school, I had to crib from a friend to get through the physics class. Now I felt as though I was getting my Ph.D.

I thought I heard Angella say something and I quickly looked up. She had turned onto her side and was facing me, but her eyes remained closed. Her finger tips were curled around the edge of the cast. I put my hand on her exposed flesh. She was warm to the touch. Her eyelids still didn't move. After a few minutes I returned to my reading, fascinated thinking of how many man-made objects were floating above us.

"Want me to bring you something from the cafeteria?"Tiny asked. "I'm going down for coffee. Reading this stuff is making me sleepy. I don't understand most of it."

"Coffee works. Black."

"Griff sent along the most recent table of orbit times. It's that small book on the ledge."

I had a thought. Fumbling through the small book, I found what I was looking for. North Korea had, in fact, launched a satellite. But it was reported not to have attained orbit.

The language of that statement made no sense. Either it was up there or it wasn't. The world could know by simply looking. It's not as if satellites are invisible. I couldn't find any times listed for the North Korean satellite, so I assumed it had failed. Or as so much that happens with North Korea, it was a hoax. Iran had put one up a few years ago. That had possibilities, especially since the people who smuggled the bombs into the country were sympathetic to Iran—or perhaps being run by Iran.

Then something caught my eye. I had seen it several times in the past hour, but it hadn't registered. Several of the satellites were named Smol. There was VLAD1, VLAD2, VLAD4, VLAD5. VLAD3 seemed to be missing and I assumed it had been launched and, similar to the North Korean attempt, failed to gain orbit.

Unlike most satellites, the VLAD series were not over the equator. From what I had just learned, most communication satellites were either geosynchronous, meaning the satellite would be electronically visible at the same time each day to a particular location on earth, or geostationary, meaning the satellite would always remain at the same location with respect to any location on earth.

However, the VLAD satellites were neither. They were in low earth orbit, or LEO, meaning, and I checked this again to be sure, they would pass over a particular location on earth every ninety minutes. Because they were not over the equator, they seemed to pass over locations at random times. Also, because of their low orbit they were less expensive to launch and not particularly well-suited for two-way communication.

"What does it all mean?" Tiny asked, after handing me the hot coffee and listening to me summarize what I had found. "You've been at this for hours. I don't understand a thing you're babbling about. Geowhats and geowheres. Afraid I slept through physics or astronomy or wherever you're supposed to learn this stuff. What we need are some geohows. Kapish?"

"Damn if I know how," I absently replied, continuing to thumb through the little book of satellite times, concentrating on the VLAD series. The book was small, the numbers packed together, made it hard to follow. After a while I got the hang of how it was organized. I said to Tiny, "Dig out your computer, or your phone, and find me the latitude and longitude of the Padre Island National Seashore."

"You thinking some satellite will drop a bomb on the place? There's not much out there. You're out of your mind. Those drugs got to you, pal."

"Just do it. Besides, dropping things from satellites is impossible. Burn up."

"How precise?"

"Roughly."

"Twenty-six point six degrees north for latitude and ninety-seven point two west longitude. Mind telling me where this is going?"

Two events then occurred, driving all thoughts of satellites, and for that matter, almost everything else, from my mind.

First, Lucinda Westminster McNaughton strode into the room. Her head was barely inside the door when she barked, "So, Cowboy, you have your partner back. Word on the street is she'll have a full recovery. Kiss her goodbye. We have work to do."

Second, Angella called my name. Her voice was husky and weak. But my heart soared. My book of satellite locations fell to the floor as I leaped to her side.

THIRTY-SEVEN

I followed McNaughton's orders and kissed Angella. The only available space was on her check, but there couldn't be a doubt in anyone's minds that the kiss was anything but a demonstration of emotional love. "It's good to have you back," I said into her mask.

But her eyes were again closed. She didn't move.

"Goodbye, Angella. Be back soon." I blew her a kiss and reluctantly followed Cindy into the hall. Not because I wanted to, but because to do anything other than what McNaughton desired was employment suicide—perhaps even extending to Angella.

"Something big is going down tomorrow," McNaughton began, not wasting time with pleasantries, "and Tiny tells me you have alternate thoughts. Can't wait to hear them."

"You did what?" I said, addressing Tiny. "You've been feeding back everything I say to you?"

"I'm your liaison. Works both ways. That's my job. Suck it up."

"Why the hell you think he's down here, Cowboy? To drive you around—your chauffeur?"

Before I could answer, McNaughton turned toward the big guy. "Stay with her. When she comes around I want a full statement, beginning with her conversation with Trich and detailed from then until Snow, or whomever, knocked her out over in Port Isabel." Cindy handed him a small recorder with instructions to record every last detail. "Push this button, whenever you get to a part you think I should hear live. I don't need to be listening to hours of details. I can do that later. Just send me the important stuff live. It also sends video, so position this lens," she pointed to a pinhole in the side, "toward her."

"Kapish," Tiny responded.

Aye aye, sir, would have been the more appropriate response.

- - - - -

Cindy McNaughton had rented the Presidential suite in the *Peninsula Island Resort and Spa* on South Padre Island. An elaborate assortment of food and drink had been set out for us. There was enough for, dare I think it, the Russian army.

I knew how jealous Angella was about Cindy, and it made me uncomfortable being here alone with her. The last time we had been together it had been in her D.C. penthouse, and Angella was peeved even though Tiny had been there with me.

The door closed behind us and my discomfort increased. Not because McNaughton had communicated a desire for extracurricular activities, but because her manner immediately switched into what I would call command mode.

Her face set hard and her eyes burned with an intensity few people can muster. "Listen to me, Redstone," she began, "and lis-

ten well! I don't know what the hell's going on with all of this—
or with you. I have reason to believe you're focusing on Angella and not on Timberwolf. You think you can do what the hell
you want, when you want. Let me once again—and for the last
time—caution you that you can't. That bone-headed stunt you
pulled before the Port Isabel operation. If the SEALs had already
jumped we would have disabled you in your car and aborted the
operation. You could have put them in jeopardy. Understand me.
Bad things happen when someone goes off the reservation. Bad
things. I also know you've not kept me in the loop, at least not
directly. That stunt with the *Origins* records. And then with the
broken window at the house. You're not a team player." I started to respond, but she held her hand up. "Let's get this straight.
When my lips are moving, yours are to be still. Understand?"

I nodded that I did, but at the same time, contemplated walking away from all of this. But Angella remained in jeopardy and I
dared not do anything that would increase her risk.

"Good. You are to report directly to me. You can use Tiny or
Jacobs, but I want to hear it directly from your mouth to my ear.
You have a theory, tell me. Understood?"

"Understood."

"Now that we're on the same page, let's go over this from the
beginning. Senator Donnlevy was murdered. You're no longer
on that case. Caused enough focus on us as it is. It is my opinion,
shared by the President, that we have a number of Congressmen
who, shall we say, have a propensity for young women. Some of
those slimes have direct control of the HS and military budgets.
That will be taken care of in a less public forum than a criminal
investigation. We also have at least one other senator who is entirely too close to Santiago. That also will be dealt with. That's
not why I'm here. And it is not your mission,"

Her lips were still moving so I locked my mouth, knowing she would eventually let me know why she had come all this way. But before she could say anything, a beep sounded and her recorder came alive.

"How did Snow treat you?" Tiny asked, his voice conversational.

"Snow?"

"The man who kidnapped you."

"The tall man?" It was Angella's voice, but still husky and labored.

"Yes. Snow. You were with him."

"I was? I don't recall. It's hard to focus. There is so much I can't remember."

"Was he threatening or just forceful?" Tiny was in his element. I had the distinct impression this was not his first debriefing.

"He only got mean when a guy named Vlad came to the house."

"Vlad? Tiny's voice asked. "What's that about?"

'Came looking for a package."

"You certain it was Vlad Smol?"

"Just called him Vlad."

"Describe him to me."

"Small man. Talks with a funny accent."

"Hair?"

"Lots of hair. But...but now that you ask, seemed weird."

"In what way?"

"More than ...I don't know, just weird."

The voice cadence was wrong. Angella never called things *weird*. She would have described what she saw. I reminded myself she had been drugged, as I had been and I don't believe I sounded like myself for a while. Maybe still don't.

"Was Vlad part of the kidnapping?"

"He seemed surprised to see me at the house, but I'm not certain." Her head turned and I thought she was going to vomit. Then she turned back to face the recorder. "He was there to pick up something."

"Any idea what?" Tiny asked, smoothly moving to where Angella was taking him.

"Sorry. No."

"Size?"

"Small."

"Pack of cigarettes small?"

"Smaller. And flatter. Looked like a small radio. I mean a real small radio. And thin. Very thin."

"Quarter, dime, thin?"

"Silver dollar thin." Angella answered. Then she turned her head and lost whatever was in her stomach.

The screen went blank for a moment and when it came back live, Tiny asked, "Before you blacked out, what did you see? What was going on?"

"Something about an implant. Something was missing and the tall guy said something about a butt."

"This is important. Try to recall the exact words."

"I'm going to be...sick." Angella again turned her head to the side and again vomited into the bedpan. Tiny held out a cup of water and Angella sipped from the straw.

"Sorry. I'm nauseous. When I move my head it starts." She closed her eyes and went silent for a moment. Then she said, "Okay, I'll try this again. Vlad asked where the others were. Tall guy said he was keeping them. Vlad got angry. Tall guy said it was no use getting angry he had already dealt with them. They were out of his reach. Vlad then jumped up and down. Like a little kid he was jumping. He screamed something in a foreign language. The tall guy then told him to get the hell out of the house, the Feds were coming. Vlad wanted the other pieces. The tall guy said it had been implanted in the hostage, to get out. They yelled back and forth at each other. I think the small guy hit the big guy, but it's all so mixed up. I can't remember the order of things. I'm sorry. At some point the little guy grabbed me, hit me in the face and threw me down. He jumped on my back and dug his nails into my buttocks. I scratched his face. He grabbed my arm and I heard it snap."

I was sick listening to Angella's account. My anger now focused on Vlad Smol. He was a dead man walking.

"The big guy pulled him off, pushed him out of the room. He then carried me to the bed and stuck a needle into my stomach. The last thing I remembered hearing was a small boat motor starting.

The tape went off. Cindy said, "When there's anything more, Tiny will stream it."

"You were about to tell me why you're down here. I would think this is most unusual."

"Can't I take a vacation? Some time at the beach?"

"Then pardon me, but I seem to be interrupting."

"President is speaking tomorrow. Leaders from around the world will be on the dais with him. Secret Service, everyone else, except for you, believes our enemies are planning something big."

"Like a bomb being detonated during the speech?"

"Or more than one. In different locations."

"Then why not cancel the talk? Or move the location?"

"That's being considered. Everything's on the table. Since you chose not to come to D.C., D.C. came to you. You have a problem with that?"

"Of course, not," I answered, studying her eyes for any sign of amusement. Finding none, I continued, "You are welcome to babysit me wherever I am."

"I prefer to think of it as running the operation from the field. My Marine training coming to the fore, so to speak. The meeting begins in a few minutes. We'll participate from here. Using the TV and a military satellite connection. I believe you've used this set-up before."

"I'm not buying the detonation," I said, going out on a limb.

"And pray tell, why not?"

"Mainly, there's been no radiation detection. I know the theory that says the radiation from the first bomb was a ruse. Don't buy it. Couple that with there is no evidence of a connection between Vlad and any bomb, and any linkage between a bomb and Snow is tenuous at best."

"What about the Iranians?"

"They turned tail and ran. I know nothing about them."

"Got intelligence on a Korean. That's our primary focus."

"Hounds are following a plastic hare. Just saying."

"Angella just told us Snow transferred something to Vlad. Could be the detonator."

"Could be. But not for blowing a bomb in D.C."

"I'm not following."

"Vlad has invested tons of money in a defense system. The most likely buyer is Washington. We know he's broke, so making a sale is high on his priority list. Blowing up the government simply doesn't help him. In fact, if anything, it'll delay any possible deal."

McNaughton checked her watch. "Four minutes 'til conference time. Eat now if you're hungry and we'll talk later. Let's see what they have going."

I used the bathroom, poured myself a Coke, and took a slice of Brie. McNaughton flipped on the TV, listened to instructions on her cell phone, then tuned to channel three hundred.

We both sat on the sofa watching black dots flicker across the screen.

"Live in twenty seconds," came a female voice. "This is two-way transmission. Please place the cell phone where it will pick up both of your voices. During roll call take turns saying your respective names. We need a good sound print of your voice for validation purposes. It'll be automatic after this."

"They have your voice print on file from your previous conversations," McNaughton explained. "Your voice print, as well a mine, has been loaded into the conference bridge. Anytime during the conference if a voice print doesn't match the channel will immediately go down."

And a sniper team will take you out, is what I expected her to add.

"Three, two, one. You're live," the female voice announced. "South Padre Island has joined the conference. Please announce yourselves."

Cindy went first and I followed.

The screen came alive and I counted ten people, mostly men, gathered around a table. At least twice that number were scattered around the room. There were computers, cell phones, fax machines, printers, and a lot of equipment I didn't recognize, positioned everywhere. Electronic wires and cables snaked among the participants and it was a wonder anyone could move without tripping. Sylvan Jacobs was the only person in the room I recognized.

I had been in many such meetings, in many such rooms, and they always smelled worse than a circus tent after the elephants had performed. Remnants of food, from congealed pizzas to what I could only surmise was a half-eaten gyro, were hanging out of over-stuffed trash cans. Empty soda cans and water bottles lay in a pile in the far corner. This meeting had been going on for a while, or so it appeared.

An elderly grey-haired man, the only person in the room wearing a jacket, responded to a statement Jacobs had made by asking, "And how did you arrive at that tidbit?" the old gent asked.

"According to the tape from Tiny's interrogation of Angella, Snow had the devices at her house in Port Isabel, Texas. From phone records we know Vlad was there at two-fifty nine in the morning. Assuming one of them headed straight for D.C., a road distance of approximately eighteen hundred miles, that would put their earliest arrival in the Washington area at about eight tomorrow morning, assuming thirty hours driving straight through."

"They could be here already if they flew," somebody called out.

McNaughton put the cell phone on mute. "I suppose they're talking about how soon Snow or Vlad could get to Washington if one of them had the detonator. They're most likely debating how long they can wait before cancelling the President's talk."

Jacobs was answering the question when I returned my attention to the meeting. "...not a chance of any of them getting on a plane, commercial or private. Both Snow and Vlad are too distinctive to miss. Also, we've been monitoring videos from airports, highway restaurants, bridges, monuments, camp grounds, tollbooths, you name it. This is an all-hands operation. Everything recorded is being run through the computers and matched against their electronic profiles."

The grey-haired guy commented, "Snow's wanted for the murder of that girl, what's her name? Lulu Something?"

"Lissalou Keller," Jacobs responded. "Goes by Lou."

"Maybe not," I said, entering the conversation.

"Who's that voice belong to?" The old guy barked, his scowl growing even deeper. "And what's he doing on the line?"

Jacobs cut short what he was about to say and instead replied, "Deputy Director Kagan, please meet Jimmy Redstone. He's with Lucinda McNaughton on South Padre Island. They just joined by video conference at my request."

"Heard a bit about you, Redstone," Kagan said. "Your partner doing better now?"

"Yes, thanks. She's been drugged. Broken arm. But she'll be fine."

"Yes, we know. Just listened to her interrogation. Seems a bit confused. Doesn't remember critical aspects. She always that...that scattered?"

"Drugs doing the talking. When the drugs clear, she'll have more for us."

"Okay, carry on," Kagan replied, dismissing my defense of Angella.

Jacobs said, "Jimmy, you were saying..."

"Sorry, I lost my line of thought."

"You questioned whether Snow killed the Keller girl."

"I know his prints were in the room. And I know he's strong enough to have crushed her windpipe, but that's not his mode. He had Trich beat up in Mexico, but he didn't kill her. He drugged me and Angella and probably Trich. Could have easily killed all three of us. So why kill Lou? And why crush her neck when a simple shot in the head would have done the trick? Or an injection of drugs as he is want to do?"

"Motive we have is jealousy," one of the people at the table commented. "We're certain he and Lou were together sexually. She was pregnant and Snow may have assumed the child was the Senator's. Got mad. Lost control."

"Was it the Senator's?" I asked, knowing the answer, but wondering if they had all the facts.

"No," came the reply. "DNA didn't match."

"Did you try Snow's?"

"No DNA on Snow."

"Try his mother?"

"And just who would that be?" Kagan asked, leaning in toward the camera, his interest obviously peaked.

"Senator's wife," I replied. "That's my best guess."

"We have no proof Sarah-Jean is his mother," Jacobs quickly responded. "You're fishing."

Pressed to defend myself I remembered the flesh Angella had been clutching when we found her. "What does the trace from Angella's hand show?"

Jacobs reached for a phone, barked some orders and turned to me. "We'll rush the DNA, but it could take three days."

I replied, "Tell them to match the fetus against what come from Angella. I've seen it done in hours."

Jacobs issued more orders, hung up the phone and said, "Where you going with this?"

Before I could respond, Cindy put the phone on mute. "Didn't Angella say she scratched Vlad, not Snow?"

"Yes, but knowing Angella, she didn't lie still when she was stuck in the stomach with a needle. She must have scratched or grabbed at Snow as well."

McNaughton took our connection off mute and at the same time picked up my cell.

I answered Jacobs. "I'm positive Snow was the father of Lou's baby. He wouldn't have killed her. Let's see what the DNA brings us."

Cindy hit the mute button again just as Tiny answered the call from Cindy.

"Jimmy, I'm in the middle..." Tiny began, thinking it was me on the line.

Cindy cut him off. "It's McNaughton! Find out if Angella scratched or grabbed Snow when he was about to stick her with the needle."

"I went over this with her. She caught hair from Snow's arm, maybe some skin, but nothing certain. She's just not coming around. Memory seems messed up. Bit scattered. She's not sure what she did."

"I'll deal with that later." Cindy hung up with Tiny and returned her attention to the TV, where Kagan was asking, "If Snow didn't kill the girl, then where are we?"

"Been giving that a lot of thought," I replied. "What if we've got it backwards? What if—"

"Never mind young man," the deputy director barked, "we don't have time for witch hunts over some kid gets herself knocked up and nobody knows who the father is. We're here to stop a mass murder terrorist attack, not to solve a local murder."

Undeterred, I said into the phone. "A hair sample from Angella came from Snow. That's confirmed. The DNA will show paternity."

"Didn't you hear me? We're not here to worry about who the hell kidnapped your partner—or who the hell killed the girl. We're here to protect the country from mass destruction. We have only a few hours before all hell breaks loose. We have a consensus opinion here and you stand alone. So pardon me, but we're not about to waste any more time talking about tissue samples and who's related to whom!"

Did Sarah-Jean Donnlevy's reach extend all the way to Kagan? Cindy was watching me carefully, as if to warn me to remain calm. Considering my options, I forced a smile so that my words wouldn't sound harsh. "I'm sure you're close to solving the terrorist mess without me, so I'll drop off and let you get on with your work. Don't wish to be a distraction."

Cindy hit the mute button, but did not hang up. "Tantrums aren't tolerated in what we do. Kagan's focused on the President. That is top priority, make no mistake. Now get it out of your system and focus with us."

Within fifteen seconds Jacobs' name popped up on my cell. I debated not taking the call, but, considering McNaughton was watching me, I hit the ACCEPT button.

"I can't say as I blame you," Jacobs began. "He comes across as a pompous ass. But he's the boss. He'll get over it. As you rightly guessed, we're stymied."

"How the hell can we get anywhere with him interfering?" I demanded. "Truth is, I'm basically a loner. You've heard the saying, one riot, one Ranger. I'm miserable with people looking over my shoulder. Committees just don't solve crimes—or stop WMD attacks. Tracking these guys is not linear and can't be solved by taking votes."

"What the hell you doing working for Homeland Security? The Government is the ultimate committee process. But let me tell you straight. It does work. One person is not going to stop them. We have more resources than you can imagine pumping data into the war room as we speak. Good as you think you are, you couldn't possibly process it all even if you wanted to. So how about playing ball and stop pouting."

"I didn't ask for this. I didn't——"

"But you're up to your lashes in it. They got your partner, you got skin in the game."

Jacobs shocked me with the lightly veiled threat that unless I cooperated with them, played within their rules, Angella would be a forgotten issue.

"Listen, Jimmy. I like you. You might even be right on this. But fact is, Kagan must make a decision about the talk. He's in a hard place and we don't have support for him."

"Ever hear of gut reaction?"

"Not when the President is involved. Got to play it safe. No other way."

"Sorry for...for throwing what has been termed a tantrum. I'm settled now." I glanced up at McNaughton, as if to say, *have I repented enough?* "I'm trying to be a good soldier, but right now my heart's focused on Angella."

"We're wasting time. Where were you going with your line of thought? It's a bit off course, but truth is, we have no course."

"Hank Stetson, Senator Donnlevy's Chief of Staff and right-hand man. What do you know of him?"

"Personally, I dislike him and all that he stands for. But I have nothing to suggest he's involved in this in any way."

"Does a senator's chief get FBI or Secret Service scrutiny?"

"Yes, but no deep background, unless they're cleared for secret material. I don't recall that he's cleared."

"So we don't know what his politics are."

"Got to assume his politics match the Senator's."

"As far as it goes. The Senator was a good friend of Santiago, a top Mexican drug king. Snow expedites Santiago's drugs into the States from Mexico. Moves around with impunity. Maybe even supplies some folks on the Hill for all we know. Senate is briefed on the plans to fly Trich into the states and someone in Mexico finds out where she is and beats her worse than she was. Find out if Stetson was privy to the committee briefing. I'm betting Snow is, or was, being directed from the Senator's office."

"You insinuating Stetson's involved? In what?"

"Shit if I know! But tell me why the Senator's wife was in the District for the first time in years? Also, going back to our previous mission, we may not have cleaned house. Bet Stetson, sitting in for Donnlevy, was briefed on everything we did."

"Sarah-Jean most likely came to D.C. to drug her husband. We now know the old boy was about to cut her out of his will."

"You get that from Donnlevy's lawyer?"

"Not in so many words. He did say he was having discussions about a new estate plan, but nothing had been formalized yet."

"So where did you get the idea the will was about to be changed?" I asked.

"From Stetson."

"Roads all lead back to the man." Then a memory came to me. I saw Stetson striding purposefully across the lobby of the Hay Adams hotel toward the elevator as I stood watching from the entrance to the Lafayette Room as Snow walked out. "Stetson was in the hotel the night the Keller kid was strangled. Need to know why."

"I'm on it. Hold a sec." I heard him say to someone close to him, "Pick up Hank Stetson. Bring him here. All out alert. National security. Priority Red. Nix the warrant." Jacobs came back on the line. "So we get Stetson, what then?"

Jokingly I said, "Waterboard him!" I waited for Jacobs to comment. But when he said nothing, I continued, "Short of that, we have to determine what, if anything he knows about a bomb threat—and possibly the murder. I don't suppose we have enough for a search warrant?"

"Not under normal circumstances no," Jacobs answered. "But for National Security we might get a judge to spring. Bet we could if we limited it to his office only. I'll clear it with the Director."

"What about Deputy Geezer? He won't like you going over his head."

"I'll tell him what we need, and the man never makes these policy type decisions. He'll buck it upward. We'll lose a few minutes, but he's predictable. Predictable people can be worked."

The phone went dead before I could give Jacobs the next puzzle piece I had finally worked out. The numbers were still in line.

THIRTY-EIGHT

I unmuted McNaughton's phone and rejoined the conference call. Not because I wanted to be on the line with them, but because the next piece involved Angella and her well-being. I had been working and reworking the question as to why Snow had drugged Angella. I coupled that with Trich also being drugged and with the comment the doctor had made about Trich's first X-Ray being black, but the follow-up was clear.

Speaking with Eileen, the Brownsville hospital pharmacist cum sonographer, had reminded me as to how we had used sonographic imaging to locate the capsule Mark had swallowed.

Drug smugglers routinely use all of the body's orifices to hide contraband. It was my guess that the igniter material, which could for all we know be radioactive, was encased in a lead shield molded to fit in a body orifice.

The folks back at FBI headquarters were regrouping. I used that opportunity to call Tiny. After briefing him on my thoughts, I added, "I'm thinking Snow implanted something in Angella. Have the hospital run X-rays, or whatever else they have, and look for something not indigenous to the body. If they find anything, let me know. Don't remove it."

Movement on the TV screen caught my attention. Jacobs had come back into the room, but instead of going to the table, he walked to a corner and flipped open his cell. Almost immediately, my phone rang. "Director told Kagan you were on a special mission from the President. Told him to cooperate. You should have seen the old guy snap to attention. If this wasn't so serious it would be funny."

I then briefed Jacobs about my suspected implants in Angella. When I finished, Jacobs said, "Assuming the X-ray shows the igniter implanted in Angella, then we need to stop her at all costs."

I'm not sure it's an igniter as we know it. I mean for setting off A-bombs."

"Go on."

"From what little I know, in order to trigger a WMD a uranium ...call it bullet...is fired down a tube to hit a uranium target. What the hell good would it do to plant a uranium bullet in Angella?"

"To transport it," Jacobs responded halfheartedly, his mind seemingly on other things. "Continue."

"They'd have to then remove it and insert it in the weapon. Besides, I don't know for sure if it would be small enough to implant. Hey, you have a roomful of experts, have someone look it up."

Jacobs put the phone down and walked over to a short bald guy who looked like he'd do well to shed fifty pounds. Jacobs bent, said something which I assumed was the question I had asked, then listened to a reply. A moment later he was back on the line. "You're right on. Not a chance of the starter being small enough. Need to highly compress the two materials. The uranium must be fired at a high velocity. He assures me it's too large to implant."

"They could have an external gun, minus the uranium," I said, arguing against my theory. "But I think not. She's got an explosive in her, but not for A-bombs."

"You're going somewhere with this. Get there already."

"A high-power explosive has been implanted. When it's detonated she blows up anyone and everything around her. The implants came in from Mexico in a shielded case shoved down Trich's throat."

I could see Jacobs' troubled look. "That's why she wasn't injured worse than she was. They leaked that info on the Korean so we'd bring you and Angella back here as well."

"Drugs would wear off, she'd be out of the hospital, perhaps sitting in that very room with you."

"Blow us all to hell! And perhaps everyone in the building as well. And while the dust was settling they'd be free to—" Jacobs fell silent. His eyes closed, worry lines appeared across his forehead.

I remained silent as he worked though his own Sudoku.

Finally, he said, "Timing's wrong. Vlad came to Port Isabel to get them from Snow. He pitched a fit when he only got one."

"Correct. And one other was implanted in Angella."

"So Vlad had one. But, as you said, Vlad has no reason to destroy the government. We don't know about Snow."

"Snow is connected to Donnlevy. That means he's also connected to Hank Stetson, Donnlevy's chief of staff. Snow might be driving—"

"Just thought of something." Jacobs again put the phone down and bent to talk privately with a woman who had just come into the room. She turned and hurried back the way she had come.

Back on the line, Jacobs said, "You triggered something that hadn't made sense. Talk about not connecting the dots! The biggest support for getting Trich out of Mexico, and, might I add, of flying Angella up here, came from the Senator's office. I sent Matti to ferret out exactly who in Donnlevy's office was pressing us. If anyone can get the back story, she can."

"Let's focus on Vlad. He has one device, whatever it is. The other was implanted in Angella. If we assume the implant is explosive, then Vlad has an explosive device as well."

"That leaves one missing," Jacobs reminded me.

"Can't yet focus on what we don't know."

"Why do you suppose Vlad was so upset about getting only one?"

"Hell! Pieces are falling! Vlad's not going to Washington! He was upset about the device being implanted in Angella, so he doesn't care about blowing up Washington. That's Snow's mission, not his." My phone buzzed, interrupting my thought.

The display read, SONOGRAM IN TEN MINUTES. Tiny was keeping us posted. He was playing it straight—or as straight as his DNA allowed—for McNaughton.

I held the phone up so that she could see. I also relayed the news to Jacobs. He terminated our private conversation and moved to the table.

"Just obtained the Stetson warrant!" a woman, sitting at a small table at the side of the room, a headphone covering her ears, announced. "I could only see a portion of her face on the screen. "Judge limited the warrant to Stetson's private spaces only. Can't touch the Senator's offices."

Jacobs called out two names. "Get a team together and get over to Stetson's office as fast as you can. Logistics, have the D.C.

police block anyone from entering or leaving the office. I want full cooperation with the locals. Brief the police chief."

A few moments later the logistics man replied, "Marshals are standing by. Police Chief's been briefed. Assured us full cooperation. Uniforms dispatched."

"Good work," Jacobs barked. "Now we wait."

Jacobs' phone sounded. His shoulders slumped and his face fell. This was a man specially selected for running national security operations, and he was visibly reacting to the information being received.

At first I thought it was something to do with the bomb; perhaps it had even gone off. But from the way he studiously kept his eyes turned away from the camera I surmised it had to do with me.

"Put it on speakerphone," I said, "so the rest of us can hear."

Jacobs hit the speaker button and said, "Repeat what you just told me."

Tiny's voice filled the room. "Sonogram's negative. Nothing anywhere in her body."

Jacobs said, "Need to rethink this from the beginning. We're halfway to hell and still digging."

"I'm positive it was implanted," I said. "All the numbers are right. Angella told us about the..."

My normally steady heart rate spiked. A wave of nausea hit me and I slumped back onto the sofa. My first thought was that the drugs hadn't fully cleared my system. My second thought: heart attack.

The nausea deepened. I bent forward, thinking I was about to give up lunch. Shivers ran down my body. But I felt no pain, only an elevated pulse.

McNaughton, flipped the TV off, pressed two fingers against my neck. "You need help? You're white as a sheet."

I tried to wave her off, but the gesture was feeble and made it worse. She reached for her cell.

I held up my hand and tried to stand. My knees were tentative. I slumped back to the sofa. "Drugs," I mumbled. "Don't mix well with adrenalin. Give me a moment." I was floating outside my body, an observer and not a player.

McNaughton, ever the general, said, "Suck it up, Cowboy. Get on with dying, or let us in on what the hell has you so agitated."

I leaned back, closed my eyes and prayed for the light-headedness to fade. I sat that way for a moment, not moving.

"Turn it back on," I managed, waving my arm in the general direction of the TV. "We all need to work this."

The picture, faint at first, came into sharp focus. Kagan was back and the table was full of people.

"What's wrong, Jimmy?" Jacobs asked. "You folks cut out. Technicians are working it. Everything okay?"

McNaughton responded, "We're fine. Just doing some thinking is all." She muted the connection. "Sit up," she commanded. "You look like you've just blown your own foot off."

I shifted forward on the sofa and my head remained clear.

"You ready?"

I nodded and the connection went live again.

"Is Tiny still on line?" I managed to ask.

"I'll get him back. What is it?"

"What a slow-witted fool I've been! Tell Tiny I want Angella's fingerprints."

Jacobs relayed the instructions, then asked, "What prompted that?"

"It's been there all the time," I admitted. "Faulty memory, lack of detail, everything!"

"What are you talking about? Kagan asked, his manner still edgy, but more deferential than before. It didn't appear as if he was about to give me much rope.

"It's not Angella! It's her sister! Name's Jayme Partridge. Fooled me when I first met her."

"You're telling us Angella remains missing," Kagan snapped back. "And most likely on her way up here. We've wasted entirely too much time already. I want her found—and stopped—at any cost. We're at war. She's to be treated as an enemy combatant. Shoot her if necessary."

I jumped to my feet. If he had been in the same room we would have had it out. As it was, McNaughton again turned the TV off. "My, you're feisty," she said. "Sit down before you fall over. Work through this logically. Half-cocked won't get us there."

Instead of responding, I called Tiny. "Make this simple. Ask her her name."

"Hold a minute. I was just bringing up the fingerprint app. Put you on speaker. Ask her yourself. Go ahead."

"This is Jimmy. Can you hear me?"

"Yes," came the still husky voice. "Hear you fine."

"What is your full name?"

Without a moment's hesitation, she replied, "Jayme Partridge."

"When did you last meet me?

"Met you only once. At Angella's house. You thought I was my sister. When we were young we did that to boys all the time. What's this…"

I snapped the phone closed.

"Confirmed," I told Cindy. "Get them back on line."

I had a thought, and Jayme was the one person outside Angella who might have the answer. I again dialed Tiny's number and asked him to get Jayme back on the line.

When she announced herself, I said, "Jayme, one more thing. Think hard back to when you saw the little guy at the house."

"I told Tiny—"

"Here's what I need to know. Did Vlad, that's the small guy, did he by chance have a wound on his neck or on the back of his head?"

"He was wearing a wig of some sort. Tiny showed me pictures of him bald. But he had hair."

"Below the hair line. Did you—"

"Come to think of it, I did see something that could have been a bandage. But it was mostly covered."

"Where was this something?"

"On his neck near the back."

"If you recall anymore, please tell Tiny. Hope you feel better soon."

The conference came live again and I said, "It's confirmed, Angella is not at the hospital. It's her sister. Must have gone there to wait for...no, that's not it. She was kidnapped from the island by that guy Buffalo Bill." I was giving the D.C. war room more information than they needed. For them, the important fact was that Angella was still missing—and had something implanted in her butt. Something most likely explosive. She now had a target painted on her back as far as national security was concerned.

"Kidnapped," Kagan said, "implies that they wanted Jayme caught. Knew about the raid. Set her up as a decoy."

"Important point is, Angella remains captive," I needlessly reminded them.

"Important point is," Kagan snapped, "she's now a danger to our country."

I started to react, but McNaughton's steel-eyed look reminded me to remain calm. Clearly, Kagan was baiting me, and like a hungry fish I was snapping at the hook.

Jacobs then said, "On another front, preliminary DNA on the samples obtained from Angella...I guess Jayme... shows a match to the Keller fetus. I remind you, this is preliminary. These tests take days to verify with any degree of accuracy. However, I think it is safe to assume either Snow or Vlad is the baby's father. Have no way at this point to know one DNA from the other. Both were under her nails."

"I'm muting this end for a few minutes," I announced. "Need to speak with Sarah-Jean Donnlevy in private. Don't want to spook her."

I placed the call, but it went to voice mail. I did not leave a message.

I tried to refocus, knowing Angella's life depended on clarity. But the specter of failure loomed large, making it difficult to concentrate.

Kagan, who had been busy on his cell phone, now said, "CIA has confirmed activity suggesting an operation is underway. Also, several ambassadors have asked whether tomorrow's ceremony will be canceled. The White House is considering moving the conference to Camp David, but that might not be workable. State is working that now."

"Any suggestions?"

Nobody said anything.

"Hearing nothing," Kagen announced, "I believe we have no real choice other than to cancel the President's speech—and cancel the conference. I'm recommending that the world leaders be moved to a safe location. If anyone wishes to voice opposition, now is the time."

Kagan looked around the table. No hands were up. He then looked directly into the camera. "And you, Agent Redstone. Do you think I'm being too hasty?"

The magnitude of the catastrophe if an atomic bomb went off in the nation's capital was too large to comprehend, my mind too small. "No, sir," I managed, not believing for a moment that he really cared what I said. "But I do have one question."

"Please enlighten us as to what is now troubling you?"

"Up to this point the President has been reluctant to fess up to an atomic weapon being smuggled into the country. Won't hustling all the dignitaries into hiding force the issue?"

Kagan glared into the camera. "Not if State can provide a plausible reason. The CIA intelligence is sufficient reason, I should suppose. No need to go into the WMD aspect."

Call me selfish, call me what you will, all I could focus on was how to save Angella. And I wasn't doing a very good job at that. I addressed Kagan. "I cannot say with any certainty that your assumption of danger is incorrect." I slumped against the arm of the sofa, my energy sapped.

Nothing made sense.

THIRTY-NINE

Jacobs studied his computer, then looked toward the camera. "President just ordered the military to full alert. The Heads of State and certain other foreign dignitaries are being moved to an undisclosed location. Several dignitaries have departed the country. Public has not been informed. I don't yet know what reason was given for cancelling."

Muting our end, I turned to Cindy. "I've spent my working life chasing petty crooks and embezzlers, sometimes even murderers, but that all seems tame compared to tracking these... these fanatics. It's depressing to realize that any one of these nutballs can destroy everything we care about. And we always seem to be a half-step behind."

Cindy didn't answer at first. Nothing in her demeanor yielded a clue as to what she was thinking—or feeling. A slight smile formed. Or perhaps it was just the relaxation of her taut facial muscles. "We all go through what you're feeling." Her tone was softer than I had expected. "The fact is, Cowboy, the better you are professionally, the worse this hits you. But know this, I've worked with these folks a long time, seems forever, and I must say the odds are in our favor. Great minds make up for the, as you put it, the half step they have on us. Everyone in that room, and I mean everyone, would lay down his or her own life for this country. Even Kagan, in his own way, is rock solid. The man's not a fool. He gets results. There might be twenty folks visible in that room, but there's over three hundred agents working this right now around the world. Not to mention the military. It's a total team effort. No one promised it would be easy, but we're not backing down."

I turned the sound back on. Kagan was asking a question directed at me pertaining to the explosive implants.

I patiently went over what I had earlier told them.

Kagan then surprised me by saying, "You could be onto something Agent Redstone. There's a recent report from Britain on implants. Been putting explosives in breasts as well as buttocks." Kagan then looked directly into the camera. "Sorry, old chap," he said, "got myself carried away before. I understand you are formerly a Texas Ranger. I'm formerly from Britain, MI Six. Seems a lot of us are imports these days."

"Takes all kinds," I answered, accepting his comment at face value.

Jacobs said, "Kagan, you're the expert on explosives. Tell Redstone what you told us earlier."

"The breast and buttock implants use PETN. Stands for pentaerythritol tetranitrate. It's an extremely powerful explosive, been used since World War One, actually. About five point one eight kilojoules per gram. Stuff's placed inside the implant bag in place of the silicone gel customarily used for augmentation implants. Even a few grams could open a hole in an airplane."

"That explains the codeine," I mumbled. The codeine was actually found in Jayme, not Angella. But I assumed Snow used the same drug combination on both.

The logistics man, Eric, announced, "The team's in Stetson's office. Got his hard drive. Going through his files. Nothing important yet."

My cell rang. The voice said, "Jimmy, its Abby."

I was slow to respond, my mind being elsewhere.

"*Washington Post.*"

"Oh, Abby," I replied, not as happy to hear her voice as I made it sound. "This is not a good time. I'll call you back." *On the other side of never*, I added to myself.

"It's never a good time. I know what's going on. My sister-in-law's down there with you. So don't give me the *tomorrow* routine."

"I'm in the middle of something. I'll ca—"

"I deal in relationships. Who knows who, that sort of thing. You promised me an exclusive, just a two-hour lead, just confirm that's still our deal and I'll give you what I have on Hank Stetson."

"Hank Stetson?"

"Don't play dumb, Redstone! FBI's tossing his office as we speak. They won't find anything useful. The man's in deeper than you can imagine. He hides it well. Lots of practice."

"You have your story, run with it."

"I've been working on this for months. I know about Donnlevy's dealing with drugs. Took me a while to key on Stetson. Underage sex is just the tip. But as far as I can piece together, drugs are not what the Senator did, despite his friendship with Santiago. But Stetson's another story. He's not what he seems to be. Donnlevy loved his country. Stetson's been a low-level agitator his whole life. Hides behind somebody of power. Then

Donnlevy suddenly drops dead and leaves Stetson high and dry. Took away his cover, if you will. Everything's blowing up in his face. Pardon the pun."

"Deal's still on. Now what do you have?"

"For starters, Stetson's been running a major drug cartel from the Senator's office. No reason to believe the Senator knew. Also, and this is what triggered my investigation in the first place, he's the half-brother of your former secretary, or whatever her title was, at Homeland Security. The one orchestrating the terrorist activities." She paused to allow that to sink in. "No reason to believe Stetson was in league with her, but it makes sense if he was."

"Didn't the FBI check him out after that incident?"

"My sources tell me he's clean with respect to terrorist activity. It's touchy investigating the man who runs the Senator's office. Senator might have intervened. FBI might have gone light."

It tied together. Stetson's connection to Santiago through the Senator may have facilitated smuggling bombs and people into the country. Santiago himself being allowed to leave the country after he was caught now made sense. Politics can explain a lot.

"I take it from your silence I hit a cord."

"Did you ever," I replied. "Did you ever!"

FORTY

Sarah-Jean Donnlevy was holding on the line. Logistics had found her and she had reluctantly agreed to speak to me. I had no idea what coercion they used, but it worked. "Thank you for taking my call," I said, trying to start off on the right tone. Out of the corner of my eye I saw Cindy McNaughton pick up the extension phone.

"They said it's a matter of national emergency, or some such thing. Mind telling me what's going on and what this has to do with me or my deceased husband? You are becoming a real pain in the you-know-what."

"You may hold the key to a major problem. Suffice it to say, time is critical."

"I can't imagine what I have that can be so damn important."

"I need to know from you—and I need you to be honest with me—just why you visited your husband."

"I told you, to support his effort with the legislation. Get off it already!"

I wasn't buying it, but badgering her wasn't the way forward. "Did you know your husband was terminally ill?"

Silence.

Did that mean she had known? Or not known? Then she surprised me by saying, "Kidney failure. He asked me to come so he could say a proper goodbye. He wanted to die here in Texas, at home, on the property he loved so much. But he refused to leave Washington before the vote. His duty to his country meant more to him than anything else. He was feeling poorly and didn't think he'd make it beyond the week. Doctors wanted to put him in the hospital. He wouldn't hear of it."

She fell quiet and I waited, invoking the old adage that he who speaks next loses. She had more to say and I was determined to wait her out. When she spoke, it was with a different voice, perhaps the voice of her younger years. "You know how it is when you've known someone a long time. To me, twelve years is a long time. I sensed he had something important to tell me, something other than goodbye. I just knew."

"So, did he?"

Again the silence.

"Please, Mrs. Donnlevy, we need to know."

Her voice was barely audible over the background din coming from the TV war room. I covered my open ear, trying to be sure I didn't miss what Sarah-Jean Donnlevy was saying. "He cheated on me, you know. But to tell the truth, I've not been a perfect angel myself. But despite his tastes, he was a good man."

"Was he involved in drugs? Using or running?"

"Good God, never! I know his friend Santiago was a drug Lord. Mathew tried to persuade Santiago to stop, but he was in far too deep. Said they'd kill him if he stopped. I tried to warn my husband on several occasions to move away from Santiago, but he wouldn't hear of it. To Mathew, a friend was a friend."

"Did you talk to the Senator about drugs, or anything connected with Santiago, when you last saw him?"

"Yes, well I was going to anyway. He died before I could say anything."

"What was on your mind in that regard?"

"I got wind of something going on, something very different. Maybe it's what you're after, I don't know."

"What did you hear?"

"Bombs. Devastating bombs, smuggled in from Mexico with terrorists."

"How did you learn of the bombs?"

"I won't talk about that."

Now that I knew she had knowledge of the bombs, we could hold her as a material witness, interrogate her at length. But the timing wouldn't work. The adamant quality of her refusal to discuss the bomb source indicated someone close to her. Something very personal. I changed the topic. "What do you believe he wanted to tell you?"

"About the baby."

"What baby?"

"The poor girl that was murdered, her baby."

What about the baby?"

"I believe he wanted to tell me it was not his."

"Why would he think you'd believe him? Like a deathbed thing?"

"I already knew it wasn't his."

This caught me by surprise. "How did you know that?"

The line went silent.

"Mrs. Donnlevy," I pleaded, "we have precious little time left. I need—"

"I've said too much already. Good night, Mr. Redstone."

The line went dead.

McNaughton, walking across the room to join me, said, "How do you suppose she knew about the bombs and the baby?"

"Snow had to be the link. The baby's father was Snow. Sarah-Jean Donnlevy knew about the baby because she was the baby's grandmother."

"That's one huge leap of faith Cowboy," Cindy said. "I'm not certain all the pieces fit. For example, how would the Senator even know about the child if the baby wasn't his?"

"Blackmail. Someone was blackmailing him. My guess, if I had to guess, Stetson. Now we need to test the theory. See if the numbers hold."

"What numbers?"

"Long story," I said. "Sarah-Jean may have known about the terrorists because Snow told her. Or possibly she overheard Snow—or Stetson—talking. They may have used her house for stopovers."

"My sister-in-law published that piece about the terrorists. Maybe Sarah-Jean got it from the article and put two and two together."

"Possibly. But I don't recall the article talking about WMD." I stopped talking. It was time to think. Snow didn't kill Lou Keller. She was carrying his baby. Lou was killed because she knew something she shouldn't have known.

I unmuted Cindy's cell phone and said to the logistics guy, "See if they found checkbooks in Stetson's office. I'm looking for one with the name of Keyston Jenkins in it. Sometimes called Keys. But I want all of his checks and the sooner the better. And I want lease documents." I then said to Jacobs. "That slime Jenkins, the so-called Facilitator, said he delivered the girls to a Georgetown pad. That could be where they're holed up. If they're in D.C. at all."

Jacobs immediately ordered a SWAT team, FBI, local police, Drug Enforcement, Secret Service, anyone he could muster to set up a command in Georgetown. Not the most convenient place to plant a bomb for devastating the Capital, but close enough.

Eric the Logistics guy came on the line. "The account information, as well as the lease documents, is on the hard drive. Unfortunately, it's encrypted with a sophisticated code. They've been working on it with no luck. They've called in NSA, nothing yet."

"Thanks," I replied. "You guys following the hunt for Angella?"

"Sure thing," Eric replied.

"Any sightings?"

"Nothing yet."

McNaughton's recorder buzzed. It was Angella's, actually Jayme's, voice from earlier in the day. She was saying, "...yes, I said Vlad was in the house. But he left before Snow. I never saw Snow leave. He stuck the needle in my stomach, that was it. I woke up here."

"Do you know why Vlad was there?"

"They were arguing. Not arguing really, but more like talking at each other. Snow seemed to be withholding something that Vlad wanted."

"Do you have any idea what that something was?"

"Vlad was upset. At one point he said, but what if this one doesn't work? Give me the others."

"And then what happened?"

Cindy's receiver showed a time lapse of ten minutes before the next response came from Jayme. Tiny had edited out the trivial.

"Snow told Vlad not to worry, that the receiver was set for the right frequency. All he had to do was get the coordinates right and the timing would be right."

Then there was another long pause. Jayme then said, "Now I recall what else he said."

"Snow or Vlad?"

"Snow. He said that as long as it didn't rain, the receiver would work fine. And that even if Vlad had all three receivers, any rain would kill them all anyway."

"And now that I have the recorder on tell me again what Vlad replied to that." Tiny was coaching Jayme.

"I'm sorry I didn't remember this before. It's all so...so hazy. Vlad got upset again. He yelled that Snow was a fool. Didn't know half what he should. Said the timing was different."

"Then what did Snow say?"

"Snow said it was too late. One was implanted in her butt and the other went east. Out of his control. Make do with one."

"Vlad then asked why I, he referred to me as that Martinez bitch, was still here and not going back east according to Stetson's plan."

"Change of plans. Bastard killed my girl. Stetson's finished."

"Vlad then said to take it out of her. Said you don't need the implant now that plans have changed."

"What did Snow say?"

"Told him to make do with the one he had. He, Snow, had made new plans for the bitch. That was his word, not mine."

"What happened then?"

"The little guy hit Snow in the stomach. I thought Snow would deck him. But Snow stepped back and told him if he did it again he'd drug him, leave him for the Feds."

"Then what did Vlad do?"

"Nothing at first. He sat on the floor like a little child with his head in his hands. Then he jumped up and hit me. Pushed me onto the bed and started scratching at my butt. Snow pulled him off. Told him to get out of the room. That's when Snow stuck me with the needle."

My cell rang. It was Tiny. "Did you receive that?"

"We did."

"Only thing I can add is that Vlad is disguised. I just spoke to Logistics at the war room. Have them looking at airport surveillance tapes. If he flew, we'll find him. Jayme's mind is mostly clear now. Hospital wants her overnight for observation. Other than her broken arm, they say she'll be fine. She's got nothing more for us. I'm packing up here and coming over. Where are you?"

I told him. Then added, "I suppose cooling your heels in this pad is better than waiting there."

"Nothing to do here. Got two uniforms standing guard. Jayme's got nothing more to tell us. I have the books you left. You still want them or should I just dump them?"

"Bring the pie."

"What pie?" The line went dead, like it always did when these guys didn't want to hear about it.

I had forgotten the books. Something flicked through my mind. The thought evaporated before I captured it. I paced the floor trying to fit the last of the numbers, but nothing made.

Tiny walked in about an hour later. One look at the TV and he said, "Nice choice of programs. Any significance to the empty table?"

Frankly, I hadn't noticed the meeting had adjourned. Deputy Director Kagan, despite his new attitude toward me, was not someone I cared to work for. His lack of concern for Angella had cast him with the bad guys.

"I'm hungry," Tiny announced. "That tray looks stale. Mind if we take an hour and get something fresh?" He glanced around, as if to check on McNaughton's presence. Lowering his voice, he said, "You look like you could use some time away. Blow the stink off you. Get us a few beers. Kick back. Kapish?"

The time was ten-thirty. Kicking back had low priority with me. All I wanted to do was focus on getting Angella back safely. But escaping from the clutches of the general held an attraction. I thought about asking her permission, but I could hear her talking on the phone. I assumed it was Jamison on the other end and she wouldn't miss me.

We headed up island about a mile to a place called *Padreritagrill SPI*. It was late, but there were still people at the bar. Two tables of folks were finishing and paying their bills. I said to the hostess, a slim woman wearing glasses two sizes too large, "Still serving dinner?"

"Order fast. We'll make it for you."

"Two of your largest steaks," Tiny said over my shoulder. "Baked potato for him, fries for me. Skip the salad. Bring two Buds."

"Bud okay with you? Or you sticking with your Skinny Bones?" We had settled at a table in the far corner. The place was arranged as an outdoor backyard and felt comfortable.

"Bud'll work," I replied. "But what if I wanted a Bones?"

"I'd drink them both. Order what the hell you want."

"Frankly, the way I feel it wouldn't make any difference if it were rat poison."

"Back at the hospital you were talking about satellite stuff. You had an idea and then Cindy interrupted. I poked through those books of yours. Nothing spun my prop."

That conversation seemed so long ago. Took me a few moments to reorient. "Forgot about that thread. That loner Timberwolf was out there recording something."

"What's your thinking on that?"

"The obvious is recoding extraterrestrial signals like Professor Butter...Buttercroft seems to believe. Singh says Timberwolf also recorded the control frequencies from the nuclear power plant."

"Planning to blow up the reactor?"

"Not likely. The recordings he made were of something in space. He happened to catch the control frequencies."

"So why was he killed?"

"He happened to catch the control frequencies." I gave Tiny time to react, but he just worked on his beer.

"Someone didn't want anyone to know about the frequencies, so they killed him and tried to take the recording."

"You think for one moment our reactors are vulnerable to every kook who comes along and knows the frequencies? I hardly believe that can be true."

"That's just it. They're not vulnerable at all. This nuclear link could just be a figment of our paranoia."

"Speaking of paranoia," Tiny said, "I suppose you know Kagan cancelled the President's talk and moved everyone of importance to a safe location. The man is a bore sometimes. But he gets results."

Cindy had said the same thing about Kagan. Sounded to me like the party line. "I'm not buying a WMD in Washington. If so, what the hell's Snow doing down here?"

"We don't really know where Snow is," Tiny reminded me. "We also don't know where Vlad is—or what he's up to. For that matter, we don't even know where Angella is."

"Consider this. Jayme said Snow gave Vlad one of the three somethings. Vlad was upset he didn't also get the backups. What did she say Vlad said? You remember his exact words?"

Tiny extracted a small notepad from his pocket. "I don't keep much on paper any more, but that part Jayme was saying about the exchange between Vlad and Snow caught my attention." Tiny flipped a few pages, found what he wanted and then began to read. "*You have the backup. Give it to me.* That was Vlad speaking. Then Snow said something and Vlad responded, *But what if this doesn't work?*" Tiny studied his notes a moment, then added, "After I prompted her she recalled, and I quote, *Snow told Vlad not to worry, the receiver was set for the right frequency. All he had to do was get the coordinates right. You'll be close enough.* There was another part to that. Here it is. Vlad said, *As long as it didn't rain, the receiver would work fine.*"

"There it is again. The word frequency. That's what Timber-wolf was recording, frequencies. It's all connected."

"I agree. But how?"

"*Close enough?* To what? Coordinates suggest a location."

"Didn't you ask me for the coordinates of the seashore where Timberwolf was killed?"

"And where he recorded the nuclear control frequencies."

Two twenty-four-ounce Texas-size steaks were placed on the table and I jokingly told the waitress that I've caught crooks who didn't stand that tall. She didn't think it was funny and neither did Tiny.

Tiny finished his and about half of mine. His beer morphed into a pitcher.

Tiny signaled for another pitcher. I waived the waitress off. "You planning on sleeping here at the table tonight? I can't carry you back. I'll be lucky to get my own ass home."

"We staying with Madam General? Or we going to your crib?"

"I've worn out my welcome. Unless she calls, we're going to my place."

"Then fill her up," he said, apparently he was only willing to forgo the alcohol if we were going back to the Presidential Suite. Tangling with the General was bad enough with full control. Not even Tiny wanted to try it half-polluted. He held up the empty pitcher and waved it overhead.

"Never mind. Let's head back. Got work to do."

As if on schedule, both my phone and Tiny's rang almost simultaneously.

Mine was from Cindy, informing me that an animal surveillance video from a place called Laguna Atascosa caught Snow and possibly Angella. The video was routinely archived in Washington and in the process the image match detector flagged Snow. She forwarded me the clip, which turned out to be only a few frames in which I saw almost nothing I recognized. Cindy then said, "Atascosa is a large natural wildlife preserve just north of Port Isabel. The preserve is run by the Fish and Wildlife Service and is about sixty-five acres of both dry and wetlands. Got that from the internet."

"Do we know when the video was taken?"

"It's collected locally and then sent to the archives. I understand not long ago. It will take some time to analyze the footage, but I have it on good authority it was taken this morning between seven and eight."

That was about fifteen hours ago. "Do we know where in the sixty-five acres this was shot?"

"No one will commit. I've been waiting for the head honcho, but I'm now told he's out of the country. The intern in charge over there won't comment, claims it's against some policy or another. I've escalated it to the Secretary of the Interior. He's a friend, and is working it. But it'll take someone who really knows the terrain to watch the video and pinpoint the location close enough to mount an operation. Do it wrong and…"

McNaughton didn't have to be any more graphic. It didn't take much to visualize the explosives implanted in Angella going off, blowing her and anyone close to her into oblivion. I said to her, "I imagine there are a lot of locals who know the area. The charter captains must know their way around."

"I've been on the Internet. Found a great site called *southpadretv.tv*. Tracked down the proprietor, a local character named Steve Hathcock. According to him, the most promising name is a woman known as the Dolphinwhisperer from the *Sea Life Nature Center* in Port Isabel. She's an expert on wildlife, photographer and a writer as well. She and her husband Captain George run a dolphin watching charter service."

"How do I find this woman? We don't have time to waste on goose chases."

"Can't reach her. Hathcock believes she's out of the country. Second best is an old salt, goes by the name of Myangel Lopez. Boat's called *Captain L*. Runs a fishing charter service, mostly up in the area of Laguna Atascosa."

"Got her number? I'll call—"

"She's waiting for you at her boat. On your right at the base of the causeway bridge. Park in the lot and walk out onto the pier. She'll find you."

Tiny and I were in sync. His call ended when mine did. "So what do you have?" I asked.

"Jacobs. Short version. Vlad rented a fishing boat at Port Mansfield at five this morning. Said he'd be out all day. Turned the boat in just before noon."

"Port Mansfield. That's near—"

"The National Seashore. The boat suffered damage to the rudder. Possibly because of grounding. Vlad was charged the repair. Charge card declined payment, only that was two hours later. Boat company called the police. Vlad's name came up on the person-of-interest register. Locals called FBI. Sometimes we get lucky."

"So why didn't we have this info ten hours ago when it happened?"

"You don't want to know," Tiny said. "You just don't want to know."

"Yes I do."

"Went on the bottom of the pile. Just a screw up's all. Feds are usually incredibly on top of things like this. But sometimes— and I mean only sometimes—they screw it up. This is one of those *sometimes*. Let it alone."

I was listening to Tiny, but having a hard time focusing. When he mentioned the National Park, I thought of the coordinates he had looked up. Then I thought of the satellites. I was trying to factor in how they could be used to disrupt things. But my real concentration was on Angella and the explosive primed to explode at any time. Kagan had been right when he suggested Angella was my main focus.

In reality, she was my only focus.

- - - - -

Captain Lopez, a squat no-nonsense woman with skin tanned to leather, stood at the head of the dock. We introduced ourselves and she said, "Who was that woman on the phone? Dealt with some tough characters in my life, but hate to meet her on a dark night. She'd make a great pirate. Just saying."

"Former Marine General," I replied, not wanting to open the tent much further. "Mind looking at a quick video? Just take a few seconds."

"That's what she said. We can do it here, or on the boat."

"Here works."

"Go for it."

I turned my cell to face her and said, "What do you see?"

"Went by too fast. Play it again."

I ran the video four times in regular motion and then twice in slow motion before she said, "Definitely, there's a man. There's a woman also. She's not moving."

"Do you know where the video was taken?"

"The sea grass indicates Laguna Madre, about five to seven miles north of here. Evidence of fresh water as well. Terrain suggests Laguna Atascosa. Yes, I'd say the national park."

"Remarkable," I replied. "Anything else?"

"Video may have been shot with a trip camera. They use them for observing the *leopardus pardalis albescens*."

"Translate, please."

"Ocelots. They're tracking ocelots up there. I volunteer on Thursdays. Motion trips the cameras. Those cameras use fast timing to get more shots per second. A few years ago they caught a mother ocelot with her kittens."

"Can you pinpoint the location?"

"There are only a few places where fresh and salt water are so close. Come out to the boat and I'll show you on the chart." We walked along the pier past several men and just as many women leaning against the railing or sitting in camp seats watching their dangling fishing lines. We walked past the hulking silhouette of the Black Dragon, a mock pirate ship used for sightseeing excursions in Laguna Madre. It was moored off to our right.

Captain L's boat sat bobbing gently midway down the pier, large fishing poles extending out over the stern. "Mostly for show," she said when she saw me eying the rigs. "They're for offshore work, and most of my charters are in the bay. Lady kingfish tournament is when we use them most."

I followed her below while Tiny waited on deck. He wasn't comfortable forcing his large frame into such a limited opening. A large chart was spread open on the navigation table. Lopez, after careful scrutiny, marked two locations. "Here or here," she said confidently, "can't be anywhere else."

"What are the exact coordinates of those locations? Give me the most likely one first."

"Not a problem. Live by coordinates."

Five minutes later Tiny had the lat/long numbers of the two locations saved on his cell. We thanked Lopez, brushed off her invitation to charter her boat, and headed back to the island. Tiny drove because I was beyond exhaustion.

Tiny briefed Jacobs on our visit with the Captain and I extracted a promise from D.C. that at first light they would perform aerial reconnaissance.

Jacobs called back before we were across the causeway to tell me the Coast Guard would overfly the area within the hour with heat imaging sensors.

"Is he serious," I asked Tiny when the line went dead, "or are they placating me?"

"You brought Jacobs into this, not I. He's your man. You tell me."

"He's FBI's man. Does what they tell him. They can paint an American flag with his blood."

"We all do what the Man tells us. Angella is only one of many priorities at this moment."

FORTY-ONE

At five in the morning, my cell rang. Jacobs had an update.

"Snow called Pittsburgh," Jacobs said. "Took us a while to gather the information, but about two hours ago he called Lou's father, Smith Keller. Apologized for missing the funeral and vowed to avenge her death."

"You didn't call for that," I replied. "You have more to that story? Or are you just checking up on me?"

"Call was traced to Brownsville. Bad connection, faded in and out. Static."

"Keep it coming." Jacobs was back to spoon-feeding and I was getting pissed.

"We located Keyston Jenkins."

"That's the guy who arranged for Donnlevy's women. I warned him not to leave the country."

"Scum bag tried to pass through security at Cleveland-Hopkins. Held a ticket to Buenos Aires. Your passport stop caught him. They've had him in detention for hours while Homeland Security tried to reach you."

"Angella set up the stop. Must have used her cell number. Mine never rang."

"Anyway, follow up with him. I'm bridging him onto this connection. Ready?"

"As I'll ever be," I said, trying to wrap my mind around all that happened since I last spoke with Jenkins. I had no idea where he fit into the puzzle—or whether he belonged in a puzzle of his own. And why Argentina?

I heard a click, and assuming Jenkins was on the line, I said, "Taking a little trip are you, Mr. Jenkins?" I forced the sleep out of my voice. I wanted to make this a pleasant conversation, at least initially.

"Need a vacation. Not bothering anyone," came the bored sounding voice of a man apparently thinking his detention was nothing more serious than a traffic ticket.

"Thought we had an understanding you were to remain in the country."

"Didn't think you meant forever. It's been a while."

"Just so we're clear on this, when we get off the phone, if they release you, I want you to head home and stay there. We're keeping your passport. Don't try to leave again until you receive your passport back. There is no time limit on this. Understand me this time?"

"You can't do that," he snapped back. "I have rights."

"Have your lawyer call me, we'll discuss. In the meantime, I have a few questions for you. How accurately you answer will determine how soon, if ever, you get your passport back."

"I won't answer any questions. I want a lawyer."

"Time is important for us. I'll make you a deal. Answer my questions and I'll let you take your vacation. Fair enough?"

He was silent for a long while. This was another of those times when the first to speak was the loser. Finally, he said, "Can I trust you?"

"Can I trust you? That's the real question."

"Okay, you hold the cards. What you want?"

"When did you speak to Snow last?"

"Around midnight."

"Where was he calling from?"

"Cell phone."

"Where? What location."

"Didn't say. Not a good connection."

"You got his cell number?"

"Yes."

"What is it?"

He gave me the numbers. Then I asked, "What else did he say?"

"Said he would get even with Stetson for killing Lulu."

"What makes him think it was Stetson?"

"Man's a snake, all's I'm saying."

"You want your vacation?"

"I've told you enough."

"I'll decide when it's enough. Give me something I can use."

"Got nothing more."

"Cancel your vacation."

"You promised."

"Deliver."

"They call me the Facilitator, but I only find the girls. He's the one supplies Donnlevy, and…"

"And?"

"And the others. Thought Lulu was going to blackmail him."

"Why."

"Maybe something I said. Maybe something she overheard."

"You running a scam on Stetson?"

"He owed me. I was trying to get my money is all."

"What exactly did you say?"

"Do I have to?"

"You want to travel, you talk."

"Told him Donnlevy got one of the girls pregnant and she was going to tell all. I said I could keep her quiet he paid me."

"Did he pay you?"

"Shit hit the fan before. Hey, man, I talked enough!"

"You know what Snow intends to do?"

"You gotta let me go!"

"Tell me what Snow intends to do."

"Didn't say. Not my business."

"We know Donnlevy had a place in Georgetown. In fact, you told me yourself you delivered the girls to his place. What's the address?"

"Don't know the exact address."

"Do your best."

"It's a standalone building with a flower shop below. Mid-block. Prospect Street, North West."

In my mind's eye I could see Jacobs signaling to the logistics folks across the room—or wherever they were now located—to get on it. In a matter of minutes the flower shop would be surrounded, nobody going in or out.

I spoke to Jenkins a while longer, asking about the relationship between Snow and Lou and what role Smith Keller played. I was keeping him on the phone so he couldn't warn anyone. But actually I was receiving good information.

According to Jenkins, Keller was an innocent dupe; his vegetable shipments were used to smuggle drugs into the country. Jenkins believed Smith Keller uncovered a shipment and told Donnlevy.

"One last question," I said to Jenkins. "What's the name of the flower shop?"

"Sally's," came the delayed reply. "The window has Sally's Fresh Flowers written on it. Am I done now? You got plenty. Let me go!"

"You are."

"Can I get my passport back now?"

"I'll mail it to you. Should have it in a week or so. Within a month anyway."

"You fucking promised!"

"I'm keeping my promise. Can't help it if the mail's slow these days. If what you gave me checks out, the passport will be in the mail. If it doesn't, then we'll arrange room, board and a fresh orange jump suit for you."

"That wasn't part—"

I hung up.

A moment later my cell buzzed again. Jacobs gave me a Web address, a logon name, a password and then said, "I'll text you the encryption code. I think you might want to see this."

It took me a full minute of fooling with the phone browser and then working through all the logon procedures, but it finally all came together.

The screen showed a city street and the camera was panning down the street. What little natural traffic there was at this time of the morning had already been rerouted. Black vans, their windows darkly tinted, were positioned at each end of the street. An armored transport slowly rolled toward the camera, coming to a stop in front of a flower store. The sign in the window read, *Sally's Fresh Flowers.*

I watched as the coordinated entry began. I thought back to the raid on Angella's house. This team worked just as efficiently as the one had in Port Isabel. No wasted motion. No verbal communication, everything coordinated using hand signals.

The image on the screen switched to the inside living quarters and a voice said, "Place is empty of people. Found a trove of weapons and enough PETN and TNT to blow half of Georgetown into Virginia. Also found laser guns, most likely used to set off the PETN." The sound faded and then the Web site went dark.

Immediately, Jacobs called, "They'll be out in a few minutes. We'll set a perimeter. If anyone returns, we'll nail them."

No one was coming back, and if Jacobs was as good as he was supposed to be, he knew it also. Changing the subject, I said, "Did you hear Jenkins? Snow's got it in for Stetson."

"Puzzles me why Snow's still down there? Doesn't that play to Stetson's hand?"

"Plans got screwed up. They're improvising. The plan was to have us bring Angella to Washington. But the plans got screwed up when they substituted Jayme for Angella. I'm stumped."

"Frankly, so are we. Let's focus on Vlad for a moment. He's also in possession of explosives that are activated by being near some coordinates."

"I'm not certain the device needs to be near the coordinates. I'm out on a limb on this, but I think Snow was trying to say the coordinates affect the timing."

"Where does that take us?" Jacobs asked, giving me all the rope I was willing to tie around my neck.

"I'm thinking Corpus Air Field is in the vicinity of where Timberwolf was killed. Or possibly the Kingsville Naval Air Station. That's even closer. He was taking frequency readings that tied into coordinates."

"So what's the connection?"

"Focus on the nuclear power feeding Corpus. Jamison is concerned about a power failure. It's all tied together."

"I'm following the dots with you. But I still don't see the picture."

"I'll call you back." I said. "Don't go anywhere."

Cindy McNaughton answered on the first ring. It was as though she had been waiting for my call. She didn't interrupt while I gave her the elevator version. I then asked her to confirm the base's reliance on the reactor.

When I finished, she said, "Hold."

The line sounded dead. A minute passed. Then two. Then a third.

McNaughton's voice broke into my thoughts. "Cowboy, you're onto something. Power to Corpus Command Center is nuclear from the dedicated generation facility with a boost from a wind farm. The base is also served by the unhardened civilian power grid. For the upcoming military exercise the assumption is that the civilian grid was knocked out. As a simulation, Corpus is now disconnected from the public grid. If the nuke plant goes down then our electronic vision into the exercise goes dark and we'll not be able to intercept the hostile incoming fighters or missiles."

"The way I have it figured, the nuke power is going down. Get the main grid back on line."

"You have support for that statement?"

"Be back to you when I have it worked out."

"Remember this, Cowboy. This is not, and I repeat, not, a one-riot-one-Ranger operation. Report to me whatever you have. Hear me?"

"Loud and clear." I had learned with McNaughton, salute first, ask questions second.

I briefed Jacobs on the electrical situation at Corpus. Then I said, "Unfortunately, not enough to know what action to take. I assume there've been no reports of trouble. I doubt if the nuke site is vulnerable to surface sabotage."

"What about from the inside?" Jacobs asked.

"The terrorists do seem to be well connected all the way up to Donnlevy—perhaps even further. Finding the mole, if there is one, will take more time than we have."

"Suggestions?"

"Timberwolf's killing took place on a barren sandbar. Nothing there."

"But we know Vlad rented a boat up that way and most likely went out there yesterday. We also know Vlad has an explosive device."

"Good point," I said. "Assume he planted the device on the sand spit. Why?" When Jacobs said nothing, I continued, "One thing we know about him is that he's built a global system to monitor hostile activities. Use's satellites. The random kind. Forgot the technical name."

"Random kind? What the hell's that?"

"They're not over the equator. They pass over an area for only a limited time. Good for observation, but not for communication. So," I said, working my way down a thread, "the explosive is now at the right coordinates and detonates at a certain time controlled by a satellite. Far fetched, but I suppose possible."

"So...so...we go blind during the military exercises. Scare the military into buying Vlad's system."

"How the hell would an explosive on a barren sand bar take us blind?"

"Don't know," Jacobs answered, "but follow the smoke. Talk to me about detonation."

My mind was racing in another direction. One of the explosive devices was implanted in Angella. It could explode at any time—if it hadn't already.

I tried in vain to feel Angella, to sense if she was alive. But nothing came to me. No vibes, nothing but agony.

"You thinking?" Jacobs asked, his voice softer, less certain, revealing stress mixed with fatigue.

"Concerned is all. For Angella, if you must know. The same signal could set them both off." As soon as I said it I knew I was right. "The same signal! Shit! A satellite could be set to pass over the area and emit a signal on a frequency. The explosives will pick up that signal and detonate."

"Short of shooting down the satellite, there isn't much we can do," Jacobs replied, the fatigue slowing his cadence even further. "Hell, we don't even know which satellite to shoot at."

"Try one of Vlad's. They're named VLAD1, VLAD2, and so forth. Just need to look up which of the VLAD satellites will be over the Gulf Coast at whatever time the exercise is."

"Any idea of how to stop this?" Jacobs asked.

"Bridge Cindy in."

I repeated for McNaughton what we had worked out. She indicated that the critical time was three hours from now.

"That's nine central time," I said. "Let's start with seeing if the military has heat-sensitive pictures of the area, say from five a.m. yesterday morning until now. Mostly mid-morning yesterday is when Vlad would have been on the island."

"I'm on it," McNaughton replied. "Call you when I have something."

I next called the South Padre Coast Guard Station and asked to speak with Mark. I was told he was sleeping. Before I could tell the orderly to wake him, Captain Boyle came on the line. "Just the man I was fix'n to call. Don't say I never give you anything. We have infrared activity on Brazos beach. Two signatures. One of them is a match to one we had there before. Nothing else moving on or off the beach. We have a patrol vessel standing off-shore."

"What about the other image?"

"Small. Probably a dog. Little cool for a dog, most likely swimming. Yesterday there were four people down there. Today, only one."

"You planning on going in?" I asked, wondering why he was giving me more than name, rank and serial number. Boyle usually passed out less information than the CIA.

"Not while the military operation is underway. Have a full plate."

"What's the time frame for that?" I asked, mentally ducking.

"Classified. You know better than to ask! Is that why you're calling Cruses? I'll have his hide if he's leaking info to you."

"I was calling to find out how his fiancée is doing."

"Got the wrong number, Redstone. This is the Coast Guard, not the friggin' hospital."

"Ask Mark to call me would you please?" I said into the phone before I realized Boyle was no longer on the line.

FORTY-TWO

I had to admit their plan had a certain beauty to it. Angella walks into the war room and at a strategic time, we're all vaporized. Nothing a civilized person would even contemplate, but yet we find it a reality. Don't even have to get themselves dirty. If they're lucky, the President or some other high officials are in attendance. If they're not so lucky, they only wipe out the folks on their trail. That supposes a random detonation. If they had control over the timing, then they could control their luck. Talk about killing fish in a barrel! By the time the FBI and Homeland Security and all the other coordinating agencies regrouped, the damage would be done.

A workable plan from their perspective. But the killing of the Keller girl and her child changed the dynamics, especially with Snow. His only concern after that was getting revenge, not destruction of the government.

My vibrating phone brought my focus back. "You know anything about a body found in the Gulf last night?" McNaughton demanded when I answered her call.

"Should I?"

"Just checking. Trawler caught him in their dragline about two hours ago. I understand from the Coast Guard he wasn't in the water very long. Fish hadn't treated him too badly."

"Know who he is? Where he came from?"

"Got the rolls reversed, Cowboy. I ask the questions. You provide the answers."

"I spoke to Boyle a while ago. He said nothing about finding a body."

"Not your business as far as he's concerned. The less you know the happier he is."

"He'll sing another song when—"

"Hold. A text just arrived." The line went quiet for a moment. "Man's name is Juarez. Don't know if it's first or last. Worked for the Atomic Energy Commission."

"Atomic Energy Commission? What are they doing—"

"He was scheduled to inspect the pump house on PINS around noon yesterday."

"PINS? Where the hell—"

"Padre Island National Seashore. I'm told that's the longest undeveloped barrier island in the world, case you care. Where Timberwolf was killed."

Atomic Energy Commission. The words played over and over, like song lyrics that just won't leave you. With a mental thud, the music stopped. "Atomic inspector! What the hell was he inspecting? What do you mean, pump house? The nuke plant is inland several miles."

"Hell if I know!" McNaughton immediately shot back. "Work it."

"Not a coincidence," I exclaimed, forcing the numbers back into order. "Vlad most likely goes out there to plant the explosive. Just his run of luck, he encounters an AEC inspector."

"So why kill the inspector?"

"Vlad was seen by Juarez. Whatever he was going to do—or did—was, if I'm to believe my own theory, for the purpose of gaining the government contract. Being seen out there blows that for him. Pardon the pun."

"So what was Vlad trying to blow up?"

"Frankly, General, I have no clue."

- - - - -

It was now eight in the morning. McNaughton had summoned Tiny and I back to the Presidential Suite for an in-person briefing. As usual, she had an impressive spread of food laid out. How she maintained her figure I had no idea.

Between bites of strawberry-laden waffle, Tiny brought her up to speed.

Our briefing exhausted, she said, "What you don't know is that the high altitude video from yesterday's pass over the coast shows someone, actually two someones, walking not far from where Timberwolf was killed. We initially presumed it was Vlad and an accomplice. We now believe it was Vlad and Juarez."

"I assume no action was taken out there or I would have heard about it."

"Not if Kagan was in charge you wouldn't. Anyway, there's no action to take. They were both gone at the next pass."

"Vlad must have delivered what he had. An atomic starter of some sort. Maybe he was burying it out there in the sand for later use. Come by in a boat, pick it up and move it to the detonation site."

"Couldn't have been radioactive or the video heat sensors would have spotted it." Cindy reminded me.

"It's small, but powerful," I said, repeating what Cindy already knew. "But now that the President's speech has been cancelled they can do what they want anytime."

"Secret Service said the same thing. But the flaw in that logic is the cancellation has not yet been made public. They don't plan to tell anyone until just before."

"That means people will gather on the mall. They could be slaughtered if a WMD goes off." I was having difficulty getting my mind around the ends our government would go to avoid disclosing an atomic threat on the homeland. Whatever happened to transparency? "But your sister-in-law knows. It'll be on the Internet, probably already has been posted."

"She'll hold it. That's how she gets her stories. Washington works that way. She's never gone off reservation yet."

"I can't believe——"

"Listen, Cowboy, if it's an atomic weapon, people will die even if they remain inside. Not saying anything may increase the casualty list, but it gives us time to——"

The TV flicked on. The war room appeared the same as it had ten hours earlier, only now the remnants of breakfast, cinnamon buns, bagels, donuts and who knew what else, had replaced the detritus of dinner.

Jacobs was in a heated discussion with a group of people I recognized from earlier sessions. I couldn't follow the points they were making. When the action cooled, I interrupted. "Mind telling me what's going down?"

"Nice of you join us, Redstone." It was Kagan speaking. I hadn't seen him until he spoke. The man appeared to have slept, if he slept at all, in his suit. His tie was gone and his collar open. Heavy bags hung under his eyes. "Pray tell, just what is it we can do for you this morning?"

I chalked up the sarcasm to lack of sleep. "What's going on?"

"If you wouldn't spend your time sleeping, or boozing, or breaking windows, or whatever else the hell you do down there in Texas, you'd know full-well what we're up against."

It was Jacobs who gave the answer. "Water pumps are buried on PINS island."

Were these the pumps that were being inspected? We were back to spoon-feeding. It must be in their genome to pass out information as if it was chocolate and I was a diabetic. "Please explain," I said, trying not to let my frustration show, "what you mean by pumps."

"Supply backup cooling water from the Gulf to the nuclear reactor."

"Got me hooked. Keep reeling."

"In the event the main cooling reservoir fails, those pumps are vital to avoid a major accident. Protocol, especially in view of what went down at Fukushima, is to bring the reactor down in a controlled fashion, before any backup is required."

If I understood this correctly, the pumps were doing nothing at the moment. But should they become incapacitated, the reactor would go off-line. It didn't make much sense, but hey, what do I know? "So all is under control at this moment. I didn't hear a big boom. So why the heated discussion?"

"If something were to take those pumps out, then..."

"Then what?" Spoon-feeding at its best. If those guys told it their way, nothing would ever get done.

"In exactly ninety minutes, enemy carriers armed with missiles, as well as several squadrons of jet aircraft, are scheduled to attack the East and Gulf coasts as part of the military war games. We need Corpus Command functioning at full capacity."

"How does—"

"High-speed imaging and intelligence processing requires massive computing. Which, in turn, requires more power than can be delivered by local backup generators. If power goes out, even for a few minutes, communication will be curtailed."

"Pardon me," I said, trying not to talk down to them, "but why not just put Corpus back on the civilian grid?"

"A combination of civilian and military politics. The President doesn't want to alert anyone that we're vulnerable. The military is playing off his concerns and for their own reasons don't want our partners to know we can't defend our own shores even when we know what is coming and when. They'll be laughed at in military circles for a long time to come. All of our *friends* are not our friends."

Political logic defied gravity and defied my limited capability as well. "So," I said, "cancel the exercise."

"Even more distasteful. Both to the President and to the military. After all, we position ourselves as the world's strongest power and can't be seen as cut and run when we have a power outage—a power outage that hasn't even happened yet. Can't deliver that message."

I turned to Tiny. "Use my satellite books to see if any of the VLAD satellites will be close within the next two hours." To the D.C. folks, I said, "Put men onto the National Seashore as soon as possible. Operation PINS, if you need a name. They're looking for a small electrical device, small enough to implant in a human, buried somewhere near those pumps."

"Pumps are housed in underground vaults," came a voice from the periphery of the conference room.

"Use GPS coordinates to pinpoint them. The device is there. Just need to find it."

McNaughton hit the mute button on her cell. "What are you thinking? They go digging around for explosives, they could set them off."

"The way I see it, the actual lethal explosives, the ones that'll take out the pumps, were planted sometime ago. Probably pretty deep. They'll be hard to find—or dig out. I'm guessing they're actually below the pumps. The detonator, that's what Vlad planted, is a small package packing enough explosive energy to ignite the main charge. The detonator contains an electronic receiver set to receive signals at a particular frequency. Need to check this out, but I think the detonator must be at, or near, the surface. When the detonator receives a signal from the satellite it blows up. This, in turn, sets off the main charge. Goodbye pumps. Goodbye reactor."

"Someone then must be controlling the satellite," Kagan snapped. "Can't we jam them?"

"Don't know about jamming, but I assume not," I replied. "The VLAD satellite is continuously sending out certain signals. When one of the signals is detected by the detonator, it goes ka-bang. That's a technical term, by the way." When McNaughton didn't smile, I continued. "But the satellite and the receiver must be within a certain coordinate distance of each other for proper timing. That's what Snow told Vlad. I have no way of knowing what that distance is."

Tiny had raced back to my condo and now my cell rang. I hit the speaker button.

"Got a pencil?"

Cindy thrust a pen into my hand and pointed to a notepad on the side table.

"Go," I said.

"Times are central. Nine-fifty. Exactly one hour from now. Then eleven-twenty. I'm assuming VLAD5. VLAD13 is the only other possibility, but its next time in the northern hemisphere is not until twelve-eighteen and it hasn't been in this hemisphere since five this morning. Then it was low, about fifteen degrees north. The others are scattered around, but nothing else will pass over North America today."

I unmuted the connection. "Best guess from here is that you have an hour." I again cut the sound so that Cindy and I could put our heads together—so to speak. The action in the war room was professional, but fast-paced. People queued to speak with Sylvan Jacobs. Some brought folders of varying colors, ranging from bright green to screaming red. Some just leaned in to ask a question or to impart information. The movement of Jacob's head was a good indicator of which direction the information was flowing.

In contrast, the line waiting to speak with Deputy Director Kagan was almost non-existent.

I turned my back to the screen.

I went live to Jacobs. "How large are those pumps?"

Immediately, someone across the war room reached for a phone, presumably to get an answer.

Cindy, not waiting for the answer from the committee, used the suite phone to call someone. She was across the room and speaking low, but it sounded like she was repeating my question.

A moment later she returned to the sofa. "For what it's worth, Cowboy, the pumps are buried in water-proof vaults deep under the sand. Air vents are camouflaged as rocks out in the water. Nothing's visible from the air."

"How many? Size?"

"Five. Each weighs three tons."

As she was talking, something else clicked. "Jacobs," I said into the phone, "you saw the video of Timberwolf being shot."

"I did," Jacobs replied. "But what—"

"Follow me here. Where did the shooter come from? And where did he go after the shooting? The view we had was from high up. There was nothing out there."

Jacobs looked around the table. Nobody spoke.

Then a voice that I recognized joined the conversation. It was General Maxwell Jamison. I hadn't known he was part of this operation, but I shouldn't have been surprised. "The reason you don't see the reactor, or the pumping station," Jamison said, "is that they're shielded from electronic penetration. The shield blocks all radiation penetration and is constructed to match the terrain. It's below ground. But even if the sand were to be stripped away, the vault would be difficult to spot."

"When it's operating it must give off heat," I said, more as a question than as statement.

"That's why the air and exhaust vents are in the water. Cools the skin. Temperature is maintained exactly consistent with the indigenous surroundings. It has no individual heat signature."

"Could Vlad Smol get his hands on the same material?"

"I suppose so," Jamison replied. "I suppose so."

"He did, sir," a voice on the line said.

"Who the hell's speaking?" Jamison demanded.

"Colonel Broderick Reilly, sir. Air Force Special Ops Liaison for surveillance. Based at Creech, but responsible for Corpus. My command spoke to Vlad about his project and his satellites. He wanted to shield them in the material. It's actually light enough. He's been in test with it."

"Then he could have carried a bomb right through security." Jamison exclaimed. "So much for national security."

"Actually, I don't think he did so, General," I said. "His plan was less risky—or so he believed."

"Okay, Redstone, give us your version."

McNaughton, who was now seated beside me on the sofa, nodded in my direction.

I took her nod as a vote of confidence. "The detonation won't be atomic," I said, "but it'll be of high capacity. His goal is to frighten the military into deploying his system of early warning. Had to do it himself to avoid compromise. He planted a heavy explosive charge around the in-ground vaults. I'm thinking he hid under a piece of the shield material after the killing. Then Vlad went up there yesterday and attached a small radio controlled explosive to the already buried explosives."

"I'm following so far," Jamison said. "But how the hell does he plan to detonate it at the right time? Need some sort of clock mechanism for that."

"A clock is a possibility. That would be the easiest. And maybe that's what he has, a clock. But…"

"But what?" Jamison snapped, clearly agitated. "out with it."

They didn't like it when I played their spoon-feeding game back on them. "But my money's on his own satellite. That's why I believe we have an hour." I checked my watch. "Fifty minutes, actually."

Tiny rejoined us. I said to him, "Timberwolf was measuring communication signals and recording satellite signal frequencies when he accidently recorded nuclear power plant signals. I bet if we go over the listing we received from Dr. Singh at Pitt we'll also find frequencies that are being sent from VLAD5."

"You saying Timberwolf was working for Vlad?"

"Just the opposite. Remember, Timberwolf was in witness protection. He was just an unlucky amateur scientist who was in the wrong place at the wrong time. Or, and this makes more sense, he got wind of what Vlad was up to and was documenting it all. Vlad killed him because the evidence of what Vlad was doing had been recorded. Also remember how suddenly the killer brought his weapon to bear on Timberwolf? We thought he heard something. But, in fact, he *saw* something. He saw his former partner. There was nothing for him to do but shoot."

FORTY-THREE

"**S**ir," Colonel Reilly's voice came over the speaker, "I have confirmation from Corpus. They're not experiencing difficulties of any kind communicating with the pumping station. All systems are go."

"What is the back-up plan if Corpus goes off-line?"

"Classified," Jamison answered. "Suffice it to say there is back-up."

"How fast can it come on line?" I asked.

The suite phone rang.

McNaughton answered it with a crisp, "McNaughton, here." She held the green receiver out to me. "Jamison wants you."

Following Cindy's lead, I said, "Redstone, here."

"This is as close to a secure line as we're going to get on such short notice. The main command is Creech Air Force Base, out in Nevada. The communications from the Atlantic, Caribbean, Gulf of Mexico and Mediterranean come into Corpus Air Station. The back up to Corpus is Tampa. MacDill."

"Then I'm wrong about taking out Corpus," I confessed.

"Not as wrong as you might think, son. In the exercise coming up this morning, we have a twenty-minute critical window. MacDill is standing by. But..." Jamison's voice lowered, "...budget cuts don't allow us to feed the raw input data to two locations simultaneously for analysis. The raw data, and by that I mean waveforms from countless sensors, seismic readings, satellite images, temperature sensors, are all being fed only to Corpus on this exercise. Corpus runs massive high-speed parallel processors on the raw data and then passes the analyzed information on to Creech. Creech handles the actual dispatching of interceptors, or missiles, whatever else is required. You following, Redstone?"

"I am."

"When the system was originally designed, back when money was no object, MacDill worked in parallel with Corpus and passed its processed information on to Creech independently. That way, if one went down, nothing is lost. Enough said. This exercise involves a mock attack on the United States involving planes and several missiles." Those planes and missiles must, at all cost, be intercepted. If they are not, then our ability to defend ourselves goes into play. When that happens it calls into question our ability to defend our allies. They will all then begin arming themselves and the cold war will reignite. That's more than you need to know. Let's go live. You have satellite info that you need to share." As is his custom when he's finished with a conversation, the line went dead.

A moment later, Jamison was back on the conference channel. "Redstone, Colonel Reilly has a question concerning the satellites."

"Agent Redstone," Reilly began, "you appear to have an extensive knowledge of satellite operations and signals. Would you mind telling us where you obtained such knowledge?"

"Partly by reading, partly from a debriefing of my partner's sister. She overheard a conversation between Vlad and another guy called Snow."

"Mind telling us the gist of that debriefing?"

I turned to face Tiny, who was just about to take a bite out of a cream cheese-smothered bagel. Grudgingly, he laid the concoction on a side table and retrieved his notebook. Moving across the suite to where McNaughton and I were sitting, he said, "I took the statement." He flipped more pages. "Here it is. It'll take me a few seconds to enter the time mark into the recorder." Tiny retrieved the recorder, powered it up, entered some numbers on a tiny screen, then said, "Here goes. This will be Partridge, Angella's sister, speaking."

"...not sure. But Vlad was upset. At one point he said, 'but what if this doesn't work? You have the backups. Give them to me.'"

Tiny entered more numbers, said, "this is a little while later." The tape then continued. There was no mistaking Tiny's voice.

"Before, you said something about a backup. What do you recall exactly?"

"Let me think. Snow told Vlad not to worry, the receiver was set for the right frequency. All he had to do was get the coordinates right. He said that would be close enough."

There was a long pause, then Jayme continued, "Now I recall what else he said."

"Snow or Vlad?"

"Snow. He said that as long as it didn't rain, the receiver would work fine. And that even if Vlad had all three, rain would kill it."

"That it?" Reilly asked when the recorder stopped playing.

"That's it," Tiny said.

"What do you make from that?" I asked.

"Three detonators," Colonel Reilly answered. "Most likely set to respond to the same frequency, but possibly not. Ultra-high frequency signals. Likely in the three gigahertz range, but not much higher."

"How'd you get the frequency range from that?" I asked, pleased, but at the same time startled that he could obtain so much information from Jayme's few words.

"Rain interferes with radio signals in the two to three giga-hertz spectrum. Higher than that, however, the atmosphere is pretty much opaque to signals coming from space. Now that I think about it, the spectrum is perhaps even lower. Possibly one to two gigs. The actual signal frequency they're using is not one commonly used, or else the device would have triggered by now. Could be a combination of frequencies, similar to the tones on your phone. But I'm thinking single frequency."

"I don't know what the hell you two are babbling about!" Jamison barked. "Let me know what the military needs to do. Until then, I'll drop off."

Director Kagan, not one to pass up an opportunity to kiss up, said, "We'll work it on our end and keep you informed, General." Kagan then turned to face the camera. Looking straight at me, he said, "Redstone, you're free to go about your business. We have it under control here. Jolly good show."

"Before I go," I said into McNaughton's cell, "is someone go-ing to track Vlad or should—"

"We'll take it from here," Kagan replied, reaching toward the camera. "You stay where you are. It's tactical from here out. Marshals will handle it just fine."

The screen went grey and Cindy's telephone displayed the words: NETWORK TERMINATED.

I stood, walked around the suite a moment and then ducked into the bathroom. Coming out, I mused, "Wonder if Vlad is just being capitalist greedy or if he's working for his former country?" It was a rhetorical question, not calling for an answer.

Tiny, his mouth full of bagel, didn't bother to answer.

But Cindy did. "It's really not important at this point. If they capture him alive he's going to jail for life. Intentionally interrupting a military exercise could be treason, could be lots of things. Not your worry anymore."

I continued pacing the room. Tiny, having finished his breakfast—or mid-morning snack—was sipping coffee by the window, his attention focused on the surf. He'd been in the business of tracking down threats to the country far longer than I and he still seemed to have a sense of humor—sometimes even of play—about him. I, on the other hand, felt remorse. Maybe it was because this operation—except for Angella—ended for me with a whimper. Nothing really happened. In the old days I would have worked weeks, sometimes years, but in the end I'd have an arrest, a trial to look forward to, something tangible. Now, the most I received was an attaboy. A jolly good attaboy, as Kagan had put it. I was becoming an adrenalin junkie.

"Cowboy, you're down," Cindy said when I joined Tiny at the window. It wasn't the surf he was watching. A woman's volleyball game was in full swing directly below us. Involuntarily, I studied the group, subconsciously looking for Angella.

"I've seen this many times," McNaughton was saying somewhere off in the background. "You gear up for combat and the enemy slithers away. To tell the truth, it's good some missions end this way. Sure, their war games will be disrupted if the pumps go off-line. But so what in the scheme of things? They'll learn from it. Harden their sites, build redundancy into the system. I think they'll even consider monitoring satellite signals in the future. You did good work. Without you, when the pumps blow, a blue-ribbon commission would spend years trying to figure out the cause."

I turned to face her. "You're overlooking the fact they still have Angella!" I snapped. The statement came out more forcefully than I had intended. "And no one but me gives a rat's whisker!"

"That's not true, Cowboy. Not true at all. Angella happens to be one of the best we've ever brought in to serve the country. She's a natural. Why the hell you think I sent the Rangers after her?"

"What Rangers? What's going on?" I was angry at the world, but taking it out on Cindy.

"Calm down, Cowboy. Military mission comes first. But I'm not down here for that. Angella is my priority."

"I didn't think—"

"It's not about you. That woman is valuable to us. Someone like her comes along once in years. We don't plan to lose her."

"So, what are you—"

"We're tracking her. That's what we're doing."

"But you waited until after I worked out the PINS details before briefing me."

"Priorities, Cowboy. Priorities. Didn't want you distracted with the rescue operation."

"No faith I could multitask," I replied, struggling to contain hostilities built up over the years working with federal agencies.

"Evidence points otherwise—especially where a lover is concerned. Need I enumerate?"

"Some people seem to manage," I shot back. "Matter of compartmentalizing."

"Touché, Cowboy. Back to business."

I glanced over at Tiny. He hadn't moved. But I knew he was taking it all in. It would all be recorded in the government's massive data bank, to be used—most likely against me—at some future inconvenient time.

"If you care so much for Angella, why aren't we going in for her?"

"We're not exactly doing nothing. Tiny, tell Cowboy what's going on."

Tiny slowly turned from the window and stood with his back to the glass. "First, we know where she isn't. Searched Laguna Atascosa. Used image sensing equipment and followed up with boots on the ground. Air Force Rangers borrowed from the Gulf operation."

"Do you know where she *is*?"

"We're pretty certain. Just haven't worked the logistics of getting her out alive."

"So exactly when were you going to tell me?" Now I was really angry. "What's wrong with you people? Where the hell is she?"

"That temper tantrum is exactly why you haven't been briefed." McNaughton responded, her eyes setting hard and her chin moving forward. I had seen that look in the past and it made me uncomfortable. "Settle yourself, Cowboy. If you're to be of any help at all, we need you thinking with your mind not your... your... emotions. Go in with guns blazing you might as well carry a body bag with you."

I made a full circuit of the room, then stopped a few feet in front of her. She was right. Anger was for amateurs. Anger got you—and people around you—killed.

Tiny came across the room to join us.

"First, we'll review what we know. Then we'll explore our options. Then, and only then, will we make a game plan." Cindy looked to Tiny, who dutifully nodded.

Then, with her eyes firmly locked to mine, she said, "And if the plan doesn't have a high probability of bringing Angella out alive, we go back to the drawing board."

It was clear, her game plan was not negotiable. So I remained uncharacteristically quiet.

The Marine General had taken command.

FORTY-FOUR

Tiny took notes as we went over all that we knew. We then made a list of options. The list turned out to be remarkably short.

Cindy's cell chirped. Judging from the manner in which she turned away, I was certain it was Jamison. My suspicions were reinforced when the communication ended without her having uttered a word.

She then snapped on the TV and dialed the conference number on her cell.

"I thought Kagan had dismissed us," I said, allowing a hint of sarcasm to creep into my tone.

"It's not Kagan we're linked to. We're on the PINS military feed. I understand this is also being monitored by the President." She waited until the picture cleared before continuing. "Rangers have been on PINS forty minutes now. Found nothing."

Indeed, there were about twenty people, all wearing what looked to be black neoprene full-body outfits. They were digging in the sand and filtering it through giant shifters. Except for the extreme garb, they looked like a bunch of big kids having a fun day at the beach. I imagined a scene from gold-rush days where tons of pebbles were filtered looking for the elusive nuggets.

Jamison's voice broke the silence. "Five minutes remaining until VLAD5 enters the earliest cone of detonation. Ten minutes until optimum position. At T-minus two we abort. Start the time count, now."

"General. May I suggest dumping water on the area. Create rain so to speak." It was Colonel Reilly, the Air Force Special Ops guy speaking. "Air Force tankers are standing by. Could be over the island in less than five minutes."

"The detonation cone could last up to fifteen minutes. That's more water than you can manage," Jamison responded. "Stand down."

"T minus four," a voice announced.

Jamison said, "Team PINS. On my command, abort according to plan alpha. No exceptions."

"T minus three," came the voice.

The operations on the beach continued. It was as if they had no care other than to dig. The concrete tops of several pump housings were now visible. Sand from around the sides continued to flow through the shifters.

"They should have hit the main explosives by now," I commented. I was pacing in front of the TV while both Tiny and Mc-Naughton sat calmly watching as if this was a pre-recorded reality show playing on the screen.

It was possible, indeed probable, that without warning these men-and perhaps women—could be blown apart. Yet the expressions on their faces revealed nothing.

"T minus two."

"Abort!" Jamison commanded.

The black clad figures immediately stopped what they were doing and ran to the water. One person, with a Ranger insignia on his back, bent to pick up something from the sand. He held it over his head as he trotted toward water's edge.

"T minus one," the count continued.

"Drop it and get in the water!" Jamison barked.

The Ranger who had been holding the small object dropped it before diving headfirst into the waves.

"T minus zero."

Nothing happened.

"T plus one," the clock keeper announced.

We were now within the time frame for possible detonation.

"T plus two."

"T plus—"

The sand at water's edge where the Ranger had stood a few seconds before exploded into a dense cloud. Nothing was visible on the ground.

It took almost a minute before the haze cleared enough for us to see the small crater that had been created at water's edge, precisely where the Ranger had dropped whatever it was he had found.

When the mist cleared further, Colonel Reilly announced, "Pump housings are intact. Corpus reports no interruption of communication with the pumping station. All systems remain go."

"All personnel have been recovered safely," Jamison reported. "Operation PINS is terminated."

Our screen went blank.

McNaughton turned to Tiny, as if nothing had interrupted her train of thought. "Show me again exactly where we believe Angella's being held?"

Tiny pointed to a map displayed on his cell screen. "Best guess. Here. Boca Chica Beach. Border Patrol, with the aid of Game and Fisheries Wardens, have it quarantined. No one can leave the beach by land."

"How do you...we...know who is out there?" I asked.

"Infrared imaging. Two people were detected on the beach. One was Angella."

"Sure it was Angella?" I asked, going over what we had discussed before the Jamison interruption. I had to force my voice steady. After seeing the damage done by the detonation at PINS I was worried about what might have occurred at Boca Chica at the same time.

"They have her heat signature from other times she was on the beach. I think it was the first time you worked with her, I don't know. But the computer gave an eighty-percent probable match. Anything over seventy I buy."

"Boyle said there was a man and possibly a dog. What gives?"

"Beats me. Signature says she's there. Don't know about a dog."

"Shit!" I was on my feet. "The dog! That was Angella!"

"Sit down, Cowboy!" McNaughton ordered. "Calm yourself."

Swallowing the temptation to lash out at her, I returned to my seat, my eyes averting the general like a school kid who had just been caught throwing an eraser. Once seated, I said, "Snow wants her alive, at least for now. He's gone to too much trouble to keep her with him."

"The dog part, Cowboy. Why do you believe her image came up as a dog?"

"He covered part of her in that shield stuff. If not, when the satellite passed overhead she—and he as well—would have been detonated."

"Then why does the new image identify her?" Tiny pressed.

"He must take it off when the satellite is not overhead. Else we wouldn't have her heat print."

"Then it's not VLAD5," McNaughton said. "The latest heat print was almost simultaneous with the PINS explosion. Signature matched the earlier one. Shield's been off for a while."

"If I recall right, the next satellite time in this area is VLAD13," Tiny said, flipping through his notebook. Finding what he was looking for, he leaned forward, as if he were about to whisper a secret. "Next pass is twelve-eighteen."

"What do you suppose he plans to do with her?" McNaughton had addressed her question to the room, but I had the distinct impression my number had just been called. Before I could respond, she continued. "What about the third detonator? He kept it. Why?"

"One for Vlad. One for Angella," I said. "And the third one for—"

"For the person who killed his girlfriend—and his child," Tiny said.

"First, he has to determine who that is," McNaughton said. "Then he has to plant it on that person."

"He knows who did it. Stetson."

Tiny's cell cut me off. A text message had arrived from Jacobs. Tiny held up the screen. KELLER'S HAIR FOUND ON STETSON'S SHIRT. REJOIN MEETING.

A moment later we had the war room back on the screen. Jacobs was talking. "...report confirms a positive match between a hair trace lifted from a shirt in Stetson's office and Lou Keller.

A warrant's been issued for his arrest. Marshals were displaced. Should have him in custody soon. We're waiting word."

"Good work," I said, and couldn't resist adding, "but I thought murder investigations were beneath your august group." Jamming Kagan felt good after being caged by McNaughton.

Kagan shot a glance at the camera, gathering himself to fire back at me. But Jacobs jumped first. "Not called for, Redstone. Join the team or sign off."

I couldn't win this battle. Shit *always* flows downhill. It's one of Newton's laws of absolute truth. So I followed with, "We've had progress on our end as well."

"If you're referring to the PINS operation," Jacobs said, "we monitored as well. Good work on calling the detonation."

Kagan said nothing. Didn't even nod in my direction.

"We have a bit more." I then proceeded to explain about the three detonators, ending with, "...and we believe the third is meant for Stetson."

"Couldn't happen to a nicer guy," someone in the war room commented.

"That'll be enough of that," Kagan scolded. "I know we're all tired, but remain on the reservation. Proceed, Redstone."

"Not much I can add, other than to suggest Stetson might, at some point, become a walking bomb."

No one said anything. I outlined the situation with Angella, and then asked, "Anyone have a reason why I should not call Snow? See if we can make a trade."

"What kind of trade?" Kagan demanded, his hostile demeanor not changing.

"How the hell would I know what he wants? He's obviously keeping her alive for some reason. Most likely, to negotiate something."

Not hearing any objection, I dialed the number.

Snow answered on the second ring. "Redstone, just the man I was hoping to talk with."

"That makes two of us. What's on your mind?"

"Your girl friend. I suppose you want her back—alive."

"You know the answer. Go on."

"Classic trade. Her for me. Stand down so I can get on my way. And immunity from prosecution."

"You keep her alive and I'll get it done."

My unilateral decision to cave on immunity went down hard around the table. Even the staid McNaughton appeared troubled. But no one said anything.

"How do you propose to arrange the transfer?" I asked Snow, certain, he had a plan to get off the beach. To the east was the Gulf of Mexico. Behind him was South Bay. To the north, less than five hundred feet from where Tiny had pinpointed him, was the Brazos Pass, the deep-water channel separating barren Boca Chica Beach from the south tip of bustling South Padre Island. The only viable way off the beach was to retrace the route from Brownsville he had come. That road was now heavily guarded.

"You come out to Boca Chica alone," Snow responded. Bring a kayak, a case of water and fishing gear. I'll trade you even up for the girl. No helicopters, no ships offshore. No nothing. Alone. One sighting and you've lost her."

"Deal," I said. Be there in an hour."

The line went dead.

Kagan become livid the instant Snow cut off. "Who the hell you think you are committing the government to immunity? He disrupted the military. Put countless lives at risk. Killed a guy out there on the beach. Better get your head screwed on straight, Redstone! We go through command. When this is over—"

"Not now, sir," Jacobs interrupted, "we have an operation to run. Redstone doesn't speak for the government. So no harm, no foul. Once the girl...Angella...is safe, we can deal with Snow however we desire."

"There sure as hell will be repercussions when the Director hears of this!"

This time it was I who cut the connection.

I turned to face the wrath of McNaughton.

But she was smiling. It wasn't an open lip, show-the-teeth smile. But rather her eyes were dancing, telling me all I had to know. My take: she disliked Deputy Director Chris Kagan as much as I did.

"Should I go with you?" Tiny asked.

"He said alone. No need to challenge him. Stay and provide logistic support. God knows, I won't get any help from those guys." I nodded in the direction of the TV. "Arrange for transportation to the hospital for Angella. Got to get that explosive out of her ASAP." We didn't know for certain which one—or ones—of the satellite broadcasts would be the detonation signal, so we didn't know the timing. "I'll need shield material, a helicopter, some..."

"Here's the plan," McNaughton said, interrupting me and taking charge of the operation. "This is not a free-for-all, improvise-on-the-spot operation. You follow the plan, or you're not going in. Period."

The answer called for a "Yes, sir!" But instead I said, "I'm listening."

"And agreeing."

"And agreeing," I repeated, wondering once again how her leash found itself around my neck.

"You're to drive down to Boca Chica Beach. My cell navigation indicates forty-five minutes. Route takes you west around the ship channel and then back east to the beach. Could airlift you in, but clearly that will spook him." She turned to Tiny, who sat taller when she glared at him. "Arrange for the supplies to meet Redstone on the way. If necessary, buy them in Brownsville, or here on the island. I don't care which."

Her hard-set eyes focused back on me. "Once she's in your custody our problems are not over. Can't take her to a civilian hospital. The device might detonate, either by a satellite signal or possibly while it's being removed. Not your problem."

"What's that mean, not my problem? She's my—"

Tiny, who had already begun working his assignment, saved me by commenting, "I've seen implants of this type years ago. Doctor was taking it out and it blew a hole in the building. Had some sort of a trip wire on it. Thirty people, seven of them doctors, died. Find out from Snow if this one is the same way. Tell him I'll personally track him down anywhere in the world and slit his throat if harm comes to Angella."

"That won't be necessary," I said. "I'll get there first."

"Enough!" McNaughton commanded, breaking into our battle. "You two sound like a couple of high school seniors trying to out-testosterone each other." She then glared at me. "Cowboy, I should know better than to send you to get her. But anyone else will cause problems with Snow. I'm warning you, remain focused on the mission. It won't end well if you revert to type."

"Meaning?"

"Stay on the team and don't go into loner mode."

My take on what she had just said was that while Angella was important to the government, she would be expendable if innocent people were put in harm's way.

She cut off my response.

"I know what you're thinking, Cowboy. But as a law enforcement officer you know we're here to protect the public. Anytime there's a choice between who lives and who dies, the sacrifice goes against us. I trust you'll abide or I wouldn't allow you to go."

Tiny broke the silence by saying, "There's another side to this as well, Jimmy. Effective logistic support depends on properly anticipating your actions. Play it straight and we'll get her out. Kapish?"

I grabbed a bottle of water on the way out of the penthouse. It tasted like acid rain as it passed across my tongue.

FORTY-FIVE

The kayak was the easy part. One phone call to Tony, the owner of what turned out to be a neat little place on the island called *UB Captain,* and he had one ready when I came by. Tony had offered to deliver the kayak to any location we selected, but that, of course, was impractical. Little did he know his kayak would not be returning. Tony even had the fishing gear I had requested.

A quick stop at *the Blue Marlin IGA* and I was on my way across the causeway, the kayak tied firmly to the car top, its bow hanging far out over the hood. Brown pelicans soared above the causeway roadbed, riding the currents as if they had not a care in the world. This was one time I envied their ability to float above it all.

In Port Isabel, just past *H-E-B*, I turned left onto highway forty-eight. I called Abby Johnson to fulfill my promise of a lead on the story. She didn't answer. I left a *for background only* voice mail telling her about the attempted power outage at Air Station Corpus Christi caused by an intercepted attempt to blow up a water pumping station buried under the sands of Padre Island National

Seashore. I emphasized that the operation was not terrorism, but rather a misguided businessman thinking he could scare the military into hiring his business for surveillance. I twice repeated my *for background only* warning.

She called back within a minute. "Is this related to the cancellation of the President's talk?"

"Yes," I responded. "They thought more was going on. My own assessment is that some terrorist group, probably Iran, is playing on our paranoia to embarrass us in front of the world."

"To what end?"

"Sky is falling routine. They act suspicious enough times, create background chatter enough times, and eventually we ignore them. They sense a lack of vigilance and wham, they take out a target."

"For your information, two foreign military fighters just buzzed Washington. No intercept in sight."

"Part of the war games," I replied. "I believe it's related to the attempted power outage."

"My sources tell me it was because the Tampa command center lost input for a few minutes. The jets slipped through."

"Tampa? I thought Corpus or Creech Air Field out in Nevada was the command point. How does Tampa fit into this?"

"My source claims they were in the process of transferring control from Corpus to Tampa. That jives with what you told me about their concern over the pumping station. Tampa hadn't trained for this mission. It's a major screw-up any way you position it. The President is furious."

"Any word of a missile getting through?"

"You telling me something?"

"Just asking?"

"Nothing yet. Thanks."

With Angella's life in the balance, I wasn't going to waste brain cycles with military screw-ups. Before Abby hung up, I gave her one last item. "Still off the record. There's a detonator, possibly explosive, set to respond to a signal from a satellite. May go off in the vicinity of Hank Stetson."

"Stetson? He's involved in this?"

"Not in the pumping station incident. But he's the lowlife who killed LissaLou Keller—and her baby."

"That's a murder story. I'll pass it along."

"Confirm it first so I'm not your source." To me, the real story was yet to unfold. Normally, I gained energy from the chase in true adrenalin junkie fashion. But in this case my normally steady emotional system was on a roller coaster ride; down—and further down.

The number ninety-two kept flashing in my mind; as in ninety-two percent of the time someone was seriously injured when a hostage is being rescued.

We had beat the odds once, but that was because Snow had been gone by the time the SEALs arrived. This time, Snow would be there. Not good odds at all.

Maybe that's why McNaughton relented and sent me. She knew it was a long shot—at best. She'd get both of us back—or neither.

Tiny called to say the beach had been sealed. I asked what McNaughton's plans were for removing the explosive from Angella. To which, he replied, "I'm out of that loop."

"So what happens when she's free of Snow? Time is of the essence."

"Call when you have her ready for transport. What happens at that point, I can't vouch for. Madam General is calling the shots—so to speak. "

"So why did you call. I already know the beach is secure. What's going down?"

"My, aren't we testy?"

"I have a right to know the operational plan."

"You can have all the rights in the world. McNaughton will tell you what she wants to tell you and nothing more."

"So why did you call?"

"Frankly, Jimmy," Tiny said, his voice barely audible, "to test your mental state. McNaughton doesn't trust you not to ad lib. Just go in, get her away from Snow, and trust the General to orchestrate the rest. She wants me to assure her you'll remain on script."

"So what's her plan if I don't behave?"

"Blips on screens come and go. Often no one knows why. Kapish?"

"That's bullshit!"

"That's the way it is. Either you convince me you're on task or...or we go to Plan B."

"That's—"

"Calls for a yes or no answer."

"Screw you!"

"Sounds like a no to me."

"Okay! Hell yes I'm on task. Tell madam General I'll recite my lines as scripted."

"Now we're talking. Keep your promise."

I wanted to say more. I wanted to say I harbored a bad feeling about this operation. I wanted to tell him straight out that Snow wasn't coming off that beach alive unless Angella was unharmed. But my words would be Exhibit A at my murder trial if Snow were to die. Especially if he died with a bullet between the eyes.

I swallowed all that, and instead replied, "Wish us luck out there."

"Break a leg," Tiny replied. "Kapish?"

"Kapish, my friend, kapish."

FORTY-SIX

The sand portion of Boca Chica Beach was long and relatively narrow. I drove north until I came parallel to the first of several ramshackle huts. They were located in the hard-packed sand and vegetation above the high water line. The decaying huts were spaced fairly far apart and, from what Boyle had said, fishermen used them occasionally.

The sand became too soft to drive, so I parked and walked north along the vegetation line.

Suddenly, movement caught my attention. A person, or perhaps an animal, had emerged from a pile of debris off to my left. A small vegetation-covered dune prevented a good view of the source of the movement.

I froze, waiting to see what it was. My hand went toward my holster. The movement was so natural that it wasn't until the fingers on my right hand touched the handle of the Beretta that I remembered I had holstered my weapon backward. If I wasn't careful, there was high likelihood of a bullet taking off a few of my toes—or worse.

Snow suddenly appeared directly ahead of me. His head was down as he picked his way through the vines. The premonition of disaster spiked when I realized he was most likely avoiding mines he had planted.

I searched in vain for Angella, but saw nothing resembling a human form. Other than a fallen hut, there was no place for her to be hidden.

Snow stepped onto the clear sand and turned to face me. We stood twenty yards apart. High noon on the beach.

"So we meet again," he called, the wind clipping his speech. "If you're thinking of shooting me, better think again. She's wired, and without me she'll blow."

"I'm well aware of the satellite signals," I said, my tone more forceful than I felt. "I also know to cover her with shield material. Give me one good reason not to put a hole in your head."

"You don't know where I hid the shield. Hey, I'll even give you a clue. It's under the sand. You have an hour to find it. Until twelve-twelve to be exact." He gestured at the expanse of the beach driving home his point.

I had no response to that.

"I'll even spot you a clue," he toyed, sensing I was defeated. "It's not in the hard pack."

"You made your point," I conceded. "What do you want?"

"First. Hand me your cell phone."

I did as he asked. He pulled the battery from the back, putting the cell in one pocket and the battery in another. He was taking no chances that the phone held a hidden microphone or a camera. He was also taking no chances that I could retrieve the phone easily.

"Behave," he said, "and you'll get it back. Screw up and it goes in the water. You'll never get her out alive without calling in help."

Did that mean Angella was injured, incapable of walking, or what? Maybe he was referring to the small time window we'd have between satellite flyovers. "I get the point, Snow. Where is she?"

"Relax, Ranger. We have time remaining before the next pass. But truth is, there's not enough time to get her off the beach even if we started now."

"Show me where she is. I need to know she's not injured, or you go nowhere."

"You got it backward, Redstone. You're not in charge out here, I am. Notice, I've allowed you to keep your gun. If I die, she dies. Simple."

"I want to see with my own eyes."

"Second," Snow said, ignoring my demand, "help me get the kayak ready to launch."

He walked past me going in the direction of the car. I again searched the area for signs of Angella and again saw nothing. I reluctantly followed him back down the beach.

It took about ten minutes to carry the kayak to the launching point and stock it with the water and other gear I had brought. The surf was strong, but if Snow was experienced, which I assumed he was, he could get through without dumping the load.

"Now we wait," Snow announced. "Take a load off your feet."

"What are we waiting for?"

"I suppose I can tell you. Seeing as how I have your phone. Hey, maybe you're wired! Let me check."

We had spoken about that back at the penthouse. Tiny wanted to rig me with a camera and microphone. CIA loves to spy on people. McNaughton had vetoed the idea, saying it was too risky. "Be my guest," I said, holding my arms up over my head.

Snow satisfied himself I was clean. He sat down on the sand and checked his watch. "Thirty-five minutes to go. Sit. Take a load off your feet."

Sitting seemed too much like a picnic. Buddies enjoying the day. "I'll stand," I replied, continuing to scan the beach for signs of Angella.

"At noon, I'll cover her with the shield. You behave, she'll be fine."

"You're sick!"

"Calm down," Snow responded. Clearly toying with me. "What's one girlfriend, more or less? Plenty more where she came from."

My muscles tensed. I was ready to take him out. Rid the world of one more slime. I moved a step closer.

Snow never flinched.

"You know, Redstone," he said, when I stepped back, "I do believe if she was anyone other than your girl, you'd sacrifice her to get your hands on me. That's real love, you ask me."

His eyes clouded and he looked away. He carried the look of a person in mourning, grieving for a loved one. Lou Keller's brutal death came to mind. "You lost a lover. I'm sorry, but what you're doing won't bring her back. Take me to Angella before it's too late." I was working from a weak hand with little chance of drawing a card that would save me. But I had to make the effort.

"I'll show you what a nice guy I can be." He slowly climbed to his feet and walked up the beach. About fifty yards north, he dropped to his knees and dug in the sand.

"This'll go faster if you help," he called. "I thought you were in a hurry."

I kneeled next to him, and like a child started throwing sand behind me. About two feet down my fingers hit something solid.

"Let me finish," Snow said. "This stuff is fragile. Been on and off your partner many times already. It wasn't meant for this type of use. Unfortunately, it's crumbling."

He pulled a tubular object out of the sand. The tube turned out to be rolled-up material and was about as long as my lower arm. The wind caught the leading edge and the material billowed up as it unrolled. I was surprised at how light and thin it was.

"Remain here. I'll do you a favor and wrap her early. No harm in that." He started toward the fallen hut. As before, he intently studied the path and he gingerly stepped through the vegetation, the shield material billowing out behind him. A moment later he stumbled forward, his left foot caught in a hole, or under a root, I couldn't see which. He reached out to balance himself, to keep from falling. A gust of wind caught the flapping material and whipped it out of his hand.

Before Snow could react, the material was airborne and going north toward the channel.

"Better catch as much of that as you can," he shouted. "That's all we have!"

My first thought was to shoot the son of a bitch. But I couldn't chance it. I focused my attention on the life-saving material being carried away. It was not just being blown north, but was being torn apart as well.

I ran as fast as I could and jumped as high as the soft sand would allow. I landed face down, my chin and nose buried.

In the process I had managed to corral a three-inch-square chuck of the flimsy material. I had no idea if this would be enough or not, but that's all I had—and all I could possibly get. The wind had carried the rest out over the water.

"Got a problem," Snow said, not displaying much concern. It was almost as if he had resigned himself to the consequences. He checked his watch. "Better get moving, time's almost up. We'll try to use what you salvaged."

"Is this piece large enough to work?"

"Maybe. Stay here." He hobbled toward the fallen hut.

He was back in less than five minutes. "She's holding it, but I have no way to be exactly sure where the explosive is planted. I put the material directly over the stitches. I'm going down beach just in case it explodes."

I grabbed his arm and threw him to the ground. "If she goes, we all go. Understand?"

"You're nuts!" Snow screamed, struggling to get away. "We'll both die. That what you want?"

"How certain are you the shield will work?"

"Reasonably."

"Okay, we wait."

"Mind getting off me?"

"Make a threatening move, and—"

"I'm going nowhere. Truth is, you still need me. You have no idea if I lied to you about the satellite time. Could be in range in five minutes. Or in an hour. Or a day."

It's never smart to let your enemy know how much you know, so I played along. "If it's not twelve-twelve, then when?"

"For me to know. My exit ticket."

"Where you heading?"

"South, if you must know."

From the amount of water he requested I assumed he intended to go pretty far south.

Snow studied the sand a long moment before looking in my direction. His eyes were begging for understanding, a look I had seen many times before, and always at a point in an interrogation when the suspect wants to be understood. Snow wanted someone to hear what was emotionally weighing on him.

I leaned back and removed my hand from my gun, trying to appear less threatening. I purposefully refrained from talking.

Snow followed my lead and eased back, leaning on his elbows. His lips remained still. But the agitation in his eyes increased.

He was deeply troubled.

I waited. He would talk or not, but only he could make that decision.

Another long minute passed. "I admire you, Redstone," he began. "You love her enough to stay close even knowing the explosive could blow you away." He looked out toward the water where pelicans were diving, presumably chasing lunch.

"I loved Lulu," he said, without taking his eyes from the surf. "She's the only girl I ever loved. Stetson took her from me." He again fell silent. When he next spoke, his face was consumed with hatred. "Death is not good enough for him!"

"You certain Stetson killed Lou?"

"Hell yes, I'm certain! Saw him come into the hotel when I was going out. Didn't think fast enough though. I was busy leading you away from Lulu."

"Why?" Open-ended questions produced better results than specific ones. He would answer what was on his mind.

"Because he thought Lulu was blackmailing Donnlevy. She wasn't. It was Keys doing the blackmailing. But Keys let Stetson think it was Lulu. Original plan was to take you in Dallas, the explosive embedded in your ass. Stetson had it all worked out. I was only the facilitator."

"You took Angella instead. Why?"

"Worked out easier all around. Her coming thorough Houston alone made it easier to work out the logistics. The idea was to get the explosive to D.C., and either of you would have worked."

"But you substituted her sister."

"I changed the plan when I finally realized Stetson killed Lulu. I wanted Stetson to think Angella had been rescued so he wouldn't bolt. The fact the sister was not taken east was a miscalculation. But it made no difference. There was nothing to explode in her anyway. The explosive was already in Angella and I wanted her to facilitate my own escape."

I heard a noise from behind me and glanced back to see what it was.

Snow seized the distraction to leap at me.

Years of training took charge and I moved effortlessly into a back-L stance, my body turning sideways toward my attacker. Text-book perfect. His fist started on its trajectory to my jaw, seemingly in slow motion.

In combat, timing is everything. Snow was out of control and I had the distinct advantage. I planned to meet his initial thrust with a rising block using my forearm, followed by a straightforward front snap kick. Typical goal was to render the adversary incapacitated—at least for an instant.

But, for once in my life, I moved backward instead of forward. This was about Angella and getting her off the beach. My score with Snow would have to be settled at a later date.

His fist flew harmlessly past its target and by the time he recovered, I was outside his reach. I said, "You want to get off the beach alive, I suggest you get yourself under control."

He slumped back to the sand. "That snake'll get what he deserves!"

I sat a few feet away and said, "You're here. He's in Washington. Big distance between the two of you." I glanced at the kayak. "You'll require more water than that you planning to paddle all that way."

"Don't need to go after Stetson." His lips quivered, and his words spit at me with venom born of deep hatred. "That low-life killed my baby! Blow his ass off the face of the earth!" He again looked away and mumbled something that sounded like, "Set to the same satellite."

Federal marshals were about to arrest Stetson. My phone was in Snow's pocket less than six inches from my hand, and without it I was helpless to warn them of the danger. There was little chance of me getting both the phone and the battery away from Snow. But, in the scuffle with him a moment ago, his cell phone had fallen out of his shirt pocket. It now lay on the sand a few feet away and behind me, out of his sightline.

I leaned as far back as I could without making it obvious what I was planning to do. My fingers were barely able to touch the cell and I worked it closer with my fingertips. The movement was painstakingly slow.

Finally, I slipped my hand around it and, glancing over my shoulder, began dialing Tiny's number.

"I wouldn't do that," Snow warned.

"Why the hell not?" I asked, continuing to dial numbers as we spoke.

"Modified it, that's why. It sends out the same frequency code as the satellite. You hit the send key and it'll set off the explosive."

"The shield's in place."

"This signal is stronger. Shield won't hold."

I paused on Tiny's last number, my finger hovering over the keypad as if making up its mind as to which key to push. I didn't believe him, but yet...yet if there was even a remote chance he was telling the truth I had to hold up.

And Snow knew it.

I dropped the phone in the sand.

"Smart choice. Here's your cell and the battery." He took both from his pocket and handed them to me. Checking his watch, he said, "Twelve-twenty. It's too late for you to do anything now anyway. No explosion out here. Means the shield held. Washington's another story."

It took an eternity for my phone to boot. When it did, I called Tiny. He listened without comment. His phone's speaker was on and I assumed Cindy McNaughton was listening also. When I finished, McNaughton said, "You're ten minutes late, Cowboy. An explosion in an Alexandria warehouse killed Stetson and four other people, one of them an undercover police officer. Marshals were minutes away."

I felt a twinge of grief for the victims. But they were far off, unseen, unknown. While McNaughton and Tiny might be focused on the dead police officer, I breathed a welcome sigh of relief knowing the satellite had passed and Angella was still alive.

FORTY-SEVEN

"**D**id I get the bastard?" Snow asked when I put the cell in my pocket.

I nodded. "You got him all right. And you managed to kill four others as well."

"What the hell you care about those low-lives? They're just mules."

"Mules are people. But, and this is unfortunate for you, one of the dead was a cop." I knew it was the wrong thing to say the instant the words came out. Amnesty was now hopeless.

The air came out of Snow. He remained silent as he worked through the new situation. Finally, he said, "This is unfortunate for you as well. I suppose they'll hunt me down now."

"The only thing I'll guarantee at this point is that if Angella is harmed in any way, I'll personally hunt you down. And it won't be pretty."

"You think I give a stinkin' damn who comes after me?" Snow scrambled to his feet. "Give me an incentive to release her? The shield won't hold up much longer. She might not be so lucky on the next pass. Or perhaps the one after that."

"How about in exchange for me not putting a bullet between your eyes? That good enough for you?"

"Think about it," he said, gaining new life. "If she were free to move around, don't you think she'd be out here?"

"Unless she's injured."

"She's not injured. She's locked up. I die. She dies. Simple."

I dove at his knees and drove him into the sand. He didn't resist, knowing full well I couldn't kill him. Not yet anyway.

I let him up. "Okay, Snow. Time to get moving. Unlock her and I'll set you free."

"The hell you will. The instant she walks out of there the Ranger in you will take over. Or your pals will come after me. I know what they do to cop killers."

Time was passing and time was not on my side. VLAD13 was in low earth orbit, which meant it circled the earth every ninety minutes. What I didn't know was its trajectory. VLAD13 could also be in the southern hemisphere for the next several passes for all I knew. But I couldn't risk it. "So, what's your plan?"

Snow reached for his pocket and almost simultaneously my right hand reflexively went to my right side.

"Something wrong with your right hand, Redstone?" Snow said, a grin spreading across his face. "You're wearing your weapon facing front. You better give up gun-fighting, you want to live to collect retirement pay—or whatever the Feds pay old cops."

What had Angella said about gun fighting? Catch them with brains—not guns? Right now I wasn't doing a good job of either.

Snow produced a crumpled business card. "If you refrain from shooting me while I dig out my pencil, I'll write down the combination and bury the card in the sand so it doesn't blow away.

Give me a thirty-minute lead before you fetch it. You touch it sooner, I use the cell. Your friends up there," Snow said, pointing over his head, "try anything funny, I hit the speed dial and she's gone. In fact, you better pray I don't see any planes at all."

"That only gives us an hour, less even. That's not enough time to get her off the beach to a hospital."

"I suggest you cut the shit and help me launch the kayak."

I nodded and after searching two pockets, he retrieved a pencil stub and wrote something on the card. For all I knew, he was writing the word, *sucker*.

Snow bent and dug a quick hole in the sand. But instead of putting the card in the hole, he stood and faced me, the trace of smirk forming. "Hey I have a better idea. Better for me, that is. For all I know that water out there is swarming with SEALs. They could flip me over, kill the phone." The smirk morphed into defiance. He held out his phone. "Swap phones. Give me your cell. In thirty minutes, I'll call you with the combination. I go over, no phone, no call. Simple."

Before Snow could react, my hand shot out and closed on the card. I yanked hard, but the injury had reduced my gripping strength. The card slid through my fingers.

Without wasting a second, Snow ripped the card twice and threw the pieces in the air. The strong southerly breeze quickly dispersed them. "Chase the pieces or help me launch. Your choice, Redstone. Your choice. Time is fleeting."

One glance at the wayward card pieces and my decision was clear. The sooner he was off the beach, the sooner I could get to Angella. The problem was that as soon as he left the beach, the military command would know it. And I couldn't use Snow's phone to give them any information. I was sure there were orders for his capture. Cop killers just didn't run free. He had most likely guessed right about the SEALs. Could be from above or below, no way to know.

With Kagan in charge I was positive the Feds would go after Snow, cross the border in hot pursuit if necessary. Aside from being a cop killer, he was a high-value target with information the Feds could use. Frankly, once Angella was safe, I didn't care what became of the weasel.

In that regard, I was certain Kagan didn't care what became of Angella—or me for that matter. I was counting on McNaughton for a measure of sanity.

I waded into the water holding onto the kayak, fighting to keep the bow pointed directly into the waves slamming against the small boat with considerable force. The boat was thrown to the side despite my efforts.

"On three." Snow began counting. "One. Two. Three."

He jumped up, landed in the kayak ass first, pulled his right leg up. Then his left.

A wave hit the bow and the kayak, despite my efforts, was thrown violently sideways. Snow slapped the left paddle hard against the water in an attempt to maintain balance. The Kayak tilted at an alarming angle. He slapped the water twice more while leaning far to his right counterbalancing the wave's force.

The kayak hung in the balance, teetering at the tipping point. I was mindful that if he went over, my chances of freeing Angella were slim. The breaking wave had taken control and Snow's fate hung in the balance.

Suddenly, the kayak disappeared. The knot that had been in my stomach now slammed into my chest. Helplessness is not a condition I am accustomed to feeling. But I was helpless—and out of control.

A flash of yellow in an otherwise blue-green sea caught my attention. But was Snow still inside? I strained into the sun, but couldn't see anything.

Slowly, the yellow materialized again, this time rising on the face of a wave. A few seconds later it slid down the far side and was gone again. But in that instant, riding the wave crest, I could definitely make out the shape of a person sitting upright.

A moment later the kayak again took focus, this time well-beyond the breaking surf, rising and falling gently as the waters of the Gulf of Mexico seemed to be welcoming the small boat. The stern was toward me and I could now clearly see Snow paddling smoothly, first on the right and then on the left. As I watched, the kayak became smaller.

I moved slowly backward, coming out of the breaking surf onto the beach, my eyes never leaving Snow. I was waiting for him to turn south.

Instead, he turned north. He wasn't heading to Mexico after all. A chill flashed down my spine as my mind went into recalculating mode; except I had no new data to recalculate.

It appeared Snow was angling back toward land. I didn't give a rat's behind which way he went so long as he remained upright with my cell dry. Circles would work for me. There was still five minutes before he would call.

Five minutes. An eternity.

Then Snow did what I had not anticipated. He turned west and headed for the jetty. He was coming back in through the ship channel. At first I was confused, then, after thinking it through, I realized there were any number of places he could land. He could even commandeer a fishing boat and take new hostages. It was a good plan, that is, assuming he wasn't intercepted.

Dolphin watching is popular on the island and I could see several sightseeing boats out in the channel, people lining their bows and looking down into the water. Dolphins typically hang around the channel, scooping up the incoming mullet.

Snow's cell buzzed.

I quickly hit the accept button.

"Redstone. I'm cutting you a break. I'm going to be busy in the next few minutes and may not be able to call. Here's the number. Left thirty-three. Right ten. Left twenty-eight." He paused, then said, "You get that or should I re..."

The line went dead.

Then it rang again almost immediately. It was McNaughton.

I didn't wait for her to say anything before I began. "What the hell's going on?"

"No time for chit chat, Cowboy. We're monitoring his phone. You switched phones. Explain."

When I did, she said, "Get that lock open. SEALs dumped him in the channel. He's under their control now."

"I'll know in a few minutes if the combination's right. She's in a collapsed shack. I'll keep the link open."

I ran across the beach and onto the hard-packed vegetation, being careful to step in the well-worn areas. Invisible sand flies were taking what felt like giant chucks out of my ankles.

The doorframe at the back of the house was the only structural part of the building still standing. I pulled the door open and found my way blocked by a collapsed wall. "Shit!" I exclaimed, looking around for another way into the rubble. But there was none.

I leaned down to brush off the sand flies. As I did so a wooden plank moved under my palm, revealing a deep hole in the sand.

Another piece of debris, a part of a collapsed wall, covered the remainder of the hole. I sat, and using my legs, uncovered the hole.

Angella sat at the bottom of the pit, her legs folded tightly against her chest. A dirty motel towel formed a blindfold and a gag, held firmly in place with a metal clamp at the back of her head. Her head slumped to the side as if she had passed out.

There wasn't room to climb into the hole without injuring her. I lay flat, positioning myself to remove the towel. "Are you injured?" I asked, silently praying for a response. "Nod your head."

Her head slowly moved from side to side.

"Thank goodness! Hold still a moment and I'll get this off."

It was not as easy as I had assumed. The clamp was locked tight with a metal twist tie and I had nothing to cut the tie with. My right hand was in spasms from trying to grab Snow's business card and I had to use my left to achieve leverage.

After several false starts, I managed to grasp an end of the tie and untwisted it ever so slightly. Not enough to completely open the clip, but enough to pull some of the towel through. That small amount of slack allowed her to gasp air.

She took several deep breaths, but didn't seem to be revived. I frantically worked the metal, finally getting enough slack to work the towel far enough out of the clip to allow the towel to slide over her head.

Angella's eyes rolled backward and her head fell to the side limp. Brain damage from lack of oxygen was a distinct possibility.

"Angella," I said, my mouth not far from the top of her head, "Just a little while longer and everything will be fine. Hang with me. Breath deep and slowly."

Her head rolled sideways. Her eyes opened. It took a few seconds, but she was able to focus on me. But she didn't say anything.

"We don't have much time," I said to her. "Need to get you out of here. Can you stand? Take my hand."

"Jimmy," she wheezed, straining to form the words. "I'm locked in. My left arm."

She was struggling to fill her lungs, and when she shifted her body sideways she winced in pain. Her eyes lost focus and her head fell.

"Angella! Stay with me! I'll get you out."

Her eyes still closed, she managed to whisper, "My left arm's cuffed." She held up her arm.

I worked the combination numbers as I had been instructed, but the lock did not open.

I tried it again, slower this time. Still nothing.

I said into the phone. "Combination not working. Angella needs medical help."

"Affirmative. ETA two minutes."

"Is that Long Legs?"Angella asked, the tiniest hint of a sparkle coming into her eyes. It faded in an instant.

"Along with a cast of thousands," I said, "There's a major operation under way. Hang on. Stay with me. I love you."

"I love you too, Jimmy." She took several deep breaths and with her head down and eyes closed, said, "I knew you would come get me. That's what got me through this." Angella's head again fell and again she seemed to be sleeping.

I put two fingers on her carotid artery. Her pulse was weak, but regular. "Keep talking, Angella. Keep talking to me. Don't sleep. I love you. Just a few more minutes."

I leaned into the hole as far as I dared go and kissed her on the forehead. I then took her left hand in mine. Her return squeeze was reassuring.

I again tried the combination and again it was futile. I even tried reversing directions, to no avail.

Her eyes opened partially, silently pleading for help, much like an animal with a paw caught in a trap. "He implanted something in my right butt. He told me to hold a piece of material over the area."

"Do you have the material?" I asked, already knowing the answer. I had seen bits float past when she reached up to touch my hand.

"I think it's lost."

"It's okay. Everything will be okay."

Tiny's voice came over the line. "Good to hear your voice, Angella. Hold on a while longer. Jimmy. You have twelve minutes."

"What happens in twelve minutes?" Angella asked, her eyes pleading with me to level with her.

"Operation will be over in twelve minutes."

"What are you not telling me?"

I decided to level with her and gave her the short version.

"Thanks for being honest. Please promise me you'll save yourself. Please."

"We're both getting out of here—together."

"It's almost over, Angella," Tiny cut in. "We'll have you out of there in a few minutes. That's a promise. Kapish?"

"Kapish, big guy. Kapish." The exchange with Tiny brought a semblance of a smile to Angella's face. In a voice low enough so only I could hear, she said, "They won't get me out of here in time, Jimmy. But, even if they do, without a shield I won't make it. Promise me you'll move out of harm's way. I don't want anything to happen—"

A shadow appeared over me. The shadow was followed by a man holding a large pliers-type device. "You want to cut her free or should I?" a voice above me said. "We're on a tight schedule here."

I couldn't figure how either of us could get down into the pit to cut the binding. I said as much to the man standing over me.

"I'm smaller than you are," he replied. "I'll do it. Miss Martinez, if you would position yourself as far from the post as you can, I'll slip down and cut that bracelet."

Angella, her head again resting on her chest, her eyes closed, slowly moved closer to where I was positioned. But there still was not much room between her and the hole sides.

I reached down and tried to help, but she was tightly wedged. "Angella, try to move your shoulders to the right?"

She did so.

"Now move your legs in the same direction. Even a little helps."

It took a while, but finally her legs slowly moved away from the post.

"A little further," I coaxed. "Once more should do it."

Ever so slowly her shoulders moved, followed by her legs and then her hips.

There was still just the tiniest of room between her body and the crumbling sand wall where the post was positioned.

"Name's Hill," the man above me said. He was wearing jeans and a nondescript tan tee. I couldn't determine which branch of the service he represented; CIA for all I knew. Frankly, I didn't care if he came from the moon. He was Angella's only hope.

Hill lay on the ground opposite me and slithered forward so that his head was over the hole. Then his head disappeared into the sand pit, causing the sides to crumble. A moment later all I could see of him were the bottoms of his boots. Sand cascaded into the hole around him.

The cuffs apparently had been made with an exotic metal that at first defied the pressure of the cutter. He tried the stake, but the cutter blades didn't open far enough. He continued working on the cuffs.

It took three agonizing minutes before Hill reported, "First one's history. There are two sets."

"Angella's eyes were closed, her breathing hadn't improved—but neither had it deteriorated.

A few minutes later Hill said," Second's not going as fast as the first."

"I love you, Jimmy," Angella, her voice barely audible, said. "You have to save yourself. Promise me, you'll get away."

"I'm not—"

"Go!" she said, mustering the strength to shout," I want you to find Snow and—"

"Second's off," Hill called from the bottom of the hole. "Let's roll."

I pulled him out feet first, using my left hand and wrapping my right arm around both legs. I pulled with all I had, and it was not until Angella's head emerged above ground level that I realized Hill had locked his arms under Angella and I was pulling them both out of the shallow grave.

The muscles across my back were stretched to their limit. My right deltoid felt as if it was about to snap.

Angella was still not completely out and I had no strength remaining to lift them both any further.

"Another few inches," Hill called, "and I'll get purchase."

I managed to continue pulling. Suddenly, Hill called, "Sand's collapsing. Can't get—"

My right arm went numb. Angella and Hill fell back about a foot before my left arm took control.

Hill must have found purchase on a hard area, because he and Angella began to slowly move upward again with only a small amount of help from me.

My left arm now hung free, with all the weight shifted to Hill. The back of my neck throbbed as I inched backward away from the pit.

Hill positioned Angella in a seated position with her legs dangling into the sand hole. With Hill's help she tried to stand, her feet at the bottom of the pit. Her knees buckled and she fell back into a sitting position.

Hill then lifted her onto his back, using the fireman's carry. My right arm was essentially non-functional and I was unwilling to trust what little strength remained in my left. Instead, I picked our way back across the low dunes, being careful to avoid traps. Once the vegetation was safely behind us I looked out toward the water, wondering how far offshore the transport vessel would be.

To my surprise, there was no boat in sight. Instead, what I did see caught me off-guard.

A field hospital had been erected just above the high tide line, all without me being aware of the activity. A large tent held a surgical table ringed with vaguely recognizable equipment. Large lights hung over the table and supply cabinets lined one wall. A scrub sink had been set up just inside the tent.

A slender black woman in blue scrubs stood near the tent opening flanked by two men and a woman, the three of them wearing green. The woman in blue, whom I took to be the leader, hurried across the sand to meet us.

Holding Angella's wrist, she studied her eyes for a moment. She produced a stethoscope and listened to Angella's chest. Her motions were smooth and practiced. "Dehydrated," she pronounced. "Start an IV, stat. Point nine percent sodium chloride."

"Two minutes." The sound came from a speaker inside the tent. I imagined a camera positioned there as well. The Feds didn't seem to go anywhere without full audio and video communications. Link in the President if need be.

I turned to the leader, "Do you know about—"

"Been fully briefed, Mr. Redstone," she replied. "Please step away. Make room for the IV. No time to waste."

While Angella was still on Hill's back, one of the men in green took Angella's arm and locked it tight against his own body. He then expertly inserted an IV needle and a moment later liquid was dripping into her through a clear plastic hose attached to a drip-bag hanging from a short pole held above Angella's head.

"Okay. Off his back. You two," she commanded, pointing to Hill and the man who had inserted the needle. "Walk her out in the water. Move quickly. Walk out as far as you can. I'll tell you when to sit her down. Once she's down, for goodness sake, don't let her buttocks be exposed, even for an instant." She then turned her head to the side and said, "Count down."

She must have been wearing a mike, but I didn't see one on her.

Instantly, Tiny's voice came back, "Thirty seconds."

"Begin ten-second countdown."

Angella was at ankle depth when Tiny announced, "Twenty seconds."

The Gulf is relatively shallow for at least fifty yards out, the sand smooth and gently sloping. The small group was already forty yards from shore, but still in relatively shallow water.

"Move faster!" the head woman yelled. "Need to be deeper."

"Ten seconds."

The water was now up to Angella's mid-calf, some waves breaking as high as her stomach. I fought the urge to run after her and push her into the water, sitting on her if necessary to keep her butt under water.

"Five seconds."

"Four."

"Three."

"Down! Stat!" the woman in blue commanded. Her voice was firm, in control. Her total focus was on the team in the water.

Hill kicked Angella's feet out from under her and the two men pushed her down into the water. The woman holding the IV pole went down on her knees, only to be knocked flat by a breaking wave. She tumbled in the surf, struggling to maintain the IV bag above Angella's head.

Hill reached out to steady the pole and caught the next wave full in the chest. His head went under, but the pole remained upright.

"One second."

My jaw clenched. My stomach tightened. My breathing ceased.

At that instant a large wave broke over the group and Angella, gagging on saltwater, instinctively tried to stand. The man on her right forcefully pulled her down. Water seemed to pour from her mouth and her head shook violently.

I started to run out to her.

The leader grabbed my shoulder. "There's no need. Takes a lot more water than that to drown. Push comes to shove, we know how to save drowning victims. Get lots of practice, sad to say. But what we don't know is how to put Humpty Dumpty together again. Get my drift?"

"Got it," I admitted, still uneasy about Angella being out there with me standing by helpless, water lapping at my feet.

"I'm Major Phillips, Chief Medical Officer, Coast Guard, Corpus." Phillips' face had softened, her eyes now almost friendly. "Been following what you two have been doing. Deserve a medal, you ask me."

I accepted her outstretched hand.

"Heard about your hand," she said when I winced. "But I thought it had been rehab—"

"Tore something pulling her and Hill out of that grave back there."

She took my right arm, gently twisted and bent it in several directions, all the while watching my eyes. She let go of my arm, and said, "Don't lift strenuously with your right hand for a few months and you'll be good as new. Teran at *Island Fitness* will take good care of you."

I was about to tell her I was already working with Teran when Tiny called out, "Minus one minute."

I dialed Jacobs, totally forgetting I would transmit a frequency that could set off Angella. But it was too late by the time I remembered what Snow had said about the signal.

The knot in my stomach tightened even more. I looked out to be sure she was still there, not even sure if I would hear the explosion should it occur.

The team, with Angella at the center, was still there, all of them battling to remain in place, the water breaking over their heads.

When Jacobs came on the line, I said, "So what happened out in the channel with Snow?" I was referring to the fact that the line had gone dead while the slime was giving me the code. I vowed to castrate the bastard if I ever got my hands on him.

"Can't talk now, Jimmy."

"Screw that! I'm tired of—"

"Shut the hell up! I'll call back in a minute."

"Call on Snow's phone," I said and hung up.

When I took the phone from my ear, Phillips said, "Take a load off your feet. She'll be out there for twenty minutes at least. Then we'll bring her in and remove that bad boy. Want something to eat?"

"Can't eat," I snapped, "stomach is in knots. I'm going out and sit with her. Least I can do."

"That's what they said you'd do. Here, take these goggles for both of you. Makes it easier to sit in the surf. That's not easy doing what they're doing, the water breaking around you. But these folks train in the water all the time."

Before I could take two steps, Snow's cell rang. It was Jacobs.

"We've only got a moment, so I'll be brief. We're now off the record. Kagan refused to allow Snow to run free. Says that turned to shit the last time we tried it. He was overruled, but it took your friend McNaughton to cash in a few chips. I think she actually got POTUS involved. The stand-down order came just as they dumped Snow. He doesn't know why the kayak flipped, never saw the assets. They stood down and allowed Snow to climb back into the kayak. Man's seasoned, I'll say that much. He's now across the bay heading for the ship channel. Fill you in when we're together. Just get Angella back—and in one piece."

Running out through the surf I once again admired the unselfishness of the men and women who serve our country. If Angella's implant goes off, they go with it. Yet, not one of them flinched.

When I arrived out where they were, it became all to apparent that each new breaker brought a fresh challenge. It was a battle just to sit upright against the relentless force of the water. Angella was leaning to the side and Hill was holding her as upright as he could, shedding saltwater from his mouth as he leaned into her.

Angella's head was bobbing wildly and it looked as though she had passed out.

I handed a pair of the goggles to Hill and motioned for him to put them on Angella.

I then positioned myself behind her in an attempt to shield my lover from the worst of the breaking waves. I placed my arms over her shoulders to stabilize her neck just as a wave took that instant to break over our heads.

The water momentarily covered us and when it subsided, Angella coughed heavily, water pouring from her mouth and nose.

She reached up and grasped my hands and pulled them tight against her shoulders.

"Just a while longer," I said in her ear, "and it'll all be over."

"Will, it, Jimmy?" she replied, squeezing my fingers tightly. "Will it ever be over?"

IN MEMORIAM

I want to publicly acknowledge Professor Emeritus John Sullivan for his many years of teaching law at Capital Law School in Columbus, Ohio. I am forever grateful to him for his dedication to his students and to the energy he brought to the classroom. He not only taught me, but changed my life in the process. He may be gone, but he is certainly not forgotten.

Other Books by David Harry

the
Padre
Puzzle

the
Padre
Predator

Naming Rights

The following character names were suggested by fans for use in this story. I trust I have not disappointed you.

Jayme Partridge
Chester Katz
Chris Kagan
Saundra
Kathleen Sexton
Myangel Lopez
LissaLou Keller

Anyone wishing to send in names for the next story can do so by going to www.davidharryauthor.com or by E-mail to david@davidharryauthor.com

THANK YOU

Thank you to everyone who provided comments on the story. A very special thank you to Kathlyn Auten for her fabulous editorial accomplishments and to Rachel Simeone for her excellent guidance. And a big thank you to Marvilyn Welton for her thorough review of the Proof.

David Harry can be reached at david@davidharryauthor.com

For information on upcoming books and other items of interest, please go to http://www.davidharryauthor.com.

You can follow David Harry on Facebook: davidharry; on twitter: david1harry and on his blog : davidharryauthor.com.

Made in the USA
Columbia, SC
23 October 2021